Love doesn't come wit

Kelly Davidson has school and get out of his small-minded, small town. But when he arrives at Hope University, he realizes finding Prince Charming isn't so easy. Everyone here is already out. In fact, Kelly could be the only virgin on campus. Worst of all, he's landed gay campus Casanova as a roommate, whose bed might as well be equipped with a revolving door.

Walter Lucas doesn't believe in storybook love. Everyone is better off having as much fun as possible with as many people as possible…except his shy, sad little sack of a roommate is seriously screwing up his world view. As Walter sets out to lure Kelly out of his shell, staying just friends is harder than he anticipated. He discovers love is a crash course in determination. To make the grade, he'll have to finally show up for class…and overcome his fear that love was never meant to last.

Heidi Cullinan, POB 425, Ames, Iowa 50010

Copyright © 2017 by Heidi Cullinan
Print ISBN: 978-1-945116-01-8
Print Edition
Edited by Sasha Knight
Cover by Kanaxa
Proofing by Lillie's Literary Services
Formatting by BB eBooks

First publication 2013
Second publication 2017
www.heidicullinan.com

Love Lessons

Heidi Cullinan

To Dr. Gregory Scholtz,
Because you were my anchor, and I'll never forget.

And to Erin, from Robert and Walter,
Because you're pretty unforgettable too.

Thanks to

Damon Suede for the talent, Dan Cullinan for the top shelf assistance, Kanaxa for the incredible covers, Sasha Knight for being the editor I never, ever want to leave, Lillie for the bibles that save me every single day, and thanks most of all to my patrons, especially Pamela Bartual, Rosie Moewe, Erin Sharpe, Lesha Maureen Porche, Sarah M., Tiffany Miller, Sarah Plunkett, and regencyfan93.

Your task is not to seek for love,
but merely to seek and find all the barriers within
yourself that you have built against it.

—Rumi

Chapter One

September
Hope University, Danby, Illinois

FRESHMAN ORIENTATION AT Hope University was an all-you-can-eat buffet, and Walter Lucas planned to gorge himself.

The adorable youngling at the student union entrance, for example, would make a nice appetizer, despite the fact that the kid looked as if he'd stepped out of Mayberry. Sex, however, would have to wait, because Walter had much bigger fish to fry—namely, figuring out where exactly he was going to be fucking all the nubile young beauties on the proverbial platter. The note in his mailbox had told him to go see the dean of students, so that was where Walter headed.

Unfortunately, he was already pretty sure this wasn't going to be a great meeting. He took the long way around, swinging by Lake Sharon to give a quick hello to Lancelot and Gawain.

The man-made lake encompassed three acres, went about fifteen-feet deep in the center, and boasted a small campanile on the far northwest side where romantically inclined coeds had gone for one hundred years to stare adoringly into one another's eyes and declare lifelong devotion. Walter appreciated the bell tower because it blocked the sun and wind, hid him from prying eyes, and made a nice frame while watching the swans.

Today as ever the graceful birds floated serenely on the surface of the water, two regal white heads bowed and moving in unison as they patrolled the perimeter of their domain. They eyed Walter with brief interest, but when they saw he had no offerings of bread or corn chips, they continued on their way. Unlike Walter, their residence for the year was already secured, their lake stocked with everything they'd ever need.

Good life if you could get it.

Walter watched them swim until he was in danger of missing the dean's office hours, and then, ready to face reality, he headed back to Old Main and his nine-month sentence.

Dean Stevens was one of those back-end-of-middle-age women who, while once lovely, had missed the memo that declared wrinkled cleavage gross, boldly wearing plunging necklines without any viable flesh to keep them from being black holes of *eww*. Though he tried not to look at her chest while she greeted him and ushered him back into her office, it drew his focus like a lighthouse. A scary lighthouse.

"Did you get the lease for the new apartment?" He took up his usual position in the chair across from her desk. "I emailed it to your secretary."

Her smile fixed a little more firmly, and that was when Walter knew for sure—he wasn't living off campus.

Dean Stevens threaded her fingers together over the top of her desk. "As a junior, Walter, I know you understand our residential policies, and I know you're committed to Hope University's community motto. I know you understand we don't lightly let our students live away from the dorms, because it detracts from that community."

"I know I lived off campus last year," Walter countered, "and I know you approved my application to do so again this time."

The smile was etched in the leather of her face. "We approved—with great reluctance—your request to live in the same residence as last year, a residence which I understand is no longer an option to you."

"It's not my fault the landlord didn't cover his mortgage. God knows we were paying him enough."

"Nevertheless, our agreement was with that lease, not a new one. I'm afraid we can't approve a student living farther away."

Walter had a fixed smile of his own. "The new place is two blocks away from the one you already approved."

"We must set our limits somewhere, Mr. Lucas. May I point out also your situation has changed. When you applied, you were living with another student, one whose graduation date was supposed to be this coming December."

Of course she *would* hone in on his one little white lie, his attempt to use Hope's own system against itself. His best friend Cara as a fifth-year senior was practically a shoe-in for off-campus digs, especially since she was engaged—with her on the application as a mid-semester graduate, their request had sailed easily through. Except Cara never intended to stay that long, and as soon as the ink was dry on Hope's approval of their living arrangements, she immediately signed up for summer classes and August graduation. It was sleight of hand no one would have paid attention to until it was too late...except the idiot landlord had stopped paying his bills and busted their plan wide open.

Walter tried to dust this detail under the rug as delicately as possible. "She managed to finish early so she could take an internship back in Chicago. That's not my fault either."

"Be that as it may, you're asking to move farther away than your last year's accommodations, alone, and at the last minute. Surely you see the difficulty you place us in? If we allow you to do this, we'll be flooded with requests to let others do the same."

They *were* flooded with requests to live off campus, because Hope was the only place Walter had ever heard of that didn't let students choose their own places of residence. It was drop-dead insane, but voicing this opinion wouldn't help his case just now.

"It's important we foster the Hope community," the dean went on. "Our students and their parents expect us to provide a safe learning environment for those attending Hope. How can we do that if they're scattered across town? Young people don't always make the best decisions for themselves. We're taking away an opportunity to fail on that score."

"I'm perfectly capable of making decisions about where I live, and as far as my parents go, I'm better suited to make decisions for them too."

He hated the way her expression turned to pity. "Yes, I'm well aware. Don't you see, though, that this is even more an argument to let us take care of you for a change? How can you argue that having to pay rent, utilities, and shop for your own meals is an advantage? Why do you need anything else to worry about?"

"I've earned the right to make those decisions for myself. I'm not some wide-eyed freshman. I'm not even a typical junior. Dean Stevens, you *know* my situation."

For the first time in the exchange, her smile cracked. Unfortunately, there wasn't a reprieve behind her mask, only another wall. "I do know, and I'm sorry, Walter. I can't let you live off campus. Even if I wanted to—which I don't—it isn't my decision. The board of regents said no. We can discuss it as long as you like, but I'm telling you as one who has been with you through this entire rocky ride, it isn't going to change. We gave you a pass because you were struggling and because you were living with your friend. Living alone is not a good idea for you."

Walter slumped into his chair. "So where are you sticking me? Because I know for a fact you can't get me in the manors with the other upperclassmen."

Stevens lifted a piece of paper and propped half-moon glasses on the end of her nose. "Actually, I could. Ethan Miller's roommate ended up as a transfer—"

"*Ethan Miller?*" Images of waking to a horny, desperate geek and a room full of science experiments filled Walter's mind. "Try again."

Pursing her lips, she scanned the paper further. "I have a handful of other spaces available. Unfortunately, they're all in underclassmen housing and all in one dorm, Porter."

Porter. Walter sat up as if a cattle prod had been applied to the base of his spine. "You can't be serious. You have four underclassmen Communist block buildings. You can't tell me the only openings are in Porterhouse."

"Porter never fills, as you well know, though this year we've come far too close for comfort. Next year won't be an issue with the new dorm's construction. For now, however, it's Porter or rooming with Ethan Miller."

What lovely options. She was offering him the choice between two circles of hell. "Talk to me about the spots open in Porter."

"There are seven vacancies there, all with freshmen or sophomores. This could be a good thing, you know. You're one of the greatest advocates against that house, and you're right, we have work to do there. You could help other young men find a voice."

"So now I'm doing community service? I hope you're comping my room." He held out his hand, and she passed over the paper. A sea of names floated before him, all of them meaningless, nothing on the page giving him a clue as to who might be a remotely passable roommate. He wanted to throw it back at her and refuse. What could they do, really? Kick him out? Did he care? He should have listened to Cara and transferred back to Chicago after all. He shouldn't have stayed, not even for Williams. He shouldn't—

He stopped, finger landing on a purple square next to one of the meaningless names. "There. This one. That's your code for *open to a gay roommate*, am I right?"

Stevens squinted at the list. "Yes, but that's a single."

"Oh." The singles were shoeboxes for one, and two was out of the question. Also the singles were more likely to house some reclusive upperclassman with an Xbox. Except there was an F, right next to the square. "How did a freshman get a single?"

"He has allergies, rather severe ones as I understand. He needs the air conditioner, and of course the only regular rooms that can support air conditioners are in the upperclassmen dorms." Stevens paused, looking thoughtful. "Though come to think of it, his parents were upset at his living alone. If you wanted to room there, I could approve it."

"Room where? Two people don't fit in those rooms."

"We've doubled up singles before. It's not comfy, but it's workable." She smiled absently, clearly warming to this solution. "Actually, this could solve a lot of problems. The mother was in here this morning as they dropped him off, almost frantic as the reality hit her of leaving her baby at college alone. They're from far out of state, and I guess the young man is just coming out. She's very worried it won't go well. He's shy, I gather."

Fantastic. Now instead of having a solo fuckfest

pad, Walter would play nanny to a shy, allergy-ridden newb who probably had backne. Walter frowned and pulled the paper into his lap, scanning it intently. None of the other open spots had purple squares, though, and if they didn't sign up for a gay roommate, they didn't fucking want one. Two of the open spots were sophomores Walter despised, and the others might well be gay bashers for all he knew. Not that they could bash at Hope. But as he'd learned to his peril—also in Porterhouse—there were many intricate ways to bully. So really, his choices were Ethan Fucking Miller and squeezing in with a freshman.

His gaze drifted back to Backne Boy.

"Worst-case scenario," Stevens pointed out, "you room there until you find a better situation on your own. You've done it every other time you've had trouble. I don't see why you can't do it now."

"I wouldn't have trouble," Walter replied, "if you'd let me live off campus."

Stevens sighed and picked up her pen. "Shall I put you down for doubling in the single?"

Walter stared at the paper a moment, then nodded, wondering what he'd gotten himself into.

AFTER THE MEETING with Stevens, Walter cut across the faculty parking lot and headed to the cracked streetlights that marked the way to the communications building.

Sitting on the farthest point of campus, Ritche Hall had been built in 1950 and never so much as been given a new curtain, though it had received an electrical and cable upgrade in 1997 when the place had nearly caught on fire. The hallways were narrow. The walls were Soviet Russian concrete block. The lights often flickered because the power upgrade in the nineties wasn't able to keep up with the needs of the current technology. Communications was the least supported department on campus, and the building that housed it made that disdain perfectly clear.

Naturally, this was the building that was Walter's spiritual home.

He passed the sad little studio where he'd taken the elective course that spawned his possibly ill-conceived degree, and he smiled. He waved at Jax, who was playing DJ for a campus radio station no one paid any attention to. Finally, he headed down the stairs to the basement offices where the communications profes-sors—all three of them—did their best not to hold office hours.

Professor Williams was at his desk, though, his lanky form huddled over the rough old wooden slab as he nibbled at a homemade sandwich, his graying and thinning hair sticking up in varying directions. Spying Walter, he waved and motioned him into the small, overcrowded space.

"Mr. Lucas. *Entre vous.*" He put down the sand-wich and moved a pile of file folders off a chair. "What can I do for you?" When Walter didn't answer right away, Williams studied him a moment before wincing. "Oh damn. They didn't give you permission to live off campus."

Walter shrugged, pretending it didn't matter. "It was a long shot."

"It was pretty important to you, as I recall." Williams sighed and wiped his mouth with a napkin. "For the record, I went to the board and the dean personally and pled your case. Though in hindsight that might have not been the best plan. They seem even more irritated with me this year than usual."

"It's okay, really."

Williams looked at Walter over the top of his wire-rimmed glasses, and Walter sighed before slouching in the chair.

"Okay. It sucks ass and not in a good way. I think I've been preparing myself for it ever since I got that notice from the bank, though."

"Still, I'm sorry, Walter." After pouring coffee into two chipped mugs from a battered thermos, Williams handed one to Walter. "Wish I kept a flask in here so I could make this Irish. Even though I'm not sure that's kosher, giving alcohol to a student no matter whether or not you're a legal eagle—today I would, because today sucks for you."

"Thanks." Walter took a sip of the lukewarm rotgut coffee and felt as if he'd gone home. Some of the best moments in his life had been in this office drinking bad coffee with Williams. "How's the family?"

"Good. Kids started school last week, so Karen's not quite as homicidal. It was getting to be a near thing toward the end of summer."

Walter winced. "Damn, wish I hadn't had to go back to Chicago, or I could have helped."

"Speaking of *that*. I know it'll be grim, but give me an update on the home front."

Walter sipped more coffee. "Mom is unstable again, Dad's blissfully ignoring her, and Tibby is at Olympic-level pouting and flouncing. Cara is in full wedding-planning mode, and Greg is neck-deep in grad school." He scraped his thumb over a chip on the rim. "They wanted me to transfer back to Northwestern, or somewhere in Chicago."

"Hmm." Williams tipped his chair back, making it creak on ancient hinges. "You sound oddly guilty when you say that. Did you *want* to transfer?"

"Not really." He rubbed the chipped mug rim again. "It would have been easier to keep tabs on my family, I'll admit."

Williams snorted. "Good reason not to transfer, then. Keeping tabs on your family has only ever made you crazy. Though you know you're wasted on Hope. Northwestern, U of C—anywhere else has to have a better communications department."

This comment made Walter frown. "I like our department."

"*Nobody* likes this department." Williams poked at his sandwich. "I'm up for tenure this year. I have a very bad feeling they're going to find a way to deny it to me. Goddamn, but I don't want to move."

"What?" Walter sat bolt upright in his chair. "Back up."

Williams looked surprised. "I'm in a tenured position, which means now that I've been here six years, they either give me tenure—essentially ensure I won't lose my job unless I retire or do something obscene with a student—or they don't, and in the case of the latter, that means you're out the door. With a black mark on your name when you try and find a new job."

"They have to give you tenure," Walter said, hoping he sounded less desperate than he felt.

"They don't have to, but it is pretty hard to deny it. Still, I've been in close contact with the American Association of University Professors, and I'm ready to appeal if it comes to that."

Walter simply sipped his coffee, though internally he reeled. He couldn't imagine finishing his degree without Williams. He'd fucking *sleep* with Ethan Miller and give Porterhouse a naked parade while they jeered before losing his advisor.

"Anyway." The professor put down his coffee and scratched at the back of his head. "I'm going to try to be a little more of a line-toer this year. Karen says that will last until about October. Probably she's right."

You're the best professor on campus, Walter wanted to say, but he couldn't because it would be too sycophantic. "If they deny you tenure, there will probably be a riot."

This made Williams smile. "Rose Manchester has already been by full of fury when she heard I was up this year, promising to start a student committee within the Philosophy Club if they deny me. Apparently there's precedent: in 1992 they denied a professor tenure, and during the appeal the students mobilized and in general made a big fit. I'm not convinced they're what turned the tide, and like I told Rose, I need to not hear a damn word of whatever they do because there's no way that will help, the dean of faculty and board of regents thinking I incited people to protest."

"Jesus, you sound as if you *expect* to be denied."

Williams's smile was almost wicked. "Well, the dean did call me a little shit just last week."

Normally that would make Walter smile, but given the current context, he couldn't. "Dean Prents is the little shit. God, that bastard is smarmy."

"*Hush.*" Williams stuck his foot out to shut the door, then stopped himself. "Be good. I can't shut the doors because Karen pointed out they'd love to revisit that debacle from two years ago."

"Please. It isn't Disney U unless someone accuses you of flirting with a student. Besides, you're old enough to be my dad."

"Hey!" Williams looked genuinely affronted. "Only if I'd fathered you under the ninth-grade bleachers, wise guy. Anyway, last time I checked, the daddy fetish was alive and well in the gay community." He turned slightly pale and pushed the door the rest of the way shut. "Fuck, I need to stop talking."

Walter laughed. "What, do you think they have the place bugged?"

"No, but—" He paused, clearly fighting some internal battle. "Here's the truth, between you and me. I'm an even bigger wise guy than you. Yeah, you find that fun, but it's probably about time, as someone old enough to be your father, that I act like a real grownup. I took this job because it was what I could get and because I had dreams of getting them to expand the program. All I've done in six years is screw around."

"You've done more than that."

"I don't mean to diminish what I've been able to give to students like you. I don't regret my time here, either. Or any of my students, even the shitheads. The thing is, at some point I should probably grow up and have a career, you know?"

"You *do* have a career."

"Sure. I'm a junior professor in a nearly defunct department at a university making its mark on the academic landscape with sky-high tuition, cutesy policies and diversity masquerading as a marketing strategy. I haven't even been pulling my punches on Hope because I agreed with them or because I was desperate to keep my job. I've been lazy. I haven't published but that one article, which right there makes tenure an uphill climb." Williams looked almost grim. "Yeah. I'm sure that sob story has inspired you to greatness. Okay, Mr. Lucas, I need to finish this syllabus. Really sorry about your apartment. Just tell me they snuck you into the Manors and I'll sleep easy."

"I'm doubling in a single in Porter with an allergy-ridden freshman."

"*Wonderful.*" Williams raised his mug in a mock toast. "Saturday night, Opie's, back room, pitcher of beer. I'll bring my wife so nobody thinks I'm seducing you." He frowned. "Fuck, I'll have to get a sitter, and Cara's gone. Jesus, I hate it when people graduate."

Walter laughed, shaking off the hollowness that the thought of losing Williams had inspired. "I'll be there."

"Though I forgot to ask. When are you moving in?

I assume you're staying at Cara and Greg's old place right now?"

"Yeah, finishing off the lease. Which ends on Wednesday."

Williams lifted an eyebrow. "It's Monday."

"You could say I'm in a bit of denial."

The professor checked his watch. "Given the time, I assume you're not moving in tonight."

"Tonight I plan to go find someone young and nubile and terrified and take him back to enjoy my last night in non-Disney cohabitation. Though I might drop by and stake my claim on my four square feet of floor space and make sure someone puts in a bunk for me. Unless I decide to stick with the futon. More room on that for bedroom acrobatics."

Williams tossed him a salute. "Go forth and fuck, young man."

"I plan to."

This time as Walter traversed the Ritche Hall corridors, he stuck his hands in his pockets and whistled, feeling a hell of a lot better than he had when he'd arrived.

Chapter Two

SOMEWHERE IN THE middle of freshman orientation at Hope University, Kelly Davidson began to doubt.

His parents had left around noon after hugging him and making him promise to call as often as he could. They'd had a nice lunch at the pizza place across the street, and they'd said their goodbyes on the shores of Lake Sharon. Kelly was pretty sure on the way to orientation a seriously cute guy—Kelly assumed he was an upperclassman, but he wasn't yet sure how to tell—had been checking out his ass.

Except now that he was finally in the campus auditorium listening to the dean of students talk about the wonders of Hope, Kelly could barely sit still, he was so full of panic. His happy bubble of utopia had burst sometime during the small group orientation circles, and the day which had begun with an Ashman and Menken soundtrack now played the theme from *Jaws*. Worst of all, Kelly couldn't point to anything specific to account for his sudden desire to run for home and dive right back into his closet.

A bump on his arm made him turn to his left, where his orientation leader beamed at him while the dean droned on in carefully modulated tones. Amy flashed her rainbow ring that went with her rainbow hair extensions and her bright green shirt that read *It's Okay With Me*. She leaned over to whisper in Kelly's ear. "Some of us from the GSA are going to Opie's for pizza and root beer after. Want to come along?"

Kelly paused, unsure of what to do. Hadn't he dreamed of joining a Gay-Straight Alliance since he was fourteen? Wasn't that exactly why he was here, to hook up with groups such as that?

He had, yes, but his orientation leader had given him the creeps the second they met. After outing him in front of the group—apparently his orientation was listed on her clipboard—she'd latched on to Kelly's arm and carried on about how they could boyfriend shop together. Her enthusiasm and rainbow regalia deepened Kelly's sense of foreboding instead of reassuring him.

Yes, he should go, but man he really didn't want to.

"I think I need to head back to my room and get some things settled. Thanks, though."

The dean finished speaking, and the audience clapped politely as they rose and dispersed. The orientation leader stayed at Kelly's side and pouted. "Aw, come on. You gotta eat, right? Double cheese pizza and root beer float tempt you?"

"I'm allergic to dairy." *And eggs, and almonds, and dust mites, and ragweed, and cats, and dogs, and down, and mold.* He picked up his backpack and eyed an escape route. "See you around." Before she could trap him again, he bolted.

Kelly didn't run out of the auditorium, but he

huddled underneath the slim weight of his orientation-literature-filled backpack, frowning as he tried to shake off the interaction. His thumb brushed the woven rainbow bracelet his sister had given him that morning as they'd left the hotel room to move him into his dorm. Was it a mistake to wear this? Was it too soon? Should he take it off? It's not as if Lisa would know he'd removed her gift. How many other people had his gayness marked down on their clipboards?

He frowned to himself as he angled toward the exit doors, so caught up in his own thoughts that when someone put a hand on his arm, he jumped. A girl with long blonde hair sticking out from a maroon knit beret kept hold of Kelly's arm and pointed to the floor. "Sorry, but you were about to walk right across the Zodiac."

Her tone seemed to hint this sentence should be self-explanatory, which only further confused Kelly. "What?"

"They didn't tell you in orientation? Usually they at least cover it as an amusing myth." She pointed to a mosaic in the floor, brass-plated symbols that looked vaguely astrological. "Don't walk over the Zodiac, or you'll fail your next test. I know, it sounds stupid now. But as one who has done it and paid the price, I can't let you start college that way in good conscience."

"Okay." Kelly wasn't sure what else to say to that. "Thanks?"

Grinning wryly, the girl held out her hand. "Rose Manchester, sophomore. Nice to meet you."

Kelly took her hand somewhat hesitantly. "Kelly

Davidson. Freshman. Though you seem to know what year I am already."

Rose shrugged. "It's a small school. Anybody you don't know at this time of year is either a freshman or a transfer."

"I don't look like a transfer, I take it?"

"Well, you're wearing your high school class ring, which most transfers don't."

Kelly tucked his thumb over his right ring finger. "Is that uncool or something?"

She laughed. "I wouldn't know. I'm kind of a geek."

He did a quick inventory of Rose's accessories—no rainbow necklace and no class ring. She did have a curious-looking necklace: a black cord bearing a heavy metal circle that read *ERASE HATE*. Jewelry seemed a safe conversation—it was working so far. "I like your necklace."

Touching it, Rose smiled, and her gaze fell briefly to Kelly's left wrist. "Thanks."

Kelly had to fight not to cover his bracelet, and as they stood there not speaking, he felt a weird kinship with Rose. She reminded him of his sister both in looks and her ability to hold graceful silence. He found himself wanting to talk to her, to capture her as a friend, but he had no idea how to do it.

He went with the necklace. "Is that the NOH8 campaign?"

She shook her head. "Matthew Shepard."

"Oh." Kelly swallowed a *cool* because obviously Matthew Shepard's plight was not.

"Normally I don't advertise," Rose went on, "but a friend gave this to me, and it reminds me of her."

Advertise. Kelly thought of Amy and tucked the bracelet higher, vowing to cut it off the second he got to his room. Then he realized what Rose had said. Wait, did that mean…? Could he ask?

Rose smiled. "I think I officially fall as a Q right now, but yes, I'm gay."

"Q?"

"Questioning." Rose shifted her backpack higher. "Somewhere between lesbian and bi at the moment, but honestly, I have no idea. I only know I don't fit the standard heterosexual mold." She lifted a knowing eyebrow. "You're just now out, right?"

He tried to laugh. "How can you tell?"

"Because you look as if you expect people to come out of the bushes and start screaming *gay* at you before they pelt you with stones. It's okay. We've all been there. Some days I still am, I think. I'm sure you've heard the spiels, but you really can relax for the most part at Hope. Just stay out of Porterhouse, and you'll be fine."

Kelly went still. "Porter? You're talking about the dorm called Porter?" When she nodded, his gut clenched. "That's where my room is."

Rose's smile died. "Ah. Well, I hope you have a good roommate."

He tried not to panic. "I don't have one. I have allergies, so they gave me a single for the air conditioner."

"That's good—no roommate, I mean. It's almost all jocks there, and I hate to stereotype, but…well, I'm sure it'll be fine." She said it in the way people say they hope things will be fine when they're sure they won't be. Fishing in her pocket, Rose pulled out a smartphone. "Here—give me your number, and I'll text you later to be sure you're okay. I'm across the way in Sandman, and if nothing else, I can flash my tits at them while you run."

Kelly laughed, but his fingers shook as he entered himself into Rose's contacts. How, after all his careful planning, had he ended up in the one bad dorm? He wanted to ask questions, lots of them, and he wanted to beg Rose not to leave him, to let him live under her bed. He might have tried if he'd thought he could survive the dust bunnies.

She took back her phone and winked. "It's going to be fine, Kelly Davidson. I'm a little bit psychic some-times, and I'm telling you, everything is going to be all right."

God but he hoped so. "Thanks."

"Anyway. Sorry for jumping you, but seriously, that Zodiac curse is murder." Stepping back, she waved. "See you around."

"Bye." Kelly watched her head into the union be-fore continuing on his way.

He put off returning to his dorm as long as possi-ble. There was a dinner in the commons for the freshmen, or so Dean Stevens had assured them during her speech, but Kelly didn't go. He wasn't hungry, and he still felt overwhelmed and off kilter.

He wandered the union instead, buying a salad in the deli and turning red when he had to ask them to make a new one without cheese and egg, even though he'd told them he was allergic. He couldn't bring himself to ask for new dressing, though, so he'd thrown the packet away and eaten it dry. As he choked it down, he tried to tell himself there wasn't anything to worry about, that living in a jock dorm all by himself would be fine.

His self-pep talks weren't working very well.

During the orientation speech, the dean of students had gone on and on about Hope's impressive legacy, about their sterling academic reputation and their notoriety for strong social unity. "We are all a family at Hope," she told the freshmen, beaming at them with slightly crooked teeth. "You are all about to take this journey together, and over the next four years you will make friends that will last a lifetime. Many of you will meet your life partners here. Many of you will send your children here. Hope is your home now. We, the rest of your family, can't wait to see what you do."

Her words kept ringing in Kelly's head as he gave up on the salad and wove through the campus pathways toward his dorm. The dean hadn't said anything different than they touted in their literature and on their website. Back when he'd applied, Kelly had taken comfort in those words, but now all he could think about was what Rose had said about Porter. What if that was only the start of things nobody had bothered to tell him?

Probably he was tired and homesick. Probably he should go back to his room, heat up one of the single-serve vegan meals he knew his mom had snuck into the fridge, and go to bed.

After pushing the ancient key code to get into the dorm door—who exactly that was keeping out was anybody's guess—Kelly went up the stairs to the fourth floor, trying not to fixate on the smell. He'd been in the other dorms during his tour, but not Porter, and now he knew why: it smelled like feet. It smelled as if five hundred pairs of feet and that many jockstraps marinated in tubs of sweat. As he'd moved in, Kelly's mother had fretted about mold and gone on and on about his allergies, double-checking his air filter about thirty times. Kelly had told her it wasn't a big deal, but he did worry, a little. He worried too about all the loud, burly guys he could hear bellowing down the hallways, wondering how he was supposed to shower with them when they knew he was gay.

How ridiculous was he, thinking being at a liberal university that promised they were all family was protection.

By the time he got to his floor, Kelly was an anxious mess. He kept his head down as he beelined for his door, key already in his hand. He could feel the stares of his floor mates, could hear the whispers, but his heart pounded too loudly inside his ears for him to make out their taunts. He didn't know how to handle being ostracized. This had never been his life. How had this happened?

How was he supposed to *live* like this?

Kelly pushed panic aside because it was starting to make his airways constrict. *No.* No asthma attacks now. He'd get inside, lock the door, and curl up in his bed until he felt better.

Except when he got to his door, it was already open.

Just a little, cracked a few inches, but it was open all the same, and the light was on inside. *Someone broke in,* Kelly thought, feeling sick and violated, and then he heard a voice coming from inside. He pushed open the door, key tight in his hand, heart pushing up at the top of his throat.

An upperclassman who looked like Flynn Rider from *Tangled* put down his cellphone, turned to face Kelly and smiled as he stuck out his free hand. "Hi. I'm Walter Lucas, your roommate."

Chapter Three

WHILE WALTER HAD fully intended to head to Moe's and cruise the new blood, once he was alone at his apartment, the urge evaporated. He'd wandered around like a caged tiger for half an hour, digesting the cold reality of all the shit he was going to have to move into storage. At the forty-five-minute mark he'd caved and started packing. There seemed no point in putting off the inevitable move. He'd shoved most of his things into storage with Cara's stuff in the garage to be picked up when she and Greg came back down, gone to the Porter resident assistant for his key, and descended back into dorm life.

As he took in his delicious newbie roommate, however, dorm life didn't seem so bad.

God Almighty, this one had it going on. Just shy of six feet, he had dark brown hair with a kiss of blond highlights—natural, as if he'd spent the summer in the sun, and it was teased into a subdued version of a messy faux-hawk. He had a medium build, not twink thin, but not cut. Maybe he worked out, but it was at home and only when he had the time. Cutie had lovely symmetrical features, nice lips with a hint of plumpness, and gorgeous eyes that sparkled in hues of pale blue and gray. He sported a suggestion of stubble reaching up to ears that, contrary to Walter's own aural appendages, lay back politely against the sides of his well-groomed head. Best of all, though, was how he was dressed. Button-down shirt with a royal blue tee underneath. Both shirts were snug without screaming *tap this, bitch*, showing off a fine, sculpted, young male form.

Then there were the jeans. The jeans made Walter want to moan, they told him so much. The jeans were tight, tighter than the shirt. The jeans had been chosen to advertise, though only to those who were shopping. The jeans hugged and molded and said, *I am a gay boy with a fine ass and nice package to go with it, and while I'm a nice boy on the surface, I truly want you to take these jeans off and fuck me. Just be nice when you ask, because I have standards.*

Walter loved Hottie Freshman's standards. He wanted to worship those standards. On his knees, with HF's perfect little mouth open and gasping as Walter showed his deep and abiding appreciation. *Talent.* Grade-A, sweet, biteable freshman talent.

At the moment, however, the talent looked scared and overwhelmed and pretty much the way Walter had felt his first night in the door, except Walter had been paired up with a pussy-pounding fuckwad who made his life miserable from the word go, and Walter had never been as shy and prone to blushes as the boy standing in the doorway.

"I don't understand." Walter's roommate tugged on his ear and glanced around nervously. "They said I had a single."

"Yeah, well, that's a long story. Short version is, you've got a roommate now, and it's me." When his roommate still looked nervous, Walter offered a softer smile. "Want to tell me your name?"

He swallowed hard before answering. "Kelly."

"Nice to meet you, Kelly. I'm sorry about bursting in on you like this. I don't even have a bed, as you can see, but happily you have a loft, and I have a futon. Going to have to see a chiropractor after hauling it up those damn stairs myself, but better than asking a jock for help." He gestured to where he'd made space against the wall. "I have a few more things I'm going to need to bring over from storage, but not much."

Kelly frowned at the futon and the now very crowded floor space. There was just enough room for him to climb up the ladder to his loft, but he'd have hell getting to his dresser. "There's only one desk."

"Yeah. They'd give us a second if we asked, but I don't know where we'd put it. I don't really need one, if you can spare me a drawer." He sighed and glared at the room. "Jesus, they're kidding themselves if they think two people can live here. What a bunch of assholes. That's Hope for you, though. If we bitch, they'll tell us this is part of being a family or some other bullshit." He glanced at Kelly, remembering he was in the presence of a freshman. "Sorry. You probably still have the postcoital glow of orientation going. Didn't mean to pop your cherry so fast."

The kid blushed again. It was kind of cute, if not a little ridiculous. "No, I…" He stopped, looking lost.

Walter began to wish he'd stayed at the apartment after all. "You don't have to stand in the doorway. This is still your room, and I don't bite. Not unless you ask nicely."

He should have known that would make Kelly nervous rather than laugh, but Kelly came in all the same, glancing around uncertainly before making a serious study of the air conditioner, fussing with one of the knobs.

Walter tried to fill the awkward silence. "That's a nice perk, the AC."

"I have allergies." Kelly frowned at Walter. "Sorry, are you…you're not a freshman?"

"Junior. I was supposed to live off campus, but it fell through. I wanted to move into a different place, but they won't take a new application. They're crazy about people living away from the dorms. Everyone else has already been given space, and I'm last minute, so I'm back here in Porterhouse with the meatheads." He pasted on a smile and settled onto his futon. "But I lucked out and got you instead of one of them, so it's not all bad."

Kelly went to sit at his desk, every motion careful as if he might have to bolt out of the room at any second like a rabbit. He reached for one of the meal bars and unwrapped it slowly, keeping one eye on Walter the whole time.

Walter couldn't figure out what to do, so he kept talking. "I noticed those bars earlier. You're vegan?"

Kelly paused. "No. Well—sort of." He had red cheeks now too. This could be a drinking game. "I'm allergic to a lot of things, including egg and dairy. I eat meat, though not a lot because my mom is vegetarian, and we don't eat much of it. Vegan products are easier for the most part, except I have to watch out for almonds. I get crazy bad hives even from a hint of them. If anything's made on the same equipment as almonds, I'm in trouble."

Sweet Christ, the guy was a hot mess. "What's the AC for? What allergies?"

"Dust mite, mold, and ragweed. And down, though the air conditioner doesn't help with that, obviously. I'm allergic to cats and dogs too, but that shouldn't be a problem here." He darted a glance at Walter's futon. "I—um, I have to encase your mattress, but I'll buy the cover. We'll have to wash bedding on hot once a week. Sorry. It's a huge pain."

Walter thought of his wonderful down comforter back at the apartment and sighed. "I'm sure it'll be fine."

Kelly broke off a piece of the meal bar and twirled it in his fingers a moment. "Sorry if I seem thrown. It was a weird afternoon, and I was hoping to just come back and crash. I wasn't expecting…this."

"I can imagine." Walter tilted his head, curious. "Why, what happened at orientation? Besides, I'm sure, some overeager fag-hag wannabe latching on to you?" When Kelly glanced up at him, surprised, Walter almost laughed. "That was a lucky guess, but I'm sorry to hear I was accurate."

Kelly was crumbling the piece of bar onto the desk, watching it fall. "My orientation leader kind of outed me to our group. I never really came out to her, either, she just—" He stopped, then shoved his sleeve down over his wrist. "She told everyone, and I don't know why, but it really bugged me."

"Probably because she made it about her, not you, and she made you everybody's focus, and you don't look like somebody who appreciates that much."

He expected at least a sad smile, but Kelly was still mangling his bar. "I only started coming out recently. I never did in high school because my hometown is so small. It didn't feel right. I told myself it wasn't long until college, that I could wait." He grimaced and pushed his sleeve back up, revealing a thin rainbow band. "I guess it shouldn't be a big deal, but it's...I don't know."

Jesus. Usually Walter was pretty tolerant about the stupid GSA, but he wanted to beat them a little right now. "It *is* a big deal. You waited forever for this moment, and then some dingbat craps all over it. You have a right to be pissed."

Kelly's shoulders slumped forward. "I guess."

Walter scooted forward on his futon. "Look, I can buzz out of here for tonight, give you your space. I'm sorry about the futon—can I get the cover in town? I'll go grab it tonight."

"No—no, it's fine. You don't have to go. Actually..." Kelly's face blossomed into a slow, shy smile. "Actually, it's nice to have a roommate. I was bummed about having to live alone."

"*Well.* In that case, I'll stay." Walter pushed to his feet, grinning. "I need some dinner. You hungry? We could head over to Moe's for burritos and a couple beers."

"Oh—I'm not old enough to drink."

Walter laughed, grabbed Kelly's hand and pulled him to his feet too. "Come on, roomie. Let's blow this overgrown locker room, and I'll give you your *real* freshman orientation."

KELLY SHOULD HAVE told Walter he didn't want to go out. He should have said he'd be fine in the room and let Walter go by himself. He didn't, because he had a feeling wherever Walter went, interesting things would soon follow.

Also, given the bellows of the jocks in the hallway, he wasn't yet convinced it was safe to stay there alone.

They went first to Walter's car, which he'd been able to park in one of the upperclassmen lots north of the union. Kelly would have been impressed enough with having his own vehicle, but to be that close to campus reminded him Walter was in an entirely different league. Not that there had been any flirting, outside of what Kelly figured was standard for Walter. Still, it all gave Kelly way too much of a thrill, because even though this meant nothing, being escorted to the mall by a hot upperclassman who was also gay and had flirted with him even reflexively was as close as Kelly had come to...well, anything.

Kelly stuffed his hands in his pockets as Walter unlocked a sleek, electric-blue Mazda3. "Great car."

"Yeah, it's okay. Hate the hatchback." Walter

winced and tossed an apologetic smile at Kelly that still managed to look incredibly sexy. "Sorry. I think that was the most entitled, suburban rich-kid thing I've said all week."

"Are you from Chicago?" Most people in his orientation group seemed to be.

"Yes indeed. Northbrook, born and raised." He put the car into gear and began to maneuver it out of the lot. "Parents divorced a few years back, and now my dad lives in some loft downtown where he boinks secretaries—so 1980—but 'home' is still my mom's place back on Wade Street. And yeah, my family has money. Nothing fancy, enough to plunk me here, pay for my sister's exotic horse to have a better room than I do, plus the whole Dad-midlife-crisis thing. My mom has a job now, but it's part-time, some weird from-home sales gig she does between living off alimony. Just another happy, fucked-up, north Chicago family." He glanced across the seat at Kelly. "What about you? I can already tell you aren't from Chicago."

He could? "How?"

That little half smile did such incredibly dangerous things to Kelly's insides. "You aren't cynical enough. You don't even have that money-up-my-ass sense of paranoid entitlement that seems to be the other way we go. You, my dear roomie, are almost fresh-faced and apple-cheeked. So spill. From whence do you hail?"

Kelly was almost embarrassed to say now. "Windom, Minnesota. It's very small, in the southwest. Not a suburb of anything."

He wasn't sure what to make of the way Walter

smiled, kind of mocking but not really. "Is it an Andy Griffith kind of joint? Dad taking you fishing on weekends, you played ball in the park, and your family had church picnics on the back lot?"

The church picnics were in the basement, but yes, the rest was dead-on, though Kelly didn't want to admit it. "It's a nice place."

"But not nice enough that you could come out comfortably?"

Kelly pressed his hands over his pant legs. "I don't like making waves, and I don't like too much attention." That wasn't quite true, he acknowledged, remembering the plays and leadership seminars he'd done in high school. He curled his fingers over his jeans. "It's not wrong to have wanted to come out in my own way."

"No, it's not." Walter drove through the neighborhood surrounding Hope to get to the main road. "It does suck that who you want to fuck is something that would be considered a big deal. That something that mundane could have ruined your high school experience. I don't know how you lived with that."

"You were out in high school?"

"Hell yes. I was out in seventh fucking grade, had my first boyfriend in eighth. Well, I say boyfriend, but mostly we were blowing each other in the locker room when we could get away with it. We liked saying we were boyfriends. Felt cool. Got over that by high school, though." He laughed. "Shit, I guess Todd was my last steady. That's hilarious. I should find him on Facebook and give him shit."

There was so much to unpack in Walter's casual reply that Kelly's head was spinning. Out in *seventh grade*? Boyfriend in eighth?

Blowing each other *in the locker room*?

No boyfriend since then? No *boyfriend*? He glanced at Walter and wrote that off immediately. No. No way Walter hadn't been with anyone since eighth grade. No. Way.

Walter caught him looking and lifted an eyebrow. "What?"

"You can't have not had a boyfriend since eighth grade."

"Not a one, and proud of it."

"But there's no way! You—" Kelly cut himself off, unable to say, *had to have had sex.*

Walter seemed to hear it anyway. He grinned that sly grin, and as usual it made Kelly's belly turn over and whine. "I've been with guys, yes. Many. But we don't date. That's awfully cute, Red, that you think fucking a guy comes with dating him."

Kelly frowned at the nickname, felt his face heat and went redder. "But why wouldn't you want to date someone? Why are you *proud* of that?"

"What the hell do I do on a date that I don't do any other time? Talk? Hell, you and I are talking right now. Go out to eat? That's on the agenda too. Doesn't mean we're sleeping together, not necessarily. Sometimes sex happens with people I hang out with, sometimes it just happens. It's a game. It's fun. Why would I want to fuck it up with some heterosexual mating dance?"

Kelly didn't know what to say to that, except that he *did* want to fuck it up with some heterosexual mating dance. He wanted a goddamn gay Disney movie, and no, that wasn't an oxymoron. He didn't think a relationship would fuck up sex. He believed it would make it better.

He also believed saying that would get him laughed at and mocked for being from a small town again, so he kept quiet.

Walter glanced at him after a few minutes. "So what do your parents do? Are they still together?"

"Yes. My dad's a vice president at Windom Savings Bank, and my mom's an insurance adjuster. My sister, Lisa, is in ninth grade."

"Bank, and a local one. He doing okay? That whole financial thing didn't wipe them out?"

"They're hanging in there. There have been tough times before, since they have a lot of farmers as clients." He felt the money thing hanging in the air, so he decided to address it. "We aren't rich. We have money, but mostly that's because my family is very careful. They'd saved for my college since forever, but Hope was more expensive than we planned for. I just hope I can help pay for my sister's round when it's her turn."

"Sounds like you guys have a perfect, happy family." Walter winced. "Yeah, sorry, asshole alert. I'm jealous, is all. We've all done our time in therapy at my place. The car and the toys and the pricey school, all of it's my dad's way of trying to buy me back. I'd trade it all in to live in a trailer park and have a family that sat down to dinner without turning into an episode of

Jersey Shore." He paused, then added, "Maybe not a trailer."

That made Kelly laugh. "We fight too. But yes, I guess we're kind of sickeningly happy. Some of it comes from both Lisa and I having health issues. My allergies used to be a lot worse, and the same with my asthma. Lisa has type I diabetes."

"Jesus, really? That would do it, everyone rallying around the sick kids. Still, I've known plenty of families with issues, health and otherwise, that tear each other apart. Give yourselves credit for simply being awesome, huh?"

Kelly smiled and ducked his head, but he felt good, not awkward for once, and he carried that feeling all the way into the parking lot of the shopping center.

"This isn't the only shopping area in Danby, but it's the best one-stop joint," Walter told him as they exited the car. "You can get food over there at Dominick's, random shit at Target, and there's even a liquor store on the end. Though don't go to that one until you're legal, because they card and they're good at spotting fakes."

"I don't have a fake ID."

Walter waved this away. "I'll get you one. Don't protest, Red. Everybody has one here. Everybody has one everywhere, because what idiots thought they'd send legal adults off to be independent but hold off the one thing they actually want to do? So. Can we get this cover thing at Target?"

Kelly wanted to get back to the ID, because he did *not* want it, but he only sighed and nodded. "Yes. They have everything we need. Their dust-mite covers aren't as fancy as the ones online, and they make a little bit of noise when you move, but they're cheap and they work. It's mostly a nonpermeable fabric with a good seal."

Walter locked the car as they headed toward the store. "What happens if we leave the cover off, use down comforters, and don't scald our sheets?"

"At first, nothing. Eventually though I swell up, especially my sinuses, and if it's bad enough, I won't be able to breathe."

Walter shuddered. "Good to know. Do you have inhalers and EpiPens and all that stuff? Should I know where they are?"

"I have those, yes, always in my pockets, but I take my meds and I know when I'm getting sick. I used to try and not make a fuss about things, especially the food, but I've had enough reactions to know I've got to. It's part of why I have the meal bars. My mom buys them in bulk because we have to make sure we have ones without almonds."

"That sounds as if it really sucks."

"You have no idea. The almonds are the worst. I eat a lot of vegan stuff because they exclude milk and dairy, but almonds they love. Vegans put them in everything."

Walter shook his head. "*You* should be in off-campus housing. How are you going to eat in the cafeteria?"

Kelly stopped walking and frowned. "They said they have allergen menus."

Walter put a hand on Kelly's shoulder. "Oh, Red. I

keep forgetting how green you are. Let's just say, keep your EpiPen handy, eh, and maybe a meal bar in your pocket."

Kelly hoped he was joking and was very afraid that he wasn't. "Why do you keep ragging on Hope? If you hate it, why are you here?"

"I don't hate it. Well, I hate parts of it, yes, in the same way I hate parts of everything. It *is* a liberal hotbed—which is where some of the weird comes from, to be honest—but the professors are great, especially my advisor, Dr. Williams. He teaches Intro to Humanities, so you'll have him eventually. Also the place really does take overt bullying seriously. Of course, they also have a ridiculously high suicide rate."

Kelly stopped walking abruptly. "What?"

"It's true. Look it up. They obviously don't advertise it, but yeah. It's the same as everywhere else in life: great intentions, grim reality. They started this joint for underprivileged Chicago youth, trying to give them a better shot. Then it became one of the first to actively recruit women. Then they sought out African Americans, and now Latinos. They've always got an angle. But it's just that, a way to look good. Actually being hopeful? That's hard shit, and it's expensive. So we get a lot of Disney."

"What's wrong with Disney?"

"What *isn't* wrong with Disney? Cute bubblegum life wrapped up in a politically correct Technicolor corporate bow. Fake acceptance and other bullshit carefully crafted to be swallowed whole and consumed at a premium price." Walter shook his head. "Hope is nothing but a bad dye job. We can't live off campus because it looks like we're a big happy family if we're all right here, and they get all that income from dorms, even when they shove the two of us in a shoebox and try and kill you over almonds slopped in your oatmeal at breakfast. They don't let people bully, not where you can see it, so they do it in other ways. Let's just say we should shower at the same time for a while, and use the bathroom at the far end until the thugs work out their pecking order."

Kelly ignored the slam against Disney and fixated on the important things, such as Hope not being what he thought it was. "I thought you said they took bullying seriously?"

"Yeah. If anyone calls you a fag and you have even a fruit fly as a witness, they're paying a big fat fine and doing community service. So they're never going to call you a fag. They're going to be subtle, and there are plenty of shy gay boys who can't take it. Now, me? Shit, I ate that for breakfast in high school. They learned to give me a wide berth, and I got out of the bad dorms fast. I transferred out of Porterhouse by Christmas break my first year here."

"But that's the only underclassmen male dorm where they allow air conditioners. The allergen rooms in other dorms were all taken by sophomores, they said."

Walter put a hand on Kelly's arm again. "Easy. Easy."

Kelly shook his arm off and pointed at himself, leaning forward to whisper angrily, "*I'm* one of those shy gay boys."

"I know, babe. I know." Walter held up his hands. "Look, I got your back, okay? Roomies, right?"

"Oh, like you're not bailing on me first chance you get." What was Kelly going to do? Classes hadn't started and he was thinking of transferring. He'd spent so much *time* finding the right place, and now—*God*.

This time Walter put both hands on Kelly's shoulders. They felt good and solid, and they meant Kelly could smell the incredible scent that was Walter, spice and cologne and man. It calmed him right down, even as it revved other parts of him up.

"I won't bail. Promise. And hey, maybe I'll be wrong. Maybe Porter has all changed in two years. Maybe you're a secret tough guy, or you'll stab them with that EpiPen or charm them. But if not—no, I'm not bailing on you."

Kelly glared at him, or tried to. Fuck, Walter smelled good. "Why not?"

If eau de Walter was hard to resist, Walter's expression turning empathetic and not at all cynical was purely lethal. "Because I would have killed to have that kind of backing when I felt the same way in high school, and it makes me feel good to be able to give it to you now."

Jesus. "So now I'm a *high school* student?"

Cue sideways smile. Kelly couldn't help it, he was starting to get hard. In Target. It only got worse when Walter scraped his thumb along the pulsing cord on Kelly's neck. "No, baby. You're one hundred percent sweet, delectable undergrad." He winked, then let Kelly go. "Come on. Let's go get those covers."

Chapter Four

THE KID WAS cute. Really damn cute, outside and in. Kelly was shy and quiet and naive and Walter was very, very afraid might be a closet Republican, but everything except for the last part was win. Making him blush was fun too. It was so easy Walter kept doing it to explore the depths of how red the guy could get.

Kelly wanted Walter too, that was clear as day, which was fun because he was embarrassed about that the way he was everything else. Slightly helpless about it, though, which really turned Walter on. He felt as if he could drag Kelly into the bathroom by the pharmacy and blow him right there, and at best Kelly would put up a token *we shouldn't* before giving up all those reserved, shy moans for Walter's mouth. He was a *pretty* boy too, and no doubt every girl in his high school had been fapping over him and imagining they'd be the one to be shy Kelly's girlfriend. Fuck, any boys unwittingly sharing Kelly's closet were right there with the girls, except whatever lucky bastards caught his eye in the locker room.

Now Walter was living with him. Fuck yeah. He could handle some shy pretty boy on tap.

"You know, sometimes I think I shop at Target because of the color scheme," Walter confessed as they trolled down the aisle. They had a cart full of anti-dust-mite bedding and a new comforter for Walter and were now simply wandering. "It's horrid suburban hell, but it has nice design, so I don't mind."

"Target's from Minnesota." Kelly pushed the cart, something he seemed to take great security in. "Head-quartered in Minneapolis."

"Which I heard is now one of the gayest cities in America. Now it all makes sense." Walter elbowed him. "So, we're here, we're queer, and I have a gold card. Let's trick out our humble abode. What are you feeling? Patio lights hung around your loft? Beanbag chairs that match your lampshade? I draw the line at mirrors on the ceiling, though a few positioned artfully on the closet door wouldn't hurt my feelings."

Kelly bit his lip. "It's fine. Whatever you want."

Walter rolled his eyes. "Seriously, I have to blow a grand a month before my dad even remembers I'm alive. Here. How about these cute mugs? They say ALOHA. I think we each have to have one, don't you? And the serving tray to match, naturally."

Kelly frowned and protested no matter what Walter put in his cart, though Walter thought his roommate secretly loved the pea-green floor rocker, and maybe the mirrored ALOHA tray Walter planned to hang on the wall near the door. Mostly Kelly seemed determined not to be a bother and to under no circumstances spend Walter's money.

Naturally, this cemented Walter's determination to pay for dinner.

They ditched the car in the lot, leaving their stuff for the way back, and walked to Moe's. It had an age minimum of nineteen to get in, but it was still early so nobody gave a shit. They ate on the restaurant side, if the handful of booths and the burrito bar could be called a restaurant. Though as Walter saw Kelly scouring the menu, he remembered the food-allergy thing and felt like a dick. "Shit, I didn't even think. Can you eat here?"

"I think so." Kelly was still scrutinizing the laminated sheet. "No cheese and no sauces except the salsa, and I need to double-check everything because I've learned otherwise I run too high a risk of hitting the hospital, but they look safe enough. It's all customized, so it's actually probably one of the better places I can eat."

"You can do all the burritos as salad, if you have the gluten thing or just don't want a tortilla."

"I thank God on a daily basis I don't have a wheat allergy." Kelly stepped forward to order, and Walter found himself hoping to hell that God thanking was ironic. If Cara found out he was living with a *God-fearing* Republican, he'd never hear the end of it.

As predicted, Kelly had a fit when Walter paid for their meal, though it was nothing compared to when Walter ordered a pitcher of Pabst and two glasses.

"I'm only eighteen."

"Do not tell me you haven't had alcohol. I won't believe you."

Kelly glared at him. "Yes, I have, but not like this. Not out in the open where anyone can see me."

"What do you think they're going to do? Storm in with a SWAT team and haul you off to the gulag?" He glanced at Kelly's hand, noticed the jewelry and laughed. "Though here's a pro tip: don't wear your high school class ring. It doesn't do you any favors in the age department." He studied Kelly with a critical eye. "You do look young in general. We'll make sure it's a good fake."

Kelly tucked the ring's stone into his palm, blushing yet again. "What happens if they figure out it's a fake?"

"Here? They'll just take it away. Tonight you're not going to need it though. If they card us, it's me they'll fry for buying beer for you."

"With *your* fake ID?"

"Actually, it's my real ID. I'm turning twenty-two next month. And yes, before you do the math, I'm older than most college juniors. I believe I mentioned my parents' divorce? Well, let's just say my mother did not take it well. At all. I was enrolled at Northwestern, and I got about a month in before I withdrew and went home because I had no idea what was going to happen. She did go to the hospital for a while, so it's probably good I pulled out when I did. I have no idea who would have kept my sister from foster care or worse."

Kelly looked at him as if he'd confessed to pulling his family from the ocean in some kind of hi-res film moment. "Wow."

"Not even close to wow. Anyway, when it was all sorted, they asked me where I wanted to go. At that point, nowhere, because I felt so old, but my best friend was here, and she loved it, and I'd visited her and thought it wasn't bad, so I said this joint. Which brings us to now."

"Is your friend still here?"

Walter shook his head. "Graduated in August. I'm two years behind my high school peers. Cara and I rigged ourselves a room together midway through my freshman year, and last year I lived with her and her fiancé off-campus, which was great. I was supposed to stay in their place this school year, but the landlord fucked that up. It's too bad. It's a great place. I should take you by to see it, since I still have the key."

"Who's living there now?"

"Nobody, and nobody will. Bank will try to sell it, which they won't be able to do because it's too close to campus. They'll probably make it a parking lot eventually. Crying shame."

"Couldn't you lease it from the bank?"

"Yes, but the college didn't like that it wasn't a year lease, which is part of their 'protect the family' bullshit, which is really them playing Big Brother. Every now and again when the crazy right-wingers bitch about socialist lefties, they get it right. This would be one of those cases." He let out a breath and gave up. "Okay, I have to ask because it's making me nuts. You're not Republican, are you?"

Kelly looked surprised and a little amused. "Does that matter?"

"Oh fuck, you are."

Now he laughed. "No. I'm not anything. Neither is my family. We vote in whatever way works at the time.

Or rather they do, I haven't voted yet. Though I know the last few times my family have voted Democrat because of LGBT rights."

"Because now it's personal?" Walter sipped at his beer. "Sure, I get that. Well, are you going to hold it against me for being a card-carrying member of the radical left?"

God, the kid had a cute smile. It made his eyes twinkle and made Walter want to suck on his chin. "I think I can live with it."

"What about religion? I have an atheist card too, and I use it."

Kelly didn't seem moved. "I'm Lutheran, but I don't care what other people believe, or don't."

"You going to go to church on Sunday mornings?"

"Probably not, but don't tell my mother."

"Fair enough." God, Walter felt a lot better. He nudged Kelly's beer at him. "What about wild sex parties? I assume those are on the menu, if we can figure out how to stack people into our—shit, you're white as a sheet. They slipped an almond into your burrito, the bastards. Where's that EpiPen?"

"No—" Ducking his head, Kelly stared hard at his plate, color coming back to his face. "I'm fine."

Kelly was, Walter realized, mortified. *Oh.* That pale expression was *extreme* embarrassment. "So no sex parties, huh? The room really is too small anyway, and we'd have to smuggle them into Porterhouse first. Do we go with the old towel-on-the-door routine, or in this century, text message? I'd crack a joke about liking an audience, but I don't want to see you pass out."

Kelly pursed his lips, then sighed so hard his shoulders drooped a little. "The thing is, I don't have sex."

"What, ever? I didn't think Lutherans were that harsh."

It was supposed to make him laugh. It didn't. "No. I want to. I would love to, honestly, but—" He glanced up at Walter, then away.

Holy. Fuck. First the boyfriend question, now this. "Red, are you trying to tell me you're saving yourself for marriage?"

"*No*. I—Damn it." Kelly took a sip of the beer, which was rather a hollow victory for Walter at this point. "Look, I get that it's not special to you, but it is to me. You can make jokes about Mayberry and my perfect family if you want, but this is who I am, and I happen to like who I am, so you can just deal. I *do* want a boyfriend. I *do* want my first time—and my second, and all the ones after that—to be special. I don't think that's impossible, either. I'm not cynical, no. I believe there are good people out there, and I want to meet one of them and fall in love and raise a family. In fact, it's what I'm going to do, and I don't care what you think about my wanting that."

Kelly looked at Walter with so much conviction it would have been beautiful if it weren't so tragic. Where the fuck the kid thought he was going to find this Prince Charming, even at Disney U, was his first challenge. That he'd find somebody remotely close on his second try—or third, or fourth, or fiftieth—wasn't the point. That kind of thing didn't exist.

He couldn't say that to Kelly, not a single word of

it though, because he couldn't work the cynicism past the lump in his throat he'd gotten from listening to that sappy, stupid speech. He couldn't be the one to burst that bubble. Because then Red would stop smiling at him, and that would break his heart.

Walter picked up his beer, clinking it against the one Kelly gripped so desperately. "Good luck."

He meant it too. He also knew there was no way in hell that fantasy would happen, but he hoped Red beat the odds. Fucking shame, though, because obviously the let's-get-it-out-of-the-way, make-out session he'd been planning on angling for before bed was off the table. He supposed he could live without knowing what Kelly looked like when he came, but it seemed such a stupid waste.

He nudged Kelly's beer again. "Drink up." When Kelly didn't, Walter looked back at him and sighed at the glare he was getting. "No sex parties, okay? I'm not playing monk for you, but I'm not a dog. We'll work something out. It'll be fine. Now drink your beer."

Kelly kept glaring. "You're mocking me somehow. I can tell, and I don't care for it."

"I'm not mocking you. You can do what you want."

"But *you* don't like it."

"It doesn't matter what I think, does it? Who knows. Maybe I'm wrong and your way is right." He snorted and refilled his own glass. "Hell, you'd be number two, because so far Cara's Exhibit A."

"Your friend who you lived with?"

"The very same. Engaged to the guy she met here,

and they're off in Northbrook picking out china patterns. Happy as little clams in a sandbar. It's not even disgusting, which in itself is disgusting."

Finally, Kelly smiled again. "See? It happens."

"Yeah. So does a lightning strike." He held up a hand before Kelly could say anything. "Don't even start about lightning rods. I get it. I just don't buy it, and it's not for me in any event. I'm going to get a good job, screw my way through whatever metropolitan area I live in, then buy myself a boy toy to amuse me in my old age. It's all arranged. You can Skype me and show me the cutesy baby you and Prince Charming adopted, and I'll send her extravagant presents. It'll be wonderful."

Not just a smile but a laugh. "Okay."

Walter glanced at his phone. "Right. They're going to start carding in half an hour, and while the owner might love me, he won't stand for you not even having a decent fake during rush hour, so chop-chop, Red. We'll go find you something suitable tomorrow. Unless, of course, you'd rather continue the traditional newbie freshman activities."

Kelly flipped him off. "I'll stick with the Cynical Atheist Orientation plan, thanks."

"Good." Walter watched Kelly's throat work as he drained his beer, feeling the beauty of it burn in his groin. Fucking, fucking shame about that sex, because they'd have had to do it twice, it'd have been that good. Whatever. There were plenty of cute freshmen to fuck. It would take him a month and a half just to get through the Grade A's.

Still, such a shame that the cream of the crop would be one bunk away and holding out for Mr. Right.

Eventually he'll come around to realizing he'd do better to settle for Mr. Right Now. Walter smiled at the thought.

Chapter Five

ROSE TEXTED KELLY that first night to make sure he was okay, and when he told her about Walter being his roommate, she flipped out.

OMG MUST DISH. I'll meet you for breakfast in your dorm. Be there at 8 with details.

Bewildered and slightly uneasy, Kelly went to the cafeteria the next day as requested. Rose waited there, her hair hidden under a leather cap, her face scrubbed clean of makeup and still slightly pale from sleep. Her eyes, however, danced. "I can't *believe* you're rooming with Casanova. How the hell did that happen?"

"Casanova?"

"Oh, so you're going to tell me you *didn't* notice Walter Lucas is sex on a stick and the biggest flirt this side of the Mississippi River?"

His cheeks burned. "I did."

Rose studied Kelly a moment, and then her eyes widened. "Holy shit, he didn't sleep with you?"

"No! We're roommates."

"Trust me, that wouldn't stop him. There's no way you're not his type. You're practically a poster child for what he usually eye-fucks on the dance floor at Moe's. He didn't even make a pass?"

It was hard to talk while being this embarrassed. "I suppose maybe he did. But it was just flirting. Nothing happened."

Kelly wondered if he should be disappointed.

"Huh. Well, I know he's not dating anyone. Ritche Hall would be abuzz." When it was Kelly's turn to be confused, she elaborated. "That's the communications building. We share a major, and an advisor, Dr. Williams." She dug into her hash browns. "Walter won't join the Philosophy Club, though."

Kelly had no idea what the Philosophy Club was, but he knew about Walter's advisor. "Williams. Yes, Walter talked about him last night, quite a bit before we went to sleep. I have him for Intro to Humanities."

"You'll love him. He's *amazing*, and not just in the classroom. His children are adorable—two boys and two girls, all of them under ten. His wife is a nurse at Danby Community Hospital. She works the night shift part-time so she can be at home with the kids." Her face clouded. "Not everyone thinks Williams is awesome, though. He's incredibly harsh when it comes to grades, really makes you work to get high marks." She put down her fork and wiped her mouth with a napkin. "He's our advisor for Philosophy Club too because we only have one actual philosophy prof, and he's a dick. Williams is the best. He's up for tenure this year, and if he doesn't get it, I'm going to personally rip that fucking dean of faculty a new asshole."

Kelly pulled Rose back to the topic that truly interested him. "So you're telling me Walter sleeps around?"

She laughed. "Yeah, you could put it that way. Just

the boys, much to my chagrin, because holy crap would I like to tap that ass. Not sure how he's going to manage it doubling in a single unless you're incredibly understanding or into voyeurism." While Kelly got more embarrassed, she eyed him speculatively. "I still can't believe he didn't try to sleep with you."

"I wouldn't have let him, and he knows that." When Rose's eyebrows lifted, Kelly fixed his gaze on his coffee and soy milk. "I told you I was just coming out."

"Yeah, but that doesn't—*Whoa.* You mean...you haven't been with anyone, either?"

"Why does that shock everyone so much?"

"Because you're eighteen years old. Virgins are a rare breed anywhere, but at your age, you're practically a unicorn."

"Well how was I supposed to go about it? I didn't want to sleep with the girls, and it was a pretty damn small town. Fooling around with a guy would be front-page news in a hot minute."

"You landed in a damn good place to start your exploration."

"I'm *not sleeping* with Walter."

She rolled her eyes. "*Hope* is what I meant. A lot of gay boys to get your feet wet with."

"Oh." Cheeks burning, Kelly picked up his coffee. "I knew that."

KELLY HAD BREAKFAST with Rose a lot. Not always, but they made kind of an appointment to meet at least once a week. When he didn't eat with Rose, he usually ate with Walter.

While Kelly had to admit Walter was right about a lot of things about Hope—unfortunately including the less-than-allergen-friendly menus—in general Hope was still a pretty good fit. He enjoyed his classes, which were all gen-ed plus a few business classes his dad had recommended. As advertised, however, Dr. Williams was great. Quirky, irreverent, and absolutely unafraid to share his opinions. He was also, it turned out, Lutheran. Kelly thought he'd ask where he went to church sometime to make his mother happy.

Unfortunately what Walter was most right about was Porter. The means Kelly's fellow residents devised to torment him hurt as much as they made him a ball of tension. They stared at him in the restrooms, looking as if they were ready to pound him into the wall, though they never did. If one of his fellow floor mates was in line for a shower behind Kelly, he waited so close to the curtain Kelly jumped and cried out when he pulled it aside. If they were loitering in the hall when Kelly passed, they blocked his path or sat on the floor and stuck their legs out so he had to weave through them to get to his room.

Not if Walter was with him, though. Then they simply grumbled under their breaths and glared. Kelly wasn't sure what magic Walter wielded, but he was glad for it.

The Porter problem was kind of a focused example of an overall stumbling block Kelly hadn't ever antici-pated finding at Hope. While Kelly made a lot of friends, they were mostly acquaintances who collected his cell number and friended him on Facebook and Twitter. Occasionally he'd meet them at the campus deli or at Opie's. They all felt slightly flat, though. The only people he really had any connection to at all were Rose and Walter.

It was so not what he'd expected to happen at Hope. He'd anticipated a horde of friends, sort of like high school but bigger. He wasn't sure why that wasn't happening, nor did he know what to do about it. Forget dating. Sure, there were guys who were cute, and Kelly wanted to get to know them, maybe even ask them out, but he had no idea how.

"Just go up and talk to them," Rose advised when he confessed his problem one morning over oatmeal. "Strike up a conversation. Don't wait for them to come to you."

Was that what he was doing? Kelly frowned, replaying his last few social outings in his head. He'd talked to people, yes, but had he initiated any conversation? He wasn't sure.

"Look, you've asked girls out, right? As cover in high school? It's the same thing, just backward, and this time you mean it."

"I didn't ask girls out," Kelly told her. "They asked me."

Rose lifted one eyebrow. "Okay, well, buck up, soldier. It's your turn."

"*How do I do it?*"

"Walk up to a guy. Say hello. If the conversation goes well, ask if you could get together sometime. Get his number. Set up a meeting. Ta-da, instant date."

It certainly sounded easy enough. Now all Kelly had to do was work up the nerve to try it. It was Wednesday, so Walter would take him to Moe's. He could practice there.

Except as they walked across campus toward the bar that night, Kelly began to panic at the idea of what he was about to do.

Walter noticed. "You okay?" He looked concerned, which only made Kelly feel more ridiculous.

"I'm fine." He fished for a distraction topic. "So you know Rose, right?"

"Manchester? Oh yeah. She's cool. Keeps to herself, and sometimes she seems sad or unusually tense, but nothing too weird. Though that could be her chosen field. She's going to be a journalist, God help her. She's never going to get a job."

They started walking again. "What's your major? I guess I never actually asked."

"General communications. That's all you can really do in undergrad. I'm figuring I'll go into PR or something, probably with a little graduate school to polish things up. No idea where yet, though." He nudged Kelly with his elbow. "Is this a fishing expedition for Mr. Right? That why you're so nervous?"

Was he that transparent? Kelly dug his hands deeper into his pockets. "I don't know. Maybe."

Walter grinned. "I'll keep an eye out for a nice trout."

They settled into a corner near the bar. Walter leaned against the wall, motioning for Kelly to take the chair beside him. When Kelly sat, Walter's hand rested on his shoulder. "I'm getting a beer. Want one, Red?"

"Just a soda."

He patted Kelly's shoulder and leaned behind him to speak to the bartender. Kelly saw Rose across the room and waved to her. As he put his hand back down, he caught a girl standing beside him staring at his ring.

"You're wearing your class ring?" she asked in the same tones she might say *you went out naked?*

Kelly tucked the stone into his palm, but Walter captured his hand, drawing it to his lips to kiss the metal. "Yes, he wears it all the time. Pretty soon he's going to give it to me so everyone will know we're going steady."

Though Kelly wanted to pull his hand away, the skin where Walter's lips had touched still burned, and he found he didn't have the strength. Walter apparently loved making Kelly blush, like right now as he put his arm around Kelly, his hand massaging idly at Kelly's waist. The touch thrilled Kelly and made him half-hard, and Kelly's panic over his reaction only seemed to charge Walter all the more.

When Walter's fingers tried to tease Kelly's nipple through his T-shirt, Kelly freaked out and batted him away. "Stop."

Walter didn't, trapping him against the table and continuing his octopus-inspired assault. "You don't want me to stop. You're sporting so much fucking wood you're going to have leaves in your ears."

It was true. Kelly pushed against Walter's chest, but not very hard. "Come on. You know I don't do this. Flirting, I mean."

"I do know. Which is why it's so fun to show you how wrong you are about it." Even as he said this, however, his assault simmered to something much more manageable and far more dangerous. He rested his chin on Kelly's shoulder. "Help me find some talent, baby. Daddy needs to get laid."

Kelly scanned the dance floor because it gave him an excuse to let Walter's hands skim his groin. He had no idea what he was looking at, just that Walter's hands were the real talent. They were almost criminal, in fact.

Walter's thumbs hooked idly into Kelly's belt loop. "Slim pickings tonight. It would be easier if this were a gay bar, but that's all the way on the other side of town, and only locals go there. Millennials, we hate labels. The gay and bi-curious boys hang out here, so this is where I fish." He stilled, leaning in close to Kelly's ear. "Ten o'clock. Tight jeans and faded tee."

Kelly scanned the crowd, uncertain what exactly he was supposed to be doing, and then he saw the guy in question. Okay, he was definitely hot. Nice butt, and his shoulders…mmm.

Walter frowned. "Ah, but wait. I remember this one. Sophomore, not that he ever goes to class from what I understand. Fairly good in bed, but dim. Also he didn't want to wear a condom, which ended things fast. I might do a BJ bare, but nobody's going in my ass without a raincoat on."

"Why wouldn't he want to wear a condom?" The implications of what Walter had said hit Kelly, and he turned to his roommate with wide eyes.

Walter looked amused. "Yes, I pitch and catch. So

do most guys I know, though there are still nelly bottoms and big alpha tops out there, I'm sure. However, since we're doing sex ed, watch for the new trend of guys wanting to ditch protection. Somehow the word has gotten out that HIV is cured. So not true. Also, gonorrhea and genital herpes? Not sexy."

"My mother handed me about sixty pamphlets. Trust me, there will be condoms."

"Your *mother* gave you pamphlets? No wonder you're shy about sex."

Kelly tried to punch him in the arm, but Walter turned octopus again, and Kelly started whimpering instead. On another attempt to get away, though, he caught sight of a beautifully stacked guy with a blond buzz near the bar. "Talent." His breath hitched as the blond met his gaze and winked. "Oh shit."

"Nice. Hook and line. You going in, Red?"

The blond touched his junk, and while Kelly got turned on, he also turned tail. He sank against Walter.

Walter laughed. "I suppose he is something of a black run. If you're passing, do you mind?"

Oh. Walter was going to fuck the blond. Feeling a bit bereft, Kelly shook his head, and Walter let him go.

"Thank you, roomie." He tipped an imaginary hat. "Don't wait up."

Kelly watched Walter walk away. It took Walter about a minute to get the blond guy out on the dance floor, but after the blond smiled at him, it was clear sex was a given between them.

Kelly tried not to be jealous and crossed the room to give a more formal hello to Rose as a distraction.

WALTER HADN'T THOUGHT it possible he'd enjoy living doubled in a single—in Porterhouse—but that's exactly what he was doing. He genuinely liked Kelly and enjoyed spending time with him. He didn't even mind, much, that having a shy virgin as a roommate was seriously cramping his love life. Less fucking, more jerking off to internet porn while Kelly was in class, and he was solid.

The Disney thing, though, threw him completely for a loop.

He'd stumbled across his roommate's guilty pleasure by accident one day when Kelly called him from the computer lab desperate because he'd forgotten to put an assignment on his flash drive and needed Walter to mail it to him before his class started. This meant digging around on Kelly's computer, which was how he accidentally ended up snooping. The desktop wallpaper was no shock: Kelly loved the artist Sia, and his desktop was a montage of her album covers and publicity photos. But Kelly was a PC where Walter was a Mac, and as he fumbled, trying to use a shortcut that wouldn't work on Kelly's recycled Dell, he accidentally triggered the screensaver.

Which was a picture of Aladdin and Jasmine.

Walter blinked at the screen. "What the fuck?" When it shifted to a screen shot from *Tangled*, he burst out laughing.

On the other end of the line, Kelly turned wary. "Why are you laughing?"

The scene shifted again, this time to Belle and the Beast, and Walter collapsed back onto the green rocker, barely able to hold up the phone through his mirth. When he managed to put it on his ear, Kelly was chattering like a squirrel, demanding to know what was going on and threatening to come back to the room if Walter didn't explain.

It had been on the tip of Walter's tongue to tease Kelly, but at the last second some deep instinct warned him this would not be a good plan. "Nothing." He got rid of the screensaver and went back to uploading the file. "You said it was right there on the desktop?"

"You were laughing at something. What were you laughing at?"

The terror in Kelly's voice tore away the last of Walter's amusement. "Hon, it's fine. Stop freaking out. You're going to be late for class. You want me to email it, right? To your usual?"

Even after they'd hung up, Kelly remained obsessed, texting Walter three times during his class, demanding to know what was so funny. Eventually Walter sent one of David Kawena's sexualized Disney hero paintings as a reply—Aladdin, because that was the most recognizable one, but man did he hover over Prince Phillip.

OMG my screensaver was all he got back from Kelly, and then radio silence until, exactly seven minutes after his class let out, Kelly came back to the room, breathless and sick with embarrassment.

Walter tried to calm him down. "Hey—sweetheart, seriously. It's fine. The pics threw me for a loop is all. No sweat."

"I forgot I'd never changed that. Lisa did that before I left as a joke."

Walter simply raised an eyebrow and waited.

Kelly folded like a house of cards. "Okay, so I have a thing for Disney movies. I always have." He held out his arms. "Go ahead. Make fun."

Walter shrugged. "Whatever. It's a little weird, but it suits you in its own way. I'm sorry, I didn't mean to laugh. It was just the last thing I thought I'd see."

Kelly leaned against the side of his loft, crossing his arms over his chest. "They make me happy. I don't think that's bad."

"Didn't say it was. Hell, I loved *Pete's Dragon* when I was younger. Always got misty when I heard Helen Reddy sing 'Candle on the Water'."

Kelly's eyes widened. "Really?"

"Yes, really. What, you think I came out of the womb this cynical?" He put his hands behind his head. "I even took piano lessons just so I could learn to play the song. It's the only thing I still know by heart."

Kelly eased into the green rocker. "That's cool. I never learned to play at all, so you're one up on me." He had his phone in hand, scrolling through until he'd pulled up the image Walter had texted him. "Where in the *hell* did you get this, by the way? There's no way this pic is Disney issue."

"You never saw that before? Are you kidding? There's a whole fucking series." He reached for his laptop and tapped out a search. "I found them a few years back, but the artist has made more since I last looked." After loading Kawena's Facebook album, he passed the computer over to Kelly.

Kelly's eyes went wide, then darkened with a quiet lust that Walter found more erotic than the photos. "Oh my God. Holy *shit*. Flynn Rider. And—*Jesus!* Tarzan. And the Beast!" He covered his mouth with his hand, but his eyes told Walter these images were burned on his roommate's brain. "If I'd have found these at twelve, I'd have needed more therapy than I already had. Either that or maybe I wouldn't have needed any at all, because this is pretty much how I saw them myself. Except somehow this is even better."

Walter studied Kelly a minute, trying to decide if he were truly that casual about having been to therapy or if Kawena's images were simply that distracting. This was confirmed when, a few minutes later, Kelly looked up with an expression that made it clear his brain had finally caught up with his mouth.

Oh, Red. So fucking adorable. Walter played it cool, propping his feet up on the desk chair. "You were watching Disney while I was drooling over Tom of Finland. Why am I not surprised?" When Kelly gave him a blank look, Walter laughed and shook his head. "*Seriously*, baby, did you grow up in a cave? Google it."

He smiled, slow and devious, as Kelly opened a search engine. Kelly went still in the same way he had when he'd seen the Disney heroes redone, except the expression on his face now was dirtier.

Good. Walter wanted to think Kelly was untutored, not a prude.

"If it helps," Walter said, "I *did* have to confess to peeking at Tom in therapy. Not because I thought it was wrong to be gay, but more that I needed help parsing out what 'real' gay was and what was fantasy. This is what happens when you grow up with a handful of half-assed role models and a whole lot of American Family Association on the airwaves."

He wasn't sure how subtle that had been, but he'd wanted Kelly to get he wasn't the only queer boy who'd needed a leg up to get through adolescence.

"Did you really cry to 'Candle on the Water' when you were younger?" Kelly asked eventually. "Or did you invent that to make me feel better?"

"Like a baby, all by myself in my room with a blanket around my head so I could hide quick if anyone came in the room." The confession made him feel too exposed, so he cleared his throat and made an impatient *come here* motion to Kelly. "Get over here and bring my MacBook. We'll alternate between Tom and Disney and finish off with a nice masturbation session."

"Not together!" Despite this protest, Kelly came over to the futon all the same, and as he settled in, Walter could tell his roommate was sporting a stiffy.

Not yet, there won't be a masturbation session together. Walter took the laptop and surfed to an untitled piece he had bookmarked, a pencil of a nude blond man between the thighs of a booted biker. *Not yet. But soon.*

Chapter Six

I T TOOK ALMOST a month for Cara and Greg to get everything out of the garage at the old apartment, but the good news for Walter was on the last run, Cara came with Greg instead of sending her dad. It was the longest stretch in two years Walter had gone without seeing her every day, and he didn't realize how much he hated that absence until she came down the campus sidewalk toward him, arms extended.

"It's so good to see you." She enveloped him in a hug, then pulled back and smiled at him a little longer. Walter drank her in like water.

"You look good." He touched the tips of her hair, which she'd cut to frame her face in a sharp bob. "Cute hair. Love the color too."

She touched the ends, making them bounce. "I miss the length, but this looks more professional, I thought."

"Internship going well?"

"Yeah. I think I might have a few leads on a job, but things are still in the air." She looped her arm through his. "So. I want to see this adorable room-mate."

"He's out at some freshman mixer. I told him it was

a waste, but every now and again he has to go rub his nose in that shit and find out I'm right."

Cara laughed. "We'll take him to Opie's later." Walter opened the door to the dorm, and she wrinkled her nose. "God."

"Smells of piss and glory, doesn't it?" Walter held the door wide and gestured for her to pass through. "After you, madam."

"It seems worse than when you first stayed here," Cara said as they ascended the stairs, the cacophony of brutish men echoing around them.

"I know. I think it's the indignity of having to return to it. Somehow that makes it smell more rank."

"I'm so sorry the apartment thing was a mess."

"It's hardly your fault."

"Still. I hate leaving you here, stuck in Porterhouse." She touched a peeling wall and sighed. "At least you have your roommate. And of course Williams. How's everything going with him?"

"Good. He's obsessed about his tenure, and so is Rose Manchester and the rest of the philosophers-wannabe. Rose is the most rabid about it, though. I think she smells a Pulitzer or something."

"No she doesn't. She loves Williams the same way you do."

They entered the fourth-floor hallway, which was unfortunately pretty busy. The guys whose rooms were on either side of the center bathroom had their doors wide open and music blasting. When Cara and Walter walked by, they wolf whistled and spoke loudly about tapping that sweet sugar ass.

They also, once Walter had cleared their vision, talked about the nasty cockroach problem on Porter 4. They emphasized *cock* with the subtlety of a sledgehammer.

Cara stiffened. "*Cock*roach? Please. Fucking apes. Why don't they just say faggot?"

"Because that will get them written up. Remember, you have to have at least a 3.0 GPA to get into Hope. These are apes who know how to compose B-level insults."

Walter let her into his room. She stopped short, shook her head, and laughed.

"Oh wow. Sardines have more room." She laughed again, but then she put her hand over her mouth, abruptly sad.

"Hey." Walter frowned and put his arm around her. "*Hey*. What's going on? Why are you upset?"

"Because I left you here. I dragged you here, and then I left you, and this is what happened." Walter started to protest, but she aimed a finger at him. "Don't. I know I did this, so you can just let me stand here and feel bad for a minute."

"How did you do this? What are you talking about?"

"What am I talking about? I totally dragged you to Hope. I told myself at the time you were miserable and lonely and you needed me, but to be honest, it was the other way around. I wanted you here, so I talked you into it. Now you're stuck. You should transfer back home. You shouldn't have to do this."

Walter rolled his eyes. "Jesus, this wedding shit has

made you a sap. You didn't drag me into anything. I wanted to come, I'm here, and it's fine."

"This isn't fine," Cara demanded, pointing to the overcrowded room.

"I'll get it sorted."

"That's what you keep telling me on chat. How, Wally?"

He had no idea. He'd dug around the first week and a half, trying to find somewhere new, but he couldn't find anything. He could have saved himself six times over, but not Red too, not without splitting them up.

"Leave it." He held out his arms to indicate himself. "I'm fine. See? Go make a tulle bow or something." He led her to the futon, then grabbed a Diet Coke out of the fridge, something he'd put there specifically for her arrival. "Speaking of bows. How come the plans? Where is the wedding of the year going to be held? You said you'd found a place."

"Well, there's this B&B on the lake I like, and I think it's where we'll end up going, unless we cave and go to the country club. Greg still clings to the idea of getting married in the aquarium, but I think it's out of our price range, thankfully."

"Yes, because every new bride wants to reek of damp and fish."

She sighed. "I know. I hate to squash the idea out-right, though. It's his wedding too, and so much of this is turning into some kind of nightmare from *Say Yes to the Dress*."

"I take it your mother hasn't settled back into sanity then?"

Cara rolled her eyes. "Yeah, right. Because she lives there so often."

Walter put his arm around her and pulled her against him. "Sorry, Pickles."

"You know that I'm used to it." She sipped at her Coke. "Speaking of crazy. Meant to tell you this yesterday, but I was so fixated on getting the trailer I forgot. Your mom got kicked out of Whole Foods the other day."

Walter went still. "What?"

"Yeah, I heard about it from my mom. I couldn't make any sense out of it, because Mom fixated on the whole Shari-Lucas-is-a-Scandal thing, but from what I could gather, it was all projection. She yelled at some clerk about stuff in the aisle, which was standard, but then she wouldn't let it go. She only stood down when the police showed up to escort her away."

Walter shut his eyes and sighed. "Tibby told me Dad showed up at the house to pick her up and had a new girlfriend."

"Bingo." Cara patted his thigh. "I didn't tell you so you could fix it. I just didn't want you to hear about it on Facebook or something. I'll take your mom to lunch next weekend, if you want. Maybe she can come with us to shop for table decorations."

"Oh Christ, that's above and beyond the call."

Cara shrugged. "I think it might be a benefit, because she and Mom would argue, and Greg and I could sneak off." She glanced at her phone and frowned. "How the hell long does it take to park a car? Is this parent weekend or something?"

"They're doing construction on Fourteenth. Started middle of August. Whole road is torn up from campus to the river."

"Oh good, because I'd hate for them to have planned that in the summer when no one would need to park a fucking car. Jesus. I don't miss this place." She leaned on his shoulder. "I miss you, though."

He smiled and leaned back, resting his head on hers. "I miss you too. Every day."

"Are you really okay with your bumpkin-boy roomie? You aren't just putting a false face on for me?"

"Kelly? He's fantastic. Naive and backward at times, but he's got a good heart. Biggest complaint is all the damn sheet washing."

Cara lifted her head and her eyebrows.

"Dust mites, you dirty mind." He pointed to the air filter. "Kelly has a million allergies. We have to wash every piece of fabric in the room every week in hot water. We clean a lot too, but that's not so bad. But hauling ass with all our bedding down to Porterhouse laundry every Thursday? Pain in my ass."

"You said he's gay, though, right?" Her eyebrows stayed lifted.

"Yes. But he's Lutheran and saving himself for marriage. Or at least True Wuve."

"Lutherans save themselves for marriage?"

"I don't think as a general rule, no, but who can say for sure?"

Cara smiled. "I think it's cute."

"You would."

"Well, it's not as if I practiced the theory. But that's cool, that he wants that."

"It's demented."

She punched him in the arm. "True Wuve happens, whether you like it or not."

"I'm not saying it doesn't. But it's rare as a dodo, and then to put First Time on top of it? Crazy."

"You're just mad because you want to blow him."

"Hell yes I want to blow him. I'm telling you, wait until you see that mouth. And those eyes. And that ass. He is grade-A talent."

"Talent." She leaned against his shoulder again. "I miss you, Wally."

He didn't say anything, simply kissed her hair and punched her lightly on the arm.

KELLY WAS AT the freshman mixer, trying to ditch the group of giggling girls he'd become surrounded by and move over to the cute redhead by the tray of cookies when his cellphone started playing "Candle on the Water", which meant Walter had assigned his texts that ringtone again.

Ditch the coffee klatch and come to Opie's. You can meet Cara and her Prince Charming and then tell me you told me so about true love being real and all that crap. I have your pitcher of root beer and dairy-free pizza ordered already.

Kelly smiled at his phone and put it away.

"Who was that?" one of the girls asked. "Your girl-friend?"

"Roommate." He tracked the redhead as he went for punch. Should he go over and introduce himself? The very idea made him sweat.

The girl beside Kelly leaned into him. "Tell him to come here and join our party."

Her hand brushed his arm, and Kelly jolted before moving away. He frowned, confused—they wanted him to invite the redhead over? Then he realized they meant Walter. "He's a junior."

"*Ooh.*" Another one of the girls leaned on Kelly's other side.

God, Kelly wished Walter had showed up personally to collect him. Of course, then Walter would watch Kelly being an idiot, not asking talent out. He cast one last longing look at the redhead, admitting he wasn't going to go introduce himself.

A third girl, the only one who hadn't been hanging on him, rolled her eyes. "Ladies, give it up. It's not going to happen. I *told* you he was gay."

"I—" Kelly cut himself off, realizing the reflex to panic was foolish and unnecessary. Still, he cast nervous glances at the girls on either side of him. "Sorry, she's right."

The one who had her hand on his arm all but stomped her foot. "Damn it." She glared at the one who'd called Kelly out. "How the hell do *you* have gaydar?"

"I have fucking eyes. He's been scoping the guy by the punch bowl."

Unable to help himself, Kelly looked that way once again. This time, as if drawn by the power of their mutual focus, the object of his affection met Kelly's gaze. He held it too, and he smiled.

"Ooh, we have a winner." The girl who had pointed out Kelly was gay nudged him in the elbow. "Go for it."

The very idea had Kelly paralyzed. *I can't,* he wanted to say, but then he remembered Rose's admonition. It was totally his turn to do this, she was right.

But what if he got snubbed?

He lifted his punch to his lips. "I will. In a minute."

The girls teased him awhile longer, but soon they drifted away, new prey in sight. Kelly watched them swarm a group of guys who looked slightly nervous but who brightened when the trio came their way. He sipped his drink while he watched the flirtations fly between them. The one who had called him out for being gay hung back, assessing, while the other two duked it out with flattery and carefully placed touches. The guys leaned into the girls, accepting their overtures, though the tall one in the center—the cutest—seemed to get most of the attention, and he reveled in it. His buddies laughed along with him, but it was clear they wished they too had girls on them.

The girl who liked to hang back caught the attention of a guy on the end, quiet, cute, but clearly shy. The girl smiled at him. He smiled back and turned to her, his posture open, hopeful.

She stepped closer into his space and put her hand on his arm.

God, could it really be that easy?

His gaze drifted back to the redhead, who was still

talking with his group of friends. This time, though, Kelly kept his eyes fixed on his prey until he turned. Their gazes met and held.

The redhead smiled, and Kelly smiled back, even as his heartbeat increased.

His phone played "Candle on the Water" again, but he hit IGNORE.

I'm going in, he thought wildly, and headed across the room.

"Hi." Kelly started to extend his hand as he approached, checked the gesture and brushed it against his leg instead.

"Hi yourself." The redhead tipped his head to the side. "I think your orientation group was next to mine in the auditorium." He held out his hand. "I'm Mason."

Kelly met the gesture. "Kelly."

"Great to meet you." Mason ducked his head and smiled at Kelly. "How are you liking Hope?"

"It's okay." He resisted, but just barely, the urge to put his hands in his pockets. Instead, he gestured somewhat feebly to the room at large. "I know it's a small school, but it's still a lot of people to me."

"Oh yeah? Where are you from?"

"Windom, Minnesota. It's not very big."

"I've heard Minneapolis is great."

"It is, but we're two hours from it. Well, if you want to go all the way into downtown. The suburbs are closer." *Redirect. Do not start talking about your idyllic small town and how far it is from civilization.* "What about you, where are you from?"

"Naperville." Mason's smile broadened. "So what do you say we ditch this party and go make our own?"

Kelly didn't just blush. He got hot, and cold, and almost paralyzed. "Um," he managed eventually, and that was all.

Mason winked. "We can start with coffee at the deli. Or, if you're feeling adventurous, we could go for pizza at that place across from campus."

Pizza. Walter. Kelly put his hand over the phone in his pocket, half expecting it to ring on cue. "Oh. Actually, I'm supposed to meet my roommate after this. Maybe later?"

"Sure. Let me give you my number."

Fifteen minutes later Kelly walked across campus toward Opie's, heart pounding in his throat, head full and dizzy, dick a little bit hard. He kept remembering Mason's smile. Mason's fingers brushing against his as they exchanged phones. Mason's wink.

Mason's entreaty that Kelly text him later.

When "Candle on the Water" played yet again, Kelly startled, and he silenced his phone, unwilling to engage. He didn't want to talk about the encounter, not yet. Walter could pull it apart when Kelly got to the pub. For right now? This was his victory, and he would savor it.

Chapter Seven

"WELL LOOK WHO finally decided to show up," Walter drawled when Kelly came around the corner to their booth at Opie's.

He looked winded, and he sank into the space beside Walter heavily. "Sorry."

Walter eyed his roommate. Kelly was hiding something, and Walter wasn't sure if he should nudge him outright to spill the deets or if he should wait and see what happened.

Cara rolled her eyes at Walter and turned to Kelly. "I'm Cara, and this is my fiancé, Greg."

"Pleased to meet you." Greg held out his hand too, though he used the other to wipe off his chin. He didn't get all the grease, so Cara dabbed at it for him, and he quickly wiped himself again. "Did I get it?"

"You're fine." Cara patted him on the arm.

Walter had tried, a lot, to hate Greg, but he might as well hate a puppy. He was so far from hottie he lived in Alaska, but he wasn't ugly either, just slightly awkward in that geeky, straight-boy way that had always turned Cara's crank. She so loved a hot mess, and boy did she have that in Greg. She also had an engineering graduate student as a husband. Her mother was over the moon.

"So you're Kelly." Cara smiled at him. "I've heard so much about you."

Kelly beamed back. "Likewise."

For a while they all did the small-talk thing where Kelly told them about Cutesy, Minnesota, and Greg and Cara and Walter mocked their own suburban upbringing. They asked about Kelly's major too, at which point Red threw a curve ball.

"I've been taking a lot of business classes, but lately, I don't know. I've kind of been thinking it could be cool to teach."

Walter put down his pizza. "As in school? High school?"

Kelly ducked his head. "Well, actually I kind of thought middle school."

"What?"

Cara swatted at Walter. "What's wrong with him wanting to be a teacher?"

"There's nothing wrong. It's just the first I heard of it. Where is this coming from?"

Kelly shrugged. "I'm not sure. I started thinking about it, is all. It probably won't come to anything."

"What subject would you teach?" Greg asked.

"History."

Cara smiled over her root beer. "Well good for you. I think you should look into it."

Kelly blushed. "It's probably a whim."

It sure didn't sound like one to Walter. But he could tell Kelly wanted to chew on it some more, so he didn't push.

After dinner they drifted over to Moe's. It was early, so they could still get a table, and they settled in the back to people watch.

"They have popcorn here now too?" Cara pointed to a machine over by the bar.

Walter swung around, blinking at it. "That's brand new. Never seen it before tonight."

Greg stood back up. "I'll get us some." He came back with four bowls, two of them balanced precariously on the others. He passed them around, and everyone munched while they waited for the waitress to bring their pitcher.

"So you're getting married soon?" Kelly asked Cara as he dug into his bowl.

"June." Cara nudged Walter and grinned. "This goofball here is my best man."

Kelly smiled. "That's cool." He flushed and reached for more popcorn. "You guys have been friends a long time, right?"

"Since kindergarten," Walter confessed. "I was scared to use the boys' bathroom for reasons I can't remember, so she took me with her into the girls'."

"It was our first scandal." Cara beamed.

"I love that." Kelly's blush was full-on scarlet now. Why, Walter wondered? "You guys have been friends that long?"

"That long, and on to forever," Walter said.

"So cool." Kelly still blushed, his whole face bright red now.

Walter narrowed his eyes. Actually, that wasn't a blush. In fact, Kelly looked blotchy. "Red? Hon, you're redder than usual. Did you get into something you shouldn't?"

Kelly frowned, then looked down at his hands. They'd started to swell. Beneath the blotches on his face, he paled. "Oh shit."

Cara came to attention. "What is it? What's wrong?"

"Allergic reaction." Kelly's whole face had puffed up now, especially his lips.

Walter floundered, not knowing what the fuck he was supposed to do. "Pen, Red. Where's your pen?"

Kelly pressed a hand against his pocket. "Here," he said, but his voice sounded funny, as if his tongue was thick. His breathing was also alarmingly raspy.

Walter stood, almost upending the table, and hauled Kelly to his feet so he could dig into his room-mate's pocket. He found the pen, which wasn't anything like a pen at all, more of a sealed syringe. It was intimidating, but even with fat fingers Kelly seemed to know just what to do, wrenching it from Walter's hand, fumbling briefly with the cap, jamming it hard into his thigh. Walter watched, terrified and helpless as Kelly held the pen against his leg, breathing labored, until he finally lifted it up and started massaging the area.

"I'm okay," he said, his voice a little more normal. He fished in his other pocket, pulled out an inhaler and took two practiced hits from the mouthpiece. When he lowered it, he was more the Kelly Walter knew. His lips weren't swollen quite as badly either.

Kelly shut his eyes for a second, his countenance a

picture of mortification. "I have to go to the hospital. Sorry."

"Fuck sorry. Jesus." Walter reached for him, then stopped, not sure that was what he should do. "Can I go get my car, or do you need an ambulance?"

"Car is fine." Kelly kept rubbing his leg, taking deeper and deeper breaths. "Just have to get there in fifteen minutes."

Jesus. Walter turned to Cara, who was already shooing.

"I'll take care of him. You go, we'll meet you out front."

Walter ran the whole way to his car, his mind still full of the image of Kelly swelling up like that. He could have died. There was no question of that, not even a little, and it scared him to death. Kelly could have died.

Fifteen minutes.

When he peeled up to the door at Moe's, Cara was there as promised, she and Greg flanking a miserable Kelly.

"I'm really sorry," he said as Cara ushered him into the front seat.

"Stop apologizing." Walter gave up and reached for his hand. "Jesus, Red, that scared the shit out of me."

Kelly didn't look scared. He looked weary and embarrassed. But he squeezed Walter's hand back.

"It was the popcorn," Greg volunteered from the backseat. "Moe used an organic oil he thought people would think was hip, and it's made on the same equipment as almonds or something. Or it has almonds in it, I wasn't clear exactly what that was about."

"Take Sixteenth," Cara said as Walter turned onto the highway. "It's faster."

Walter followed her direction and glanced back at Kelly. "What happens in fifteen minutes?"

Kelly sagged into his seat. "The epinephrine wears off. But it'll be fine. I've done this before."

It became Walter's new mission in life for this to never happen again.

At the hospital, Cara got out with Kelly and explained what was going on to the nurses, but when Walter would have parked the car, Greg stopped him and said to hand over the keys, to Walter's great relief. He stayed with Kelly as he checked in, but none of them could go back with him into the exam rooms. Kelly waved as he went away, telling them they could go home and he'd text them when he was done.

Cara didn't even ask, just settled Walter on a couch in the waiting area and pulled out her phone, heading straight to WebMD.

"It says they're going to give him breathing treatments and antihistamines. He should be fine. It's pretty standard stuff, I guess."

Walter stared after the place where Kelly had disappeared. "That was horrible."

Cara gave him a long look, then a funny smile.

Walter glared at her. "What?"

"Nothing." She waved her phone at him. "Get out your ear buds. We'll watch YouTube."

They watched quite a bit of YouTube, sharing an ear bud each between them. Greg took field trips to the cafeteria for coffee and bags of chips. Walter wanted to go ask the front desk when Kelly would be done, but they wouldn't tell him anything, he knew, so he waited, glad that at least Cara was there.

Eventually Kelly came back out, red now from embarrassment instead of hives—in other words, back to normal. He gave them a weary, awkward wave. "Sorry. You shouldn't have stayed."

As if he'd have been anywhere else? Walter messed up Kelly's hair and put his hand on his back to nudge him toward the door. "Come on. You have a date with your bed. Unless you don't want to climb up into yours? You could have the futon for tonight."

"I'm fine," Kelly said.

"You're shaking."

"It's the pen. They had to give me another shot, and I'm jittery."

Kelly seemed annoyed, and that annoyed Walter. "Well, you scared the piss out of me."

"I *know*. I'm sorry."

Cara slipped between the two of them, linking their arms as they went out the door into the parking lot. "How about we go back to our hotel room and hang out? They gave us double queens. You guys can crash on one if you want."

Walter didn't want to go to the hotel room. He wanted to go lock Kelly in the dorm and stand over him like a paranoid idiot all night long, making sure he could breathe. Which Cara probably knew. He sighed. "It's up to Red."

Kelly hesitated, then said, "A beer sounds really

good."

"Beer can be had." Greg put his arm around Kelly's other side and nodded at the car. "Let's go."

KELLY WASN'T SURE if it was wise to drink after an allergic reaction, but right now he honestly didn't care.

He was in a foul mood all the way to the liquor store and to Cara and Greg's hotel, and the fact Walter kept hovering only made him surlier. Kelly *hated* that he'd had an attack in front of everyone. Half the school went to Moe's, and they all saw him turn into a fucking pufferfish. Thank God he hadn't had to call an ambulance. He'd ruined everyone's evening too, making them sit in the emergency room while he sucked on a nebulizer and all the usual crap. Even having Professor Williams's wife as his nurse hadn't done much to ease the ignominy.

Though he'd had plenty of accidental exposure to his severe allergens, it had been a while since he'd put on such a performance, and it was his first time at college. His allergies always made him feel different, separate, and tonight they really upset him. He didn't want to feel separate. He'd felt so good, so normal, included. He couldn't even finish the evening, though, without being reminded he wasn't *really* one of them.

Okay, that was horribly pouty, he admitted to himself. So he drank beer until he didn't feel pouty anymore.

That took about two and a half bottles, at which point he was giggly, leaning on Walter and half falling off the bed as Greg did *Star Wars* impressions that really weren't that funny but made Kelly laugh all the same. The best was the Jawa—*utinni!*—and the Tusken Raiders. God, they just tickled Kelly's funny bone.

"You're *giggling*." Walter shook his head and grinned at Kelly.

"Sorry." Kelly giggled some more.

"It's adorable." Cara was half in Greg's lap, looking relaxed and happy, as if she was at home. *I want that*, Kelly thought.

"*Bantha poodoo*," Greg said in his Jabba the Hutt voice, and Kelly giggled again.

At his fourth beer Kelly was more than a little stupid. He'd slid onto the floor at some point, and now he lay on his back, listening to the sound of the others' voices, drifting away and coming back occasionally as Walter's foot nudged his leg. He would admit he did a fair amount of brushing himself, because it felt good. He missed touch. His family was a touchy family, always hugging and snuggling on the sofa. The warmth and pressure of Walter's foot was a paltry substitute, but it felt heady and bold, and he kept courting interaction with it.

Then Walter himself leaned down, looking bemused. "Hey there, drunk boy."

"Hey." Kelly grinned and waved. Drunkenly.

"Maybe you want to climb into this bed, get comfy?"

That was all he said, and he didn't even say it lewdly. In fact he was soft and quiet, very gentle, the same way he'd been gentle with Kelly all evening. Even so, it hit Kelly like a hammer.

Get into this bed.

Kelly couldn't breathe, and it didn't have anything to do with allergies.

Walter reached down to Kelly and pulled him upright. "Up you come, kiddo."

Kiddo. That hurt, and Kelly wanted to protest it, but the world spun alarmingly as he came to his feet.

"Easy, easy," Walter said, and Cara and Greg said something too, but all Kelly could focus on was Walter. Walter who, he realized, would go to bed with him. The idea made blood rush to his groin.

Except Walter only tucked Kelly into the bed on the far side away from Cara and Greg, and though Kelly'd had a moment's thrill of thinking Walter might undress him, he entered the bed fully clothed. Walter didn't climb into the other side, only went back to sitting on the edge, talking to the others.

Kelly lay there, aroused, confused, aching. He wanted Walter. *Wanted* Walter. This ache was new, different than anything he'd felt before. He'd looked at guys and thought they were cute. He'd lain in bed and fantasized about men. He'd fantasized about Walter a few times. He'd wanted Mason when he saw him too, but abstractly. All his crushes had been distant and full of vague longing.

There was nothing vague about the way his whole body ached for his roommate right now. He stared at Walter's back, silhouetted by the hotel room lighting, and Kelly wanted him *now*. Wanted to touch him. Wanted Walter to touch him back. Wanted Walter to smile while he touched him. Wanted Walter to put his arm around him while he talked to Cara, the same way Greg and Cara held each other. Some of it was that he just wanted somebody to hold him.

A lot of it, he realized for the very first time, was that he wanted Walter to be the one who did that holding. And so, so much more.

Kelly lay in bed, half-asleep, aching, yearning, his beer-soaked mind fueling murky fantasies of Walter sliding under the covers and pulling Kelly to him. In his fantasies neither of them wore any clothes—except underwear at first, because even Kelly's subconscious was shy, but eventually as they rubbed against each other, those evaporated too.

Abruptly his fantasies faded and real-life Walter slid beside him, wearing boxers and his T-shirt, which made Kelly want to pull him closer. He didn't though, not drunk enough anymore, too worried what Walter would say, what he would think, whether or not he would laugh.

Walter didn't laugh. Keeping his back to Kelly, he lay on his side, far, far away.

The next thing Kelly knew, it was morning, and his head was pounding. Walter stood over him looking sleep-rumpled and bleary but a hell of a lot better than Kelly felt.

"Come on," Walter whispered. "Let's head back to the dorm."

He offered Kelly a hand, and Kelly took it, wondering if the touch would give him the same thrill it had the night before. It was there, just muted, dulled by a reality sobriety provided.

Walter Lucas was hot, sexy, fun, and a good friend—and the wrong place to look for a boyfriend.

Kelly vowed he would start looking elsewhere a lot harder.

Chapter Eight

THE WEEK AFTER Cara and Greg's visit, Kelly was weird. When Walter would ask him what was going on, usually because his roommate had a funny look on his face, something sad and full of longing, the expression evaporated. "Nothing," Kelly would say, and mumble about needing to study.

Walter didn't press, but he tracked his roommate carefully from then on, trying to work it out. Kelly was almost *dopey*, really. He stared at the wall at odd moments, and when Walter called out to get his attention, he blushed, like he'd been doing something he shouldn't.

One day Walter caught Kelly checking his phone, blushing at texts, and recognition dawned.

Oh. Red had his eye on someone.

The realization didn't sit well with Walter. He wondered who had captured Kelly's virginal interest, and he did his best to discreetly find out. It wasn't easy. No one was overtly flirting with Kelly, not when Walter was watching. A few times Walter even made sure no one knew he was watching, and he still couldn't see anything.

Who the hell was this loser?

One night Walter stole Kelly's phone after he'd gone to bed, took it to the bathroom and read the messages. When he saw the name of Kelly's mystery texter, he swore.

Mason. What was he, a set of jars? *Mason.* Mason Gallagher. God. Walter rolled his eyes. He pulled out his own phone and did a Facebook search too, lip curling when he saw the smarmy freshman's grin. At least he was talent. Walter scanned Mason Gallagher's public posts and looked him up on Twitter. Well, he was boring all around, wasn't he? Cute, maybe even good in bed, but boring.

Walter stilled at the thought, then relaxed. No. He'd know if Kelly had gotten laid. Hell, he practically had a neon sign when he'd masturbated.

Had there been a date, though?

A thorough scan of the texting exchange said there hadn't been, only lots of near misses. Gallagher never dropped a chance to invite Kelly up to his room, the perv. Jesus, what did Red see in him? The guy was about as interesting as a mixed drink. Conceptually a good time, but the actual consumption wasn't worth much more than getting off.

Seriously, why did Kelly swoon over him? They weren't making jokes. They weren't having fun, just flirting like awkward junior high girls and not hooking up.

Walter pondered the situation long after he'd replaced Kelly's phone in its charger and gone back to bed. He watched Kelly even more closely over the next few days, and when he spied Mason Jar outside the campus deli one day, he lingered to inspect. No, Mason live wasn't any more interesting than Mason the text.

Mason caught Walter watching and gave him a coy smile.

Rolling his eyes, Walter pushed off the wall and headed to class.

Still, the limbo of dreamy Kelly without an actual date lingered the rest of the week, alternately making Walter feel relieved and tense. Should he say something? Give flirting advice? Point out this was going to be a disaster? He didn't know the answer to this one, and it was driving him crazy.

Then he realized how obsessed he was with his roommate's lack of a sex life and took a pause. What the hell? Shaking his head at himself, he vowed he'd go out to Moe's as soon as possible—alone, though he wouldn't stay that way. He needed to get fucked, and right now, thanks. He needed to clear his head.

Unfortunately, when he was getting dressed to go, Kelly came back to the room. He looked a little rough, though when he saw Walter getting ready, he seemed almost relieved, if not still off his game. "Oh, are you going out?"

Walter swallowed a groan. He'd thought Kelly had been on one of his joiner benders, heading to campus film night. "I can stay in."

Kelly glared as he collapsed into the rocker. "I don't want to wreck your *plans.*"

Now Walter stared at Kelly, hard, because that was way out of character. Had something happened with old Mason Jar? "You okay?"

Cue blush. "Just a frustrating day."

Definitely something with Mason Jar. "I can stay. It's fine, really. I don't mind."

Kelly gave him a long, angry look. "Seriously, go. It's not a big deal. I'll call Rose."

Walter hesitated, still not sure, but Kelly was already on the phone, waving Walter impatiently away. Walter threw up his hands and headed out the door.

When he got to Moe's, though, he was almost immediately bored. A few guys flirted with him, and they weren't ghastly or anything, but he wasn't interested. He felt restless and cranky and, after a few drinks, lonely. Since his friends here were part of the problem, he called Cara.

"Where are you? It's so loud."

"Moe's." He slumped on the bar. "Something's wrong with me. I can't find anyone to sleep with. And Kelly is being cranky."

Cara laughed. "Well, I think I can guess why Kelly is cranky."

"Really. All the way from Northbrook, you know why my roommate is cranky? Let's hear it."

"No, because you're being an ass."

Walter snorted. "What's new? Tell me, oh wise one."

"No, I don't think I will. Where's Kelly? He with you?"

"He's back in the room."

"I think you should go back to the room."

"I wanted to get *laid*." When Cara was silent, he rolled his eyes. "I can't fuck Kelly. We've been over this." He was drunk, but he could still put two and two together. "You think that's why Kelly is mad? You think he *does* want me to fuck him?"

"Not like that, no." Cara sighed. "Forget I said anything. Just go find a guy and blow him."

God, everyone was a bitch tonight. "Fine, I will," Walter said, and he hung up.

He didn't blow anybody, though, and nobody blew him. He did get a text from his mother, something vague and desperate and boner killing.

Because he was stupid, he nipped out into the quiet of the back patio at Moe's and called her.

"Walter. It's so good to hear from you."

Some of Walter's tension bled from his shoulders. His mom wasn't a drinker, but it felt as if alcoholism was what was coming next. "How are things going?"

"Terrible. I'm giving up my business. It's a stupid waste of time."

Oh God, that wasn't good. Walter was never sure what it was exactly his mother did, some kind of professional perfume party thing, kind of a modern suburban Avon gig. All he knew was that without it, his mother would have nothing to do but mope around.

"Oh," he said, because he didn't know what else to say.

"Not that it matters what I do. Your sister is always off with Pony Club, and you're at college."

That comment dug. "Mom, what do you want me to do, come home?" *Again?*

He regretted the words as soon as he said them. What if she said yes?

"No." The sulk went out of her voice, and she was simply sad. "No, that's not what I meant." She went quiet for a minute. "I don't have anything to do, Walter. I don't know what to do."

Walter didn't either. "I'm sorry, Mom."

They spoke awkwardly for a few more minutes, and Walter had the strong suspicion his mom was going to go off and cry. When they hung up, it was only twelve thirty, but he went back to Porter, horny, guilty, out of sorts, and confused.

Rose was over, and she and Kelly had fallen asleep on the futon, Rose wrapped up inside the circle of Kelly's naked arm.

Walter stared at them for a long time, trying to sort out why he felt betrayed and angry. The garbage was crammed full of Opie's pizza boxes, and they'd finished off a six-pack of root beer. Kelly's laptop was propped on his chair at a perfect angle for the futon, which meant he and Rose had been watching movies when they fell asleep.

Jealousy stabbed him hot and hard, and it wasn't just because Kelly wasn't wearing a shirt. He'd seen that a thousand times, and he appreciated the sight of the bare chest his roommate boasted, the slightly toned arms. Arms looped around Rose. Obviously, *obviously* this was a platonic embrace, and it wasn't that he gave a damn if it hadn't been, but—yeah, it bugged him. A lot.

He thought about what Cara had said, about how Kelly wanted him, except that he didn't, or that Walter shouldn't do anything about it. Standing over his own bed, Walter admitted *he* wanted to be snuggled by Kelly. And then he wanted Kelly to shift his hand lower, straddle his thigh…

Grumbling, Walter got undressed down to his boxers and climbed into Kelly's loft. He was still horny, so he jerked off quietly in the dark.

He told himself he imagined Kelly jacking him because he was in Kelly's bed, surrounded by the smell of Kelly on the sheets. No other reason would be tolerated.

IN HINDSIGHT KELLY probably should have seen it coming, but seeing Mason making out in the Sandman lounge hurt. He was only glad he'd been able to keep it together in front of Walter long enough to call Rose. He hadn't cried, but he had been a soppy mess. She'd been a rock and watched *The Little Mermaid* with him instead of lecturing—though he hadn't realized she was saving that for the next morning when they ate breakfast together.

"I didn't even know you were dating him," Rose said, her tone accusatory.

"No. We weren't. But I thought we were heading there." He slumped and stuck his spoon in his oatmeal.

"Well, he's a jerk and doesn't deserve you, if he's going to flirt with you and make out with someone else. When was your date supposed to be?"

Kelly averted his eyes and fiddled with his napkin. "We…we had a hard time finding a time."

"What, between your dueling CEO schedules?"

"Okay, it was more that he kept inviting me to his room, and something about the way he said it made me uneasy, so I kept trying to meet him other places. We did have coffee once. It was nice."

"So, wait. You're telling me you did have a date, but then you wouldn't go back to his room?" Rose tilted her head forward and looked at him meaningfully from beneath the brim of her leather cap. "Seriously, Kelly. This isn't the Victorian era."

"I know." Kelly blushed hotter and ripped off the corner of the napkin. "I just...I wanted to get to know him first, okay? I don't see that as so bad."

"You couldn't get to know him in his room?" She leaned back in her chair, frowning. "You probably came off as a prude."

The words hurt, but since Kelly had been thinking the same thing, he figured he deserved them. He slumped deeper into his chair.

Rose stroked his shoulder. "Sorry, that was harsh."

Kelly shrugged. "It's not. You're right, I *am* a prude."

"No. I shouldn't have said that. You're not a prude, but I think you're going to have a hell of a time, being a shy, virginal, gay man wanting a 1950s-movie kind of courtship."

Kelly had worked that much out on his own. "So what, I shouldn't even try? You sound like Walter."

"Interesting, isn't it, that your two closest friends are both cynical about relationships. Though honestly, I can't see what you saw in that guy, outside of his being cute. You're smart, you're funny, and you're kind. You knew all Mason wanted out of you was a lay, and when you held out, he lost interest. You could do so much better, probably while sleepwalking."

"I can't find anyone, though, and I want to be with someone."

She ruffled his hair. "Well, be smarter about it next time. Pick somebody worthy."

Walter's sideways grin flashed in Kelly's mind, but he quickly snuffed the image out. "And if there isn't anyone worth my time?"

"Then welcome to the cynical relationship express. I'll save you a seat." She nudged his tray with her finger. "Hey, I know. How about you come with me to a party tonight over in the Manors? It's a bunch of lesbians and bi girls, and while there'll be drinking, it's not mandatory."

Kelly raised his eyebrows, highly dubious. "Why would I want to go to *that*?"

"Because there's no pressure, no boys to sigh over. Just music and good times." She grinned. "Bring your iPod, and you can show off that artist you keep telling me about."

It still sounded a little crazy, but Kelly couldn't say no, not when Rose had been so nice the night before. "I'll think about it," he said.

She aimed her spoon at him. "You'll go," she corrected.

WHILE KELLY HAD every intention of wheedling out at the last minute, he forgot how well Rose had his number. Not only did she text him all day, she promised to come hunt him down if he didn't show up by nine. When Walter caught him groaning over that last text, Kelly showed it to him, hoping he had a way out.

To his surprise, Walter laughed and looked intrigued. "She invited you to a party at Luna's? Shit, honey, you should go. And you should take me along." When Kelly did a double take, Walter waved impatiently at him. "Sometimes I forget you're a freshman. Luna is a senior on the endless-year program. She's a crazy lipstick lesbian and absolutely adorable. Every now and again she bribes her floor's RA and throws a killer party, invite only. I've heard about them but haven't ever been."

"Then how am *I* invited?"

"By Rose, it seems. Which means she's sleeping with Luna, if she's able to toss out invitations that freely. *Very* interesting." He nudged Kelly's elbow. "Text her back and see if I can come along."

Kelly still couldn't get over that Walter wanted to go watch a bunch of lesbians dance, let alone that he needed Kelly's inside connection to do so. Overwhelmed and a bit confused, he did as Walter ordered, and half an hour later they were both heading across campus, iPods in their pockets and a tote bag of alcohol slung over Walter's shoulder.

"Aren't we going to be in trouble if someone catches us?" Kelly eyed the bag nervously.

Walter raised his eyebrow. "For what? Drinking? I'm old enough, and so's Luna."

"Most people at the party won't be though, right?

Rose and I are underage, and the college knows that."

"The Manors are pretty small—they're set up in pods, sixteen units total, and my guess is she invites the whole building to the party. When she lived in junk housing like us, she had to be more creative, but the thing is, even when parties get shut down, everyone just goes home. Campus security shines a flashlight and looks stern, and everyone heads to bed." He bumped Kelly with his shoulder. "Stop fussing. It'll be fine, and you can get drunk and have a good time."

"I don't want to get drunk. What if something happens?"

"To a gay boy in a room full of lesbians? Nothing. You need to let your hair down, Red. You seem uptight. Tell you what—I won't get any deeper than tipsy, and I promise to keep your virtue safe. Deal?"

Kelly shrugged, embarrassed but not quite sure why. He didn't plan to get drunk, whatever Walter said.

That resolve quickly slipped as they went down the steps to Luna's dorm and Kelly took in the riotous feminine debauchery spilling out of the front door of Ashburn Manor. Kelly hadn't gone into the upper-classmen dorms during his campus tour, only driven by on the street. They were a little village, four sets of four buildings to each pod, the sections connected by a series of walkways, though each entrance was a sunken pit in front of a kind of communal picnic area. The whole design was so 1970s it might as well have a disco ball hanging in front of it. Though no sooner had he thought that did Kelly spy one spinning slowly inside the lounge of the building where the party was to be held.

He glanced around the quad, taking in the other three buildings in the pod, wondering if any of the residents minded all the noise. He read the names off the individual houses in front of their front doors: Ashburn, Chaney, Clark, Dahmer—

"*Dahmer?*" Kelly repeated, scandalized.

"Vernon, not Jeffrey." When Kelly looked at him blankly, Walter winked. "You must not have gotten there in your humanities course yet. All the manors are named after dead civil rights activists."

"Oh." Kelly blinked, relieved but still a bit thrown. "That's...different."

"That's Hope, honey." Walter put his hand on the small of Kelly's back. "Rose is going to throw her back out trying to wave you over. Go say hi. I'll catch up after I thank Luna for letting me crash."

It turned out Walter wasn't exaggerating—Rose hung out the window of one of the lower floors, a red Solo cup in one hand and a long necklace banging against her cleavage as she gestured wildly to Kelly. For the first time since he'd met her, Rose didn't have on some kind of hat. Her long hair was curled, even, and she wore makeup.

There was also a *lot* of cleavage. He stared at it, realizing he hadn't noticed how well-endowed she was before.

She caught him looking and laughed, leaning heavily on his shoulder. "Kelly, sweetheart! I'm so glad you came. I was too drunk to come get you." She waved her red cup, sloshing some of her drink onto herself. "Come on in. I'll get you something."

"What room are you in? I'll come around and—" He yelped as she put down her cup and dragged him in through the window.

The room was full of women, all of them as drunk as Rose. Several of them were snuggled together, one group a threesome. They smiled up at Kelly, waving as Rose introduced him. It was the usual get-to-know-you chitchat, Rose's friends asking where Kelly was from, making the Mayberry joke when he said Minnesota, and they all announced they were from various Chicago suburbs. A few of them started telling random stories about Chicago—at the same time—but when Kelly realized two of the girls in the threesome had their hands down the third girl's pants, actively getting her off, he shot to his feet and gestured at the door.

"I'm going to go find Walter," he said to Rose, and beat it the hell out of Dodge.

He found his roommate in the main lobby, sipping water from a bottle as he talked to a cute, short blonde with perfectly applied makeup, more cleavage going on than Rose, and purple streaks in her hair. She waved as he came over.

"Hi, I'm Luna. You must be Kelly. Rose told me all about you. Oh good, I see you already got something to drink."

Kelly looked down at the glass in his hand, surprised to see it there. "Rose gave it to me, I think."

Luna laughed—wickedly. "Yeah, she's been hitting the hard stuff. She's going to be *fun* tonight."

While Kelly tried not to actively recoil from all the lesbian imagery, Walter took the drink from his hands and sniffed the rim. His eyes went wide, and he handed it to Luna. "Babe, do you have something a little less toxic? My boy's not a heavy."

"Sure thing." Luna set Kelly's glass down and gestured to a makeshift bar in the middle of the room. "Help yourself. Music's down in my room, number four."

She drifted away, and Kelly watched her go as Walter guided him to the table of alcohol. "I can't believe she and Rose are sleeping together. She never even said anything about dating someone."

"If I know Manchester, and I do, I can't say I'm surprised. She plays everything close to the vest. My money's also on this being a weeklong romance at best." He sipped at his water and frowned at the table. "Hmm. Your options are either hard liquor or white wine. Warm white wine, but it's shit white in a box, so who cares, right?" He filled a glass and handed it to Kelly. "Drink this and stop looking so nervous."

"It's just weird. We're the only guys here."

"Oh, more will show up. Trust me. Not our kind, though." He linked Kelly's arm through his. "Let's go find the music. I like dancing with lesbians."

Kelly thought at first that was either a joke or a euphemism for something, but it turned out Walter meant that comment literally. No sooner did he have Kelly set up with a trio of not-that-drunk (and not making out, thank God) girls on a sofa, he disappeared into the middle of the room, where he began dancing with an abandon Kelly hadn't ever seen him exhibit, not at Moe's, not anywhere. Kelly watched Walter move, transfixed.

"He's so cute." The girl next to Kelly—Tricia, Kelly thought her name was—leaned her head on Kelly's shoulder and smiled as Walter shimmied behind a laughing girl who moved in sync with him. "Except he's gay, dammit."

"And you're a lesbian," the girl on her other side said, and they all laughed.

Kelly felt dazed. God, Walter just…*moved*. For a long time Walter danced and Kelly watched him, sometimes talking to the girls who sat next to him—they kept getting up and new ones sat in their places—and then after about a half hour, as a song ended, Walter came over, sweat-soaked, and collapsed next to Kelly.

"Shit." He laughed, relaxed and happy, and he glanced at Kelly's glass. "You need another?"

Kelly peered into his cup. It was empty. Huh. That would explain why he felt buzzy.

Walter popped back to his feet with a wink. "Be right back," he said, and he was, with a new glass for Kelly and another bottle of water for himself. He was about to sit down when a girl grabbed him and hauled him back onto the floor.

Kelly had half a minute to observe them, that odd feeling of longing stirring in him again, and then someone grabbed *his* arm too.

He danced stiffly at first, but soon the wine and the gentle teasing of his partner relaxed him, and he began to loosen up. It *was* fun to dance with a bunch of lesbians or nearly lesbians, because yeah, nobody gave a shit about what he looked like or how badly he danced. Even when a girl with shock-red hair plastered herself tight against him, her tits mashed to his chest and his— limp—cock squashed along her thigh, it was so clear neither of them were turned on *at all*, and as such they could both let go and be total sluts. Laughing, he tossed up his hands and danced. Someone handed him another drink, this one smelling tart and intense, but he drank it anyway.

He was having *fun*. So much fucking *fun*.

When he heard the familiar thumping beats of "Wild Ones" begin to play—they'd finally picked his iPod, apparently—he gave a hearty *woot* and threw himself into his boogie with an abandon he didn't know he had in him. Somehow he'd become the center of a circle—he could see the straight boys now, mingled in amidst the girls, all of them looking slightly lost and out of place, and it was funny so he laughed. Hands slid down his arms, making him shiver, and as someone pressed against his back, he caught the familiar scent of cologne.

Walter's thumb brushed Kelly's wrist. "You're having a good time."

"Yeah." Kelly tried to smile over his shoulder, but Walter's hand skimmed his hip, and he jerked, glad Walter couldn't feel the sudden erection that sprang up at the contact.

Walter gripped Kelly's hip more firmly, holding him in place. "Hey—it's just me, goofball. What, you can't dance with me the way you were dancing with Sally?"

No, Kelly couldn't. Except as Sia's voice boomed out over the room and Walter led him into a sway, Kelly started to wonder if maybe he could. *It's only dancing,* he told himself. Because the truth was, he did want to dance with his roommate. He wanted Walter to dance with him the way he'd been dancing with the girls, and Kelly wanted to let go enough to be the way he'd been with his own partners. He wanted to be able to feel that relaxed with Walter.

He couldn't do that, though, because then Walter would know. Hell, he'd feel, because even *this* subtle contact had Kelly hard as a rock.

"Hush." Walter's lips grazed his ear, making Kelly shiver. That made Walter laugh, though not unkindly. "Is that it? You're being self-conscious because I'm turning you on?" When Kelly said nothing, Walter snorted and pulled Kelly against his body.

Kelly shuddered. *Hard*—Walter was as hard as Kelly was. "Walter," he croaked, his entire body turning to jelly. Except his screaming dick.

Walter kept them moving, his touches gentling, soothing, even as they kept in time to the beat. "Babe, it's fine. We're both guys. We both like guys. We're both hot, so we get turned on by each other. Big deal. You don't have to be embarrassed about it."

He turned Walter on? He was a hot guy? Kelly angled his head around, needing to see Walter's face.

Walter looped his arms around Kelly's neck and shook his head. "Oh, Red. You're precious, you know that?"

No, Kelly didn't. "You confuse me," he confessed, because he'd had too much to drink.

Walter laughed, but it wasn't a mean laugh, not at all. "*You* confuse you, Red. Turn your head off for ten minutes and dance with me. I don't care if you come in your pants. Just let go for ten fucking minutes."

Kelly's whole body felt hot. "I can't do that. Not with you."

"You can't flirt with me?" Walter gave him a *come on* look. "Red. You can *totally* flirt with me."

Wait, *what*? Kelly shook his head, trying to clear it.

Walter sighed and began to speak in the tone of someone teaching a child something simple that they'd made complicated. "Walk it through, babe. You're tipsy. You're turned on. You're having a good time, and it feels good to be turned on. You're at a party full of lesbians, and me. Is there anyone here you're going to let take you to bed tonight?"

"What? *No.*" It came out so automatically he couldn't stop it, but rather than be upset, Walter seemed to be waiting patiently for Kelly to figure something out. Kelly frowned, still not getting it.

Walter rolled his eyes, but he laughed too. "Jesus. Red—you can flirt with me, you can do whatever you want, because we're not sleeping together. So stop worrying about it. Just have a good time."

The music slipped into the chorus, and Walter dragged Kelly bodily back into the dance. He forgot to be upset or confused or anything else, and within a few bars he was moving in time to the beat with his roommate, brazenly sliding his arms around Walter's body. He tried to stay loose, to not think about how hot Walter made him, how bad that was. *We're not going to sleep together* kept ringing in his head, though, annoying him.

The music shifted to Pink's "Raise Your Glass", and the room erupted in drunk, enthusiastic people singing and dancing along.

Most of the girls jumped up and down and did some drunken version of headbanging while they belted out the chorus, but Walter kept tight hold of Kelly and pulled him close, alternating between sensual thrusts with his thigh into Kelly's groin and shimmying them in deep dips that nearly ran them into their neighbors. Kelly could feel Walter's hard cock against his hip, and he knew Walter could feel his erection too. He could smell Walter's sweat, could sometimes taste it on his tongue. The wine and whatever else he'd been drinking filled his head, heightening his senses, making him think he could *feel* Walter on his tongue.

Suddenly he wanted to. He really, really wanted to.

Raise your glass, the room shouted as one, Walter too, his shout reverberating in his chest beneath Kelly's hands.

Kelly shut his eyes, drew in a sharp breath through his nostrils and buried his face in Walter's neck.

He thrilled when Walter stilled, and he laughed, the sound rolling in his belly before he opened his lips over the throbbing pulse and sucked. Walter gasped, his knees wobbling, and his hands tightened against Kelly's hair and waist.

Running his tongue along Walter's skin, Kelly felt his cock pulse inside his jeans at the sharp, salty taste of his roommate's skin.

Walter jerked and tried to pull away. *Fuck no,* Kelly thought, and turned his grip into a vise. He stopped kissing Walter's neck, but he nipped at his jaw, heady at the thrill of making *Walter* the awkward one for once.

"Stop thinking," he murmured, and ran his tongue along Walter's stubble.

"Jesus." Walter sounded shattered. He turned his head, and for a second their mouths almost brushed together. Walter kept that from happening, pulling Kelly's head away from his own mouth. "Kelly, don't."

The refusal shafted Kelly, and all the self-consciousness alcohol had kept at bay returned in a tidal wave. "You drive me crazy," he said to Walter's chest, because he couldn't look him in the eye.

"Sweetheart, you're drunk. Really drunk. If I let you do what you're doing, you'll hate me tomorrow, and I'm not going there."

Some distant, wine-slogged part of Kelly acknowledged Walter was right, but that didn't mean Kelly enjoyed hearing it. "You think I'm a stupid, dumb kid." He just wanted Walter to kiss him, to push him onto the couch and...do stuff.

Walter drew Kelly in close and kissed his hair. "I don't think you're stupid. Or dumb. Or a kid."

Could he stop being so reasonable and nice for a second? Kelly sank against his shoulder defeated. "I'm so confused."

"I know, baby."

Walter was stroking Kelly's back, and his butt, and it felt so fucking good. "I want you to fuck me," he whispered.

Though Walter stilled, he didn't let Kelly go. "I want to fuck you too, baby," he said at last. "But we can't."

Why couldn't they? Kelly wanted to ask, but he was starting to feel dizzy. Were they spinning? He opened his eyes, which helped, but the more he thought about it, the more he realized he felt queasy.

"I don't feel good." Kelly's stomach gurgled, and he clutched at Walter, all thoughts of fucking forgotten. "I think I had too much to drink."

Something brushed his hair—a kiss?—and Walter patted his butt. "Come on, sweetheart, let's get you home."

Kelly thought that was a good idea.

Halfway across campus, he threw up. Into a bush, and Walter held his head as he knelt and puked.

"I'm sorry," he slurred as he tried to wipe his mouth on his sleeve. God, he was gross.

"I think you got some of that Everclear they were passing around, hon. Sorry, I should have paid closer attention."

Kelly tried to point out Walter didn't have to babysit him, and then his stomach heaved again.

He wasn't sure what happened after that—it was as if there was a sort of gap in his memory—and all of a sudden he was lying on Walter's futon, sweating like a pig and opening his eyes blearily. Someone kissed his forehead, someone sweet and gentle.

"Mom?" he whispered, but then Walter chuckled, and Kelly drifted back off to sleep.

When he woke in the morning, he wished he were dead, feeling as if someone had dragged him backward through dog shit. When he remembered what he'd done with Walter, he nearly got sick all over again.

"Oh my God." Kelly would have covered his face with a pillow, but he hurt too much to move.

Walter only laughed, gently, and passed him some water. "Congratulations, roomie. That was quite a bender you put on last night. Though from what I hear, it's nothing on what Manchester tied on."

That was all they spoke of their night out—Walter brought Kelly a meal bar to nibble on as his stomach would tolerate it, kept the water coming and acted as if everything were perfectly normal.

Except every so often Kelly remembered Walter whispering, *I want to fuck you too, baby,* and some part of Kelly knew, no matter how they pretended, things wouldn't ever be the same.

Chapter Nine

THINGS WERE A little weird between Walter and Kelly after the party at Luna's, but Walter told himself it wasn't anything he couldn't handle. Kelly had been drunk. Really, stinking drunk, and Walter felt like a shit heel for not watching Kelly's glass. It was too bad, because if not for that Everclear, it would have been a magical night. Walter hadn't ever had that much fun dancing.

Right up until Kelly had licked his neck.

Licked it.

Every time Walter let himself think about that moment, every bit of wiring in his brain short-circuited, and he stood still, motionless while the memory played again and again. Once it happened while he was in line for a soda in the cafeteria, Kelly standing right beside him, and he caught a whiff of Kelly's cologne as he stuck out his arm to put his cup under the ice maker.

Except he knew Kelly didn't wear cologne and had unscented, non-allergenic, all-natural, hippie deodorant. Which meant he was smelling Kelly straight up and getting hard. And thinking about Kelly running his tongue down his neck.

Over. And over. And over.

"Walter?"

He blinked, coming out of his trance right before the Dr. Pepper overflowed his glass and spilled all over his fingers. Swearing, he tipped some of it out, set the glass on his tray and shook off the sticky residue.

Kelly gave him a wary look. "You okay?"

Walter rolled his eyes at himself, grumbled under his breath and headed for their table.

The one good piece of news was that Mason Jar had moved permanently out of the picture. The texts had stopped, and when Mason walked past them in the union, Kelly went stiff as a board and quickly fixed his gaze on an external window. Mason didn't even seem to notice Kelly was there.

"Everything okay?" Walter asked, just to be sure.

"Fine," Kelly replied, in a very not-fine voice, but he didn't offer anything else, and Walter didn't push.

He was still worried about Kelly, though, so the next time he Skyped Cara, he brought it up. What did *she* do? *Laugh.*

Walter glared at the screen. "What the hell is so funny?"

She gave him a long-suffering look. "Oh please. You're practically a mother hen over Kelly. You didn't fuss this much over me."

"I'm not fussing."

"You're not just fussing, you're obsessing." She rested her chin in her hand, looking wicked. "Walter, do you have a crush on your roommate?"

Walter refused to dignify that with an answer, only

crossed his arms over his chest and waited for her to stop being an idiot.

Now she looked wistful. "Oh, Wally."

"Oh, Pickles. I think your veil is on too tight. Be reasonable. Just because it would make you feel better if I were trotting off into the sunset like you are, don't go hooking me up with whoever you think makes me a cuter matching set."

Their conversation ended shortly after that, and now Walter felt frustrated and guilty in addition to feeling confused. So he did the only thing left he could do. He went to Williams.

It was Saturday afternoon, but Williams was in his office. Two of his kids were making iMovies in the studio across the hall, and Williams was at a command viewing performance when Walter stuck his head in.

"Walter!" Paul, the youngest, beamed and waved him over. "Come watch this. We're turning a bug into a bird."

"Oh yeah?" Walter stood behind the table with the professor, not faking much of his praise as he watched a cockroach morph into a chicken pecking at the ground. "Wow, how'd you do that?"

"A five-dollar app," Williams murmured. "Don't tell the dean." He clapped his hand on Paul's and Mary's shoulders. "Okay, guys, I'm going to go into my office with Walter for a bit. Don't break anything, and don't do any more shopping."

"Okay," they said in chorus and made the cockroach morph again.

Williams poured Walter a cup of coffee and nodded

at the chair beside his desk. "Sit. I can tell something's up. You've been off in class too. Please tell me it's not your mother."

He'd been off in class? "It's not." Walter took the mug and sipped. The coffee was almost warm today, but it was still rotgut. "Well, she's not great, but no, that's not it." He put the mug down and shifted in his seat, trying to get comfortable. "It's Kelly. Or really, it's not Kelly. It's everyone."

Lifting his eyebrows, Williams cradled his mug, leaned back in his chair until it creaked, and waited.

Walter tried to explain about Kelly's desire to date and the near train wrecks Walter endured on a daily basis. "He's going to get his heart broken, and it makes me insane. When I say that to other people, they have knowing smiles and tell me I'm falling for him. I'm *not*. Even if I were, that's not what this is about. He's so fucking clueless it kills me. He doesn't notice when people do flirt with him, and the only guys he gives the time of day to are the ones with bad pick-up lines who want to get in his pants. Which would be fine, except he acts as if he lives in a goddamn Taylor Swift song."

"He does seem a bit hung up on the ideal in pretty much everything. I've noticed that in how he responds in class." Williams cocked his head to the side. "Wouldn't you consider that part of his relationship evolution, though? Maybe he has to get his heart broken a little bit in order to have those rose glasses adjusted for clarity."

"Yeah, well, then I have to watch it happen. I don't want to."

Williams's gaze gentled. "Walter, you *do* care for him. He's your friend. More so than Cara, I think."

Why did Williams saying that make Walter's skin feel tight? "I've known him a few months."

"And you talk about him constantly." When Walter stiffened, he held up a hand. "No, I'm not going to make cutesy comments about how you're in love with him. It's worse than that. You love him, period. Friend or lover is irrelevant. You care for him, and the people who fall under that category for you have a horrible track record. They all leave you or go crazy. Especially lately."

Walter swallowed hard and averted his eyes.

A heavy hand rested briefly on his arm, squeezed, then lifted. "Talk to me about your mom. You haven't mentioned her, just keep telling me she's fine, which is the biggest pile of bullshit this side of your sister's horse barn."

Walter couldn't laugh at the stupid joke. He kept his eyes on Williams's bookshelf. "She's melting down at the grocery store and crying to me on the phone. Nobody loves her, nobody needs her, there's nothing for her to do." Williams said nothing, and the rest came spilling out. "I broke down last week and called Dad. He got mad at me, and now I only ever get his voicemail or secretary. The one he's fucking. Cara says she'll check on Mom, but there's nothing she can do, and she's stupid busy with the wedding of the year. There isn't anything anybody can do."

"You do get that this includes you?"

"She calls me and texts me all the time. If I don't

call back, she sobs and talks about how I am abandoning her. What, am I supposed to follow through?"

"You're supposed to get the college education she already stopped you once from having. You aren't her parent. You're her son." When Walter said nothing, Williams shook his head in disgust. "Honestly, sometimes I could smack your parents upside the head and feel nothing but gleeful at their pain."

A headache began to bloom in the back of Walter's skull. He set the coffee aside.

Sighing, Williams did the same. "If I didn't have the kids, I'd say let's go get a beer. All I'm doing here is alternating between stressing over my tenure application and wondering what hell my children are bringing down upon the department."

Walter thought about the beautiful fall day he'd walked through to get to Williams's office. "We could take them to the park and get coffee on the way. Real stuff that doesn't rot our intestines."

Williams grunted and pushed away from his desk. "I'll get my coat."

KELLY DIDN'T GIVE up on relationships, but he did try to be smarter, as Rose had suggested. He continued to go to the freshman social events and school-sponsored "fun breaks," but he forced himself to be choosier about his affections. He gave considerable attention to a young man who wasn't talent but had a nice smile. Dave was incredibly eager to talk with Kelly, and he never winked and suggested they go to his room to make out.

Dave was a perfect, if slightly geeky gentleman. And God save him, but Kelly wasn't interested in him at all.

His failure with Dave made him feel particularly lost, and in a fit of desperation, he stayed after Intro to Humanities one day and asked Dr. Williams about the Lutheran church. The professor seemed surprised but pleased, and he acted as if he and Kelly were already good friends. This turned out to be Walter's fault.

"I've heard so much about you. You've single-handedly turned a disappointment into a pleasure for Walter, I think, as far as that whole room thing goes."

Kelly didn't know what to say to that, so he didn't say anything. The next class was filling the auditorium, so the professor motioned for Kelly to follow him out the lower-level door, talking to him all the way down a hallway Kelly hadn't been in before. "So you're wanting to go to church, are you? I have to say, I love that Walter's best friend is a believer. That has to keep him up at night, and things that keep Walter up at night are good for him."

Best friend? Kelly had no idea how to respond to all this. He stuck with things he could talk about without getting flustered, like church. "Well, originally I thought I'd go because it'd make my mother happy, but now I'm kind of wanting to go for me."

"You sound surprised by that realization."

Kelly shrugged. "I don't really need to be in church to feel okay with God or my faith. But..."

"But now you're starting to realize that a lot of going to church was about community and comforting ritual, not getting up close and personal with God?"

"Pretty much."

Williams held the door for Kelly. "How are you finding Hope?"

"It's okay." Kelly realized that sounded lackluster and tried to amend his reaction. "I mean, it's fine. It's a good school."

Williams laughed. "I'm not going to report you to Dean Stevens if you tell me it's not going well."

Kelly shrugged. "I know. It *is* fine. Nothing's really wrong. It's a good school. It's more that school isn't what I thought it would be."

"Interesting comment. How is it different than what you expected? What *did* you expect?"

"I'm not sure. Certainly not what I got, though." Kelly worried he should stop talking, but there was something about Williams that made him want to continue. "I feel a bit stupid most of the time. As if everyone gets the joke about life but me."

Williams's smile was knowing. "Ah. Yes, I know that feeling well."

Kelly gave him a hard look. "Not like that. I mean, I feel like a bumpkin." His cheeks heated. "Well, I guess I kind of am."

"Mr. Davidson, you're a young man in his first year of college. You're a long way from home—Minnesota, I think Walter said—and you're the eldest in your family, as you said in one of your essays. All your close friends are upperclassmen or bright sophomores. If you didn't feel lost and confused by the middle of October, you'd be doing it wrong. However, I have great faith that by this time next semester, you'll be feeling the wind under your sails again, perhaps a bit tentatively, but there all the same."

"Why?" Kelly asked.

"Because in addition to all the aforementioned, you're also intelligent and good-hearted." He pushed open yet another door, this one leading to the outside, and winked at Kelly. "I'll look for you on Sunday."

Not sure if he felt bolstered or not, Kelly watched his professor go.

KELLY THOUGHT ABOUT what Williams had said for several days, sometimes taking heart in the conversation and sometimes being frustrated by it. He didn't go to church that Sunday, partly in a kind of protest, though he'd admit it was a rather useless one. Mostly he simply couldn't bear to be around people and smile and answer questions about himself. He wanted to sleep more, but his thoughts jumbled and turned on themselves, and the only result in the end was that he was too awake to go back to sleep.

Walter was still unconscious, and after a few minutes' consideration, Kelly decided to brave the Porterhouse fourth-floor showers on his own.

As he made his way down the hall, Kelly kept his eyes fixed on the distant point of the shower doors, ignoring sly comments they murmured under their breath about stepping on cockroaches. When he went down with Walter, the jocks still made the comments

they were making now, but Walter and Kelly usually
ignored them and chatted, Walter pointing out talent
sotto voce to make Kelly blush. Alone, Kelly felt slightly
vulnerable, but he knew how to run this drill: no eye
contact, no comment, no trouble.

The one redeeming quality of Porter was its shower
stalls were just that, stalls, with private dressing areas
staged before single units with their own walls and
secondary curtain. Apparently in Sandman the male
floors had two mass shower units with six heads each
aiming out for true communal action. While in theory
the setup sounded like a porn film, in reality Kelly was
pretty sure he'd have been showering at midnight just
to keep from accidentally sporting wood in front of a
nice ass or set of pecs. Here in Porter 4, there were
seven private stalls, and as fortune happened to favor
him that morning, two of them were free.

He lingered under the spray, stroking himself. As
had been his habit since the night at Luna's, he gave in
to the guilty pleasure of fantasizing about sex with
Walter, even though he knew it was stupid and possibly
dangerous. In the privacy of his shower stall, he allowed
his fantasy self to pull out his cock while sitting on
Walter's lap, let Walter do the stroking for him. He
switched to pretending Walter was with him in the
shower, and he imagined Walter murmuring into his
ear, his own hard body pressing Kelly into the wall.

The trouble was, Kelly couldn't help remembering
the way Walter smiled at him in real life, the way he
teased, the way he was always there for Kelly. As a
friend, he knew—but when he masturbated to the idea

of Walter, friend and lover blended oh so easily. Especially when he remembered what it was like to kiss Walter's neck and make him lose his cool.

His dream Walter moved Kelly's hand to his own cock. *I want to fuck you, Kelly.*

Kelly came all over the tiles, wiping up the mess with his washcloth after. His cheeks were still red when he got out of the stall and dried off before stumbling back into his sweats.

When he tossed his towel over his shoulder and opened the curtain, Walter was standing there, holding his shower tote in hand, glaring.

"Walter!" It was a good thing he had the excuse of the shower for being flushed, because Kelly was never more embarrassed in his life.

"Why didn't you wait for me?" Walter demanded. He looked sleep-bleary, and his hair stuck out at odd angles. Kelly wanted to rub his hands in it.

Down, boy. "I didn't know you were awake."

Walter grunted, but his eyes lost some of their bleary nature as he ran his gaze up and down Kelly's recently-showered form. Kelly braced for teasing, but all Walter did was pinch Kelly's ass on his way into the cubicle, hard enough that Kelly could still feel the memory of it as he grabbed his backpack and hustled off to breakfast.

Rose was already seated at their usual table, wearing a blue beret today, and she smiled and waved as he entered. Her eyes were a little bloodshot, and as he saw the puffiness around them and realized that smile wasn't going all the way to her eyes, he wondered if her relationship with Luna had gone exactly the way Walter had predicted. Kelly waved back as he picked up a tray and headed through the line, determined to hurry so he could wring the story out of her. He made himself ignore the pancakes, delicious as they looked, because he knew damn well they weren't vegan. He considered the potatoes, but a glance at the spatula of the student worker manning them told a story of many omelets, so he continued on his way. When he saw the soy milk was empty, he got himself a dry bowl of cereal, some black coffee, and tried to swallow his bad attitude before he got to the table.

Clearly it didn't work, because Rose looked at him in concern, then glanced at his tray. "Oh, honey, I'm sorry." She slid her heaping plate of food away.

Kelly stopped her gesture with his free hand. "Don't. It's not your fault." With a sigh, he sat down and poked at his cereal. "I should go and ask for soy milk. I probably will in a minute. I just...I get tired of it sometimes, even though it's been most of my life. It's not any fun when the rest of the world can eat and you can't."

Rose patted his hand. "If it helps, the food sucks, same as always."

Kelly took in her red eyes and sobered. "Is everything okay?"

Rose folded up like a picnic blanket and all but pasted a *no trespassing* sign on her forehead. "Fine."

Kelly tried to figure out how to nudge the story out of her, but before he could Walter appeared, slouching into the seat beside Kelly.

"What the fuck is this, you won't even wait for me?" Walter nodded at Rose. "Hey, Manchester. Kelly, what the fuck is this you're eating? Christ. Let me guess, no soy milk. And polluted hash browns. Fucking idiots."

He rose from the table and stormed off toward the food counters. Kelly, who hadn't even been able to set down his coffee and manage a reply, sat with his cup in midair and watched his roommate turn into a tornado.

Rose sipped at her tea, eyes twinkling. "You and Walter are such a couple, and it's adorable. I know. You're not dating. Except that you are. It's almost as if you skipped dating and went straight to married."

"Walter doesn't date." Kelly had said this to her before, but it felt like a lifeline right now. *Remember that, before you hurt yourself.*

Rose had a wicked look about her. "Walter takes better care of you than anyone I've ever dated, slept with, or simply called a friend."

"I want to date." Why did he feel so panicked? "I don't just want to fool around when one of us is horny. I want to have a boyfriend."

Now Rose looked intrigued. "You've been fooling around? With Walter?"

"No." *Do not think about licking his neck. Do not think about licking his neck.* "This has nothing to do with Walter," he lied. "I want the full package. I want to meet someone at a restaurant and wonder if we'll kiss at the end of the night. I want a sweet first kiss, and I want to lie in bed wondering when we're going to have sex. I want it to feel special."

Rose snorted into her coffee. "Honey, you want a fantasy. Which is fine, except you need to remember that life isn't a fantasy."

"What's wrong with wanting what I want?"

"Nothing—except you want the experience, not the person. Relationships aren't mail order, and people don't have tidy little boxes to check off. I know you've been trying to be more discerning since Mason, and I applaud that, but—come on. Are you telling me you scan guys and think about whether or not that one or this one will open the door for you, and that's how you decide if you'll date them?"

Kelly did, kind of, but the hell he was going to admit that with her making it sound like a bad thing. "So what if I did that?"

"Well, it's a free country, so do what you want, but I'd sure love to know how is that any different than Walter eyeing their asses."

Kelly was so thrown by her question he could only blink. He was still trying to form a response when Walter came back to the table, brandishing a tray of clean hash browns, a bottle of ketchup and a paper quart of soy milk. He had a wild look about him, and he put down the tray with a bit of satisfied flourish.

"They're making a tofu scramble with clean utensils. It's too bad I'm not straight, because I think the vegan girl behind me in line was about to blow me on the spot. I'm having them hold a plate for you, and I'll pick it up when I go back in line." He glanced at Rose, as if just now realizing she too might need to be cared for. "Hon, you need anything?"

Rose lifted an eyebrow and eyed him with open lechery. "One of you that comes in bi and poly."

Walter laughed and openly fondled his crotch as he did a brief, exaggerated porn wiggle for Rose. "I'll be right back, baby, and all this is sitting right next to you, throbbing like a mighty hunter."

Rose laughed, and Walter grinned. He put a hand on Kelly's shoulder and nudged the disappointing tray out of the way for the one he'd prepared. "Eat up, Red. I hear you need to replenish some fluids and nutrients after your shower."

Kelly was so embarrassed the room spun, and when he recovered himself, Walter had already walked away. Even before Kelly looked at Rose, he could feel the weight of her meaningful stare.

"He doesn't date," Kelly said, almost desperate this time. Thank God she couldn't know how his shoulder tingled from Walter's touch or how the murmur in Kelly's ear had made his insides churn into gooey butter.

Rose said nothing, just kept smiling and staring as she drank her coffee.

Chapter Ten

ON THE LAST Sunday before Thanksgiving, Kelly went to church.

Even though Williams was right about his wanting to feel part of a community, Kelly didn't actively try to engage with any of the parishioners. He was polite when they introduced themselves and inquired about him, but he left things at that. Being in church, hearing the comforting murmurs of call and response, that's what he'd come for. The service wasn't the same as the one he attended back home, but it was close enough to be a balm.

He saw Williams across the sanctuary, his entire family in tow. Williams's wife was beautiful in a way that reminded Kelly of his mother: no makeup, only striking features and a plain but pretty style. The children were an adorable mob, each one towheaded and apple-cheeked from the cold snap that had taken Danby by surprise that morning. Though Williams waved, Kelly didn't close the distance between them, choosing simply to wave back and observe the happy clan from across the room.

As he headed back to campus—a mile-and-a-half trek leaving him plenty of time to think—he pulled out his phone, rubbing his thumb against his ring as he scrolled through. No messages, no texts, not even from Walter.

None from any potential boyfriend.

He'd gone to lunch with a nice guy from his econ class, someone as bored and lost in the back of the room as he was, and everything looked great until he'd found out Jason already *had* a boyfriend, and he couldn't wait for Kelly to meet him.

Worst of all? They'd met by being *roommates*.

The fall wind whipped around his ears, making Kelly shrug the collar of his coat higher. He stared at the leaves as they swirled in soft eddies around his shuffling feet. The crunch of leaves and cold burn of wind soothed him, reminding him of walks through his neighborhood back home, the same walks that had helped him first come to terms with his orientation. Kelly wanted to keep walking, keep letting his mind spin slowly, quietly, with no one and nothing to impede it.

He walked so long and far that he missed the cafeteria lunch service, so he swung through a deli on the highway in front of campus and grabbed a soup and sandwich. He watched the couples of all ages, noticing the ones who clung to each other didn't seem half as connected as the older couples who barely touched at all. He found he couldn't stop watching an elderly pair who barely spoke, the woman fussing to get more coffee and napkins for her husband whose eyes seemed slightly cloudy and unfocused—all until he looked at his wife. Kelly saw the affection he had for her, his gratitude, his love.

As he finished eating and headed back onto campus, past the lake to say hello to the swans, his insular world felt ridiculous and strange, more so than usual. He wished the rest of the day could be as quiet and pensive as his walk had been, so much so that he took the long, outdoor, and out-of-the-way path back to his dorm, which was why he passed Ritche Hall and saw Williams hurrying inside.

Kelly followed.

Though he hesitated at the professor's open door, Williams beamed at Kelly. "What a lovely surprise. Come on in." He regarded Kelly as he sat down, and his expression schooled to concern. "What's on your mind?"

Kelly hadn't really known why he'd gone into the building until that moment, but at Williams's inquiry, all became clear. "I've been thinking more about what I expected and why Hope has been a little disappointing. I think I've figured it out."

"Oh?" Williams settled back in his chair in a half slouch and laced his fingers over his midsection. "Let's hear it."

"I think I expected, or really, assumed, that going to college would mean growing up. That everything about being at college, at Hope, would be moving me toward that. Except I don't always feel like it is. Sometimes it is, but sometimes it seems even more ridiculous than high school."

Williams's expression was wry. "I hate to break it to you, but that doesn't go away after college. It's pretty much a constant state."

"But *why?*" Kelly could feel himself almost whining and tried to rein himself in, but it was difficult. "I don't understand. If I'm not supposed to grow up in college, when the hell am I?"

"Ah. That right there, Mr. Davidson, is where you begin to go wrong. There is no *supposed to*. There's no magic ruler by which we're all judged and weighed, not in this life. If you wait for someone to tell you it's time to grow up, you'll wait forever. Some people, quite happily, do just that. They don't do anything until they're forced to by circumstance."

"Well, that's awful."

"You might see if you can squeeze in a few philosophy courses next semester. I know they've cut that department down to nearly nothing, but I think you might enjoy the academic exercise."

It seemed an unsatisfying response to people being lazy and awful by definition, to take a course about why they might be so, but Kelly didn't want to point that out. "I'm not sure I'll have time. I was planning on switching over to history education, and I hear that major has a really tight timeline."

"*Teaching.* Well, far be it from me to countermand the education department, but my advice, as an educator myself? Make the time for that philosophy class, Kelly, if you truly do plan to be a teacher. Because those people who wait forever to grow will be all over your schoolroom."

Kelly was starting to feel more depressed by the minute. "So you're saying don't bother trying to help them?"

"Not even close. I'm saying get inside people's heads a little before you try to fill the spaces there."

"Isn't that psychology?"

"It might be. It might be both." Williams's smile was slow and knowing, and something about the back end of it made Kelly's skin prickle. Like Williams knew a secret, and if Kelly were very good and patient, he'd let him in on it.

Kelly, however, wasn't feeling very patient. "How am I supposed to find out?"

"Have you heard of the Philosophy Club?"

"Yeah, Rose has talked about it a few times." She'd tried to get Kelly to come, but the reading list made Kelly's eyes cross.

Williams pulled out a piece of paper and handed it to Kelly. "We're having a meeting on Tuesday afternoon in the back room at Opie's. Why don't you come? You don't have to do the reading. Just show up and see what you think." He winked. "I'll buy your dinner, though, if you can rope Walter into joining you."

Kelly still wasn't sure about this, but he supposed at the very least he'd have something good to eat. "Okay."

"Great. See you there." He leaned back in his chair. "I'm serious about that meal. Round of drinks to go with it. Root beer, of course, though I know Walter got you an ID."

"I've never used it," Kelly said, blushing.

Williams laughed. "Tuesday."

"Tuesday," Kelly agreed.

Chapter Eleven

WALTER HAD STAYED away from Philosophy Club for good reason, which he remembered within three minutes of attending the backroom meeting at Opie's with Kelly. For starters, all the club members were overeager nerds with inflated senses of importance—Ethan Miller, ten o'clock—and weighed down by nagging self-doubt. The only professor there Walter could stand was Williams, and he was the only one not officially a member of the philosophy department. Everyone in the club—professors included, except for Williams—did a weird battle for attention that drove Walter crazy. Worst of all, though, was the way the students didn't have the first clue about philosophy outside of parroting back what their professors said or they read on Wikipedia. This was what had driven him away two years ago, and none of it appeared to have fixed itself in his absence.

Unfortunately, Kelly seemed to find it all intoxicatingly wonderful, and not just because Rose welcomed him like the prodigal son and brought him deep into the flock. Eyes wide and posture upright, Kelly sat in the middle of the fray, alert and eager, trying to keep up with conversations, joining in tentatively when invited. He accepted flirtations from girls and boys both, returning them with polite overtures of his own. He brought the same good-boy earnestness he always did, and somehow that brought up the level of the whole affair, at least as far as Walter was concerned. Either that or the show Kelly put on was simply that good.

Except underneath the nice-boy mask, he was still the Kelly Walter knew. Allergic, idealistic, I-hide-that-I-masturbate Kelly who watched *Doctor Who* and *Big Bang Theory* torrents with Walter until they were passing out against each other on the futon.

Philosophy Club was stupid as ever, but Kelly was there. Walter stayed. He drank root beer and ate pizza. He took the handout dictating next week's reading list.

He argued with Ethan Miller about Michel Foucault.

He hadn't meant to let himself be lured into that mess, but he couldn't help it when they were doing such a hack job of arguing Foucault's positions. Williams was no help, feeding them the line he and Walter had spent an hour debating just one week prior: Should, as Foucault says, life be about nothing more than finding one's true self? Should complete individuality be the sole purpose of life?

"Absolutely not." Miller stuck his nose in the air as he said this, casting several *watch me, I'm so cool* glances Kelly's way. "Nihilistic philosophy gets us nowhere. We're meant to work together, or everything is chaos. Society is mutual sacrifice for a common good."

This was the same prattle Miller had offered up the

last time Walter had come, and it didn't piss him off any less now. "For fuck's sake. Foucault isn't nihilistic. He may be influenced by Nietzsche, but he didn't sit in his damn lap. Of course, are you arguing metaphysical, moral, or existential nihilism? I'll give you the moral argument, but then everything short of religious faith is nihilistic if you want it to be."

Miller looked ready to do murder but could only sputter. Most of the table had gone slack-jawed, though a couple sophomores were flipping through their notes as if they might find a foothold in the conversation there. Walter sank back in his chair, annoyed, mostly at himself. That's right, this was the *other* reason he never came to Philosophy Club.

Before Walter could check to see how Kelly was taking all this, Williams jumped in. "So you agree with Foucault, Walter, that our life's purpose is to find our true self and nurture it?"

Williams knew damn well his thoughts were more complex than that, and he knew now this whole evening was a trap, because this was one of Williams's favorite arguments. This was his advisor trying to drive home his opinion that Walter and everyone else in the world needed a nanny, that nobody could function completely alone, that it wasn't healthy. Which was fine, Walter would do this dance anywhere.

Except he found he did not want to do it in front of Kelly, not without being able to understand how Kelly would take his answer. Out of the corner of his vision he could see Kelly's eyes widening, but without out-and-out staring him down, he couldn't get a good read. Was Kelly impressed? Turned off? What was he thinking?

"Do you think life is a search for our true self, Walter?" Williams leaned over the table, eyes dancing with mischief. "If you do think so, do you think it matters how we achieve that search for self?"

Walter stopped trying to read Kelly and faced the professor down. "I think searching for self is all anyone does, yes, but probably about two percent of the people alive actually think of it that way. As for how we achieve it—well, that's the crux, isn't it? Of course it matters, but the problem is everyone thinks they're a saint, because everyone can justify their own actions." Williams gave him the eyebrow, but Walter barreled on. "Everybody's the hero of their own story. So sure, they're living their true self, or fighting it. Why are they doing it, though? That tells you more of who and what someone is than whatever weird script they're following."

Rose Manchester—green bandana today—leaned forward and frowned curiously at Walter. "So what do you think of the original question, then? Should complete individuality be the sole purpose of life?"

Hadn't he just said this? "Everyone's going to live an individual life whether they think they are or not. Join a church, a cult, follow a flag, be a hermit—you made that choice, and that's your search for your self. Everyone's going to be faced with Kool-Aid. They'll drink it or refuse it, and depending on the context of delivery, the consequences will mark their life."

"So what do you think matters, then?" Miller

asked, his tone so snide he didn't have to add *wise guy*. "If everything everyone does can be explained by their own justifications, where does morality come from?"

"You can't find universal or absolute morality any more than you can find universal or absolute truth. I live with my beliefs. You live with yours. You believe sweater vests are sexy and will get you laid, even though it's never worked. It's a truth for you, so you go with it. Some people go to church. Other people get high. Some of us get laid. Some of us open our eyes and some of us force them shut. Everybody copes however they can. That's life. Search for self, hide from it—*that* is what life is."

Miller was all but in a lather, but Williams stayed as cool as a cucumber. "Not allowing one's self connections, commonalities within social circles—rejecting moral and religious forces *isn't* nihilistic?"

"Well, you count every moral system that doesn't have a daddy at the top nihilistic, don't you?"

Several of the clubbers gasped. Miller looked ready to pop a zit from excessive internal pressure. Williams grinned, looking pleased.

Kelly looked…blindsided.

Walter retreated from the argument then, too focused on Kelly. Gone was the happy, socially adept young man Walter had brought into the back room. This Kelly was a deer in the headlights. Time, Walter decided, to end this stupid farce.

"Hey." Walter nudged Kelly with his elbow and nodded at the door as the others continued to argue around them. "Want to bail?"

Kelly glanced down at his hands. "You're having a good time."

"What? No. I want a real beer. Come over to Moe's with me. I mean—unless *you're* having a good time."

Shaking his head, Kelly eased a little. "No, I'll go to Moe's with you."

Good. Walter tossed a salute to Williams and a wink to Manchester as he followed his roommate out of the restaurant.

WHILE WALTER HAD known something was wrong with his roommate, he hadn't realized quite how serious it was until Kelly not only failed to object when Walter ordered him a beer but drank it down as if his new goal in life was to get himself smashed.

"Whoa." Walter pulled his own beer closer to himself and sank onto the stool next to Kelly. "Slow down there, sailor."

Kelly glowered into his now half-empty glass. "No. I want to get drunk."

"You're making a good start on that, I'd say." Walter took a sip of beer, forcing himself not to think about what had happened the last time Kelly got drunk and how much that still confused him. *Focus on right now. Why is Kelly wanting to get drunk?* "Okay, I clearly missed something back there at Opie's. What's going on?"

Kelly's glower deepened. "Nothing," he grumbled, and finished off his drink. "Another one, please."

Well, this was interesting. Walter picked up the

pitcher of Pabst and replenished his roommate's glass, continuing to sip his own moderately as he watched Kelly go at his second glass with the same enthusiasm of his first. It went down a little more slowly, but within fifteen minutes of beginning to drink, Kelly was angling, quite adamantly, for a third helping.

"No, I don't think so." Walter pulled the pitcher more firmly out of Kelly's reach. "Red, what's going on here? What the fuck happened?"

"Nothing happened." Kelly shoved the glass away from himself, his pretty face screwed up in disgust. "I figured out the truth, is all, and I don't like it."

"Truth at Philosophy Club? That has to be a first. What was it?"

Kelly's face was red, partly from alcohol, partly from fury, and partly, Walter realized as his roommate's countenance transformed once more, shame. "I'm *stupid*. That's what."

"What? Come on." Walter shoved Kelly lightly. "Seriously. What happened?"

"What happened? What *happened*? I sat there like a moron, that's what happened. I had no idea what anybody was talking about." He hunched over his stool. "I couldn't even come close to following what anyone was saying. I was the valedictorian of my fucking class, but I couldn't follow anything going on. And *you*." He glared at Walter as if he held the sword that had stabbed him.

"Me?" Walter put his hand on Kelly's shoulder, but Kelly shook it off.

"*You*. Oh my God, I thought they were bad, but

you were ten times worse. I swear you were speaking a foreign language." He propped his elbows on the bar and shoved his hands in his hair. "All I wanted to do was hang out with Rose, and you, and Williams, and feel as if I belonged, but now I feel worse than ever. I don't belong here. I don't belong anywhere."

What the fuck? Walter wanted to touch Kelly again, but he didn't want to be rebuffed, so he moved closer instead, gentling his voice and lowering it so it was almost a whisper. "Red. Honey. You belong. You were great. They loved you."

"I had no idea what anyone was talking about."

"Well of course not. Most of it was bullshit. Remember, I've got almost three years on you for school, and I thought I was going to be pre-law before, so I read all kinds of weird crap while I was home with my mom. I got into philosophy because it helped me think about things, helped me figure out what was important in life. It's not rocket science, but yeah, you have to read it to get it. Sometimes multiple times."

"I tried to read it," Kelly murmured to the bar. "I couldn't even get through a page."

"So I'll help you, if you want. Or we forget it. It's not as if you need to read philosophy to survive. Most of it's common fucking sense, as far as I'm concerned."

"Common sense that I can't understand."

"Okay, now you're just whining. Which is fine, but—" He filled Kelly's beer and passed it back over. "Here. Sip this time, buddy."

Kelly did sip. He stayed hunched over, his anger bleeding into sorrow. "Nothing's the way I thought it would be. Nothing."

Walter gave in and put his hand on Kelly's back, making slow circles. "What isn't the way you thought it would be? And don't say everything."

"It *is* everything. School. Classes. *Guys.*" He took a bigger drink of beer. "Don't tell me you told me so, either. I feel like a fucking failure. I don't know what it is I want to do instead of this. I don't want to go home. I mean, I do. But I don't."

"Kel, there isn't a freshman alive who doesn't get to this point of college and feel that way. And take it from someone who *did* go home: that doesn't help."

Kelly frowned at Walter. "I thought you went home because of your mom."

"Yeah. Well, that wasn't the only reason." Walter drained the last of his glass and stared out toward the dance floor, which was starting to fill up. "You want to talk about feeling stupid? I was at Northwestern, hon. Everyone was so serious and so fucking smart I was sure I should be taking out their garbage, not going to class with them. I couldn't even hook up with a guy without feeling as if we were competing. So when things went bad at home, it was a great excuse to bail. Except it was the stupidest thing I'd ever done. Everyone else was off at school. Everyone else was moving forward." He ran his finger around the rim of his glass. "It still feels weird most of the time, being the wrong age. It's especially shit this year, with Cara gone. I can't shake the feeling I got off the merry-go-round and can't quite get back on."

"I don't know that I ever got on it." Kelly's fingers

tightened around his glass. "I'm always waiting. Always having an excuse. I can't go out for football, I have asthma. I can't come out, I'm from a small town. I can't, I can't, I can't. But I thought I'd come here and it would all be okay. It's not. I still can't. Can't go take a shower without getting harassed. Can't eat the same pizza as everybody else. Can't have a double room because I have to have an air conditioner. Can't eat in the cafeteria. Can't go to a club meeting without feeling like an idiot. Can't date because I'm a fucking chicken."

"You're not dating because you have standards," Walter corrected.

"No. I hardly try. I keep hoping some magic guy will walk up to me so I don't have to do it. Sometimes I think maybe I should let someone fuck me, let it mean nothing, but then I get scared of that."

What the shit was this? "Well you fucking should be scared. You don't want it to mean nothing."

"That's what *you* do."

Walter sighed and ran his hand down Kelly's back, letting it fall away. "No. I don't go up to some random guy and let them fuck me. It does matter. I pick guys I think I can have a fun time with. It doesn't mean *nothing*, certainly not the black hole in your tone. It means a good time. A release. An escape from the shit of life for a little while. That's not the same thing as nothing."

"Well, I don't know how to do that." Kelly spun his glass clumsily on its coaster. "I wish I hadn't told you I wanted to save myself for dating. I wish you'd have flirted with me and taken me to bed the way you do everybody else."

Walter went still, his body running hot and cold. "What?"

Kelly watched his glass as he turned it round and round. "I wish I'd been one of your freshman conquests. I wish I wasn't sitting here a stupid virgin on top of everything else. I wish I weren't so fucking scared. I wish I could have fun for a little while."

Walter had no idea what he was supposed to say. He didn't know what he *wanted* to say. Kelly was smashed, he reminded himself. Upset. He needed Walter to take care of him right now.

I wish I'd been one of your freshman conquests. I wish you'd taken me to bed. The words stirred the memory of Kelly making love to his neck. They reminded him too that he *wasn't* taking everyone to bed this year. He'd put in a good few weeks of man-whoring, and now...

Now...

Walter swallowed hard. "Kelly," he whispered, the name almost a plea.

Kelly clenched his fists against the sides of his head, hunching over the bar. "I shouldn't have said that. Now it's going to be weird again between us."

Wait, *what?* "When has it been weird?"

Kelly lifted his head to give Walter an accusatory look. "Only since Luna's party. You know, the last time I was a drunken idiot."

Walter was totally lost now. They'd been weird? "We haven't been weird. We're fine."

Kelly kept glowering. "You're weird. I'm weird. Because I fucked that up too."

Enough of this shit. Walter shoved the beer away from his roommate, turned him forcibly on the stool and gripped his shoulders hard as he looked him squarely in the eye. "You aren't weird, and you haven't fucked anything up."

"You told me no." The hurt on Kelly's face cut Walter like a knife.

"You were drunk," Walter pointed out.

"You'd tell me no now."

Fuck. "Honey, you're drunk now too."

Not that drunk, though, not as drunk as Walter had thought, and as Kelly stared him down, Walter got chills. "If I could work up the courage to ask you sober, you'd tell me no again. Because you don't want to sleep with me."

Not for the reason you're thinking, baby. Walter managed, just, not to say that out loud.

Except he'd heard it, and he *did* know the reason why. And it scared the ever-loving shit out of him.

He tried a new tactic. "You'll feel better after you go home tomorrow for break. You'll be with your family, and they'll restore your confidence, and you'll come back and kick the ass of that stupid Philosophy Club."

"I can't go back there, ever. I felt like an idiot."

"I'll help you make sense of it." Why was he en- couraging Kelly to go there? He didn't know, just that talking about that was safer than why he couldn't sleep with him.

"You'd have to dumb it down pretty far for me to

get it. You have to dumb everything down for me."

Walter was starting to get annoyed with all this self-pity. "I don't dumb anything down for you. I like you how you are, Kelly. Just how you are."

"How? I don't know how I am." He waved a drunken hand back at the general vicinity of Opie's. "I don't know what my life is supposed to be about. I don't know what my true self is or whatever it was they were talking about."

"Nobody does, Red. Don't let Foucault make you crazy."

"*He* knew what he wanted, I bet."

Walter snorted. "Yeah. He wanted to infect cute gay boys with AIDS."

Kelly startled. "What?"

"He was a crazy leather daddy. He was HIV positive and deliberately had unprotected sex with young men and didn't tell them he was passing on a death sentence. On purpose. He said, 'To die for the love of boys, what could be more beautiful?' He was smart and visionary. And an asshole." He nudged Kelly. "You're not an asshole. You're not dumb. You're kind and smart and funny and fun to be with."

"Then why doesn't anyone want to have sex with me?"

Oh, honey. Walter saw the red lights of danger begin to flash, but he couldn't stop forging ahead. "People want to have sex with you, Kelly. Trust me on this one."

Kelly waved this thought away with a gesture so drunken and effeminate Walter ached. "No. That's not what I mean."

"What do you mean?"

Kelly stared hard at his nearly empty glass, sighed, and let himself sink sideways against Walter. "I don't know."

Walter put his arm around Kelly and pulled him closer.

Kelly snuggled into him. "I want to have sex. I do. I don't even want it to be pretty and Disney the way you're thinking. I want someone to come up to me how you go up to guys. Except I want them to mean it."

Jesus fuck, Walter was right back in the soup again. "I do mean it."

"But you tell me no."

Fuck fuck fuck. "You want me to say yes? You want me to screw you, drunk, really? Then you want me to walk away? Because I'm not buying what you're selling."

Kelly sighed and turned away from Walter, sinking back onto the bar. "No. No, *dammit*, I don't." He rubbed at his head. "I need to go home and go to sleep. I have a class in the morning, and then I have to go back to Minnesota."

And I have to go to Northbrook. The thought made Walter feel hollow, and he rubbed at Kelly's back. "Let's get you to bed, Red."

Nodding, Kelly stood and let Walter help him out the door and toward the dorms.

"I'm sorry," Kelly said as they passed the parking lots and started to cut across the main lawn.

"What for?"

"For always getting drunk and coming on to you. For you always having to babysit me."

Walter slid his arm around Kelly's waist and took a slow, deep breath of Kelly's hair, hoping he didn't notice. He didn't say anything, because he couldn't. Because he wanted to say things such as *I can't sleep with you because it wouldn't be like the other guys I fuck. I can't sleep with you because I already think about you way too much, care way too much, and if I sleep with you, I'm scared to think about how bad it would be if things didn't work out, if you went away too, the way everybody else always does.*

He couldn't say any of that, which meant he couldn't say anything at all.

Chapter Twelve

THE NEXT MORNING Kelly woke early. His head hurt, but only a little, and while he was aware of how much beer he'd consumed, he felt no urge to vomit.

He remembered, quite clearly, everything he'd confessed to Walter. He lay awake a long time, staring at the ceiling, cheeks burning as he remembered how whiny and childish he'd been. He remembered telling Walter he wanted to sleep with him.

He remembered Walter telling him no. *Again.*

Shutting his eyes, Kelly prayed the bed would swallow him whole so he didn't have to face his roommate.

"You up, Red?"

Walter's sleep-rough voice startled him. He thought about pretending he was asleep, but he'd have to face the music sometime. "Yeah."

"Feeling okay?"

"Yeah. Sorry I was such a whiny idiot last night." *I swear, I'll never ask you to sleep with me again.*

"You were fine." Kelly couldn't get a read on his tone, so he leaned over the edge of his loft. Walter lay in bed, scrolling through his phone. "What are you heading out?" When Kelly didn't answer, he glanced up. "Your dad is coming to get you this morning, right?"

"Afternoon." God, even with bedhead, Walter looked so good. *Stop thinking about Walter that way.* Kelly sat up and began the process of descending, hung over, from his bed. "About one."

"Cool." Walter put the phone down and rubbed at his cheek. "We could do the laundry here. I could do it for you, since I don't have anything going on. There's no need for you to haul it all home."

Kelly shook his head as he sorted through his medicine bottles on his dresser. "It'd be better if I washed it right before I came back. Anyway, if I don't bring it home, Mom will fuss."

Funny how that seemed to make Walter's expression cloud. "Sure. Well, I'll do my own. I definitely know the drill by now."

"Okay."

A weird, heavy silence hung over them for a few minutes, and Kelly's heart sank. See, he'd fucked things over between them. He shouldn't have let himself get drunk and confess stuff. It had wrecked everything, just like the last time.

Walter groaned and stretched. "Well, I suppose I should pack."

He made it sound as if he was getting ready to serve a death sentence. Kelly remembered what Walter had said about his family and realized the awkward silence might have nothing to do with the night before. "Are you not looking forward to going home?"

Walter's laugh was a sad snort. "In a word, no." He

ran a hand through his hair. "In fact, if I could get out of it, I would."

Kelly couldn't imagine not wanting to go home. He was looking forward to it, and not just to get away from the weird sexual tension with Walter. "I'm sorry," he said, because he didn't know what else to say.

"Yeah, well." Walter stood and headed for the closet.

They packed in mutual silence, no discussion of the night before or of their upcoming visits to their respective homes. The silence was more than a little awkward, even through breakfast and again when they were back in the room together after classes. When Kelly's dad finally arrived and they said goodbye to Walter, he was almost relieved.

Dick Davidson didn't talk much and never had, but the one place he was known to break that pattern was in a car, especially during a long ride. Both Kelly and Lisa had taken advantage of this when they needed advice or help from their father, inventing something they needed in Minneapolis and insisting he was the one who had to drive them. Kelly was acutely aware he had his dad in his talking chamber for a very long time, and he had plenty he wanted to talk to him about. The trouble was, he didn't know where to start.

Happily, his dad took care of that too.

"Your mother mentioned you were thinking of declaring a major."

Kelly was driving at that point and flexed his hands against the wheel. "Yeah. History education."

"You sound a little unsure."

"Well, I am. I don't know that I'd make a good teacher. Are there any jobs? I know teachers get paid poorly. How will I help with Lisa if I don't make enough?"

"You don't worry about paying for your sister's school. That's my job."

Kelly frowned. "But Hope is so expensive. I took more than my share."

Dick smiled and shook his head. "Your sister is going to end up at the University of Minnesota. She's going to want a big place but not too far away."

"How do you know? She's just a freshman."

"I know my kids."

Kelly thought about this for a while. "So does that mean you knew I was gay before I told you?"

"Hmm." Dick thought about that for a second. "Well, I knew you were upset. That you felt set apart and were scared to talk about why. I didn't know it exactly, but when you told us, it made sense to me."

It was funny how much that relieved Kelly, when he hadn't even known he was nervous to hear. "You weren't upset?"

His father took a long time before he replied. "I was nervous for you. I didn't like what the world might say to you when you told them who you truly were."

Hmm. "Hope is pretty good about that. It's not perfect, but it's a good place to be myself."

His dad nodded. "Good. I thought it should be, but it's nice to hear for sure."

Kelly drove awhile before voicing the darker niggle behind his desire to teach. "Do you think it's okay to be a teacher if I'm gay? I mean, I know it's actually okay, but am I going to end up fighting that instead of teaching?"

Another thoughtful pause. "I hope not. I suppose it would depend on where you ended up, and how quickly the world changes."

"See, that's what I mean about jobs. I can't just look for one wherever. I have to look for one where I'll be okay."

"Anywhere you couldn't be who you are isn't somewhere you'd want to be no matter what. It might feel more limited, but that's not all bad. Sometimes less choice only makes the right choice more clear."

"Except in dating," Kelly murmured.

He felt his father's gaze on him. "That not going okay?"

Kelly's ears heated. "No. It's really not."

"What about Walter? Does he have a boyfriend?"

"No." Kelly felt the unspoken question hanging in the air and sighed. "No, and he's not interested in one."

His dad frowned. "He seems like a very good friend. And you did say he's...?"

"He is. Both a good friend and gay." Kelly swallowed hard and gripped the wheel. "I think I'm falling in love with him."

His dad nodded, as if he wasn't surprised. "But you don't think he feels the same way?"

"I don't know. I'm not sure how to tell."

"It might not be a bad idea to let him know how you feel."

The very idea made Kelly's stomach knot. "Except

he's said flat out, many times, that he doesn't date, doesn't do relationships. What if I say something and it wrecks what we have? I'd rather have him this way than not at all."

"That sounds about right."

"Right for what?"

"Some advice, son. You need to let him know, but you don't have to use words. Sometimes the ones we love are like butterflies, flitting all over, and we have to sit and wait patiently for them to land. Sometimes they never do, and that's a risk we take. But sometimes what they need most is to see us sitting still, patient, waiting. To understand that we're going to be there no matter what, that we're the ones who are always sitting there waiting, loyal, loving. Sometimes that's more powerful than any words."

Love seemed an awfully strong word. It scared him a little actually. "How long do I wait? What if he never notices?"

"That's the hard part, I'll admit. Because sometimes they don't. The right one, though? The right one will."

"Is that how it was with you and Mom?"

Dick's smile was wistful. "It was. Still is."

As they rode awhile in silence, Kelly thought again about Walter, about how much he enjoyed being with him, about how good it felt to see him at the end of a long day. He thought about the way Walter teased him, taunted him. He thought about how Walter had reacted when Kelly had kissed his neck.

He thought about what Rose had said, about how Walter treated him. He thought about all the times they'd hung out together, laughed, teased or simply talked. Was that the same thing his dad was talking about? Kelly didn't know.

He really needed to figure that one out.

AS SOON AS Kelly left the dorm room, Walter collapsed on his futon and stared at the ceiling.

Porter 4 was a third as noisy as it usually was, the standard raucous athlete call and answer replaced by more sedate shuffling as the residents took off. Everyone was in a rush to head home except for the international student at the other end of the hall. He was hunkered down with a friend from Sandman, talking animatedly in Urdu.

Dick Davidson hadn't been what Walter had expected. Walter continued to stare at the ceiling and thought about how Kelly had brightened at the sight of his father, how the older man's eyes had danced and he'd opened his arms to hold his son even before Kelly had started toward him. Dick had been warm to Walter, if not a little reserved as he assessed his son's roommate.

Lying on the bed, Walter couldn't help but wonder if he'd measured up or been found wanting.

His hand skimmed down the front of his shirt as his musings drifted to the thing he'd been trying not to dwell on, things about Kelly. Things he hoped Kelly's dad hadn't been able to see.

Walter shut his eyes.

He didn't open them until the dorm floor was quiet. He must have dozed off, because the room was dark with shadows and he could see the gray of the late afternoon through the window. That got him up and moving, gathering a few toiletries and clothes. Kelly had forgotten to take his bedding after all, so in addition to the futon cover and his own sheets, Walter grabbed Kelly's things too. Though he picked up his phone to send a quick text to let his roommate know he was taking care of the laundry, he only stared at the screen with Kelly's name a few minutes, reading.

Red, I'm hungry. Where are you? Are you eating or what?
Sorry got caught up talking. Meet you at the caf?
Sure. Will make sure they have food.
Thx, W. See you soon.

OMG, this class is never going to end.
Hang tight, Red. We can spring for burritos for supper once you survive. My treat.
Have a thing, actually. Meet up later?
Sure. Laundry tonight, since we're going to be gone for the holiday?

That had been the last text, yesterday before the Philosophy Club. Not wanting to think about that anymore, Walter scrolled back further.

Are we going to Moe's tonight?
Nah. Don't feel like trolling. Unless you're still shopping for boyfriends.
No. Let's watch more D. Who. I need a Tennant fix.

Just not the Martha eps, please.

Gag. Donna Noble. Oh, I know, let's watch the library one. River Song AND Donna.

And Tennant. I'll leave the lube on your bunk.

You would not believe what I'm seeing right now. Whole Philosophy Club is trying to make a human pyramid in one of the studios. I don't even fully understand why.

Not feeling the pyramid love?

Fuck no. I'm documenting for posterity. Will send a pic.

Maybe I should be a comm major. This econ course is going to kill me. From boredom.

I can send you nudie pics to keep you entertained.

Who of?

Who would you like?

Shit, prof eyeballing me. Gotta go.

Walter shut the phone without sending a text, grabbed the laundry basket and his duffel, and bugged out of the room. After packing the Mazda, he headed across campus to Lake Sharon, where the swans were huddled in a corner of the lake, heedless of the icy water, too wrapped up in each other. They were beautiful in the reflected lights of campus, and Walter stood a long time beneath the shelter of the campanile, watching them.

When he finally headed out of Danby, he didn't put on any music, riding in silence all the way to Peoria. After a pit stop to hit the bathroom and grab a

Starbucks, he scrolled through his phone and put on some Adele. A soft rain began to fall as she crooned about needing to make her partner feel her love, and somehow the double dose of melancholy allowed Walter to relax into his disquiet. It wasn't that he knew home was going to suck, that he'd be enduring four days of his mother's manic depression and his sister's fits for attention. It wasn't that listening to Cara talk about the wedding and pull further away from him and toward Greg alone was going to hurt. It wasn't that he'd be lucky if his dad so much as called him, let alone met up with him for a coffee.

It was that he missed Kelly already.

Feeling slightly pervy but way too depressed to care, Walter reached behind him and fished in the laundry basket until he found one of Kelly's pillowcases. Walter clutched it on his lap for a minute, then gave in and went full-on pathetic as he drew it up to his nose to inhale his best friend's scent.

A voice in the back of his mind whispered that this kind of behavior went well beyond simply weird, that it meant something a lot scarier than being a pervert, but Walter pushed the voice firmly aside. He wasn't mooning over Kelly. He wasn't a pervert, and he wasn't weird.

He was...sad.

Inhaling the pillowcase one last time, Walter clutched it in his hand and kept it there all the way back to Northbrook.

Chapter Thirteen

ON THEIR WAY back from his grandparents' house on Thanksgiving, the Davidsons' car broke down.

It became quite an adventure, calling Dick's brother to get a ride back to the house and arranging a tow. When it was clear on Friday the car wouldn't be fixed until the following week, however, things got interesting. How was Kelly going to get back to school?

"We still have my Datsun," Dick reminded them as they sat around the table brainstorming.

"Yes, but then Lisa and I won't have a car until you get back. And she has that church thing on Sunday afternoon," Sue reminded him.

"Can't we get her a ride?"

Lisa looked mortified. "We're delivering baked goods people ordered for the fundraiser."

"Surely they'll understand the circumstances," Dick said.

"Can the truck even get to Illinois?" Kelly hoped not. He wasn't excited about being crammed into the tiny cab with his stuff flying loose in the back end.

"We could rent a car," Sue suggested.

Kelly shook his head. "I might as well fly, for the expense."

"But are there any flights because of the holiday?" Sue pressed. "And didn't you tell me the airport was an hour away from Hope?"

It was. Kelly bit his lip. "I could ask if Walter minded picking me up."

"That's an awfully big inconvenience."

"I don't think he'd mind." Kelly was pretty sure of that, despite their weird parting. He was starting to root for this idea. How fun would it be to ride back with Walter, even part of the way?

Dick frowned and fussed with his laptop a few minutes before looking up. "Didn't you say your roommate lived in Chicago?"

"A suburb. Why?"

Dick turned the laptop around to show some airline listings. "There's a red-eye on Sunday morning from Minneapolis to O'Hare. Four hundred dollars."

It was a lot for such a short flight, but it would be only slightly more than renting a car, and that didn't include gas and hotel and the general pain in the ass that was driving all the way to Danby and back again. It would also mean seeing Walter earlier and riding back to campus with him—all the way, at least from Chicago. The idea had Kelly both excited and anxious.

Sue looked doubtful. "I don't know. It seems terribly presumptuous."

"How?" Dick asked. "It's not out of his way, one assumes. And then he'd have someone to share gas."

"O'Hare is a big airport. I don't care for the idea of Kelly there on his own."

Kelly balked. "Mom. Seriously."

"Sue, I think you're being a little overprotective," Dick said.

Sue sighed. "I probably am. But I still don't like this. I wish they could fix the car so it wasn't an issue."

They couldn't fix the car, though, and the flight to Chicago was the only solution they could come up with. Kelly was charged with calling Walter to make sure the arrangement would be acceptable. He took his ring off and played with it in his palm, trying to keep his nerves distracted as he dialed.

"Kelly!" Walter's greeting was brighter and more eager than Kelly would have predicted, and it made the butterflies the call had stirred do odd things inside him. "How'd your Mayberry Thanksgiving go?"

"It was good. Ate too much, fell asleep on the couch, played lots of board games with my cousins. You?"

"Ah." The light went out of Walter's voice. "It was okay."

"Have you had a chance to see Cara yet?"

Walter cleared his throat. "No. We were supposed to do lunch tomorrow, but I think that's getting ousted because of a wedding-prep thing."

"I'm sorry. I know you were looking forward to seeing her."

"Well, I was never too attached. They're trying to please everyone, so they have about eighty Thanksgiving dinners to attend. And she really does need to pin the location down. She's left it way too long. This is supposed to be some scouting mission at a bed-and-breakfast. Or something. Honestly, I'm trying not to get involved."

Something about the phone amplified Walter's tone, parsing out the wry wit and revealing a hint of sadness underneath. Kelly wished his dad had found a ticket for Saturday instead so he could hang out with Walter. Had he even looked for one? Kelly turned his dad's laptop around and tucked the phone against his shoulder so he could type as he talked. "So, I'm actually calling because I have a favor to ask."

"Sure. What do you need, Red?"

Kelly's heart flipped a little as he saw not only was there a flight on Saturday, but it was a late-afternoon one and a hundred dollars cheaper. He dug his fingernail into the edge of his ring, tracing the smooth stone. "Well, I was wondering if there was any way you could give me a ride back to Hope." He explained about the cars and the idea to fly to Chicago. "If it doesn't work, that's okay," he added as he finished.

"Of course it'll work. I'd love to come pick you up. It's a dead boring drive by myself. When do you fly in?"

God, Kelly's heart was beating so fast. Why was he so nervous? "Well, that's the thing. I can get a flight on Sunday morning getting in to O'Hare at 7:30. Or...or I can come in on Saturday. That one's cheaper and comes in at five in the afternoon. But that would mean I'd need to crash at your place, and I don't want to impose—"

"You should totally come on Saturday. Not only would we not have to get up at the crack of dawn, but we could go out that night. Or not. I mean, if you'd rather stay another day with your family—"

"No, that sounds like fun, going out with you." Kelly's cheeks went up in flames. "I mean—so if it's okay to come Saturday, I'll book that one."

"Great. Text me the details, and I'll be there to pick you up."

Now the butterflies in Kelly's stomach were doing backflips. Jesus, he needed to get himself under control. He hurriedly clicked through and booked the ticket, fumbling with his mom's credit card. "Awesome. I will."

"I guess I'll see you tomorrow then." Walter sounded a lot brighter.

"Guess you will." Kelly could feel the conversation closing off, and he found he didn't want it to end. "Thanks. This is totally helping us out."

"Me too." Walter coughed. "I mean, it'll be nice to have something to do Saturday, and company on the way back."

"Yeah." Kelly wished it were Saturday right now.

"Great." A pause. "Well, I should probably let you go back to your family."

"Yeah, I guess." Kelly shifted his grip on the phone. "Okay. See you tomorrow?"

"It's a date, Red."

Kelly's whole body was hot this time, and he kept the phone to his ear a moment even after the connection was dead, closing his eyes and savoring the words. Finally he laid the receiver on the table and headed to the kitchen to tell his parents about the change of plans.

AFTER THE PHONE call, Walter vacillated between feeling eager for Kelly's arrival and anxious about it. On the one hand, simply thinking about seeing Kelly had him feeling happier, and the idea of a night in Boystown with him was so delightful it made his body hum.

On the other hand, having Kelly stay one night, even spending most of it out of the house, meant exposing him to the toxic-waste dump that was Walter's family.

The house itself was pretty lethal too, the more Walter thought about it, and as he dwelled on the matter Friday night, he realized he needed to de-dust the place or risk having Kelly get sick. In fact, as he did a walk through with an allergen/asthmatic eye, it became quite clear what he was going to be doing for the next twenty-four hours. The nice part was he knew exactly how to proceed from living with Kelly for almost three months. After scanning his mom's cleaning supplies, he made a Target run and started in.

First order of business was his room. It was the only place Kelly could sleep, because the spare bedroom had become catch-all for Walter's mom's home businesses, much of which had been doing nothing but collecting dust. Walter figured he'd sleep in there, so he'd keep the door closed after doing a cursory clean.

Next was the bathroom he shared with Tibby and the bathrooms off the kitchen and family room in the basement. Theoretically they were mostly clean, but Walter wanted them to look decent, plus he remembered there was a mold thing too. He did a thorough job on the toilet rims, the faucets, and the grout.

After that, Walter felt slightly lost. His mom had a cleaning service, so he'd expected the main rooms to be good, but when he did a deep-clean check he realized things weren't remotely close. Sure, the oven knobs gleamed in the kitchen, but the curtains in the living and dining room were so full of dust even Walter sneezed when he shook them. Same for the top of the china cabinet. When he checked the HEPA filter on the vacuum, he about gagged. He wrote down the number on the part and went out to the stores again, but it took him three tries to find the right one. He very nearly bought a brand-new vacuum, but that felt excessive. It was just one night.

Still. He wanted it to be a good night.

Walter clipped on the attachments to the vacuum and got to work. He wasn't sure suctioning off the curtains would do much good, but the alternative seemed to be hauling them to the dry cleaners—which he considered but dismissed because he worried they wouldn't be done until he had gone back to school. His mom was giving him odd looks enough as it was.

She came into the dining room as he climbed down from wiping off the top of the china cabinet, hands on her hips. "Walter, what are you doing?"

"Cleaning." He shifted the stool and climbed up again so he could get the tops of a few picture frames, though he wondered if he should take them down and wipe the whole business off. "I know you have a service, but this dust-mite thing is serious. And honestly, given how much grit I've been finding, I think you should try a different company."

His mom almost looked ready to laugh. "Walter, he's here for *one night*."

"I know. But I'll feel like shit if he has an attack, and it doesn't take much of this stuff to set it off." He glanced over his shoulder and raised his eyebrows. "Besides, you want to try to tell me you're annoyed at having free housecleaning?"

This time she did laugh, and the smile lingered in her eyes as she spoke. "No." She brushed off her hands and put them on her hips. "Okay, give me a minute to change, and I'll help."

Walter paused with his rag on the top of the frame. "Mom, you don't have to do that."

"You trying to tell me you want to do this all by yourself?"

She was still smiling, sort of. She looked almost eager. Walter felt something heavy inside him shift. "No. I'd love your help. Thanks."

"Give me ten minutes."

It took her fifteen, but once she came down in sweats and a T-shirt, she was all business. Walter explained the dust-mite rules: they lived in cloth and carpet, loved humidity. "Don't shampoo the carpets. They love that, apparently."

"So his family has to keep their house that clean all the time? Good God, that sounds horrible."

"Yeah." Walter swiped a dust mitt around some knickknacks. "He's got a pile of allergies. Milk and egg too."

His mom paused with a damp cloth on the wall. "I

don't even know how to cook without eggs."

"There's a replacer, but he says flax eggs are better. Don't worry, we'll be gone before lunch, and I want to take him to Pie Hole Pizza Saturday night. So oatmeal for breakfast and we're set. I already got him some soy milk."

Shari went back to wiping down the wall, but she had a soft smile on her face. "You take good care of your roommate."

"He's the best. I can't imagine having to room with anyone else." He scrubbed slowly at the face of a china figurine. "Rooming with him is better than Cara, even."

His mom stopped wiping again. "Walter, are you...?" She shook her head. "Never mind."

Walter set the figurine carefully back on the shelf. "He's shy and quiet and a little naive. I guess I get focused on making sure he's okay. He has this look about him. It would break your heart to see him sad."

"Is he cute?"

That question was a landmine, but there was something so lulling about the conversation. He couldn't think of the last time his mom had been this interested in his life. Middle school, maybe? It made Walter hungry for more. "Yeah. Like a button."

His mom just kept smiling. "Straight, I suppose?"

"Gay. But we're not dating."

"It sure sounds as if you should."

Okay, now the conversation was getting uncomfortable. Walter reached for the expandable duster to get the chandelier. "Don't want to screw anything up."

"I suppose." Shari dropped her rag into the bucket and frowned at it. "Not that you should take relationship advice from me."

Walter put down the duster. "Dad's the asshole who left."

No more smiles now. He dared a longer glance and saw the clouds had returned to his mother's face. How pathetic was he that he ached over the loss. What, he'd thought ten minutes of small talk about Kelly would fix everything?

Stupid.

Shari put the bucket on the table and pursed her lips as she reached for the vacuum. When she fired it up, Walter went back to his duster job, and when she finished, he didn't bring up his father again.

Things got lighter when they moved to the living room, but it was getting late so they quit after that. Tibby came home from a Pony Club meeting and found the two of them covered in dirt and grinning as they recapped their cleaning adventures—the look of wariness on his sister's face reminded Walter that happiness in this house was an unusual thing. He decided he wanted more of it. Especially when Kelly arrived.

When he woke the next morning, it was to something unusual: the smell of something cooking. Something really good cooking. His mom was making vegan pancakes.

She was frowning over her iPad when Walter walked in. "Smells great."

"Hey, you. Thanks." She poked at the screen. "So, I

liked this first batch I made, but wondered about this one with honey. It wants flax milk, though. I had no idea there was such a thing. I wonder if soy would be fine?" She glanced up at Walter. "Does he eat meat?"

"Some. His mom's vegetarian, so they do vegan most of the time when he's home, but I've seen him pack away pig. I'll eat it, in any event."

"Bacon it is. And hash browns." She smiled, but there were shadows again. "This will be fun. And much better than oatmeal."

Walter took the plate of pancakes she handed him and poured on the syrup. "Damn. These are great."

"I know. But I really am curious about the honey. And I feel kind of gross making vegan pancakes with cheap crap sugar. Whole Foods would have—" She cut herself off, and the dark clouds returned in full to her face.

God, it was sad how desperate Walter was to chase them away again.

"I'll go out and find maple syrup and flax milk," Walter volunteered. "Anything else you want me to get while I'm there?"

"I'll make a list." Shari stroked his face, some of her shadows lifting. "I miss you when you're not home, honey."

I miss you too. Especially this you. "Maybe I can talk Kelly into visiting over Christmas break, and we could try out all kinds of crazy recipes together."

"Maybe." Shari's smile came back, small but present, and she nudged him with her elbow. "Eat your pancakes."

WHEN KELLY LANDED at O'Hare, it was complete chaos. He was pretty sure he'd feel like a BB in an oven even without the holiday travelers making things worse, but right now he was all about survival. The hallways were narrow despite the vaulted glass atrium ceiling above. Would it have killed them to make the ceiling shorter and the walkways wider?

Someone wearing too much perfume walked past Kelly, and he felt his lungs yearn to contract. Oh, that's all he needed—an attack on top of it all.

His phone began to sing to him, and he pulled it out of his pockets with shaking hands.

It says you've landed. I'm right here at the security exit.

Kelly's entire body sagged in relief. All he had to do was get to Walter. He texted back.

On my way. Way too many people and too much perfume.

Though Kelly knew he should have started walking, he lingered against the wall, hoping for an answering text. He didn't have to wait long.

I'm not far. You're on one side or the other of a Y. Where it meets, head straight until you get to the public area, and there I am.

Kelly felt equal parts ridiculous for being such a ninny and relieved that it was Walter he was heading for.

Okay. Be right there.

Putting away his phone, he gripped the handle of his carry-on and joined the herd heading for baggage claim. Walter's directions helped, and it really was that easy. Soon he was moving through the gauntlet leading out of the secured area. His heart beat faster as he searched for Walter. He tried not to let his eagerness show, tried not to give away how he'd spent the last day being equal parts nervous and excited.

When he saw the familiar shock of dark hair, however, he couldn't help breaking out into a grin. When Walter grinned back, his usual sly, I'm-causing-trouble smile, Kelly's heart soared a little. Walter wore a black leather jacket he'd never worn at school. He looked good. Really good.

"Hey, Red." Walter had his thumbs looped at the edges of his pockets, but his body posture opened as he came up to Kelly. "Good to see you."

"Same." Kelly knew he was flushed, but he tried to brush it off. "Crazy in here."

"Yeah. Let's get out of here." Walter's hand fell on Kelly's upper back as they walked. "You have a bag checked?"

God, that hand felt good. "No. Mom saw the fees on the bags and said she'd ship everything. Though that means half this carry-on is meal bars."

"Because you can wait for clothes, but not food." Walter massaged the center of Kelly's back briefly and let his hand fall away. Kelly tried not to feel bereft. "Car's not far. I got lucky with my spot."

"Was it a long drive?"

"This is Chicago. Everything's a long drive."

"Oh. I'm sorry."

Walter rolled his eyes and grinned before punching Kelly lightly in the shoulder. "Red, Red. I didn't know

I could miss you so much in three days."

Their eyes met, and Kelly could see Walter hadn't meant to say that, not that way—but there were shadows in his countenance that made something deep inside Kelly resonate. *I missed you too,* he wanted to say, but instinct told him that would be a bad idea. He couldn't think of how to lighten the moment, though, so he changed the subject. "I'm starving. Want to find dinner on the way back? My treat."

"Oh no. I have plans for our dinner. But it'll be a while, so we should find you a snack."

Kelly grimaced at the airport chaos around him. "Not here. Airports and airplanes never have food I can eat."

"What do you feel like?"

"A seven-course meal. I'm starved."

"Well, if you can wait a couple of hours, there's the best pizza you'll ever have in your life. Totally Kelly legal."

Kelly's stomach rumbled. He pressed his free hand against it. "Can we go now?"

Walter laughed. "No. We have to stop at the house, get dressed for the night, and then we'll head out." He frowned. "Unless you'd rather stay in."

Something told Kelly Walter *really* wanted to go out. To be honest, Kelly did a little too. Going out with Walter sounded fun. Not that he didn't do it all the time, but this was *Chicago.* "No, I'll just have a meal bar to tide me over. Where are we going? Downtown?"

"Boystown, baby. Local gay mecca. I think you'll

enjoy it. Besides, how can we not?"

"They really called a section of Chicago Boystown?"

"The neighborhood is called Lakeview, but the gay district is Boystown. Kind of like Liberty Avenue in *Queer as Folk*, except it's North Halstead. And it's real."

Kelly had watched pirated clips of *QAF* in high school. It was good Liberty Avenue wasn't real, because a few desperate times he'd thought about running away there. "It sounds great. Is there a diner too?"

"Probably, but not the same as the show. Pie Hole Pizza is there, though."

Kelly's stomach rumbled again. "Let's get back to your place so we can go eat."

He did steal a meal bar out of his bag before they stowed it in Walter's hatchback, and he'd wolfed it down before Walter got the car started. Walter noticed and grinned.

"How about a big soy mocha on the way out? There's a Starbucks before we hit 294."

"You're on."

Walter bought their drinks, probably because he knew it would annoy Kelly. The drive back was pretty thick with traffic, both on and off the interstate, but according to Walter it wasn't bad at all.

Kelly decided he would never live in Chicago.

Northbrook was nice, though it and Walter's housing development pretty much screamed *suburb*. Wealthy suburb, he added as he noted the cars lining the drives and the level of decor in the yards. Everything felt like a competition of wealth, one Kelly couldn't come close to matching.

"When I was little and we first moved in," Walter said, "I used to be so afraid of getting lost in our neighborhood because all the houses were the same. It's not as bad now, because it's been twenty years and people have changed the color schemes and the foliage, but man, at first it was so Stepford it was creepy."

It was pretty Stepford now. "They're very nice houses."

"Not really. Expensive and posturing, mostly." Walter nodded to a blue house coming up on the left. "That's us with the light on."

Kelly couldn't help but notice that Walter grew tense as they pulled into the driveway, and he became worse as they approached the door. Remembering Walter's sarcastic comments about his broken family and the evasiveness he gave every time Kelly tried to ask about them, he wondered what he was about to walk in to.

It turned out to be a pretty normal house, if not more elegant than Kelly's own home. It was meticulously clean, and he took his shoes off at the door when he saw the gleaming white tile.

"Oh, you could have left those on." Walter grabbed the carry-on and motioned him toward the stairs. "Here, I put you in my room."

"Walter?" A woman in her late fifties came around the corner into the living room. She looked slightly haggard, but she brightened when she saw Kelly. "You must be Kelly." She came forward with her hand extended. "I'm Shari, Walter's mom. Nice to meet you."

Kelly shook her hand. "It's a pleasure, Mrs. Lucas."

Shari and Walter exchanged a quick glance. She smiled, but for some reason she seemed a little sad. "I know Walter has a big night planned for you two, so I won't keep you. I have a pizza in the oven for Tibby and me, but let me know if you need anything."

"Thank you," Kelly called out as he followed his suitcase to Walter's room.

Walter's room was, unsurprisingly, very Walter. The bed was a sleek double with a dark, modish headboard and footboard and matching end table and dresser. Posters—framed and mounted—decorated the walls, one of his favorite British band, Saint Etienne, one of the Scissor Sisters, and one that was some abstract art piece full of greens and browns. The room was incredibly clean, the same as the rest of the house.

Though now that Kelly thought about it, the house *smelled* incredibly clean. As in, someone had recently cleaned it.

He cast a sidelong look at Walter.

His roommate was busy setting Kelly's suitcase on the bed and didn't notice. "I'm in the guest bedroom down the hall, and I already took out whatever I'll need, so I won't bug you. Bathroom's just across, and my sister's staying over with a horse buddy, so nobody else will be using it. Mom's bedroom is downstairs, and she has her own bathroom." He turned to Kelly and rubbed his hands together. "Do you need anything to drink? Anything else to eat? We have apples and carrots and all that. I could make more coffee too."

Walter was so hyped up Kelly feared what more

caffeine would do to him. "I'm good." He rubbed his arm, trying not to feel self-conscious. "I'll change, and we can get going."

"Okay." Walter stood there a second, still looking like he was a jack-in-the-box ready to pop, then seemed to realize what he was doing and jerked to attention. "Right. I'll get dressed too and meet you downstairs."

He left.

Kelly sat on the bed and stared at the door for a few seconds, trying to work out what was going on.

Nothing was going on, he decided at last, and peeled off his shirt. Walter was being Walter. He knew after three months of living with him that this was how Walter rolled, taking care of people. Giving up his bedroom. Cleaning his whole house. After checking the pillowcase, Kelly knew that yes, Walter had bought dust-mite covers because Kelly was going to sleep in his bed for one night.

Sleep in his bed.

Kelly shut his eyes and moved away from the pillow. *Alone.* Sleep in his bed *alone.*

He got dressed with somewhat shaking hands, though, and he took extra care fixing his hair in Walter's mirror. When he was done, he stared at his reflection for several seconds.

Somehow it felt huge, to be in Chicago with Walter. To be going out with him not at school because they were bored, but to Boystown because they were…friends. Because Walter wanted to show it to him. Because Walter wanted him to try some pizza place. Walter had gone out of his way to clean for

Kelly. It sounded so benign, but it felt huge. All the fantasies Kelly had been quietly quashing since Tuesday came raging back, and this time he didn't know how to keep them at bay.

"He isn't going to date you," he told his reflection. "This isn't to woo you. It's just Walter being Walter. Don't fuck it up."

He looked stern as he said it. He tried to carry his own warning with him as he walked down the stairs, but all it took was one look at Walter, who was still wearing his leather jacket but now sporting a tight black T-shirt and soft blue scarf to boot, and Kelly almost lost his knees.

He was going to fuck this up before the night was over. He'd be willing to bet money on it.

Chapter Fourteen

KELLY LOOKED LIKE fucking sex on a stick.

Walter kept his eyes on the road as they traveled down 90/94, but his brain kept playing the mental movie of Kelly coming down the stairs. Kelly in his tight jeans and tight, *tight* shirt. It was old and soft red. It made Walter want to bite his nipples, which were neatly outlined by the fabric. He hadn't bitten, though, not even metaphorically. He'd simply told him he looked great and escorted him to the car.

He could see Kelly out of the corner of his eye, though. And those nipples.

"So." His voice cracked, and he cleared his throat. "I thought, after we eat, we'd do a little tour. A lot of the shops stay open until later, and there are the bars too." He glanced at Kelly. "You did bring your ID, right? The one I got for you?"

Cue blush. "I keep it in the back of my wallet, so yes."

"Thank God. I was ready for you to tell me it was in your drawer at Hope."

"No, because you always got annoyed when we wanted to go and I'd have to go to our room first. I'd meant to take it out before I left for Minnesota, but I forgot."

"Well, move it to the front of your wallet. I'll take you to Roscoe's later." He glanced at Kelly again. "Have you ever been to a gay bar?"

"No. I mean, outside that one time you took us to Sparks in Danby."

"God, Sparks does not count. Hell, we'll make a circuit then."

"Okay." The reply came out nervous.

Walter reached over and squeezed Kelly's leg. "They're not scary. I promise."

"No, I—" Kelly looked down at where Walter held on to him.

Walter let go and put his hands back on the wheel.

"I'm not nervous about the bar," Kelly said, sounding very nervous. "It's just…I don't know. Ignore me. I'm weird tonight."

Weird? Why? Walter frowned. "We can skip the bar and go back to the house after we eat, if you want."

"*No.*" Kelly sighed and sank a little in his seat. "Never mind, really."

Walter tried not to mind, but it was impossible. Before long they were on the streets of Lakeview, which kept him alert, and then he was on a mission to find a parking spot. On the way, Kelly got an accidental tour of the neighborhood.

"They have rainbow pillars?" Kelly asked, glued to the window. "Oh, and there's a pizza place."

"That's not Pie Hole. It's on Broadway. There's a great music store down the street, and we're going to pass my favorite grocery store here on the left: Treasure

Island foods. It's a dive, but I love it. And there, that's Pie Hole."

"Cool." Kelly looked around at the street crowded with cars and people. "Where are we going to park?"

"That's always the problem down here. I think I may cave and go back to one of the garages on Halsted, if you don't mind walking."

"Sure."

They didn't have to go far up on Halsted to find a ramp, and there was still plenty of parking inside, thank God. Walter led Kelly back down toward Broadway again, this time via Cornelia.

And Gaymart.

Kelly laughed when he saw the store. "Gaymart? For real?"

"For real. All the rainbow kitsch you could want, some fun T-shirts and an excellent comic memorabilia collection."

"But do they have *Doctor Who* stuff?" When Kelly saw Walter's nod, his eyes went wide and he headed for the door.

Walter grabbed his arm. "Pizza first. Now I'm starving too."

Pie Hole was one of Walter's favorite restaurants, not just because the food was good but because it was fun and quirky and cute and incredibly gay without making the gayness a meme. There was a logo on the window, "Pie Hole" with the O missing and an invitation that patrons "Twitter their hole", and Walter as usual did as instructed. He pressed his mouth in place of the missing vowel, forming an O of his own against the glass, and he had Kelly take a picture so he could post it online. Kelly wouldn't reciprocate, but he did let Walter take his picture holding a T-shirt that read, *I want a large sausage.*

Walter decided he'd buy it later and give it to Kelly for Christmas.

The place was crowded, so Kelly and Walter stood together at the bar along the wall after giving their order. Kelly kept taking in the decor as they waited, pointing things out or letting his gaze linger on talent, of which there was plenty. Most of the patrons were slightly older than Walter, gay men about to hit the town but fueling up on pizza first.

"I wonder if I'll ever have this kind of life," Kelly said around his drink straw.

Walter leaned an elbow on the counter. "What kind of life?"

Kelly gestured to the room. "One where I go out with my friends in the city. Laughing and making bad jokes and heading off to the bar." He paused, tossing a shy smile at Walter. "I mean, we do that. But not this way. Not with jobs and apartments. Real life."

"I had a taste of that when I lived off campus." A stool freed up behind them, and Walter passed it to Kelly. "I know what you mean. It felt like air. I had space around me to breathe. Admittedly, sometimes too much space, when Greg and Cara were gone."

"How did you ever get the school to let you live off campus as a sophomore?"

Walter grinned and stirred his soda. "I didn't. I paid for a dorm room but lived with Cara, paying a third of the rent. It was the only way they could afford it."

"Your parents never noticed you were spending that much extra money?"

No, they hadn't, not until March. Walter's smile died. "I told you, it's a grand before Dad remembers my account is even there."

Kelly frowned. "I'm sorry."

"What for?" Walter tried to brush it off, but Kelly reached for his hand. His fingers were warm against Walter's cool ones, and he met Walter's gaze without faltering.

"I'm sorry," he said again, more firmly this time.

Walter should have pulled his hand back, but, well, he didn't feel like it. "It's okay."

"It isn't." Kelly still didn't let go. "I'm sorry you had to go through all that, paying double just to find somewhere decent to live." The corner of his mouth lifted up a little. "I'd say I'm sorry they didn't let you live off campus this year, but I'm not."

"That's okay." Walter squeezed Kelly's hand, letting his thumb catch the underside of his wrist. "I'm not sorry either."

"Okay, lovers." The call came from a waiter as he settled their plates on the space between them. "Order's up. Don't fuck in the restroom, and if you do anyway, be sure to clean up, or Doug'll be pissed."

This time it wasn't only Kelly who blushed.

GAYMART PROVED TO be as awesome as Kelly had

hoped, and his biggest problem was figuring out what *not* to buy. He had fifty dollars' worth of merchandise in his basket at one point, mostly *Doctor Who* figures, but he ended up putting everything back except for the Rory one. He hesitated over several T-shirts, feeling oddly drawn to one that read *Corruptible*, but mostly he had to fend off Walter's offerings of shirts suggesting people *Try the Sausage* with an arrow pointing to his crotch, or ones with a picture of a rooster and *COCK* emblazoned over the animal. In the end he got the Rory figure, a Dalek, and a raunchy lesbian card for Rose. They ran his purchases back to the car, and on the way to Roscoe's they stopped at another store which Kelly never saw the name of but was full of the most awesome club clothing and kitschy jewelry he'd ever seen. When he got to the retro leather in the basement, though, he nearly swooned.

"You'd look good in this," Walter suggested, handing him a leather motorcycle jacket. "You'd look good in the chaps too, but I know better than to think you'd try them on."

The chaps were sexy, but Kelly didn't dare admit that. He couldn't resist the coat, and when he got a peek at himself in the mirror, he shivered. "Oh God. It's amazing."

Walter stepped up behind him, placing a hand on his waist. In the mirror, Kelly could see his admiration. "God, you look fuckable in that. You have to get it."

Kelly wanted to get it, and now he wished he hadn't bought anything at Gaymart. It *did* look amazing on him, and better yet, it made him feel amazing. He fished for the tag, hoping for the best but expecting the worst. He found it, but before he could catch the price, Walter closed his hand over it.

"No. I got this."

"What? No." Kelly met Walter's gaze in the mirror, trying to be outraged, but Walter had such a hungry look on his face, it was hard to focus. "Walter, you can't buy this for me."

"Fine, then I'll buy it for me and make you wear it."

Kelly started to protest, but Walter nuzzled his ear. *Stop,* Kelly thought, but couldn't bring himself to say the words. He let his eyes drift closed, swimming in the sensation of Walter's touch. The hand on his waist tightened, and Walter's breath on his ear sent him the rest of the way to fully erect.

"It's just money." Walter's lips were still on Kelly's ear. "It's better than that shirt you kept picking up. You don't look corruptible in this jacket. You look already corrupted."

Kelly's eyes blinked open, slowly as if he were waking from a dream, except he didn't wake, not from his lust. He caught sight of Walter in the mirror, watched Walter ogle him, and he realized, yes, Walter was right. He was already corrupted. He wanted to let Walter buy this for him, and he'd wear it every day because he'd think of Walter every time he did, knowing he'd given it to him. The only way it could be better would be if Walter wore it occasionally so it smelled like him.

Every time he wore it, he'd think about how much he wanted Walter, and how he'd never have him.

Oh God, he was in so much trouble.

Pushing away from Walter, Kelly shrugged out of the jacket. "No. I don't want it."

Walter seemed hurt, which annoyed Kelly, and he didn't stick around to argue with him because he was afraid of what he'd say. He headed back up the stairs and browsed through a rack of costume jewelry without seeing any of it until Walter came up behind him. He didn't touch Kelly.

"Ready to head to the bar?"

Kelly couldn't read anything in the tone, if Walter was angry or disappointed or what. Kelly tried to respond in kind. "Sure."

There was a small line at the door, and Kelly worried he'd have trouble getting in with his fake, but if the doorman suspected, he didn't say anything. In fact, he winked at Kelly as he stamped his hand. "You boys have a good time."

Kelly glanced at Walter, who wasn't touching him, wasn't even looking at him. Something told him a good time wasn't on his agenda.

"You drinking?" Walter's voice made it clear he was still annoyed.

Kelly wasn't exactly happy either. "I'm drinking." Why not? It wasn't as if if he got drunk and threw himself at Walter anything would happen. It wasn't going to happen if he stayed sober, either.

It wasn't going to happen, period.

"Yes. I want a drink," Kelly said, more forcefully this time. "But not beer."

Walter's eyebrow lifted. "What do you want, then?

A Mike's?"

Yes, a Mike's Hard Lemonade sounded good, but the mockery lacing Walter's tone pissed Kelly off. "No, I don't want a Mike's."

Now Walter seemed amused. "What do you want, then?"

Kelly had no idea. He tried to think of the names of drinks he knew. Not whiskey, that was for sure. Rum and Coke? He'd had a sip of Walter's once, and he'd hated it. What else was there? Bloody Mary? Martinis? "Gin and tonic."

Walter was still amused, but he was surprised too, so Kelly counted it as a win. "Gin and tonic it is."

He started for the bar, but Kelly pulled him back. "No. I'm getting it." He glared at Walter. "What are you drinking?"

Now Walter looked annoyed too. "Is that what this is about? You're pissed because I tried to buy you a jacket?"

"No," Kelly shot back.

"Then what the hell, Kelly?"

Kelly turned away from Walter before he could get a good look at his face and figure anything out. "I'll get you a rum and Coke."

He bought the drinks, not even feeling nervous this time, he was so angry. A cute guy tried to flirt as he waited for his order, but he was older and from Chicago, so Kelly just nodded at him and went back to glowering. When he got his drink, he took a liberal sip before returning to Walter. The burn of the alcohol helped a lot, but he still felt moored in the dangerous waters between angry and desperate.

He drank more, hoping for the best.

The bar was nothing like Babylon on *QAF*, but something told Kelly nothing ever was. The music was good, and as the gin forced him to unwind and the music crawled under his skin, he felt better.

"I'm going to dance," he declared, and headed out onto the floor.

He had no idea if Walter followed him or not, and he didn't let himself pay attention. He didn't know the song being played, but it had a good beat, and he let it lead his body. He didn't hold back either, not even a little—he danced as he had in his bedroom back home, back when he'd been afraid if he looked too into it people might suspect he was gay somehow. He danced the way he hadn't danced even at Luna's. That night he'd still been partially aware of Walter's presence, but tonight he was so pissed at Walter he didn't care.

Pissed and hurt, and he knew he didn't really have a right to feel either emotion.

Stop thinking and dance, he scolded himself.

He did.

Kelly danced with abandon, first by himself and then with anyone who put their arms around him. Young guys, older guys, hot guys, and guys who were so far from talent it wasn't funny. He wanted none of them, but he appreciated their bodies to dance against, so he shoved aside the part of him that felt lonely and let down and made himself let go. Maybe Walter was right. Sex with strangers was the same as dancing, except he got off. Sure, it didn't match his idea of love, but it was better than nothing.

It was better than pining foolishly for somebody he knew wasn't ever, ever going to be that rosy person for him.

When the arms came around his back, Kelly knew it was Walter behind him. He meant to treat Walter like just another guy who danced with him, to enjoy it quietly, almost perversely, but he got a whiff of Walter's aftershave and couldn't. No, if he danced with Walter, he'd give away all his secrets. He faltered and tried to step out of Walter's embrace.

Walter's arm tightened and kept him close. "So you'll grind against everyone in the room, but you won't dance with me?"

He sounded pissed, which made Kelly that much angrier. He spun around, ready to say no, he wouldn't, but then he got a good look at his roommate's face.

Walter wasn't just pissed. He was hurt.

What?

Walter's jaw was tight as he spoke, making his words come out clipped. "I didn't buy you the jacket, okay? What more do you want?"

The jacket? "I don't care about that."

Walter only got angrier. "Then *what*? Why are you so pissed?"

Kelly tried to be angry, tried to retreat, but he couldn't. Maybe, he decided, he shouldn't. Maybe the only way out of this was the truth. But when he opened his mouth to speak, the words choked him, and he deflated.

"I can't," he whispered.

"Can't what?" Walter's grip loosened even while it seemed to pull him in closer at the same time. "Kelly, baby, tell me what's wrong so I can fix it."

Oh God. Kelly's hands tightened against Walter's shirt. "Stop," he whispered. "Please. I *can't.*"

"Kelly."

Fingers pushed Kelly's chin up, and he gave in, looking Walter dead in the eye. Let him see whatever he would, let him laugh or be disgusted or whatever he was going to do, just so it could be over with.

Let his heart break, so he could move on.

Except Walter didn't laugh, and he didn't seem disgusted. Kelly didn't know what that look was, but he did know that when Walter's thumb scraped gently along his jaw, he thought it was an outright miracle he didn't melt into a puddle on the floor.

Then the hand fell away, sliding back to his waist. "Come on," Walter said. "You should dance. It's your favorite song."

It was? Kelly glanced toward the DJ, not so much that he thought he'd see the name of the song flashing above his head but that he could maybe focus when he wasn't distracted by Walter, and it did help. They were playing "Titanium", the David Guetta mix with Sia, which was, yes, his favorite song. Ever, in the whole world.

As the soft guitar opening bled into the first verse, Sia's voice drifting pleasantly into Kelly's ears, Walter pulled him closer, swaying to the beat.

It wasn't an easy song to dance to, too many shifts in tempo, and Kelly was surprised the DJ played it at all. Walter didn't hesitate, though, just kept them sliding together on the floor expertly. He bled Kelly's nerves away, all but the center core of his tension, his uncertainty over what was happening, what would happen next.

Because it felt like Walter was doing a hell of a lot more than flirting with him, and he knew that would never happen.

Except that maybe it was happening right now.

"Relax," Walter whispered, pulling him closer.

Kelly couldn't. "Walter," he began, then broke off. His heart was clogging his throat again. He shook his head, clearing a bit of space for speech. "Walter, I can't. I feel things when we do this that I shouldn't." He shivered as Walter's hands skimmed down his body. *Say it. Get it out, so you can get it over with.* "You don't feel those kinds of things, not with anyone."

Walter nuzzled Kelly's neck, then his ear. "Maybe I do, with you."

Kelly's legs all but folded beneath him.

Walter caught him, bore him up and pulled him closer. The song drifted into the bridge, and Kelly melted into Walter as their dance turned into a slow, sultry sway as Walter's words echoed crazily in Kelly's head. He knew he couldn't have heard right. He had to be dreaming, except he knew he wasn't. This was happening. Walter had said those words, and they were dancing, and this was happening.

"I know you dated a couple guys. Stupid Mason Jar at the very least." Walter's lips brushed Kelly's ear. "On any of these dates with those losers—did any of them ever kiss you?"

Kelly's heart, still at his throat, swelled, rose and fell, and did a backflip. How did Walter know about Mason? Except he didn't, because he thought there had been dates. There hadn't been any.

"Did any of them kiss you?" Walter asked again.

Jesus. Unable to trust his voice, Kelly shook his head.

Walter pulled Kelly tighter against him. As the song drifted back into the chorus, he nuzzled his way along Kelly's jaw.

Kelly was so lost he was barely sure of his name. Walter—*Walter*—was holding him, asking him about kisses, and maybe, maybe, working up to one. Slowly, sultrily. He was, Kelly realized, waiting for the moment in the chorus when the music swelled.

Probably Walter was the reason the song had been played.

Maybe I do, with you.

The music shifted into its climax, and Kelly turned to meet him.

Walter's lips were soft, and wet, and when his tongue stole out into Kelly's mouth, Kelly forgot to breathe. He let go of everything, his fears, his inhibitions, his guarding of his heart, and he threw his arms around Walter's neck, opening to him, inviting him deeper. Walter dove in, slanting his head and tipping Kelly's in the other direction as their lips made a seal.

They didn't stop dancing. They broke the kiss a few times to change direction, to move arms, to let Walter press his thigh between Kelly's leg for him to ride it.

Kelly did, with abandon. The music screamed in his ears, the beat pushed against his soul, and Walter held him so tight they felt as if they were one person.

Kelly never wanted it to end.

Eventually, of course, it had to. The song finished, bleeding into another club tune without a break, but the spell that had held them in place on the floor broke with the shift. They kept dancing, but they pulled back enough to look at each other. Kelly didn't know what he looked like, but whatever it was prompted Walter to stroke his face.

"It's okay," Walter whispered. Kelly wondered if he was reassuring himself too.

Kelly slid his hands back up Walter's chest. He felt as if he should say something, but he was too wild, too raw.

Walter brushed a kiss against his eyebrow. "Want to go home?"

The very idea filled Kelly with terror. He didn't trust the magic to last. Even if this didn't all turn out to be a dream, at some point they were going to have to talk about what this meant, what they would do now. He had no idea what would happen then, and he was afraid to find out.

He shook his head. "Dance with me some more?"

Walter smiled and pulled them back into the music again.

Chapter Fifteen

WALTER DIDN'T KNOW what he was doing with Kelly at Roscoe's, but maybe if he kept moving and didn't let himself think, maybe, just maybe, everything would be okay.

He hadn't so much as touched the rum and Coke Kelly bought for him, too busy being green with envy as Kelly made out with every other fucking guy in the bar while Walter watched. Then he'd been busy trying to figure out what the fuck was going on, and then...

Kelly. He'd *kissed Kelly*.

He'd been Kelly's *first kiss*. Every time Walter thought about that he short-circuited, lost in wonder, victory, and sheer, unadulterated terror. What was he doing? Why had he done this—with *Kelly*?

What in the *hell* were they going to do now?

"You're doing it again." They had stopped dancing to get some water, and Kelly had lost his languidness, sliding back into his earlier tension. "You're going to close up on me and things are going to be weird, aren't they?"

"I've never closed up on you," Walter said, then realized he'd pulled away from Kelly, muscles tightening as he drew his arms against his body as he...closed off. He swore and sat on an empty stool, shaking. "Kelly, I can't do this."

"Damn it, Walter, *you* kissed *me*." Kelly's fist rested on the edge of the bar. "I was trying to leave it alone, but you kept pushing. This isn't my fault."

Walter gave him an incredulous look. "Whoever said it was? This is me being an idiot. I didn't say you couldn't. I said *I* can't."

Kelly threw up his hands. "I don't even know what it is we can't do. Because you're making it sound as if you can't kiss me or get too close to me, and after months of watching you fuck your way through campus, that hurts. It fucking hurts."

"This is about a lot more than kissing you." Walter laid his hands flat on the bar, staring at his fingers. He'd only had water, but he felt drunk. Crazy. Lost. Sick to his stomach. "I don't want to fuck us up. I couldn't stand losing you."

Kelly stilled. "How is kissing me losing me?"

"Because I want to do more than kiss you. More than have sex with you." Walter's fingers faded out of his vision as it clouded over, obscured by the haze of his emotions. "I want to have a relationship with you, but I've never had one, and I know they're hard, maybe impossible, and I can't do *regular* relationships right, so how would I not fuck this up even worse? I can't do this. *I can't.*" He dug his fingernails into the slick surface of the bar. "Except the more I try not to do this, to not be with you like this, the more it seems as if it's the only thing I *can* do." His throat grew thick, and he shut his eyes. He felt sick to his stomach. "I have to get out of here."

Kelly took his hand and pulled Walter from his stool, toward the corner where they'd left their jackets. Walter followed Kelly all the way outside, where Kelly led him to a snug alcove against the side of the building, pressed him against the brick and hugged him tight. Kelly's head tucked in on Walter's shoulder, his face against Walter's neck in the same place it had been that night at Luna's, and everything inside Walter went still and quiet, desperate to keep Kelly right there. Forever.

For a long time they stood there, embracing and breathing slowly. Eventually Kelly spoke. "I don't want to screw this up either. You're the best friend I've ever had. You…you're everything."

The words cut Walter open, both what he longed to hear and what he feared to hear at the same time. Everything about Kelly undid him, made him feel lost and found at the same time. He stroked Kelly's hair, letting his thumb catch on his ear. "So what do we do now?"

"I have no idea." Kelly shivered. "Maybe we start by heading back to your car and turn on the heater?"

Walter didn't want to leave that spot, didn't want to break the moment, but it *was* cold, and it was still quite a drive back to the house. He nodded and took Kelly's hand as he led them back to the garage, telling himself they could talk on the way back to Northbrook.

Except as they pulled onto the streets and aimed for the interstate, no one spoke, not for several miles. Walter didn't plug in his phone to play music, because he knew nothing would cut his anxiety, not right now. He was on the verge of babbling, blurting out anything to stop the damn silence, and then Kelly spoke.

"I know what you mean about not fucking this up. I didn't get what you were saying at first because you've always said you don't *do* relationships."

Walter swallowed hard. "I don't."

"But you're saying you want to with me?"

He took a deep breath, focused hard on the road and nodded.

In the darkness of the car, Walter could see Kelly turn toward him, felt his hand touch Walter's own against his leg. He said nothing, only held Walter's hand.

Walter soaked that up until he could breathe normally, until he didn't feel quite like a rubber band about to snap. "You have no idea how long I've been trying not to go here."

After he said that, he worried it came out wrong, but to his surprise, Kelly laughed. "I've been trying not to go here longer, I bet."

"How long?"

"The night Cara and Greg went out with us. When I had my stupid reaction and had to go to the hospital."

Walter glanced at him. "You figured out you had feelings for me while you were having an allergic reaction?"

"*No.* At the hotel. When I was on the floor and you helped me up."

Walter didn't remember this. What had he done? "Was I particularly gallant or something?"

Kelly shook his head. "No. I just...that was when."

Walter found Kelly's fingers, lacing their hands together as he soaked in the knowledge that Kelly'd had feelings for him since the beginning of October. It made him feel good, and it inspired him to make some confessions of his own. "Honestly, I've been going crazy every time you start talking about dating. Then there was goddamned Mason Jar."

"Mason—wait, I never told you about him. On purpose. But you mentioned him before too. Did Rose tell?"

"Uh, no. That would be me scamming your texts." When Kelly tensed and he could feel the outrage coming, Walter lifted his free hand off the wheel in a quick *stop* gesture. "I know. I shouldn't have. But I could tell it was going to go to shit, and I couldn't stand it."

Kelly frowned. "How? How could you possibly know that anything was happening?"

"You looked dopey, like you were in one of your damn Disney movies."

"You read my text messages because I was *happy*?"

"No. I read them because you were...because..." He sputtered a few more seconds before giving up. "Because I was jealous."

Jesus, confessing had been a stupid idea. If thinking about being the right person for Kelly was bad, talking about how he felt and why he'd behaved the way he had was ten thousand times worse. Walter would have been more comfortable naked in the middle of campus with a dunce cap on his head and a searchlight highlighting his location. He changed lanes because his exit was coming up, and the fact that they were almost back to the house made him realize the next awkward moment was going to be what they did when they got there. Did Kelly expect them to sleep together now? Or no, because of the virgin thing? What the fuck did they do *now*, as in not just tonight when they got back but tomorrow in the morning and back at school and—

"Walter, are you okay? You're shaking."

Swallowing hard, Walter gave a wooden nod and moved into the exit lane. His head hurt. His hands felt clammy. Jesus fucking Christ, he wanted out of this.

Except he didn't. *Fuck.*

"Walter?"

Swearing, still shaking, he pulled off onto the first side street, put the car in park and collapsed forward onto the steering wheel. His initial plan had been to stay curled up until he either died or got over whatever the hell was going on with him, but when Kelly touched his back, he started talking.

"I don't know what to do." Walter opened his eyes and stared through the gaps in the steering wheel to the floor of the car. "I don't know what you want to do. I don't know what I want to do. I don't know how to behave, what to say around you now. I think I thought back at the bar if I just gave in, things would be better, but now every single thing I think of saying or doing seems like it could fuck us up, and I can't take that. I don't want that. But I can't be sure that won't happen, which makes me crazy, and I'm not making sense and talking too much and this can't be helping my cause *and I can't stop—"*

Kelly grabbed him, hauled him upright and kissed him hard and fast on the mouth, stopping the rest of the verbal vomit. It wasn't an artful kiss, or even a particularly passionate one—it was simply Kelly, keeping him from tripping over himself, pulling him back to the ground.

Walter eased into the kiss, part of him thinking how he could turn it deeper, use it to move them into something familiar and sexy and less vulnerable, but that part got drowned out fast. Yes, part of it was that this was only Kelly's second kiss, but it was for Walter himself that he let Kelly keep leading, let the kiss be untutored and clumsy but oh so sweet.

Yes, this, that deeply buried part of him whispered. *I want this. Sweet and simple and Kelly.* The kiss wasn't just something he'd never had before—it was something he'd never allowed himself to yearn for. It felt like a dangerous door opening to a land of tigers and demons and darkness.

Kelly was there, though. That truth alone made opening that door worth the risk.

They kissed for a long time, the car idling, Walter's pulse beating at the back of his skull, quieting his headache, bleeding out his tension as Kelly kept making more and more space for him to be okay. Eventually they did pull apart, though, Walter heavy lidded and soft as Kelly smiled against his lips and nuzzled their noses together.

Walter nuzzled back, only a little hesitant. "Sorry. Lost my shit there for a second."

Kelly's laugh was soft and tickled the base of Walter's spine, making him come unspooled just a bit more. "Is it bad that I'm glad you did? You're always so put together. Nothing ever bothers you."

"That's because I work to avoid things where I can't fake it." He stroked Kelly's cheek. "I'm not going to be able to be that guy in this instance. Sorry."

Saying that out loud made Walter feel as if he'd peeled the skin and muscle away from his chest, exposing himself all the way to brittle bone. Kelly only smiled and kissed him again, softly, which was a relief. He'd worried Kelly was going to say something about how that wasn't what he was attracted to. Because that was bullshit. Nobody was attracted to a hot mess.

Walter would simply have to work hard to not be a hot mess when it came to being with Kelly.

Brushing one last kiss across Kelly's lips, he shifted back into his seat. "We should probably head back to the house."

"Probably so." Kelly reached for his seat belt.

Walter still didn't know what they were going to do when they got there, but he wasn't as panicked about it now. Must have been the kiss that lightened him up.

Good to know, he thought, and angled the Mazda back toward home.

WALTER'S MOTHER WAS in bed when they tiptoed into the house from the garage, which was good on the one hand because Kelly wasn't in the mood to make small talk, but on the other hand it made the awkwardness between himself and Walter that much bigger.

Obviously the big question hanging over their heads was whether or not they were going to go to Walter's room and continue what they'd started on the dance floor and renewed in the car. Or rather, what Walter had started on the dance floor and Kelly had renewed in the car. He still felt a little thrill when he realized that not only had he been the one to kiss Walter, but his kiss had calmed Walter down and given him something he needed. Kelly kept playing that over in his head, not only because kissing Walter was awesome but because he'd sort of reacted, not thinking, and he wanted to work out what about that had worked so *well* so he could do it again.

Right now as they milled around uncomfortably in the kitchen, Kelly knew he couldn't start anything at all because he was so self-conscious he wanted to stick his head in the oven.

"You want anything to drink?" Walter asked as he opened the fridge door. "Looks like we have Diet Coke, lemonade and vitamin water. Oh, and soy milk and flax milk."

"You have soy milk? *And* flax milk?"

"Well, I got the soy milk for you, and Mom has some pancake thing she wanted to make for tomorrow morning that takes flax milk." He leaned back out of the fridge and waggled his eyebrows at Kelly. "Would you care for a glass, sir?"

It was funny—Walter was trying hard to go back to his usual carefree self, so hard that Kelly could see the gears turning. That realization made Kelly smile, and ironically it eased him a little bit. "I'm good, thanks."

Walter shut the door, and now that Kelly knew to watch for it, he tracked the fleeting glimpse of panic as Walter tried to redirect. "I suppose we should go to bed. With the drive and all tomorrow."

He said this, but he also glanced sideways at Kelly, his gaze searching to see if this was what Kelly wanted, or if he was expecting something else.

Kelly found helpless Walter achingly endearing, and he couldn't stop a smile. Funny too how the more nervous Walter got, the more confident he felt. "I'm not super tired yet, I have to confess."

"Oh?" Walter stilled, those visible gears trying to shift and predict the new direction. "What...what did you have in mind?"

Good question. Making out sounded fun, but coming out and saying that was more than Kelly had in him just then. What else could he say to do that would let him subtly move them in that direction? Or let the evening play out longer? "Um...well, I have a couple movies on my laptop."

Walter's slow, knowing smile made Kelly's heart constrict and his pants get tighter. "These wouldn't happen to be *cartoon* movies, would they?"

Busted. Kelly faltered, then ducked his head to hide his embarrassed smile. "Yeah. Though *Enchanted* is only partly a cartoon."

"I love that you're a Disney nut."

That made Kelly look up, his expression dubious. "You do?"

Walter had closed the distance between them, his

sly smile no longer forced. "Yeah. I do. It's so...Kelly."

Kelly wasn't sure if that was a compliment or not. "I still can't believe you want to be with me when I'm the one who was scamming on animated Tarzan while you were getting off to Tom of Finland."

Something went soft and almost sad in Walter's face. "Kel, that's *exactly* why I want to be with you." Kelly frowned, but Walter didn't say anything more, just reached up and stroked his cheek. "Let's go watch *Enchanted*. I hear Amy Adams is pretty good. If you tell me Susan Sarandon chews up the scenery, it'll probably be my new favorite film."

Kelly didn't have high hopes that Walter would enjoy even a minute of the movie—mostly he figured they'd laugh a bit at Kelly's expense, snuggle on the bed, and start making out. Which was why he was so surprised when Walter laughed in actual enjoyment. He was in tears during "True Love's Kiss", and when Sarandon's cartoon character walked onto the stage, he flipped onto his belly, elbows buried into the mattress as he settled himself in front of the laptop.

"I had no idea this was a *farce*. Do they seriously keep up with this, making fun of their own genre?"

"Oh yeah. Wait until you see the singing and dancing scene in Central Park." Kelly repositioned himself on the bed so he could lie beside Walter. "It's about to shift to live action, which is when it really gets good. Also, Giselle meets Robert."

Walter raised an eyebrow but didn't turn away from the screen. "You mean Edward wasn't her prince?"

"Nope. He hooks up with Robert's fiancé. It's kind of a love quadrilateral."

Grinning, Walter glanced at Kelly, but after a moment his smile turned a bit wry. "Sorry. Something tells me this movie was only supposed to be a cover activity and I'm ruining the plan."

Kelly blushed, but he smiled too. "That's okay. I *do* love this movie."

Onscreen, Giselle started to squeal as she was hauled down the New York Streets in her extreme poof gown, and Walter's focus shifted back and he started giggling. *Giggling*.

This was better, Kelly decided, than making out.

They did snuggle, sort of—their arms pressed together, and behind them their feet kept rubbing against each other, linking at the ankles as they swayed back and forth together. Kelly watched the movie, but more than that he watched Walter, having possibly too much fun tracking his reactions. He laughed, but it wasn't all in mockery.

"So Robert is the cynical man who doesn't believe in love, and Giselle will convince him it does exist by the end, so they can live happily ever after?" Walter asked.

"Sort of. She has to come to terms with stuff too. The whole thing where she's promised to Edward but she falls in love with Robert is a bit of a tough nut too."

At this point Edward made it through the manhole, changed from cartoon to live-action, and Walter laughed so hard that he fell against Kelly.

"Holy shit, he's so fabulously gay. This is perfect."

Then the chipmunk started to chatter, and Walter lost it.

He giggled too, and Kelly decided this was his new mission in life, to find ways to make Walter giggle. Eventually he had to reposition himself because his arms were hurting from leaning on them, and when he shifted on the bed, Walter moved too, lying on his side and pulling Kelly up in front of him, wrapping an arm around his body and encouraging him to nestle in close. Kelly did. With Walter behind him, he didn't have to pretend to watch the movie, either. He could shut his eyes and drink in his scent, let all his focus settle on the way Walter's hand moved along his forearm and how amazing it felt when Walter slid a leg over his, trapping him lightly in place with a delicious pressure. It was perfect, lying there with him—could he call Walter his boyfriend? He wondered how it would be best to ask that, or if he even should. Maybe when the movie was over, since Walter was in such a good mood and they were both relaxed, he'd bring it up.

However, before the movie ended, in the middle of Giselle and Robert dancing the King and Queen's waltz—just after Robert started to sing to her—Walter's lips brushed Kelly's ear. When Kelly turned to look at him, he had one moment to register the desire in Walter's face, and then there was no space between them, because Walter's lips were on his.

Funny how he'd been kissed three times that night and each one was completely different and none of them ever what Kelly had expected a kiss to be like. Yes, he'd admit to being one of those boys who had rewound kisses and watched them over and over, and the few he'd been able to find on YouTube that were gay had him mesmerized. He'd always figured kissing would be engrossing, as if he were sliding inside someone. Completing a connection.

It was, but it was also scary and thrilling and such sensory overload that it took Kelly by surprise every time. This one wasn't as dramatic as the one in the bar or as bumbling as the one in the Mazda. It was slow, and sweet, and it sent Kelly spiraling into something new, something that made him feel hot and cold at once, made him want to lie flat on the mattress and pull Walter on top of him. The kiss made his cock hard and hopeful, even as that development made his heartbeat kick up and flutter inside his rib cage.

Kelly moaned, a quiet sound that escaped his lips. Walter kissed him deeper, opening his mouth over Kelly's and stealing inside.

Whimpering, Kelly opened wider to let Walter in. His eyes rolled back into his head behind his lids and he let go into Walter's embrace, shivering at the wicked feel of Walter's tongue beside his own. Walter's fingers brushed his jawline before he changed the angle of the kiss, went in *even deeper* and shifted his body tighter against Kelly's, pressing him into the bed.

Kelly moaned again and slid his hands up the front of Walter's shirt, fingers along the slope of Walter's neck.

Nothing about Walter was self-conscious now as he shut the laptop, took a brief moment to reposition Kelly flat on his back, and resumed the kiss, pressing their frames together chest to chest, thigh to thigh, groin to groin. Electricity ran across Kelly's skin as Walter's erection pushed hard against his own—when Walter thrust gently, rubbing them together like bits of tinder. Kelly thought he might combust any second, and it didn't take much frotting to have him gasping into Walter's mouth and clutching at his shoulders.

"Walter," he whispered, breaking the kiss long enough to speak. His hips, no longer taking orders from his brain, kept undulating in time with Walter's. Kelly bit his own lip and nuzzled Walter's chin. "Walter, I'm going to—*in my pants*."

"Me too. It's okay—we can do a load of laundry." Walter nuzzled back, then caught Kelly's bottom lip lightly in his teeth. "Come with me, Kelly. Right now."

He nipped at Kelly's lip again, harder this time. Shutting his eyes and holding on tight, Kelly let out a shuddering cry and did as he was told. He came in his underwear, in his jeans, humping against Walter without an ounce of shame. He wasn't even fully back in his body before Walter did the same, his mouth sealing over Kelly's as his body tensed, jerked, then melted against Kelly in release. As Walter dragged a weary kiss down Kelly's cheek, they lay there together, breathing hard through their recovery.

It was fantastic, unreal, amazing—all except for the sticky, awkward, and increasingly cool mess inside his briefs.

Walter nuzzled behind Kelly's ear. "We'll want to go clean up. Dried come is nothing to fuck with." His lips brushed Kelly's nape. "Hope that was okay."

Was it okay? God it was *epic*. Kelly felt that was too silly to say, so he nodded and kissed Walter's cheek instead. "It was great."

Walter's smile made Kelly's heart flip over, though it ached as Walter climbed off the bed and held out a hand to help Kelly up too. As soon as Kelly stood, though, feeling the cold squish inside his pants, he made a face and shivered. "Oh, *ew*."

"Yeah, and it only gets better the longer it sits there." Walter squeezed his hand and tugged him toward the door. "Come on. We have a date with warm washcloths."

Cleaning up was a little embarrassing—it wasn't as if he hadn't stolen a peek at Walter's cock before, but he'd never stood half-naked beside him in a bathroom and wiped spunk out of his pubic hair. Naturally, Walter wasn't embarrassed at all, which worked out well because he had Kelly giggling and relaxed in almost no time at all. They shimmied into sweats, brushed their teeth together and headed back to the bedroom. That was when Walter went awkward again.

"Do you want me to go?" He nodded toward the guest bedroom. "I mean—I don't want to…" He trailed off, looking lost and uneasy.

This Kelly could fix. Happily. He took Walter's hand and led him back to the bed. "Please stay."

Walter relaxed, but not all the way. "We can just sleep. Or—" He rubbed at his jaw, then sighed. "I don't care what we do, or don't. I only want to be with you. If that's okay."

Kelly smiled, heart swelling. "Totally okay." He

tugged Walter into the bed and pulled the laptop back between them. "Come on. You need to see the end of the movie."

Chapter Sixteen

WALTER LAY AWAKE a long time, watching Kelly sleep.

It was ridiculous, he knew, but he was afraid to close his eyes for fear he'd wake up and this would be a dream. That he'd wake in his room, without Kelly, with his mom banging around in the kitchen, either putting on a fragile smile when he came down or ripping the veil away entirely and weeping because he was leaving, going to school and leaving her alone. That he'd find out he hadn't picked up Kelly from the airport, kissed him in Roscoe's and made out with him with a Disney movie as background noise.

It was ridiculous. He knew this. Even so, he fought sleep as if it were a devil, letting it claim him only for long, heavy blinks before he woke himself with a sharp bite against the inside of his cheek. He traced the soft contours of Kelly's face as he lay still and serene in his slumber beside Walter, ran his fingertip down the line of his neck, across his clavicle and around the collar of his T-shirt.

He'd done it. He'd told Kelly how he felt. Some of it. They'd kissed, made out.

Now what? Walter still didn't know. Part of him

was convinced this had been the biggest mistake of his life, bigger than staying home with his mom those two years.

Part of him ached so badly for this he wanted to cry.

He didn't, but his throat was thick and his gut queasy as he kept tracing Kelly's skin, as things he'd promised himself he wouldn't think about stirred like dead leaves inside him. That was the funny thing about feelings. He'd learned this years ago, even before college—he could lock things away, but it was a hard turn, that valve. He had to shut whole parts of himself off when he closed it. This had been discussed, at length, in the therapy he'd allowed himself when things with his mother had gone particularly sour. *You can't shut your heart off forever,* the counselor had warned him.

Turned out she was right.

Walter skimmed his hand over Kelly's chest, lightly so as not to wake him, but enough to let himself feel, to learn those planes he'd been longing for. It was important not to wake him, because Walter wanted to blurt out everything, all his secrets that weren't anything at all, stupid old wounds that upset him. Things he could look back on now and see were problems, scars he carried that got in his way even now, events that if he hadn't been so young and clueless would have told him a lot, could have kept him from feeling so lousy. Sad truths about how sick his mother was—oh, not sick enough to be a real danger, no, but sick enough to make life lonely and confusing. Ugly truths about his dad and how fucking inattentive and selfish he was, how his dad's worthlessness mixed with his mother's Russian roulette was a nightmare roofie cocktail. Unfortunate truths, about how maybe it wasn't terribly brilliant for a fourteen-year-old to go cruising for daddies, no matter how mature and put together those boys thought they were.

Walter shut his eyes, swallowing the darkness back down. No, he wasn't telling any of that to Kelly. Funny, though, how being happy brought that crap out. This wasn't the first time it had happened, either—moments of something this good, this unexpected and off his usual path, they always dredged up old shit, as if somehow happiness came with sorrow as its anchor. In Walter's case the chain had gotten all tangled, and the whole business came up or stayed down together. Which was why he preferred not to get involved with people, especially not like this.

Yet here he was. Involved. Really fucking involved, and he didn't think he could walk away now, even if it was the right thing to do.

Eventually he had to give in to sleep, but before he did, he tossed out a different kind of anchor. Pulling his phone from the nightstand, he punched out an email to Williams, using the professor's home email, not the one he used through the college.

Weird break. Lots has happened. Good I think, but I'd love to reserve some time in your garage workshop next week to talk it through. Love to the wife and kids.

Some of his anxiety bled off simply by typing that. He took a moment to breathe, to let his lungs release, then added one last line to keep the tone light and redirect a little focus off himself.

And stop worrying about your tenure. It'll be fine.

Hitting send, Walter curled up beside Kelly, wrapped an arm carefully around his waist and slid into sleep.

WALTER WOKE THE next time to find Kelly already awake and staring at him. Smiling shyly, Kelly ran a hand down Walter's arm beneath the sheet. "Hi."

Walter smiled back, body still heavy with sleep. "Hi." He bent his hand and captured Kelly's fingers, tugging them down to tangle over his chest. "Sleep okay?"

Kelly nodded, fingers moving against Walter's. He had a bashful look about him, and he nibbled his lip a few times before he spoke. "Can I ask you kind of a dumb question? One that makes me sound like a stupid, sappy tool?"

"You are not a stupid, sappy tool." Walter brushed his thumb along Kelly's wrist. "Ask."

Kelly caught Walter's hand. "Are we...boyfriends?"

Walter had to shut his eyes in a long, slow blink as he wiped the crazy riot of emotions that question stirred, but he didn't do a good enough job, because when he opened them back up, Kelly looked abashed and miserable.

"I'm sorry. I shouldn't have asked. I told you—"

Walter let go of Kelly's hand to stop that babble with his fingertips. "Hush. Kelly, you can't be sorry for asking that question."

Kelly's face still radiated extreme embarrassment. "It's just that I know you don't do that, and I know you said you would for me, but you can't mean it, not really, not when I'm a clueless virgin and you're—"

Fingers weren't enough. Walter had to stop this tide with his mouth, but part of that was because he needed another minute to hide, to get himself together. God, he thought he'd put this away in the middle of the night, but clearly not. What was he supposed to say? *Kel, I'm more clueless than you'll ever know. You could do so much better than me. I want to tell you that, want to confess all the ways I'm a mess and then some, to show you that if I wanted to, I could give you a real run for your money on that stupid, sappy tool business.*

He couldn't say that, no. So instead he whispered against Kelly's lips, "I'm your boyfriend. That's what I am." When Kelly started to protest, he kissed him again, hard and fast. "No. No more fishing for compliments, not until I get something to eat. And unless my nose deceives me, there are vegan pancakes and bacon waiting for us downstairs."

The smell of food only got stronger as they opened the door. Walter sent Kelly to take a shower first, and after a quick, silly goodbye kiss, he headed down to the kitchen. Walter could smell the pancakes—and the bacon, and he thought, perhaps, hash browns. As he approached the kitchen, the prospect of good food mingled with the bliss that was waking up with Kelly, and Walter allowed himself to savor the golden moment.

Of course, he should have known a moment was all he'd be allowed to have.

Though his mother was indeed cooking, she wasn't the smiling, happy, let-me-make-breakfast-for-you mother he'd left waving them off the night before. She looked harried and grim, and she'd clearly spent a considerable portion of the night and possibly the morning crying. When she saw Walter, she wiped at her eyes and put on the fakest, most pathetic smile he'd seen in a while.

"Hi, sweetheart. Breakfast is almost ready."

She moved back to the stove before Walter could go to her, leaving him to stand impotently at the breakfast bar. "Mom? What's wrong?"

"Nothing," she said, her voice very full of *something*. Yearning, mostly, if he had to guess, and loneliness. As usual, it tore at Walter's heart. Especially as she added, "I shouldn't bother you with my problems."

She said this almost petulantly, as if she knew they were the right words but hated them for being so. Those were Walter's cues to countermand her, to assure her that no, he wanted to hear why she was upset. It was a game they'd played for a long time, a game many people had tried to get him to stop playing, but he'd never been able to successfully manage it.

Until today.

For the first time in a long time, Walter didn't play. His lack of response hung in the air, and his mother paused, waiting for them, like a cue someone had missed in a play. Walter kept quiet, feeling guilty but obstinate. He'd had the best night of his life, and a pretty damn fine morning until this. He didn't want Kelly to see his mom in one of her fits. If Walter wasn't supposed to hear what was bothering her, then she should keep it to herself. Otherwise she should just tell him because she didn't care if she upset him or not. She shouldn't make him give her permission to ruin his day with whatever had her upset this time.

No sooner did he think these thoughts, however, than the guilt became too much, too acute, and he caved. "What's going on, Mom?"

He listened woodenly to a recycled tirade against his dad—for a second he'd convinced himself it would be something new, something significant, but no, it was the same tired line about how she was always left alone, how no one cared. It made Walter angry.

"What do you want me to do, Mom? I'm not quitting school again. You might notice I came home for break. I did Thanksgiving with you." It had been a nightmare, but he'd done it. "Apparently that doesn't count as caring, in your book."

Of course this speech turned out to be a tactical error, because with a smooth downshift she went from *poor me* to self-flagellation, and now she sobbed and carried on about what a bad mother she was, how Walter deserved better, how Tibby probably hated her too. The self-hatred was so thick Walter panicked, worried she was more depressed than he'd known and would kill herself or something equally awful.

"Mom," he pleaded, but she only sobbed and went off to her bedroom down the hall, slamming the door.

Walter could hear her muffled sobs through the barrier, and they tore at him.

Their breakfast sizzled on, giving off a scent that promised burning without swift attention. Moving stiffly, Walter took up his mother's place, flipping cakes and turning bacon, half his focus on the bedroom, where soft crying drifted out on occasion. He felt the hard dome he all too often hoisted over his emotions in the face of his family start to rise, but no sooner was it about to lock in place than Kelly came into the kitchen, hair damp. He radiated a glow that made Walter ache and fumble at the same time. The dome of protection retreated all on its own, and Walter stood there, raw and unsure of how to behave.

With one look at Walter, Kelly's smile died. "What's wrong?"

On cue, Shari wailed from the bedroom. When Walter winced, Kelly came around the breakfast bar and took his hand. "Hey." When Walter didn't react—he couldn't, he was so close to the edge—Kelly took the spatula from Walter's hand, turned him around and pulled him into a tight, comforting embrace.

God, it felt good. Too good. "The food," he croaked, his voice too thick to work right.

"Fuck the food."

Walter wanted to shut his eyes and sink into Kelly. The thought of doing so made him ache even as he warned himself he shouldn't. "It'll make it worse, if this is burned on top of everything else."

Not fully letting go of Walter, Kelly reached for the spatula, flipped the last pancakes onto the plate bearing the others, moved the bacon and hash browns to cool spots and turned everything off. He came back immediately to Walter, squeezing his hand tight like an anchor. "What happened?"

Walter shut his eyes. "Same shit, different day."

"What shit? What happened? Is she okay?"

Walter snorted in derision. "No. Nobody loves her, she says. So she cries at me, and I don't know what to do."

Fuck, he was not supposed to say all that. Walter tensed, ready for this to go to shit because of his damn over-sharing.

Kelly held Walter's hand a minute, then brushed a kiss against his cheek. "Let's grab some food."

Walter had no idea if this meant Kelly regretted asking or what, and he sure as hell wasn't hungry, but he ate anyway, taking the plate Kelly filled for him and reciprocating by getting him some coffee with soy milk. His mother appeared shortly after they sat down at the table, eyes red but wiped clean, and she sighed as if she had handily put all her troubles behind her.

"Thanks for finishing up, Walter." She smiled at Kelly, clearly trying to put on her best face. "Hope you like it."

"It's great," Kelly assured her. Walter combed the two words for tone, nuance, trying to figure out if Kelly was really fucking sorry he'd asked what was wrong or was smoothing the waters. He couldn't get much of a read, and it managed to kill what remained of his appetite.

Pushing away his plate, he rose. "I'm going to

shower quick. We have to get on the road soon."

He didn't linger to hear how this disappointed his mother.

The shower soothed him a little, but not enough, and he dressed rigidly, trying not to catalog all the ways his confession had fucked everything up and failing. After chastising himself for his weakness for several minutes, he moved quickly on to admitting this whole relationship thing was a bad idea, which led to panic over how in the world he could get out of it now without making everything worse. By the time he came back downstairs, he was popping antacids to ease the acrid storms inside his gut.

Back in the kitchen, Kelly and Shari chatted together while Kelly helped her put away the remainders of the meal and organize the dishes. Kelly was at his Minnesota Nice best: polite and deferential, which still didn't tell Walter a damn thing. Walter lingered a minute, wondering what he should do, eventually giving up and heading upstairs to pack.

He tried not to think, tried to focus on getting together what he needed for one month more at Hope, tried telling himself everything was fine, that he'd make it that way, but there was a Kelly-shaped elephant in the room he couldn't ignore. What the *hell* had he been thinking, starting anything up, and with Kelly of all fucking people? He should have let him flirt with whoever he wanted at Roscoe's. He'd have come home in a foul mood to match his mother's moping, and maybe this would be out of his system. He wouldn't have this god-awful ache across his arms like he was empty. Because even if he hadn't already fucked up with Kelly, he would soon, and he'd be alone.

It would have been better not to have ever started anything. Better to have left things as they were.

Even though it had nearly killed him, watching those other guys mack on Kelly.

Even though watching a Disney movie together and holding him close while they slept had been better than any sex Walter had ever had in his life.

Gripping the clothes in his hand, Walter shut his eyes and made himself draw slow, steady breaths until the searing pain across his chest was little more than a dull ache.

When Kelly came up to pack also, Walter tensed and got the lies about being fine all prepped and ready to roll off his tongue. Kelly didn't inquire how he was, though, only put his few belongings back in his backpack and asked Walter if he needed any help packing. When Walter shook his head, Kelly touched his arm, a brief, sad brush of fingers, and went back downstairs.

Walter wanted to throw up.

Trying to get that dome of indifference back in place, Walter hurried through the rest of his packing, loaded the car with their stuff, and kissed his mother without really looking at her. She was going to play for more sympathy or reassurance, and he couldn't do that, not right now. Not when everything was shit.

When they got to the car, though, Kelly threw him a curve ball by climbing into the driver's seat before Walter could.

Kelly held his hand out for the keys. "I'll drive."

Walter didn't hand them over, only glared at Kelly as he stood in the propped-open door on the driver's side. "You hate driving in traffic."

"I can survive." Kelly kept his hand out.

"You don't have to do this." Walter knew he was a little curt, and he cared about that, but he was about done with shit he wasn't expecting. What was Kelly trying to pull?

"Give me the keys, Walter." Minnesota Nice had left the building, and there was an edge to Kelly's tone now that said *don't fuck with me, Lucas.*

Fine. Kelly wanted to drive? He could drive. Walter tossed the keys in his lap and muttered to himself as he went around the back of his car to the passenger side. Even as it felt weird to sit there, he had to admit it would be nice to do nothing but drown in his chaos, rather than do that and drive too.

Except he knew Kelly *really* hated traffic, so he felt guilty for not insisting he at least drive out of town. He still didn't know why Kelly was doing this, what had brought it on, what it meant, and what it did to the two of them.

Fuck, he was going to throw up.

Kelly had pulled the GPS out of the glove box and was affixing it to the dash. "I don't suppose you have Hope entered in here?"

Walter did, because sometimes he let the computer route him around thick traffic or construction. Instead of saying this, though, he pulled the faceplate to himself, punched in the coordinates for Hope and frowned. "This is routing you over to the expressway,

which isn't something you want to experience. Here."
He nudged the path farther west with his finger. "You'll
take 294, then 88, then 355, *then* 55. That'll take us all
the way down to Springfield, where we'll catch 72 over
to Danby."

Kelly scanned the GPS monitor, then nodded.
"Four and a half hours, this says."

"Yeah, that's if we never stop. Figure we'll get there
around five or six, depending on how we lollygag." He
cast a sideways glance at Kelly. "You're not driving that
whole way."

Kelly glanced back at him, an odd, almost suggestive look that made Walter shiver. "I might. You never
know."

Walter wanted to surrender to that teasing, which
was why he pushed back. "I can drive."

"Me too," Kelly replied, and pulled out of the garage onto the street.

Chapter Seventeen

KELLY DROVE LIKE a grandmother, which made Walter crazy, but whenever he tried to get Kelly to pull over, the request was met with such a sharp rebuke that finally Walter gave up and retreated into his seat. When traffic got hairy and Kelly's shoulders started to tense, Walter did what he could to help by turning around to check lanes, keeping an eye out for exits, and to frequently say inane things such as, "You're doing fine," and "Good job, babe," which he couldn't tell if Kelly appreciated or not, but it made him feel as if he was doing something, so he kept it up.

For his part, Kelly said next to nothing, keeping all his focus on the road ahead of him and on the GPS. There was one tense moment when Walter knew its directions were wrong and he had to manually guide Kelly into the right exit lane, but that went more smoothly than he'd feared, and soon they were out of the worst of the snarls. When they finally made it onto I-55 and much, much easier traffic, Kelly sank back into his seat and visibly relaxed.

"Okay," he said, his voice shaky. "I should have let you drive."

Walter wanted to ask why he hadn't, but he could

feel talking coming on, and he had a feeling it was going to be a nightmare. He stared out the window, hoping he was wrong, knowing he wasn't.

"So," Kelly began, getting some of his composure back by degrees. "Talk to me about your mom."

His mom? That wasn't what he'd expected. Walter shifted in his seat. "What do you want to know?"

"I want to know why you got so upset this morning. You said it was more of the same. Except you've never told me about her. You've said your family is a mess, but I didn't get how seriously you meant that until now. I want to understand. Because you left the bedroom happy and lit up, and ever since you're...I don't know. Withdrawn. Upset." He slid his hands to an easier position on the wheel. "I can tell you don't want to talk about it, but you were upset, Walter. It made *me* upset. I don't want to make you bring up stuff you'd rather leave alone, but can you...I don't know, fill me in?"

No, Walter didn't want to talk about it, but at the same time he really, really did. The idea of dumping some of this crap off his plate and letting someone else help him sort through it was a powerful draw. At the same time, he was painfully aware that was how his mother operated, and the hell he'd ever be her.

"Is she in trouble?" Kelly pressed. "Is she sick?"

"She's depressed. Cara thinks she's manic-depressive, but I really don't know. She sees a shrink, and I figure they'd treat her for that if that was her diagnosis, but maybe not. Maybe it's not working, or maybe she's not taking her meds. She's good at lying about what she's thinking and feeling, putting up a front. Not to me, though. I get the whole hot mess." He stopped and grimaced. "I shouldn't be telling you this."

"I'm not going to tell anyone else, Walter."

Walter waved this away. "It's not that. You don't need this, Kel. This is deep crazy, this bullshit."

"Then tell me about it."

"No. There's no way to fix it."

"All the more reason for you to get it off your chest. Because it's killing you. Maybe I can't help, but I can sure as hell listen."

"I'm not going to be her and dump all my problems on other people," Walter snapped.

Kelly let go of the wheel to briefly squeeze Walter's hand. "You aren't the same as her, Walter. Not even close."

How could Kelly know that was what he was afraid of? How had he figured that out without knowing his mom, not knowing what Walter would dump if given the opportunity? Obviously he was saying it because it was the thing to say. Except God, Walter loved hearing it, and yeah, he wanted to spill his guts. Which was all the more reason he shouldn't.

Maybe he could tell Kelly a little. He took a deep breath, held it, and let it out.

"I don't know how it started. Because it was happening before they got divorced, her trying to dump everything on me, but I didn't listen then because I wanted to be loyal to Dad too. I didn't want to take sides. Plus I was thirteen and full of my own problems."

He ran his thumb along the inseam of his jeans. "It wasn't so bad in high school, either that or I was numb to it. Things got bad when I went to college. That's when Dad cheated on her too, which sent everything into a tailspin. I felt like a heel because crap, hers had been the right side. Which was part of why I came home. I felt as if I'd betrayed her."

"How is that betraying her, if you were simply being fair? And why do you have to take sides?"

God, he sounded like Williams. "Because she *is* all alone."

"You didn't make her that way."

"I went away to school."

"Well, yeah. That's what you're supposed to do."

"She fell apart, Kel. It was ten times worse than what you saw." Though it was only a little worse than what Walter had seen before Kelly came downstairs. His insides began to knot back up.

"Okay, but—" Kelly cut himself off and frowned at the road for a minute. "I mean, I get it. I'd leave Hope to help my family if they needed me, same as you did. I'd do whatever I had to. The thing is, I don't—" He cut himself off and frowned harder.

"You don't what?"

Kelly kept quiet for almost a full minute before replying. "I guess what I keep thinking of is the way you looked when I came downstairs. It wasn't right. I mean, I know I'm naive. I do get that. I've been really lucky, and even with the gay thing, I've had it easy. So I might just not get it. I might be wrong. Yet I can't help thinking you shouldn't be the one to have to save your mom. It's one thing for me to be careful with money and help out around the house, but if I came home and Lisa looked as upset as you were just now, I'd want to know what the fuck was going on. And maybe I'm thinking a bit more of myself than I should, because maybe you changed your mind, but I also can't help noticing you were different to me before you went downstairs and after. As if you'd decided, for some reason because of your mom, you didn't want anything to do with us. That's not right either."

Walter stared at the dashboard awhile, letting Kelly's observations sink in. The last one rang in his head, and he said, "I was thinking some of that, I suppose. Which isn't fair to you at all."

"Walter, it's not fair to *you*. If you didn't want to...date, or whatever this is, I could accept it. Yeah, I'd be sad, but I'd get over it. Still, it's one thing for you to decide that, but another for you to push me away because—I mean, how does that even work? Why does your mom being sad and clingy mean you can't be happy?"

Why not, indeed? Walter sank deeper into his seat and pinched the bridge of his nose. "It's not that." He had the distinct feeling he should shut up, but he kept talking anyway. Why not? Blow it up now before things got too personal. "It's more her breakdown reminded me I shouldn't rock the boat."

"Because you think if you date me you'll turn into your mom?"

It sounded so insane, when Kelly said it. "I don't know. But I don't ever want to be that. I don't want anything to do with that kind of pain."

"'Life is pain, princess. Anyone who says otherwise is selling something.'"

Walter couldn't help a small smile. "Yes, Dread Pirate Westley."

"See? I watch more than Disney movies. Besides, it's true. Avoiding pain doesn't make everything okay. It means you're avoiding pain instead of living." Traffic had spread out, and Kelly relaxed and took one hand off the wheel. "I thought about that a lot over Thanksgiving. Here and there I saw people from high school, and the word has gone out that I'm gay. They look at me different now, and they whisper. Basically they're doing the things I was afraid they'd do. In high school that fear seemed so important, and I had all this justification in my head. Mom didn't help either, because she freaks out about everything and concocted scenarios where I got beat up behind the bleachers or dragged behind cars. I let that be my excuse too. Honestly, though? What I was afraid of was rejection. I liked how people saw me, and I was willing to trade my whole high school experience for that acceptance. An acceptance of bullshit, I realize now. And I don't care. I don't give a damn what those people think of me. I see them when we fill up our car at the gas station or go to the grocery store."

His jaw grew tight, his eyes hard, and he shook his head. "I can't believe I gave them so much of my life. I can't believe I let them convince me to be embarrassed about myself, to become so socially backward that while everyone else is hooking up I'm all doe-eyed and gooey like an eighth grader, because I was too busy hiding in actual eighth grade."

Kelly wasn't embarrassed at all now, but he did seem sad, and it broke Walter's heart. "You can't look back from here and say it would have been fine. Maybe you were right. Maybe you were smart to do it the way you did." He thought of all the stupid things he'd done in eighth grade and shook his head. "Better to be cautious."

"Not according to Cher. She says do everything now, that you can always look back and say you shouldn't have done something."

"She also says she wouldn't take her own advice, because advice is kind of bullshit." Walter settled into his seat, distracted for a moment by thinking about Cher and her all-over-the-map, crazy life. "Though she's really done it all, hasn't she? And now she's Queen of Weird Twitter."

That was supposed to make Kelly laugh, but he had this determination about him now, and as he spoke he stared at the road, clearly seeing something more than lanes of pavement and traffic. "I really do regret playing it safe now. I'd almost rather have been beat around a bit and been myself and been proud of who I was than hide. It cost me so much. Now not only am I behind everyone else, but I lost years of my life." He shook his head, his jaw going tight. "I gave up my *life*, Walter. My *life*. I'm never doing that again, ever, not for anyone." He wiped at his eyes, a quick swipe, like he was embarrassed. "You shouldn't, either. Not for your mom. Not for anyone. It's *her* life. And you have yours.

What is it you think is going to happen if you don't make yourself happy as some weird kind of solidarity with her? What is it you're supposed to get?"

Walter wasn't doing it out of solidarity, he wanted to argue, but he knew Kelly would say what it was about then, and they'd be back to the life-is-pain thing. "Wouldn't you want company if you were lonely?"

"She's not lonely. She's in a bog, and if you give her a chance, she's going to pull you in with her. Then all that will happen is we lose two of you senselessly."

Walter couldn't think of a retort to that, so he sat there for a few miles, soaking in everything Kelly had said to him. Including the Cher quote. For someone who thought he was naive and clueless and got intimidated by Philosophy Club, he was pretty damn wise.

Probably he should tell Kelly that, but instead he spied an exit and nodded at it. "Pull off here."

"Why?" Kelly asked, even as he aimed for the off-ramp.

"Because life may be pain, but you hate driving and I'm out of my funk now, so let me. You don't have to suffer quite that much." He caught Kelly's hand and brushed his thumb over the bottom of Kelly's palm. "Besides. I want to kiss you a hell of a lot harder than I safely can while you're behind the wheel."

That made Kelly swerve, but it made Walter smile. When they were parked at a gas station, Kelly turned to Walter—shy, eager, hopeful—and Walter caught his chin before kissing him with all the passion and gratitude that he felt. He let the last dregs of the idea of pushing Kelly away drown in that kiss, let himself sink into the space Kelly had made between them. When they finally parted, Walter pressed their foreheads together and stroked Kelly's cheek.

"Thanks," he whispered.

In answer, Kelly kissed his knuckles. Then he climbed out of the driver's seat and came around to the passenger side, looking relieved, before Walter could even undo his belt.

Chapter Eighteen

IN HIGH SCHOOL, when Kelly had needed to tell himself a story about *someday* in order to get through right now, a boyfriend had been a mythical, magical creature he pulled out of a box. A boyfriend called him on the phone, texted him, sent him supportive, suggestive emails. A boyfriend held his hand, touched him, and gave him special smiles. A boyfriend took him out on dates, to the movies, and to dinner. A boyfriend brought him presents and noticed things he needed. A boyfriend kissed him and filled in the gaps between Kelly's fantasies of sex and the snippets of online porn he'd watched with the sound off underneath his covers.

Except Kelly realized that since almost the moment they'd met—as Rose had said—by that definition Walter had *been* his boyfriend, except for the kissing and sex. The weirdest part was how slowly the kissing-and-sex bit was getting folded into their dynamic.

Kelly had assumed that Walter—sexually experienced, I-cut-my-teeth-on-Tom-of-Finland Walter—would try and take him to bed that first night they got back to Hope, and Kelly had been frantically processing whether or not he was ready for that. The very idea that

Walter would move *more slowly* than Kelly wanted had completely stunned him.

They made out on the futon—but that was it, kisses and a bit of groping. At first, Kelly assumed this was them going slow, Walter being noble or something. Except instead of adding to their repertoire of making out, Walter seemed to be cutting it off. He was staying out late too, as if he was avoiding Kelly. It made him nervous.

So he talked to Rose.

"You should be talking to him, not me," was what she said.

Kelly didn't dignify that remark with an answer, simply stared at her over his breakfast tray.

Rose sighed and rolled her eyes. "I know. But it *is* what you should do."

"You're telling me, with a straight face, that I should sit Walter Lucas—*Walter Lucas*—down on his futon and tell him I'd like us to talk about our relationship?"

"Fine. You're right, that would never work." She moved her empty tray to the side and cradled her coffee cup in her hands. "So let's review. You went to see him at Thanksgiving break."

"All I did was ask for a ride back. It was legit, because my family's car broke down."

She nodded. "Right, good point. So he turned *can I get a ride* into *let's go out on the town.* He took you to Boystown, out to pizza, out shopping, and to a gay bar."

"He tried to buy me this crazy expensive vintage

leather coat first. That was when we started fighting."

"Interesting." Rose leaned back in her chair. "You fought over him buying you the coat?"

Kelly nodded. "I was going crazy, because I'd realized just how much I care about him while I was away, and I was trying to be good and not let it show. But he takes me on a freaking date, then tries to buy me things. Then, while I'm almost rigid from trying to resist him, he takes me to a gay bar—and gets mad when I dance with other guys."

"That's when he put on your favorite song and made out with you on the dance floor."

"Right."

Rose raised an eyebrow. "This is pretty textbook fairy tale so far, hon."

"Yeah, well, I'm starting to realize they're leaving out a hell of a lot, ending at the kiss in the castle window."

"Less Disney and more *Shrek*." Rose sipped her coffee. "Obviously things have not been all HEA since the bar kiss. Give me the lowdown on that."

Kelly told her about the ride home to Northbrook, about Walter running hot and cold and freaking out. "He said he didn't know how to behave. He was all wigged out, and he wouldn't stop, so I kissed him. Then we went back to his house, watched *Enchanted* on his bed, then made out and went to sleep. There was this weird stuff with his mom the next morning. I still don't understand everything that happened, but that's when he shut down. I came down to breakfast, and it was like I'd caught him trying to brick himself in. His mom was crying—crazy crying—in her bedroom. I guess that happens a lot." He stirred his hash browns with his fork. "He's always so cool and snarky. He wasn't then. Not even on that map. It broke my heart. I tried to help, got him to talk a little."

"But he's been weird since then? Putting that wall back up?"

Kelly nodded. "It sucks, because he's more distant now than ever. In the car on the way back, I thought we'd be fine, but now that we're back, it's changed again, and not to what we were before Boystown. It makes me mad that he kissed me, that we started on this, because I'd rather have our old way than nothing." He put down his fork, feeling suddenly sick. "God, I had a boyfriend for three-point-five seconds, didn't I? And now I've lost my best friend too."

"Jesus. *Stop.*" She took his hand. "You haven't lost him. But, sweetie, you're going to have to talk to him. Ask him what's going on."

"I can't! Don't you get it? I did that. It's when he got super frosty." He sank back in his chair, his stomach making him sorry he'd eaten at all. "Anyway, he keeps ignoring me. He's out late. He was great the first few days too, but now he's all reserved. How can I live with him and hardly see him, especially in my shitty-small room?"

"Make a date with him. Stay up late or text him or something and get him to commit to Friday night. Even if you don't want to talk to him, go do something together. Or hell, just fuck."

Kelly snorted. "That'd be nice, but I'm not holding

my breath."

Rose gave him a look that told him, quite plainly, that he was being pitiful. "Try getting naked. I bet that will get things started without much additional effort."

Kelly gasped. "I couldn't!"

"So you won't talk to your boyfriend and find out what's wrong, and you won't seduce him." She picked up her tray and stood. "Good luck with that, Minnesota."

WALTER KNEW THIS thing with Kelly was a bad idea—he'd known it since the moment he'd realized the only way to be with Kelly was to date him. Somehow in Chicago that certainty had slipped. He couldn't do this. He couldn't be a boyfriend. He *especially* couldn't be Kelly's boyfriend.

Except he couldn't break up either, because it would break Kelly's heart. Which meant he was fucked. *Fucked.* Fucked, and nobody but nobody could help him get out of the hole he'd dug for himself.

Certainly not Cara. *Jesus.* Walter had called her up, given her the backstory, and from then on all Cara heard was that Walter was dating someone and wasn't that so sweet that they were both hooked up now. She refused to see the problem, and the more he tried to explain it to her, the more tense their conversation became until he had no choice but to hang up on her.

Which was awkward, because before they'd gotten to the Kelly part of the conversation, he'd agreed to be her First Attendant—the millennial version of best man/maid of honor. He'd be paired with Greg's sister, their only other attendant. Walter was genuinely eager to be that for her too, which made their fighting One More Goddamned Thing he had to deal with.

That, at least, he could talk about with Williams.

"I was afraid of this," the professor said, reaching into the bag of microwave popcorn Walter had brought over for them to share. "I'd hoped with you and Cara it would be different, but given how many factors you're up against, that was probably foolish on my part."

"Factors?" Walter prompted.

"Yes. First," Williams began, ticking the incidents off on his fingers, "you have the fact that you're still in college and she's not. It's a milder but significant version of that break you have after high school with your peers. You might have had an easier time if you'd graduated together and moved to the same town, but even then you'd be making adjustments. It's the same kind of mental makeover everyone does at semester and summer break. Ever notice how everyone comes back with some new article of clothing or haircut or *some* physical marker of change? It's as if we have to mark the cycles with something physical, but if you really watch people, you'll see they change internally at those moments too. Little cycles get little change. Big cycles get big change."

This wasn't exactly helping. "I don't see how this explains why Cara's suddenly turned into a bitch."

"She's female and she's joining the biggest, fattest relationship cult we have as a culture. I've seen it fell the most counter-cultural of women. Even if they don't get swept up in it, they expel fantastic amounts of energy rejecting the pull to succumb to the bride lure. So what I'm saying is that between all the different things hitting Cara, and you, it's frankly a miracle you're still speaking at all."

"Golly, Dr. Williams, you really know how to cheer a guy up."

Williams rolled his eyes and took the popcorn into his lap. "It's not like things can't turn around. All relationships take work and patience. So." He paused to munch a handful of popcorn, but the waggle in his eyebrows told Walter what was coming. "Speaking of relationships."

Walter sighed and stole the popcorn bag back. "Please. Not you too."

"Are you kidding? Even the professors are talking about it, how the nice young man from Minnesota charmed Casanova."

Walter rubbed at his temples. "I thought you were trying to play nice for the tenure people. Doesn't asking about your student's sex life count as a no-no on that count?"

"I didn't ask about your sex life. I asked about your relationship with Kelly. Big difference." He helped himself to a liberal handful of popcorn. "But if you're feeling fragile, I don't want to push you."

Had there been sarcasm in that tone, Walter could have handled it. He put the popcorn bag on the desk and gave in with a slouch. "I'm not fragile. Things are just...weird." He sighed and rubbed at the bridge of his nose. "Never mind. I should stick to not thinking about it. Keep busy with something."

"Well, that's always been a popular strategy in your book. You've ever been the shark that has to keep swimming to avoid death, at least in your own mind."

Walter raised his eyebrow at that, then decided he'd dissect that one in the privacy of his own head later. "I can't date him, Williams. I'm not a dating kind of guy, no matter what Cara thinks."

"Why do you say that?"

"Why can't I date? Jesus, where do I start?" Walter trained his focus into the popcorn bag, into the half-burned kernels at the bottom. "For one, I have no idea how to do it."

"From what I gather, neither does Kelly."

Walter glared at him. "Right, so he deserves some-one who isn't stumbling around in the dark. Plus, he's a virgin in every way. I'm so far from that it's not even funny."

"But you care about him."

Williams was staring hard at Walter, and it made him twitch. "Of course I do. Don't you get it? That's why I have to find a way to end this. Before he gets hurt."

Now Williams frowned. "Don't you think that's up to Kelly to decide?" His gaze turned knowing. "Unless, of course, the concern for Kelly is just a front."

For a second Walter stared at him blankly—then frowned as he cottoned on. "Get off. This isn't about me."

"Isn't it?" Williams laced his fingers together, rest-ing his elbows on the arms of his chair.

Walter flipped him off. "*Please*. What, you think I'm scared?"

Except that was supposed to come out a lot stronger than it did, and the crack at the end of the question didn't do him any damn favors.

He shut his eyes. "I want to do right by him. I don't want to fuck him up. I don't want him to end up like me, especially by being with me."

The hand on top of his head surprised him, and he held still as Williams gave his hair a gentle tussle before withdrawing again. "Walter, someday I hope you're able to look back at the man you were at this moment and realize how proud you should have been of yourself." When Walter gaped at him, Williams grinned. "Yeah, Lucas. I just rubbed your head and called you a good boy. Get over it. You deserved it."

Walter reached for more popcorn. His cheeks, he knew, were as flushed and bright as Kelly's were wont to be. "So, this tenure shit. When are they going to let you off the short leash so you can chill out?"

"Last day of finals week." Williams slumped back into his chair. "God, I think I'm going to go out and get drunk, either way it rolls."

"It's going to be fine. You told me yourself, they have to have a really damn good reason to deny you, and if they try, you already have that in with the AAUP. You're worrying over nothing."

"I sure hope so." Williams reached for the popcorn bag, but he didn't take any, just flicked the edge of the wrapper and sat back again. "I sure hope so."

THE FRIDAY NIGHT after their return to campus, Kelly sat in the green rocker waiting for Walter to make it back from class. In the hall were muffled male curses and guffaws as their floor mates prepared for a night of partying, but in room 412, Sia's *We Are Born* album played softly from Kelly's laptop speakers. He stared at the underside of his loft while he rocked back and forth.

He'd set up a date as Rose suggested, and any second now Walter was due back to the room. At which point Kelly had to figure out what to do with him. He kept trying to think of how best to start the *let's have more sex* conversation, because it was the only one that felt safe. Except he had no idea, and the more he thought about it, the more knotted his stomach became.

When the door finally opened and Walter came inside, Kelly turned to smile at him, hoping for last-minute divine intervention. He got a good look at Walter, and his smile died.

"Hey." He sat up in the rocker. "What's wrong?"

It was a little surreal to watch Walter wipe his face clean of the heaviness Kelly had glimpsed there. "Nothing." He nudged Kelly with his toe. "What do you want to do tonight? Stay in? Go out? Watch online porn?"

The last one was tossed out to make Kelly blush, he knew—and distract him, Kelly realized. Walter didn't like that Kelly had caught him vulnerable.

Which was maybe why Kelly said, "Sure, porn sounds good."

Walter paused, backpack suspended over the futon. Glancing over his shoulder, he raised his eyebrows at Kelly. Kelly knew he was blushing, but he kept his expression as even as possible. Something was up with Walter, but Walter wasn't telling him. Something told Kelly it was all related to the sex thing. Or maybe that was just his ego.

Whatever. He was tired of being a predictable virgin. Watching online porn with his boyfriend seemed out of that territory. He was going for it.

Drawing his laptop into his lap, Kelly tried to play it casual. "You have anything particular in mind?"

"Why, do you?"

Walter was laughing at him, Kelly could tell—and it irked him. Kelly said nothing, only opened the locked Word document in the folder he kept very deliberately buried, retrieving a few web addresses and loading them into his browser. "This site isn't always great, but it has a few of my favorites."

His heart pounded as the Man Hub video began to load—at the last second he remembered to turn down the volume, just in time for the bartender to tell his waiter friend to "Suck on it." It was loud enough still for Walter to hear, however, and though Kelly kept his gaze on the screen, he trained one eye on Walter, watching his roommate come around to stand behind Kelly. For a minute they stayed that way, Kelly with the porn going in his lap, Walter behind him. Kelly waited for a wry comment, for Walter to tease him.

What actually happened was that Walter squeezed Kelly's shoulder and said, "Scoot forward, hon."

Kelly did. It wasn't easy, because moving forward on the chair made it rock with him, but Walter caught the back and pulled with counter force until it was his body keeping the chair in place. His groin bumped against Kelly's ass. Walter took the laptop from Kelly with one hand and nudged Kelly's thigh with his other, helping Kelly climb into his lap. When Kelly settled down, it was to sit in the center of Walter's crotch.

He eased back against Walter's chest. He still watched the screen, but all his focus was on Walter— Walter's body around him, Walter's reactions. How Walter slid a hand down Kelly's thigh, lightly stroking. Kelly assumed he watched the show, but he didn't know for sure until Walter said, "This is one of your favorites?"

"Yeah." Kelly felt his cheeks burn, but he didn't let self-consciousness get the better of him.

Walter kept stroking. His voice was soft, gentle as he spoke. "What is it you like?"

Kelly considered a minute. "The production value. It's not harsh lighting and raw." He watched the waiter crawl over a barstool, taking the bartender's cock into his mouth. "It's not teasing, though, either. It's a guy getting his cock sucked." He remembered the rest of the video, what was coming up next, and his own cock got a little harder. "And rimmed."

Walter's stubble brushed Kelly's ear. "I didn't know you had rimming fantasies, Red."

He did. Kelly was pretty sure that would feel amazing. "They do get the internet in Minnesota, you know."

Walter's free hand had been sliding up Kelly's arm, but as Kelly spoke it stopped, and so did Walter's ear nuzzles. Kelly sensed he'd stumbled on the reason Walter had been hesitant with him. The trouble was, he didn't understand it, not completely.

"Walter," he said, giving up. "What's going on?" The thought he'd been trying not to think rose, and it escaped before he could reel it back in. "Are you sorry we did this? Dating?"

"No." Walter said the word with such conviction Kelly couldn't doubt, but he still seemed tense. He sighed and rested his head against Kelly's. "I'm not sorry—but I worry you should be. Or will be." He stroked Kelly's arm sadly. "You deserve better."

Kelly turned too, so Walter could see the irritation on his face. "What am I supposed to say to that?"

A loud groan came from the laptop. "*Yeah, suck that cock,*" the bartender said. "*Next I'm gonna rim that ass.*"

Kelly blinked, glanced at Walter, and they fell against each other, laughing, nearly sending the laptop to the floor.

"Okay," Walter said between giggles. "I admit it. That was stupid." He pulled Kelly back against him, righting the computer at the same time. "I just…I suck at this, Kel."

"Well, it's not as if I would know." Onscreen, the bartender stuck his hand down the back of the waiter's pants, and Kelly drew in a sharp breath. "God. I love that part."

"That's just it. You *should* know. You shouldn't

settle for me."

The waiter gasped and jerked as the hand at his backside—one assumed—found pay dirt. Kelly bit his lip and resisted the urge to adjust himself. "You do realize that you're trying to talk about our relationship, and I'm getting uncomfortable in my pants while I watch porn? I haven't had Psych 101, but I think this is role reversal."

Walter said nothing after that, and Kelly was free to watch as the waiter's moans became more and more desperate, as the waistband dipped lower and lower. There were several nice cock shots too of the bartender—he was shaved because it was that kind of porn video, but Kelly didn't think he'd have cared either way. What really had his attention was the fact that, though he'd watched this video a million times, this was the only instance where he was in another guy's lap while he did so.

Walter was quiet, and mostly still, his hands brushing over Kelly's skin on occasion. His breath was hot against Kelly's neck, coming a little bit faster now, and the bulge pressing the back of Kelly's ass got bigger all the time. They watched as the blow job continued, as the waiter's pants slid farther and farther down his ass.

When the scene shifted to the waiter leaned over the bar, buck naked save his socks, knees wide as the bartender spread his cheeks apart, Walter jolted. "Shit."

Kelly glanced over his shoulder. "You're not going to convince me this is hardcore for you."

"No." Walter had a funny look on his face, half-wary, half…hopeful? He was still so hard to read. "I would have assumed it was for you, though."

Now Kelly glared. "Who do you think I am? No wait, don't answer, because I know. I'm a repressed Republican from Mayberry who thinks sex happens in the dark with the lights off to swoony orchestral soundtracks. Jesus. *I'm not.* Just because I blush frequently doesn't mean I don't want sex or that I need it pretty. Just because I'm a virgin doesn't mean I need everything watered down. I mean—you were a virgin once too. Maybe you were looking at Tom of Finland when you were thirteen, but you weren't getting rimmed." He paused and added, "Were you?"

The way Walter's expression shuttered told Kelly he'd stepped in something, but he didn't know what. He tried to cover with self-depreciation and a rueful laugh. "Okay, maybe you were. My point is that even though I'm a late bloomer, at some point you were a virgin too, and you had to learn—"

"My first time was with a guy who could have been my dad."

Kelly stopped laughing, the porn soundtrack behind them suddenly not so awesome. Kelly turned fully, trying to get a better read of Walter's face. It wasn't easy. "Was that good or bad? I mean—" *Shit, Kelly, shut up.* "Were you…forced?"

The corner of Walter's mouth quirked up. "No. At the time I thought I was hot shit, doing it with a thirty-year-old. There was nothing rape about it, not as far as I was concerned. Legality of course is another story altogether. The guy took a horrible risk. Really, he was as fucked up as I was. I didn't think that at the time. I thought I was the fucking coolest kid on the block. I didn't just have sex with him, either. I had a lot of great times and in some pretty crazy places. I took stupid, *stupid* risks." He rubbed the line of his jaw and averted his gaze. "That's what I mean, when I say I don't think I'm right for you. You wouldn't ever do anything like that. I did. Until a few months ago, I still was doing shit, albeit in a safer, more grownup way."

Kelly threw up his hands. "So you're saying you don't want to be with me unless I go out and have stupid sex first?"

"What? *No.*" Walter glared at him. "I don't want you to *ever* do anything so dangerous."

"So I can't be with you because I'm pure and you're tainted? Who has the Disney fetish now?"

"Kelly, that's not what I mean. I'm telling you I'm fucked up. You aren't fucked up. You shouldn't do this. If you came to me as a friend and asked if you should date a guy like me, I'd say hell no."

Kelly went cold. "Are you breaking up with me?"

His heart tightened as Walter hesitated. The whole world came into sharper focus, and for a moment Kelly wanted to run, hide, to cry. Just for one moment. Because the moment after that, he got pissed.

Fuck this.

Grabbing the laptop from Walter's hand, Kelly closed it and set it aside before turning back to face Walter. "Here's the deal. I'm going to make out with somebody tonight. Someone's going to get their hand down my pants and their tongue down my throat. Who knows what else comes after. You get to decide,

boyfriend, if that's you or some random guy at Moe's."
When Walter gave him a dubious look, Kelly only got
angrier. "Don't test me. I'm serious."

"You wouldn't make out with a stranger. That's not
who you are."

"Then I'm going to become that guy, and fast."
Kelly dug his fingers into the leg of his jeans. "That's
why you've been weird. You have this stupid idea about
who I am, and you're writing me off."

"I don't have a stupid idea about who you are—*you*
don't know who *I* am. You don't want me, Kelly. You
don't—"

He didn't get to say anything else because Kelly cut
him off with a hard kiss. All his anger, his hurt, his fear
went into it, and when he finally came up for air, he
was shaking.

"I want you, Walter. I don't care who you slept
with or how old you were or they were or anything. I
don't care if you're the rimming champion of Illinois. I
want you. For more than holding hands." He nuzzled
Walter's nose. "You're right, I couldn't do it with a
stranger. But it's not because I don't want to make out
or am afraid of it. It's that I want it to be with you." He
felt Walter try to pull away, and Kelly panicked at the
thought that he'd called his own bluff. "That doesn't
mean I'm not going to bully you into making out with
me."

Walter paused, half smiling. "Oh? This I want to
see."

Kelly thought fast. "If you don't make out with me,
I'll go down to the vending machines in the lounge and

buy a Hershey's bar. With almonds."

Walter stopped smiling. "That isn't even funny."

"I'll do it. I swear to God." He'd end up in the hospital, but hopefully it didn't come to that.

"I'll take your money."

"I'll borrow some from the RA."

Walter cupped Kelly's cheek, and it wasn't gentle. "I'll lock you in our room."

"How? I can open it from the inside."

Those fingers dug into Kelly's skin. "I'll hold you down."

Kelly's whole body went soft in Walter's arms and filled with want. "Okay."

The rigidity in Walter's face softened a little, but he still gripped Kelly tight. "Kelly."

Sensing an opening in Walter's wall, Kelly went at it with everything he had in him. "I'm not a Disney princess in a castle. I'm—" He fumbled as he tried to think of an appropriate metaphor. "I'm Luke Skywalker wanting to get it on with Han Solo." They'd been bought by Disney. The metaphor held.

Walter laughed, and his hand slid down to Kelly's neck. "You're so much hotter than Mark Hamill."

Kelly shifted in Walter's lap, trying to figure out an elegant way to maneuver into a straddle. There wasn't one. He gave up and put Walter's free hand on his hip.

Walter kneaded it. "Is this your way of telling me you want to play waiter and bartender?"

Kelly nodded, feeling his ears heat. "But if you say one more word about me being too precious to make out with, it's milk chocolate and almonds."

Chuckling, Walter bent to nuzzle Kelly's cheek. "Now you're just begging to be tied up."

He paused though, and Kelly knew they'd shifted back into that same stupid space. "Have you done that? Tied someone up?"

"I was tied up. Once." He nuzzled again.

Kelly thought about Walter tied up, and he shivered. Deliciously. He sure hoped that wasn't one of those bad/good memories. "Was it fun? Because I've always thought it sounded fun—with the right person." Walter didn't answer, which wasn't great because the image of Walter bound and naked was wreaking havoc with Kelly's ability to be patient and understanding. "I don't know if that right person would be me, with you, but God, I bet that was hot."

The hand on Kelly's hip tightened, and when Walter nuzzled Kelly's neck, Kelly felt the dampness of his boyfriend's lips. "I couldn't let you tie me up, not when you're threatening to eat that candy bar."

"If you were tied up, I'd forget all about death by almonds in chocolate." Kelly gasped as Walter's mouth opened over his neck, and he clutched at Walter even as his legs went slack and his thighs parted. Somehow he'd ended up lying prone in Walter's arms.

Walter kissed his way along Kelly's jaw, his hand tracing the outline of Kelly's hip. "You've gone all limp noodle. Like overcooked ramen."

Not all of me, no. Kelly found Walter's hand and moved it—somewhat awkwardly—over the non-limpness in question. Walter lifted his head, his eyes wary and lustful at the same time.

Kelly forced Walter's hand to knead him. "How about you eat me up?"

God, but it cost him every ounce of courage he had to be that bold, and for a moment he worried it had been for nothing. Walter looked almost stricken. *Fuck,* Kelly thought, and made his cock twitch under Walter's hand.

Walter paused, then kneaded his palm.

Kelly gasped and rocked up into Walter's touch.

They stilled, gazes locked. Walter seemed to be doing some sort of deep internal wrestling, and Kelly tried to think of what he could say to push Walter over the edge.

Then it occurred to him that perhaps he shouldn't say anything at all.

Letting go of Walter's hand, he flicked open the button of his jeans and carefully undid the zipper. Face beet red, heart thudding so hard against the wall of his chest it hurt, Kelly took up Walter's hand again, drew it to his waistband, and lowered it inside.

Chapter Nineteen

WALTER'S HAND ON his cock was the most amazing thing Kelly had ever felt in his life.

He bucked up into it, but when Walter's fingers shifted, getting a better grip on him, his legs went limp again, his stomach flexing. He shut his eyes and turned his face into Walter's shoulder. "Shit," he gasped.

Walter nuzzled Kelly's forehead, nipping at his hair while his hand continued to work steadily on Kelly's dick. Kelly felt like he was a greased fish trying not to flop in his lover's arms, if fish embraced and got stiffies. He tried to be a cool, suave lover, because it was his inexperience that had Walter so spooked. He tried, but it was impossible. Because he'd never had anybody's hand on his cock before, and it felt *so amazing he could die*. He wanted to thrust wantonly into Walter's hand. He wanted to grab Walter's neck and kiss him hard and wet and sloppy. He wanted, more than anything, to let go, not think and just *feel*.

This was what Kelly had thought of sex being: an extension of the movie kiss, of letting go and getting lost in somebody, and his few forays into it so far, that theory was holding water. Except at the same time he was also realizing it wasn't that simple, at least not with

Walter. It wasn't just their heavy, nearly nuclear discussion before he'd successfully gotten Walter's hand into his pants. If Kelly was a greased fish, Walter was a machine operating on halting gears. One minute he'd carry on blowing Kelly's mind, and then he'd stop, his movements retreating and hesitant, as if he'd remembered what he was doing. It was unexpected and strange.

Weirder still, though, was Kelly's growing conviction this wasn't, as he'd initially feared, Walter being awkward because Kelly was a virgin. Whatever this was seemed to be all about Walter. Something that, Kelly had to assume, didn't get in the way when Walter was taking random guys back to their rooms. Something messed up that only came out with Kelly.

It was a backhanded compliment, basically. *I can only be this fucked up in bed with you.* What Kelly couldn't decide was what he should do about it.

He went with instinct, and instinct told him he should under no circumstances let Walter end their make-out session. Which meant he had to be the seducer in this particular scenario, which—well, God help them both.

Kelly decided his first order of business was to get them onto the floor so he could climb on top. If they had a real dorm room, all they'd need to do was kick the rocker out of the way and get busy, but in their crowded space, lying beneath the loft involved bending their knees or contorting into L shapes. If they lay stacked and didn't mind whacking their elbows, they could lie in front of the fridge with their feet toward the door, but it also meant lying on top of the extension cord. Really, the only place to make out was on Walter's bed.

So they'd move there.

Wriggling out of Walter's arms, Kelly stood, grabbed his pants with one hand and Walter's hand with the other. "Come on," he said, out of breath, and hauled Walter over to the futon. When Walter had that look again, like he was going to launch into another lecture about how Kelly should keep himself pure or some other bullshit, Kelly grimaced and shoved his boyfriend onto the mattress. "No talking," he declared. "I'm going to ravish you."

As he'd intended, this made Walter laugh. He relaxed too, easing back onto his elbows and letting his legs fall apart. "Do you even know how?"

Kelly shrugged. "Feel free to offer pointers." When Walter got *that look*, though, Kelly held up a warning finger. "Just remember. One wrong move, and you'll have to figure out where I hid my EpiPen."

But they were right back to annoying noble sacrifice, because Walter sobered. "Kelly," he began.

Kelly pushed his pants to the floor.

He got so embarrassed he was dizzy, but the move was worth it because oh yeah, did Walter shut up. Riding the wave of success, Kelly stripped his T-shirt off too, and before he could retreat into self-consciousness, he climbed on top of Walter, sitting naked on his lap and bracing his hands on either side of Walter's head. Kelly was fully naked, except for his socks, and Walter was fully clothed. Probably he should have simply kissed him and gotten to business, but he couldn't check the compulsion to study his lover's face. Kelly didn't figure it got a whole lot more vulnerable than climbing naked on top of your reluctant partner. He needed reassurance.

Walter's expression was a good start. He appeared to be battling reservation and lust, and lust was winning. His hands skimmed down Kelly's sides, his gaze fixed on Kelly's cock lying erect on Walter's stomach. When he gripped Kelly's hips, Kelly's elbows buckled, and he lowered himself to Walter's mouth.

The kiss was hot and greedy and extra erotic with Walter's hands—no more hesitation, not even a little—roving over Kelly's ass and thighs. Because Kelly had his knees on either side of Walter's legs, his cheeks were spread—he thought of the porn video and the way the bartender fingered and licked the waiter. Just thinking about Walter doing that to him made his balls draw up tight and his dick get so hard he feared he'd come before anything happened. *Focus,* he reminded himself. This had to be about Walter.

At the moment Walter seemed to be doing fine. He had control of the kiss, nibbling and thrusting and making Kelly whimper, but the real stars of the show were Walter's fingers, which were drifting up and down Kelly's crack, teasing closer and closer to his ass. They never made it to the place Kelly wanted them most, though, only came close and only a few times. Eventually Kelly moaned into Walter's mouth, shuddered, and lifted himself enough to speak.

"Please," he begged. "Please, please. Touch me."

Walter's fingers brushed close enough to stimulate the downy hair, but that was all. "What else, baby?" Walter teased again, his mouth mimicking the light touch at Kelly's neck. "How far are we going tonight?"

To the moon and back. Kelly thrust into Walter's belly, the sweet friction sending lightning up his spine. "I want to feel your mouth on me," Kelly whispered. "Your hands on me." His heart thumped hard, an erratic beat that clanged at the back of his throat. "In me."

Walter huffed against Kelly's neck in response, his fingers brushing Kelly's entrance. It made Kelly jolt, whimper, and shiver. When Walter touched him again more deliberately, Kelly turned his head and found Walter's mouth.

He wasn't thinking anymore. He couldn't. All Kelly could do was push back on Walter's fingers and dive into his mouth. He was aware of his nudity, of his hardness scraping the waistband of Walter's jeans, his nipples, hard and pert, brushing hard against Walter's shirt. He wanted more skin, needed it. He pulled off Walter's mouth and leaned back, working at Walter's shirt. The motion, though, had the effect of making him sit on Walter's hand. The tip of the finger that had been teasing him pushed a little ways inside, and Kelly froze, eyes wide and locked on Walter's. When Walter tried to withdraw, Kelly tensed his sphincter and clamped a hand on his arm.

"Don't," he whispered. He clenched again, feeling the finger still there. He shivered, and his cock bobbed with a new swell of blood. "Oh God."

"We need lube." Walter's voice was rough, and it thrilled Kelly.

"Where?" God, that *finger*. It was so different than touching himself. More than anything in the world, Kelly wanted it to push inside. "Where is it?"

Walter jerked his head toward the plastic crate serving as his nightstand. "Tube right there. Black."

Kelly leaned over and pawed through, trying to find it. Walter didn't take his finger out, which was good but distracting, especially when he pushed deeper, making Kelly clench and falter, knocking over the box of tissues. That turned out to be good, because the lube was behind it. Grabbing it, he pulled himself back onto the futon.

Walter had gone quiet, his gaze dark. Kelly wanted to please him, to do whatever he needed to keep this going. Placing the lube on Walter's chest, Kelly's fingers trailed over the T-shirt.

"What should I do?" Kelly asked, aware of that fingertip. He kept his gaze on Walter.

Walter took the lube with his free hand, the other pulling out. Kelly could feel him fumbling from behind, and his cock and balls got heavier thinking about what was coming next. Even anticipating it, though, he gasped and jerked when the slick, cool fingers pressed against him.

Walter laughed, still massaging. "It says it's self-warming, but it's always cold at first." He teased Kelly's opening, and Kelly drew in a sharp breath. Walter watched Kelly's face carefully. "You're okay?"

Not as good as I'll be when you push inside me. "Uh-huh."

Then the finger pushed back in, faster, deeper, slicker, and Kelly lost his mind.

He made soft noises, moved back and forth against Walter, gasping and clutching at the mattress and blindly seeking Walter's mouth. When he found it, he plunged in, kissing him hard and desperate, moaning as Walter began to thrust in and out of him.

It blew Kelly's mind, blew it clean out of his skull. So slick, so hot, so...wicked wonderful he thought he'd die. He took Walter deeper, chasing what he wanted, and eventually he got it—Walter pushed in deep, so deep, tickling him from the inside, seeking, seeking—

Walter's fingers brushed something, something small and wired to every nerve in Kelly's body, and he came unglued.

The kisses became carnal, Kelly whimpering and thrusting with his tongue even as he spread his knees, taking Walter in deeper. Sharper pressure told him a second finger had come into play, and Kelly shook with the joy of it. He grabbed Walter's shoulders and pulled on him, trying to draw him closer, trying to...something, he didn't know, just knew he wanted to eat Walter alive and take him so far inside he couldn't ever get out.

Somehow Kelly ended up on his back—he had one last glimpse of Walter's dark, seriously fucking sexy face before he bent his head and took Kelly's nipple into his mouth. Kelly cried out and clutched at Walter's shoulders, digging in as the fingers inside him started thrusting again, fucking him slowly. Kelly whimpered.

He didn't want slow. He wanted more, harder, deeper—

He didn't realize he'd been yelling that out loud until Walter put a hand over his mouth. "Shh," Walter said, then licked Kelly's nipple, making him cry out. Kelly groaned into Walter's fingers. Walter teased the sensitive tip with his teeth, and Kelly all but arched off the futon. When he came back down, he was shaking.

Walter nuzzled his way to Kelly's pecs. "Too much?" His voice was rough. "Do we need to slow down?"

Kelly wanted to beat him about the head. He settled for pulling on his hair. "No." He did his best to swallow Walter's fingers with his ass. He felt wild, unchained. He felt as if everything he'd waited his whole life for was right here, right in front of him, and he longed to grab it and never let it go. He yanked Walter's mouth to his and gave him a carnal kiss before whispering against his mouth, "Fuck me. Please. *Please.*"

Walter kissed him back hard, but when he lifted his head, he said, "No." Kelly dug his fingers in, but Walter pinned him with his forehead. "Shh. Not yet."

"Walter, *you have to.*" Kelly was whining, but he didn't even care. He bit Walter's bottom lip.

Walter let him, then caught Kelly's upper lip and treated it in kind. "I want to go slow."

"*I don't.* I've gone slow enough." Kelly let out a frustrated breath. "Why are you doing this to me? Why will you fuck everyone else but not me?"

"Because you matter." Walter ducked his head and

nuzzled Kelly's ear, but it wasn't sexy. More needy, insecure. "You matter so much, Kelly."

Too stunned to reply, all Kelly could do was kiss Walter back.

The kiss went on and on, slow and sultry, a banked fire. Kelly felt dizzy, but only a little of it was what Walter did to him. Most of the spinning inside his head was what he'd heard. *You matter so much, Kelly.* Even remembered, the words made Kelly melt.

He slid his hands inside Walter's shirt, needing to feel his skin—he traced his hands down Walter's chest, over Walter's back, into his waistband. *You matter. You matter.* He fumbled with Walter's fly, trying to be suave, trying to be quick too so Walter couldn't tell him no—Walter didn't say no. He lifted his hips to give Kelly better access. But he never broke contact with Kelly's mouth.

He hissed when Kelly took him in hand, his fingers pushing in a little deeper. Thrusting into Kelly's grip, he broke from Kelly's mouth, breathing hard. Kelly kept stroking him.

"Tell me you want to, at least," Kelly whispered. "That you want to fuck me."

In answer, Walter nipped his neck. "Like you wouldn't believe." He sucked at Kelly's ear, moving his fingers and hips in time to each other. "I meant to blow you tonight. I meant to make it amazing, but you keep making me lose my focus, you're so hot."

Kelly shut his eyes and thrust too—his penis was caught between the back of his hand and Walter's cock in a snug little pocket. God, he bet they'd feel good together. "I want to blow you too. I want to do every-thing." He brushed a breathy kiss against Walter's hair. "Mostly I want you to never tell me we shouldn't do this, ever again." He paused. "I'm not sure that came out right."

"I know what you meant. And I promise. You're too good and I'm too bad. If you're this determined that I corrupt you, I can't say no, only drag it out a little." Walter nipped his ear, then drew on the lobe. "Get the lube beside me on the bed. Put some in your hand and grab us both together."

Oh yeah, that was a plan. Kelly fumbled to com-ply—tricky, one-handed. "You have too many clothes on."

Walter laughed, a low, dark sound. "It's hot, having my clothes on with you naked."

"Except for socks," Kelly pointed out, and rubbed one against the back of Walter's shin.

"That's my favorite part." Walter lifted up as Kelly slipped a lubed-up hand between them. As Kelly took their cocks in hand, Walter winced and abruptly pulled out of Kelly.

"Hey," Kelly complained, pausing mid-stroke.

"One moment please." Walter shimmied as he wig-gled his jeans over his ass. Then he sighed in relief. "Okay. You were right, less clothes. A zipper on my balls does not sexy make."

Kelly laughed, though he stopped when Walter's fingers found him again. "Ooh."

"Ooh, indeed." Walter thrust inside Kelly's grip. "Keep it nice and tight, baby. Nice and tight."

Kelly did, though he kept losing his concentration as Walter's fingers worked their magic inside him. He was distracted, too, by the discovery that Walter's bare ass was open and available for fondling. Teasing Walter's crack elicited the same jerky-shaking reactions that the action did in Kelly. Inspired, Kelly let go of their cocks, did a quick lube up behind Walter's back, then put both his hands back at their respective stations.

Holy shit, was Walter hot inside. And man, did he jump when Kelly wriggled in.

Walter laughed too, and that was how they fumbled toward release: laughing, gasping, thrusting, and kissing, until first Kelly then Walter seized up and went over the edge. They glued themselves together with their semen and lay spent, the air smelling of musk and sweat and sex. It was glorious.

Kelly stared up at the ceiling, smiling and stroking a still-panting Walter lying sprawled over his chest. "I did it. I had sex."

Walter lifted his head up at that, grinning too. "You did. And you did it very well."

Kelly nipped at his nose. "I want to do it again."

Walter laughed, but weakly, and he fell back down. "Give me a few hours, okay?"

They gave it about six. They cleaned up together, brushed their teeth, made a quick visit to the bathroom, and snuggled back in Walter's futon together. Usually he slept with it as a couch, but they opened it up full, pushing the fridge and dresser against the door so they could lie together. Though they fell right to sleep, Kelly woke in the middle of the night to find Walter kissing his chest. Their eyes met.

Walter smiled, laced his fingers against Kelly's and trailed his mouth down Kelly's sternum, carrying on toward his waist.

When Walter's mouth closed over him, Kelly cried out so loudly he had to smother himself with Walter's pillow to keep the whole floor from hearing him. *Oh my God* but it felt good. He whimpered, he arched, he begged and murmured incoherently. When Walter added a lube-slicked finger to the orchestra, Kelly came like he'd been on a trigger. Right into Walter's mouth.

Not only did Walter not even balk, but he still had a little spunk on his lips when he came up to kiss Kelly. And that was so crazy hot he felt as if he could come again.

He didn't. He went back to sleep, drowsily protesting he wanted to give as well as he received, but Walter just smiled, stroked his hair and promised he could do that and then some in the morning.

It was a promise Kelly fully intended to keep.

Chapter Twenty

WALTER STILL WASN'T sure it was wise to let things keep going with Kelly, but since Kelly's standard response to Walter's doubt was to get naked, it was getting harder and harder to resist. He was developing a full-on association: relationship doubt equaled getting laid. It all got confused in his head, and eventually he gave up and went with it.

It was nice, really, so long as he didn't let himself think about all the ways dating, especially dating Kelly, was a bad idea. When he focused on the right now, not the potential hell to come, things were great. Trouble was, Walter had never been a fan of the now. He liked to peer several miles down the road and see what was coming.

Of course, his now had an enthusiastic boyfriend determined to master the fine art of blow jobs. Now had a lot going for it.

Cara continued to plan out Walter's wedding for him in addition to her own, which was annoying, but after Williams's comments, Walter began to understand a bit better. Williams also seemed to be nudging Walter toward something serious with Kelly, but his endgame was harder to predict. Walter understood the next

Philosophy Club meeting topic had been picked just for him—the moral philosophy of Jane Austen—but he couldn't understand why. Perhaps it had been simply a nod to Walter's report of how lost and frustrated Kelly had been at November's meeting—prepping Kelly for the discussion was as simple as queuing up the right film adaptations on his laptop.

They took a week to work through them, starting with *Pride and Prejudice* because Kelly loved the Keira Knightley version, unsurprisingly. They read a bit of the novel together too, Walter pointing out passages he thought would get brought up at the meeting. They took on *Sense and Sensibility* next, because the Emma Thompson adaptation was so exquisite and the book was Walter's favorite, and then, feeling they were ready, Walter took them to *Mansfield Park*.

"This one is a little boring," Kelly admitted as they settled in.

Walter smiled and nipped playfully at his hair. "BBC production values aren't often *Doctor Who*. There are other adaptations, but they aren't half as accurate to the text." He nodded at the screen. "*Mansfield Park* will get a lot of billing at the discussion. It's Williams's favorite, plus it has a lot of the romance stripped out. Which obviously will make it not your top story, but it means you can easier see the moral aspects. Fanny is your guide through this world: watch how everyone engages with her and what happens to them through the whole of the movie. *Mansfield* is thick with human foibles and consequences for bad choices. Watch too how Edmund helps her, and what happens because of that."

They watched in silence for some time, first Kelly snug in Walter's arms, but after a break to use the bathroom and brew coffee, they settled in with Kelly in front of Walter, Walter leaned back with Kelly's head pillowed against his chest.

Kelly hated Mrs. Norris just as Walter thought he would. He frowned at her trying to block Fanny getting a horse, but when she planned to plunk her at home while they all went off in the barouche, Kelly lost it.

"She's such a bitch!"

Walter caught his hand and stroked his wrist soothingly. "Some of it is of the times. There was something of an excuse of separating Fanny from the other girls, because she was of such a lower social status."

"Yes, but how is that okay? They treat her like a drudge. They go too far."

"They do, which I suspect you were meant to notice."

"I hate Mary. She's a snake. Edmund and Fanny should be together."

That did surprise Walter. "Usually modern readers and viewers want to see Mary and Edmund together, because Mary is a bit of a roguish Elizabeth Bennet."

"She's too mean. Edmund is being led by his nose. Fanny is better."

When Mary began to monopolize Fanny's mare, Kelly threw up his hands.

"See? *Bitch*. God, and Lady Bertram is a dingbat. Edmund is too, when he's under Mary's influence. Otherwise he's so good to her."

Walter reached back and stroked Kelly's hair and neck.

It was a long movie, more a miniseries in fact, and once Kelly got over the slower pacing, he seemed to settle in. It was interesting to track his empathy—he hated both Crawfords, despite the fact that Walter still bet Henry saw his share of young men when in London, and to engage a rather specific kind of billiards. Kelly was sorry for poor, fat, clumsy Mr. Rushworth, declaring Maria should have been glad to have him. While the play didn't strike him as particularly awful, he didn't care for them pressuring Fanny, and he got very upset at Maria and Henry's kiss backstage. He groaned at Edmund and Mary making Fanny read for them together.

When the movie ended, with Fanny and Edmund properly matched, with Maria shamed and Mary shunned, at least by Edmund, they lay side by side on the futon, talking.

"I feel a little bad for Maria," Kelly confessed. "She was a spoiled princess, but I wouldn't wish her that kind of ruin. And of course that jerk Henry got away with the whole thing."

"That was the times." Walter stroked his arms. "You don't regret poor Mary being turned off, just for wishing for what is now modern sentiment?"

"No. She only ever used Fanny."

"Wouldn't she have been improved, for being helped along by him?"

"I suppose." Kelly trailed his fingers over Walter's own, tangling his hand beneath, pressed his ring into

Walter's palm. "The thing is, you could tell right off they were supposed to be together, Fanny and Edmund."

Red was full of twists and turns, wasn't he? "So if Austen had opened with Mary and Edmund, you'd have rooted for them?"

"God, I don't know. Maybe." He rubbed his ring again, nudging it against Walter's palm. "Except it wouldn't have worked. It's the same as Fanny with Henry. She was smart the whole time—okay, so maybe having a fit about a play is stupid now, but God, look what they all did with it. Really, she carried it all off, being the moral example even when Sir Bertram had lost his way. She deserved the happy ending."

Walter smiled and turned around in their embrace, which meant he lay on his back while Kelly loomed over him. "You do realize you're dating Henry Crawford. Minus the infidelity."

"What? I am not." Kelly tweaked his nose. "I'm dating Elizabeth Bennet, thank you very much."

Walter laughed. "Does that make you Darcy?"

"God, no. I'm afraid I'm Colonel Brandon. Not a fine match on your end, Elizabeth."

Walter stroked Kelly's cheek. "No. You're Edward Ferrars. And I think I've made a perfect match."

This earned him a kiss, and then another—and they stopped talking philosophy or anything else, after that.

THEY SPENT THE last days of finals week making out

and mapping potential scenarios for visitation over break, deciding they wouldn't commit to anything specific until they'd been to their respective houses and taken stock of familial crises. At the very least, they'd meet up for New Year's Eve and hang out the rest of break if they could.

Kelly left on Wednesday of finals week because he didn't have anything set for Thursday and his dad could get away to pick him up. The three of them went to Opie's for vegan-cheese pizza and what ended up being a quiet interviewing of Walter by Dick. This embarrassed Kelly, though when they made their private goodbyes later, Walter said he enjoyed it.

"I never thought I'd be the guy being grilled by an overprotective father for anything. I loved that he didn't give a damn that I was gay but wanted to know if I was good enough for you."

"You are. You're more than good enough." Kelly sighed when Dick tooted the horn. "We have to get going. I'll text you, okay?"

Walter kissed him, long and lingering. "Go on. Don't let your father blame me for making you late."

Kelly got into the car, Walter's kiss still burning on his lips.

Immediately, he realized something was wrong.

In hindsight something had been going on all afternoon, something that had nothing to do with Walter. When Kelly saw how much whatever it was bothered his dad, he found he was afraid to get the details.

Despite this, they weren't in the car five minutes

before Kelly turned in his seat and said, "Dad, what's going on?"

Dick's mouth flattened into a thin line before he expelled a heavy breath and said, "It looks as if your mom's going to lose her job."

The news hit Kelly in the center of his chest. "What?" His mom worked in a small independent insurance office with the owner and their shared secretary. "You mean Gary's going to run the place on his own? He's what, seventy?"

"That's just it. He's looking to retire and sell the business. We can't afford to buy it. Likely the business will get absorbed by another firm. Maybe they will take your mother, maybe they won't."

Kelly stared at the dash, the hollowness in his chest slowly expanding. "Let me guess: there's not much work for insurance adjusters in Windom."

"Not so much, no. She's got her ear to the ground, but she's trying to play it cool in case Gary doesn't sell or she can end up keeping her job. I asked at the bank, but they frown on spouses both working there, especially when they have differing seniority. It's a long shot anyway, because we don't have much open except the occasional teller, and that doesn't pay what our family needs."

"So are we in trouble for money?"

"Not yet." Dick paused. "I hate to ask this of you, but we're going to have to cut expenses for school as much as we can. And if your mom can't find a job for an extended period of time or she has one with a reduced salary, I'll need you to get a job this summer."

"I can get one now." Kelly tried to think of where he could apply off campus.

"No." Dick's tone brooked no argument. "I want you focused on school. She hasn't lost her job yet, and I don't want your attention divided."

Kelly wanted to argue that he could do both job and school, but he decided he'd look around on his own and see what he came up with. He wanted to punch stupid Gary Johnson in the face for putting them through this. It wasn't as if they had a lot to spare anyway, and now this. He slumped in his seat. "I'm sorry my school is so expensive."

"Don't do that." Dick glanced away from the road to give Kelly a heavy look. "This isn't your fault. I hate that I have to even ask you to help us economize."

"I'm still in this family. Of course I'm going to help."

"You're not to think your school is a problem. The last thing your mother and I want is for you to let this affect your studies. We worked hard to get you to Hope, and we're going to keep you there."

He knew his dad hadn't meant it that way, but Dick's phrasing made Kelly realize if things became bad enough, he'd have to leave Hope. The idea made him feel cold and small.

It wasn't Hope itself, of course, that he'd miss.

Dick reached over and patted Kelly's leg. "No more worrying about it, all right? All there is to do right now is watch our pennies. Christmas will be a bit light on gifts this year, and your mother's been doing some amazing jujitsu with rice and beans for most of our meals, but other than that, nothing has changed."

"I don't need anything for Christmas. Take my stuff back and save the money."

Dick glanced at Kelly over the top of his glasses. "I'll let you try and sell that one to your mother yourself." He turned back to the road. "New conversation. Tell me how your finals and such went, and school. You've been quiet this last month—must have kept you busy, we figured."

Oh, Kelly had been busy. His cheeks stained as he recalled how. "My finals were okay, nothing that bad." He bit his lip, then added, "I think you've figured it out, given the way you interviewed him at Opie's, but Walter and I are dating."

Beaming, Dick reached over and lightly cuffed Kelly's shoulder. "There you go, didn't I say you had to be patient? I know how much you liked him, and he seems as if he's a good young man. Congratulations, son."

"Thanks." Kelly's face was still flushed, though now it was with pride and pleasure at having pleased his father. "We were hoping to get together over break. We hadn't decided if we were going to his place or mine or both—he's insisting on giving me a ride back to school."

"We'd love to have him at the house. We'll talk to your mother about when would be best."

"If it's okay, longer would be better." Kelly hesitated before divulging his next thoughts. "His family life is rough. Parents are divorced, and his mom has a really hard time. He worries about her, but I don't think it's good for him to be there too long, because there's not much he can do to help, and it only tears him up. I'd been kind of thinking if he didn't stay with us from New Year's on, I'd go back with him from whenever we left until school went back on. I think he needs the distraction."

"I'm sure we can work something out, though I'm sorry to hear about his family."

"It's awful. He's started telling me about what goes on there, and it makes me so sad." He shook his head, remembering some of it. "I never realized how lucky I was, having you and Mom as parents."

Dick ruffled Kelly's head, and when he spoke, his voice was gruff. "We're lucky to have such amazing kids, is what."

Kelly leaned into the touch, wishing they weren't in the car so he could hug him properly. He vowed to do so later. "We're going to be okay, Dad. No matter what happens with Mom, we're going to make this work, and we're going to be okay, school and everything."

Dick grinned into the setting sun ahead of them. "Now you're talking like a Davidson."

WALTER TUCKED HIS hands in his pockets and wound his scarf tighter against his face in deference to the cold as he walked back across campus, humming softly to himself. He planned to leave in the morning after his last test, and for the first time in a long time he was almost eager to go. Maybe, if he laid the right seeds, he could finesse Tibby and his mom so their family would

be functional enough to have Kelly over for an extended stay. His sister had a horse show that weekend, he
knew—maybe he'd go, because she'd like that. Maybe
for Christmas he'd take his mom on a date, something
fun and exotic that she couldn't make into a sob story
about how nobody loved her.

Maybe he could fucking pick up the moon and put
it in a gift box. Because he felt so damn good, he
thought maybe he could manage it.

Spying Williams's light on, Walter ducked into
Ritche to wish his advisor a merry Christmas and give
him one last pep talk before the tenure news on Friday.
He heard voices as he approached, and when he came
around the corner, he saw Dr. Holtz, the English
department head, sitting in Walter's usual seat. It was
odd, because Holtz wasn't usually on Williams's staff
hang-out list. When Holtz saw Walter, he stopped
talking.

"Hey, sorry to interrupt," Walter said, leaning into
Williams's office. "Just wanted to wish you—" He got a
good look at Williams's haggard face and cut himself
off. "What happened?"

The two professors exchanged heavy glances, and
Walter tried not to freak out. Eventually Williams gave
Holtz a nod. "Give us a minute?"

Holtz stood. He didn't leave, though, until he'd
put a heavy hand on Williams's shoulder. "I'll make
some of those calls while I'm out."

Walter didn't even bother hiding his anxiety, and
he damn well didn't sit down when Williams offered
him the chair with a haggard gesture.

"What the fuck is going on?" When Williams only continued to look heavy and bleak, as if somebody'd lined up his kids and shot them one by one, Walter began to spin out. "*What?* It's not tenure, I know that, because you said it's Friday, and I know those assholes don't work any faster than they have to."

"It's not tenure. I won't be getting tenure, and I won't be denied it either." Williams kept staring down at his desk, haunted and defeated. "They've cut my position. After the end of the next term, the communications department will merge with Language and Culture, and they're cutting the faculty there down by two. One of them is me."

Walter stared, dumbfounded, then shook his head. "They can't. That's crazy. That doesn't even make any fucking *sense*. What about communication majors? What, are they cutting my major out too?"

"No. It doesn't affect the majors, only the faculty." Williams looked up at Walter with a desperation he knew he'd never forget, not for the rest of his life. "I've lost my job, Walter. There's no appeal. It's simply gone. No matter how you slice it, I only have one semester left here at Hope."

No, Walter wanted to shout, to cry, to scream, to pound the walls until they fell down. He didn't do any of it, though, only collapsed into the chair Holtz had vacated, legless, as the rock he hadn't even known he'd been clinging to rushed out of his grasp and into open sea.

Chapter Twenty-One

AFTER HE LEFT Williams's office, Walter wandered all over campus, ending up at the campanile. The swans were nowhere in sight, however, which felt like a terrible omen.

He still couldn't quite get his head around the fact that Williams was gone. Would be gone. Thoughts ricocheted inside him, denials, rages, plans, but nothing stuck. He didn't know what to think, how to act, what to do.

The one light in the darkness was that Holtz didn't seem to think the matter was settled. He had his hand well inside the board of regents, and as a thirty-year veteran professor, he was a favorite of scores of alumni. Holtz didn't think Hope grads would appreciate losing an entire department, especially communications, and he didn't think Hope would stand their ground on such a controversial decision under the scrutiny of a scandal.

"It looks especially bad when they're building new dorms and pushing the international student program so much. There's no guarantee we can change their mind, but we can make a hard push in the next few months and see what we can get," Holtz had said.

"They always announce such things over a long break, hoping furor will die down in the shift. We'll see to it, Jay, that it doesn't."

Holtz was Walter's candle right now, and he clung to his vow all the way back across campus toward Porter. Halfway over the green, though, he changed direction and headed to Sandman instead, hoping against hope that Manchester hadn't gone home already.

She hadn't, because she had a big final in Communications Law the next morning. For half a second, Walter considered not telling her until after her test. Then he realized what he'd think of someone who withheld intel on Williams's trouble from him, and he told her anyway.

Rose cried.

It was weird how much that helped Walter—all of her reactions bled him a little, really, first her tears, then her rage, then her mad plans on how they would rally the troops to stop the insanity. He rode along on the tide, mostly relieved to be with someone else who felt outraged and betrayed, but when she pulled out a binder labeled *Ways to Help Williams*, he had to call time out.

"You mean you've been compiling this all year?" He flipped through the pages of potentially influential alumni, donors, and page after page of documents on academic tenure. She also had no less than six drafts of articles on why Williams deserved to keep his position and *ten* dummy letters to the editor. "Holy shit, Manchester. You're a fucking force."

"Except I never saw this coming." She took back the binder, looking ready to cry again. "I don't know how much of this will translate to the cutting of a position." Grimacing, she shook her head. "I'm going to have to redo three-quarters of this over break."

"Well send me some of it, and I'll help. I'll use this list you have here to start a Facebook group tonight—a lot of the grads will be on there. We can have the administration sweating before they go to their holiday party."

"No—I mean, the Facebook group is a good idea, but we want to go carefully. Better to launch after the holidays when people are bored and lonely, not busy. This will give them something to do. And us time to plan." She wiped at her eyes again. "I can't *believe* they did this. I'm never going to sleep tonight."

"You need to study for your final. Comm Law isn't a walk in the park. Let me get started on this."

"Don't you have a final?"

"Digital Media. I just need to show up at nine and breathe." He held his hand out for the binder. "Rose, you know I'm good for this. If there's a way for us to save Williams, we're going to fucking do it."

She gave him the folder and kissed him hard on the cheek. "Oh my God, if you weren't gay, I'd fuck you so hard right now. If you weren't dating Kelly, I might at least try to blow you."

Walter couldn't help a grin. "No worries, my dick's been well sucked today." He glanced around the room. "God, it's amazing how much more space a real double has."

"Sandman's bigger than Porter too. You and Kelly should've tried to move over break."

"Air conditioner. Only Porter and the Manors have physical plant approval for them, and then only the singles. Which I think is bullshit, but, whatever. Besides, I like an excuse to make him sit in my lap." He used the binder to give her a parting salute. "I'll keep you posted on my progress."

"Why don't you stay here and work?" Rose nodded to her computer. "I'll put on a pot of coffee, and for breaks you can reward me with signs of your progress. You can even crash on my roommate's bed if you want. She left yesterday."

Walter was about to tell her no, but then he thought about heading back to Porter, where the RA was ignoring at least three parties and the empty room would remind him Kelly was already gone. "I'll go get my stuff and come back then." He'd planned to leave after his final—nothing would give him greater pleasure than being done with his damn dorm earlier than previously scheduled.

He set down the binder, and Rose caught his wrist, squeezing it briefly, her eyes filling with tears again. "Thank you for coming to tell me. It means a lot."

Walter winked and waved as he left the room, but he also had to wipe his eyes on the way down Sandman's back stairs.

WALTER DIDN'T END up telling Kelly about Williams until he was driving back to Northbrook, partly by accident and partly by design. He was too busy organizing Rose's notes, altering them to fit the new situation, lining up a potential information loop. By the time he saw Kelly's text announcing his arrival in Windom, it was after midnight. Maybe Kelly was up, maybe he wasn't—at that point Walter didn't think he could stand to rehash it all without at least a few hours of sleep, so he sent a benign, *glad you're safe, call you tomorrow on my way home*, and declared it good. As soon as he got into his car, though, he set up his hands-free speakers and dialed Kelly's number.

Kelly could tell something was wrong right off the bat.

"I'll tell you," Walter promised, "but first I want to hear how things are for you."

"Well, my dad dropped some news on the way back."

Listening to Kelly tell about his mother's job crisis hit too close to Williams's troubles, and he quietly hated the soulless bureaucracies that ignored the fact that real people with families held the jobs they so casually tossed out the window. He realized Williams was probably home with his wife this morning, doing the same thing Kelly's family was doing: trying to figure out how to live on one salary, trying to decide where and how to build their hopes.

When it came time for Walter to share his bad news, it got to him more than he'd intended to let it. He wasn't quite as bad as Rose had been, but there wasn't any hiding how much it upset him.

"I've never seen Williams looking so low. It made

me ache, Kel."

"I can't believe they're collapsing the department. That's crazy."

"No shit. They just hacked a big chunk off the value of my degree and anyone else graduating from communications at Hope. Not that it had a lot of value to lose."

"You said there was talk of fighting if they denied him tenure. Can they fight for this?"

"Well, funny you should ask." Walter told Kelly about Rose's binder of aggression and the work he'd done on it so far.

Kelly listened while Walter bared his soul for over an hour, flipping from strategy to outrage to nervous predictions about what this all might come to. It hadn't been what Walter intended to do, but once he got going, he couldn't seem to stop himself, not until he was past Bloomington. That was when he realized how long he'd kept Kelly on the phone, how long he'd been gabbing on.

"Jesus, I'm sorry. Do you need to be with your family?"

"Oh no, it's fine. I'm here alone until four when Lisa gets home, at which time I get to drive her to youth group and come back to start dinner. Well, I don't have to do the last part, but with everyone so stressed out, I thought it would be a nice surprise. Besides, apparently I'm going to be eating a lot of rice and beans unless I go find us some affordable vegetables."

"In Minnesota in winter. Good luck with that."

The idea that the Davidsons were penny-pinching made Walter feel guilty, especially when he knew he'd probably blow a few hundred dollars in junk takeout over the next few days. "When I come see you, I'll bring a belated Christmas present of gourmet almond-free vegan goodies from Whole Foods."

"God, could you come now?"

Walter wished he could. He'd had one passive-aggressive text come through from his mother this morning already. "Soon as I can, baby. Let me know when will work."

"I think pretty much whenever you want after Christmas. Except I'll warn you now my dad's going to try and pay for your gas at least one way."

"That's crazy, but I get it. Manly pride. Well, I'll slip a gas gift card in the food basket."

"I miss you, Walter."

Kelly's confession wasn't plaintive, only slightly wistful, which somehow made it wedge that much harder into Walter's heart. "Miss you too, Red." *Like an arm.*

"Don't ever hesitate to call or text. If I can't answer, I'll call back as soon as I can. I want to hear how everything goes at home. And don't let your mom get to you. You can be there for her, but you don't need to bleed too."

"Yes, sir." The words didn't come out quite with the mockery he'd wanted. He shifted his grip on the phone. "You call me too, anytime. I want to hear what you make for dinner, to start."

"How about I call you later tonight," Kelly said, his

voice dropping to a seductive—if not slightly shy—tone.

Slow heat unfurled over Walter's weary worry. "How about you do that. With your door locked and your pants off."

"Mmm." Kelly sounded less embarrassed now. "You know, I always wanted to try phone sex."

Walter just bet he did. "I haven't done it either. We'll be virgins together."

"God." Kelly sighed. "I know this is pathetic, but I really hate that it's going to be a week at the very least until I see you."

Walter smiled, aching heart warming. "Well, that makes two of us who are pathetic, then."

Chapter Twenty-Two

IT TURNED OUT Kelly and Walter were a natural phone-sex couple, and Walter went to bed that night sated and more comforted than he'd expected after witnessing his mother and Tibby's row at dinner. He wondered, as he drifted off to sleep, if that technique could work all break long.

The next morning, however, ushered in a full day of undiluted family, making it clear the confrontations and meltdowns would continue to jar his day at any given moment and usually when he was the most vulnerable. He was weak after fielding an upset call from Rose or realizing he was going to be lucky to see Cara once during his entire break, unless he skipped his Minnesota visit and hung around her back door. The few emails he'd exchanged with Williams didn't help matters either—not that much would happen between the announcement and the end of break, but inactivity felt like lost ground. By the end of the first weekend he'd convinced Rose to let the Facebook group start, and it was heartening to see more than eighty people join in the first thirty hours. Everyone was full of outrage and ideas, and most of them had letters drafted, ready to submit to the school paper, or already submitted to the board. Mostly they continued to make plans, but it was progress, and progress was good.

His mom and Tibby were dual lead weights putting drag on any momentum toward even fleeting happiness at home. Worse, somehow Walter had internally become a drama queen—little things, sometimes tiny events, upset him. Each subtle dig they took at each other over breakfast, each fit over when Tibby would be allowed to go to the barn or buy Harper a new blanket set him on edge. Every one of his mother's sighs while she washed dishes or flipped through a magazine made him tense up. He felt stupid, because there were no more big fights after that first night, but Walter reacted worse to that somehow than bloody knock-downs at every meal.

Kelly tried to soothe him, but that he needed soothing at all made Walter feel that much more ridiculous, so he took to soft-pedaling his reactions even though he ached to vent the odd emotions he couldn't seem to control. He kept his focus forward, on his impending familial obligations and on his now-established trip to Windom on December twenty-seventh. They'd decided to stay in Minnesota through the third of January and would make up their mind about spending the last six days there or in Chicago later.

In the meantime, unfortunately, Christmas had to be dealt with.

Walter had fun shopping for Kelly and the Davidsons—he still planned to get a big food basket on his way out of town, but in the meantime he dealt in non-perishables, such as the vintage leather jacket in

Boystown that had started it all and a swath of *Doctor Who* figures Kelly had picked up but put back down. He bought the *Corruptible* T-shirt too, and a less suggestive but still sassy *Registered Princess* one for Lisa. Never mind that Gaymart generally sold that one to proudly swishy gay men. Kelly's parents were more difficult, mostly because he knew they'd be upset if he spent too much, though Walter very much wanted to give a token to each to show his willingness to please and impress them. He ended up getting Dick a handsome desk set at a Lakeview gift shop and a gorgeous mirrored chotskie box for Sue. Both were actually quite pricey but still seemed humble—they were exactly the message Walter wanted to send.

Presents for his own family was the usual circle of hell, which made him sad, that he'd been so happy shopping for near-strangers but depressed making purchases for his flesh and blood. Part of the problem was nobody in his family wanted for money or things, so to make a splash with a gift he had to blow a serious wad, which wasn't practical en masse and tended to make the next shopping season that much more impossible. As usual, he had to stick to predictable and boring. His sister was easy: listen for fifteen minutes about what it was she wanted from Dover Saddlery and then run to the internet. His dad was even easier: golf balls, a few assorted crap ready-made gift sets from the internet, and a big gift card. None of it was inspired, none of it would make them smile beyond the traditional thank-you version, half of it they'd not use or change their mind on by Christmas Day. Walter didn't let himself care.

Grandma Marissa, his mother's mother, was always the worst, because Shari Lucas hadn't gotten her dark view of the world from a vacuum. After hours and hours of combing stores and online shops, Walter ended up ordering a handmade quilt from Etsy and hoping for the best. Probably she'd think it was shoddy construction or decide it was infested with bugs or something equally dismissive. If she didn't like it, though, it would end up in Shari's spare bedroom, and Walter could steal it for school.

Might as well be practical.

Grandma and Grandpa Lucas were moderately difficult, though that was only because they lived in New York. Since his parents' separation, he'd barely seen them at all because they were angry with their son, though they hadn't ever cared for his wife. Grandma Claire wrote Walter letters every few months, and originally they'd intended to come to Chicago over New Year's, but they'd started waffling on that even before Walter committed to Minnesota. It would have been nice to see them, but not nice enough to skip Kelly for. They spoke on Skype instead a few days before Christmas.

"You look tired, Walter," his grandmother said, frowning at her screen. Walter wished he could look into her eyes. She had soft, gray ones that had always made him feel she was magic. In fact, when he'd been a kid he'd called her his fairy grandmother.

"It's been a little rough here," he confessed to her, immediately wishing he hadn't been so forthcoming.

Why did he keep spilling his guts like that? He didn't want her to worry.

Claire frowned. "Is it your mother? Or your worthless excuse for a father?"

"No, it's fine. Just Christmas crazy." He decided to distract her with something she'd love to hear. "I'm cutting out of Chicago right after Christmas too, so I'm getting ready for that. Heading up to Windom, Minnesota for New Year's."

"Minnesota?" Claire pulled a face. "Goodness, what for?" Walter smiled slyly in answer, and she gasped. "Walter Andrew, you scamp, do you have a boyfriend?"

"I do, Grandma," Walter confessed.

It was fun to watch Claire clap in glee and pull Grandpa David over to look awkwardly happy for Walter too. In fact, for a full fifteen minutes Walter only had to grin and enjoy his grandmother melting down over the fact that she could finally talk about her grandson's gay love life at the club.

"*Walter*, this is so wonderful. I'm so happy for you. You have to send me a picture. I'd ask if he's cute, but with you, I know he must be."

"He's adorable." God, now he wished he were going to see them. "If you guys come to Chicago, how long are you staying? Maybe I can arrange for you to meet him."

Claire's face fell. "It's not going to work this time, honey, I'm sorry. But we're going to make it work sometime in the spring, and I'd better meet your young man then."

"Well, if we're still dating then, sure," Walter said,

not wanting to tempt fate.

Claire waved an angry finger at him. "Don't you even try that. You made me wait this long, you're going to date him long enough for me to meet him."

Walter laughed. "I'll do my best."

Claire's smile promised trouble. "You know, we have gay marriage here in New York now, and I know the perfect place for a ceremony."

"Grandma."

She laughed, but the scary thing was Walter knew she wasn't kidding. "I do want that picture. Regina Nelson has been bragging about her lesbian daughter dating a former model, and I want to at least keep pace."

"I'll email it as soon as I'm done," he promised.

He ended up sending them a luxury gift basket full of wine and chocolate, which was less personal than he'd have liked, but it was clear his forwarded photo of himself and Kelly mugging for his phone was the gift she'd truly wanted.

GRANDMA MARISSA ARRIVED the same day as the present for the family from her ex-husband—not Shari's biological father, but the father of her heart. It was the usual explosion of things none of them needed but desperately wanted, luxurious food, drink and condiments, iPad minis, noise-cancelling headphones, gift certificates to truly posh horse suppliers and tech companies and department stores, with a handful of exotic shops from Harrods of London to push the whole thing truly over the top. It was always this kind of a deposit, and the fact that it arrived on the same day as his ex-wife and her meager trolley of carefully hoarded and unwanted toys, was the only present the manipulative old bastard needed. Not that any of them but Shari shopped for him any longer.

Predictably, Marissa superseded all other meltdowns by locking herself in the guest bedroom and sobbing for hours while Shari knelt outside of it and wept with the determination of one still learning how to properly fall to pieces. Unable to stand it, Walter took Tibby to the barn and out to dinner afterward. His sister seemed appreciative but distant, and Walter understood the reaction: while it had probably been a very welcome move, she didn't want to get too attached to the idea of him doing it again.

Walter felt guilty because even knowing he'd be abandoning her, he was still glad this was the case.

When he got back to the house, to put the icing on the cake he'd missed Cara stopping by—why she hadn't texted to let him know she was coming, he would never understand. She brought a fruitcake—a fucking fruitcake—and a gift card to Amazon.

Grabbing a bottle of vodka, a shot glass, and a bag of chips, Walter headed to the basement den to get drunk. He was pretty close to smashed when, at nine thirty, Kelly called.

"Hey, you," he said, trying to scramble back into happy. "I didn't expect your call tonight. I thought you were at your grandparents."

"I am, but I still have a phone."

Walter shut his eyes and drank in the beautiful sound of his boyfriend's voice. "God, but I've missed you."

"What's wrong? And don't give me that dismissive crap you keep giving me. Something's really wrong this time, I can tell."

Walter shut his eyes tighter. "No, it's just collective. And then I got drunk, which I think may have made it worse."

Kelly's frustrated sigh was a balm even as it made Walter feel guilty for causing it. "I wish you were here, or I were there."

"Three days," Walter reminded him. He hadn't started counting the hours yet, but he wanted to.

"You can come earlier if you want. You can come tomorrow."

Why was it Kelly's offerings always made him feel good and bad at the same time? "I'm not interrupting your family stuff. Besides, I have my sentence in hell to finish out first. Including a purgatory dinner with Dad tomorrow night."

"There's nothing left to interrupt here, and you wouldn't have anyway. It's just us tomorrow and Christmas Day, and everybody's going crazy talking about meeting you, except for Dad who keeps getting grilled over the two hours he's spent in your company. You don't have to wait until the twenty-seventh. Come anytime you want. Let me know you're on the way as you leave."

"Maybe I'll come on the twenty-sixth," Walter said, the vodka unfurling his resistance to barging in on the

Davidsons.

"Awesome. I'll tell Mom." Kelly's voice went soft and sad. "Take care of yourself, Walter. Don't let them drag you down. And stop lying to me about how much it's bothering you."

Walter's throat was thick. "It's not only you I'm trying to lie to."

There was a long, heavy pause on the line. "Come on Christmas Day. Please. For me. Because I'm going to be a wreck until you're here. I don't care if that sounds pathetic or clingy or if you hate it. I'd beg you to start out tomorrow, but I know skipping Christmas Eve and Christmas morning will make things worse. Maybe you can't come Christmas Day, but God, I want you to. Just come. *Please.*"

The word cut across the center of Walter's chest, and he said, his voice almost a whisper, "All right."

The rest of the conversation was Kelly babbling excitedly about what time he should leave and what the weather was like and how he should respond if it upset his family that he was leaving early. Walter heard about a third of it, caught up in the spinning sensation of relief that came with realizing he was about to get the hell out of hell. He went to bed that night not entirely sure it hadn't been part of a drunken hallucination, but in addition to one mother of a headache, he had two emails and seven texts from Kelly with further weather updates and admonishments for him to not go back on his promise to come on Christmas Day.

The kitchen rocked with the drama between his grandmother, mother, and sister—they were making cookies, ostensibly, but mostly this was the backdrop for a *Real Housewives of Northbrook* episode—so Walter slipped out to bring home dinner for them from Whole Foods and prepare his long-coveted gift basket for the Davidsons. It proved more difficult than he'd thought, and he nearly broke down twice in the frozen section because he couldn't quite work out how to get chocolate coconut ice cream to Minnesota without it melting. He ended up at a low-rent grocery buying a massive cooler and enough dry ice to stop global warming, then went back to cleaning Whole Foods out of everything he thought Kelly and his family might ever possibly desire.

He ended up dropping eight hundred dollars on the food basket, not including the two hundred he spent on a handcrafted wicker container from a boutique next door to put the whole thing in—and it wouldn't all fit. It barely fit in his hatchback, and God, but he hoped the dry ice would last that long. It was far, far too much.

It didn't feel even close to enough.

By the time Walter got to dinner with Tibby and his father at Fogo de Chão, he was so strung out he could barely eat. Kelly texted him every hour, demanding reassurance that Walter was okay. Walter wasn't, but he kept both of them sane by reporting everything as it happened, that his mother and grandmother had made his gift of dinner into a sign of how badly their family had fallen apart and retreated to their rooms, that Tibby seemed wooden, and he worried, that his dad had brought his girlfriend and it was beyond awkward. Before heading back home after with Tibby, Walter texted Kelly his longing to reach out to his sister, but admitted he feared teasing her with more help than he could give. Kelly suggested he take her out to the barn for Christmas Eve to see Harper, which was so brilliant and perfect Walter felt dumb for not thinking of it. It turned out to be ten thousand times better than the present he had under the tree. Watching his sister love her Friesian had a side effect of healing Walter too, and when they finally got home for the night at eleven, they both went to bed with smiles on their faces.

In the light of Christmas morning, he doubted the wisdom of leaving that day. He couldn't comfortably get away until after lunch, and that would put him at a Windom arrival of nine thirty at the earliest unless he drove like a bat out of hell the whole way—which given the fact that he'd face at least two bands of snow flurries en route, seemed stupid as fuck. He was debating whether or not to try for a midpoint hotel at least as a backup due to weather when they sat down to open presents after breakfast—and there his grandmother and mother tossed the flaming turd that finally broke Walter's back.

Shari had opened Walter's gift to her: a high-end silver photo frame with gorgeous cutouts and collage space for photos, which Walter had painstakingly filled with images of himself, Tibby, and his mother and grandmother, images ranging from Shari's birth until the day before when he'd been able to snap the three women smiling before another snarling match. It had been the project he'd done in his room to save his sanity, and as he watched his mother open it, tears in her eyes for its beauty, he wished he'd have taken even more time to polish it and make it the best offering he could. For that moment, the gift was everything Walter knew how to be.

Grandma Marissa leaned over Shari's shoulder, sniffed and tipped her mimosa to her lips. "You look at it and feel Cal's absence like a knife, don't you?"

Shari blinked, then blinked again, and as Walter watched, all the light and happiness he'd put there drowned in the return of her pain.

It was too much. It was too far. It was such a smack across the face Walter didn't even yell, didn't so much as cut his grandmother a glare. He only rose, went to his room and started to pack. He barely had three items in his duffel when he heard someone at his door. Stiffening, he readied himself to face his mother or worse, his grandmother. When he turned, however, it was Tibby who stood in the doorway, looking tired and sad and a lot more grownup than she had a right to be.

"I'm sorry," she said, giving an apology for the other women she had no business having to deliver. "It's a beautiful frame. I'm going to do my best to convince Mom Grandma is a piece of shit and that we should hang the collage over the mantle, especially because Dad isn't in it." She spied the duffel on Walter's bed and grew sadder. "You're going to Kelly. You're leaving now."

Walter paused with a pair of socks in his hand. *I can stay for you,* he wanted to say, should have said, but when he opened his mouth, all he could manage was, "I can't take it. I'm so sorry." He looked away. "I should stay for you, I know, but—"

"What?" She sounded almost angry. "What the hell would that accomplish? That we'd both be miserable?" She curled her lip and shook her head. "I mean, God, I'm so jealous of you being able to get away I'm sick with it, but it's not as if you being here would change anything. Just one more person to fight with."

"I don't want to leave you here alone."

"Well, you're not taking me with you unless you bring Harper too." Her face softened. "Thank you so much for taking me to the barn last night. That was the best, seriously."

"If I were here, I could take you more often."

"Please. I'll bum a ride or use my Christmas money from Dad to take a taxi. Besides, I get my license in three months. I plan to sugarcoat Dad and his bimbo until they buy me a car. Or I'll hoard my allowance and buy some piece of shit that gets me from here to there and nowhere else."

"I'll help you if you need it," Walter promised.

Tibby smiled, still sad, but she looked a lot stronger than Walter had realized she was. "It's going to be okay. I promise you: it's going to be okay. You're going to go to Minnesota with your boyfriend, and I'm going to get my ass to the barn this afternoon if I have to hitchhike. We're all going to be fine."

He ended up taking her on the way out of town—they grabbed Chinese takeout for brunch, enough to hold her over until dinner if she could get away with staying that long, and he left Tibby heading for the barn lounge burdened with bags of tack and gifts and food, seeming ten thousand pounds lighter than she'd been in the living room with their family.

Walter watched her go, remembering what she'd told him yet again as he'd dropped her off, their mother and grandmother's cries of betrayal and abandonment still ringing in his ears.

"We're going to be okay," he whispered to the snow falling gently against his windshield. "We're going to be okay."

He let the words echo for a minute, then pulled out his wireless handset and dialed Kelly as he headed north for the interstate.

Chapter Twenty-Three

UNTIL WALTER'S MAZDA pulled into his family's driveway, Kelly was a raving mess.

He started out okay, all but sitting on his cellphone and spinning his class ring around his finger as he waited for Walter's intermittent reports and chat sessions until traffic or weather dictated he hang up. The only way Kelly survived those radio silences was by reminding himself that every mile Walter put between himself and Northbrook seemed to make him lighter. Until Walter was in front of him, however, visibly put together and happy, he wasn't going to be able to completely relax.

"I have the soup on," his mom told him when Walter lost service in western Wisconsin. "Black bean, the one with the tomato base that's kind of a chili, and I have some bread and salad. I was trying to decide what to make for dessert. Got any ideas? Or should we just go with cookies?"

"He's addicted to my chocolate coconut milk ice cream. Do we have any?" It was a stupid question, he realized too late, because of course they didn't. That shit was five dollars a pint. "Sorry."

She rubbed Kelly's arm and gave him an encouraging smile. "If the store were open, I'd have your dad go pick some up. We still do treats, Kelly, and this is Christmas."

"I wish he were here, that it wasn't so far. God, he sounded awful when he first called. I hope I never meet his grandmother, because I'll probably deck her instead of saying hello."

"You do that and I'll paddle your behind." She let go of Kelly's arm and rubbed his shoulders. "I'm sure he's fine, hon. In any event, he's on his way here now, and we'll all do our best to help him put his bad holiday behind him. I just wish I'd have gotten him more than one gift to open."

"Trust me. If we sit around the table and have real human conversation and play a board game afterward, that'll be better than a million dollars."

"I think we can manage that." She clucked her tongue and stopped rubbing Kelly's shoulder as she moved back to the kitchen. "Poor boy. Maybe I'll make cornbread too, that new recipe I told you about that uses masa flour and pumpkin. Nothing says love like good cornbread."

Kelly ended up helping his mother put the recipe together to distract himself. It wasn't hard, but it was fun, because it involved the cast-iron pan in the oven, which Kelly always enjoyed. It smelled delicious, and Kelly couldn't wait to eat it. Not just because when he got to, Walter would be there.

At seven thirty he arrived, finding the house no problem thanks to his GPS, and Kelly went out with only his dad's rubber-soled slippers and a sweater as nod to the cold. He didn't need anything else because as soon as he saw that dark mop of hair and that bright face emerge from the car, he had all the warmth he needed.

The hug wasn't bad as a fire starter either, and neither was the kiss. It tasted of longing and cold weather and desperation, but also relief. It became Kelly's mission to rout every last one of the shadows in his boyfriend's eyes by the time they went to bed.

Which was one of the first driveway conversations he needed to have with Walter.

"Mom did this weird contained freak-out over where you were going to sleep. Normally she'd have you stay in my room in the sleeping bag, since we don't have a spare room, but because we're dating she feels as if she shouldn't. Then she said she felt ridiculous because she knows we sleep in the same room at school, and then she mostly went red and murmured about not wanting to have this conversation. The thing is, my room's in the basement, and they're all on the second floor, so my thought was to have you officially take the blow-up mattress in the TV room but pretty much spend the night in my room."

Walter seemed oddly happy about this. "That's so sweet. So old-fashioned. I'll do whatever—I don't want to upset your mom."

"The thing is, I think this was what she kept trying to suggest, that we give her some window dressing so she can lie to herself easier." He pulled Walter closer to him. "You're coming to bed with me at least part of the night, though."

Walter's grin went a bit wicked. "Works for me," he said, and kissed Kelly again, a different kind of desperate this time.

Kelly helped Walter bring things in from the car, pausing to introduce everyone. They got to chatting, so Kelly went back to the car to bring in another load—and he saw the food basket. And cooler.

"Whoa," Lisa said from behind him.

Kelly couldn't speak, too busy riding a cascade of emotions and thinking very quickly on his feet. Shaking just a little, he turned to Lisa, keeping one eye on the door of the garage. "Okay, I'm going to prep them. Can you keep him occupied, maybe help him bring this in but be a little slow so I can lay groundwork? Act impressed, by the way."

"I'm not going to have to act. Holy shit, there's a Le Creuset casserole dish in there. Are you dating a sheik?"

"I know. Play it cool, okay? Don't freak."

"*Dad* is going to freak."

"I *know*. Which is why I need a minute."

Lisa gave him the thumbs-up sign. "All over it."

Kelly disengaged his parents from Walter by claiming to need to talk to them desperately about *something*, and they followed him into Dick's office. Kelly shut the door and spoke as quickly as he could.

"Okay. So you mostly have to trust me on this, but you need to know that Walter brought a lot of presents. I mean, a lot of presents. It's my fault because I told him about the job thing, and he worries, and when Walter worries he goes a little nuts trying to take care of things. But the other part is I know it's been driving him crazy that he can't save his family, and I think he's trying to save ours or something, and the gift basket is crazy over the top but *please, please,* don't take it badly because I think all he wants is to save somebody and make them happy, and his grandmother was a shit this morning with that picture thing like I already told you about, and I just want him to be happy, so please, please let him give this to you."

He had to stop talking then because he ran out of air, but it kind of covered everything, so he simply pleaded with his eyes after that.

In the end, he wondered if he would have had to even go through that kind of prompting, because when they came into the kitchen, the basket of insanity was exploded all over the table, overflowing and gaudy and so beyond over the top it needed a new zip code to get the job done. There were six kinds of pasta, all of them high-end label and promising the kind of crazy health benefits Whole Foods loved to do. There was more produce than could fit in their fridge. Lisa was busy unpacking enough chocolate coconut ice cream for Kelly to eat his weight in it from a cooler they could have stored a small body in. They might as well have been survivalists, Walter coming to replenish their stock for the winter and part of the summer too.

Walter stood behind a chair at the table, lit by the overhanging light, looking down at his offering as if he were horribly embarrassed by it and as if it were paltry all at the same time. Walter, who never let a damn thing bother him and rarely even let Kelly know if he was upset, stood there more naked and raw than Kelly had known he could be. Kelly wanted to hug him, to haul him downstairs to his bed and wrap him up tight in a down-alternative blanket and make everything better.

He didn't have to soothe Walter because his family did it for him.

Sue pressed her hands over her face and approached the basket as if it were the baby Jesus's cradle. She touched each item in awe and wonder, murmuring Midwestern silliness like "for goodness' sake" and "my word," all until she found the Le Creuset, and then she burst into tears and hugged Walter so hard she nearly knocked him over, thanking him and asking him how did he know, how had he known that was what she wanted most for Christmas, because she hadn't even told Dick, let alone Kelly? It was so genuine it had to be true.

This seemed to be the cue for them all to start pawing over the food, holding up their favorite things and grinning, and in the case of a rather phallic butternut squash, laughing. All but Dick, who stood at the end of the table with a quiet, reverent look on his face. Walter watched him, holding his breath.

Eventually Dick turned to Walter, as if he'd known he'd been watched all along. Countenance soft but serious, Dick held out his hand to Walter, gave him a small jerk of a Minnesota nod and said, "Well done, son."

He shook Walter's hand when he put it there, then pulled him in close for a steady, man-pat hug. Walter stayed stiff for a second, then when Dick let the embrace linger, giving Walter space, Walter let himself sag for a moment and closed his eyes in relief.

At that point Kelly had to look away, or *he'd* start crying.

"I think we fixed his Christmas," Lisa whispered in his ear.

Kelly started to say he agreed, but he ended up howling in mock rage instead because Lisa poked him with the phallic squash, laughed and ran away, begging him with a grin to give chase.

He did.

IT DIDN'T TAKE but three hours for Walter to figure out that the Davidsons weren't as good as he'd thought they'd be: they were better.

Seriously, if he didn't love them so much, they'd make him sick. Their happiness made him feel happy simply by watching them. That part surprised him. He'd braced himself against their camaraderie, thinking it would make him feel lonely and left out, but it didn't, and not just because they included him as if he were one of them. Their goodness was like one of those candles in the window in the old Christmas stories. It eased him and gave him hope.

Dinner was amazing, and after three bowls of soup, and more cornbread than he should have tried to stuff into his belly, he played a few rounds of Scrabble with Lisa, Sue, and Kelly while Dick did the washing up. After, he curled up on the couch in the basement next to Kelly to watch some mindless TV by the light of a small, beautifully kitsch Christmas tree. He texted Tibby to make sure she was still doing okay, then leaned back into Kelly's hands as he gave him a slow and more than slightly arousing massage.

He tipped his face back, stroked Kelly's cheek and pulled him down for a kiss.

They made out languidly, not taking things too far because they could still hear everyone moving around upstairs. It was almost better that way, tension building, knowing they'd make love later in Kelly's bed but still able to touch and fondle each other now. Walter drew on Kelly's lips, tongue stealing inside, winding him up but never taking him anywhere.

"We could go to bed," Kelly whispered huskily against Walter's lips, sliding his hand down Walter's thigh.

"I'm not going to scandalize your mother just because you're horny." He nipped at Kelly's bottom lip. "Besides. I still have to give you your presents." He'd given everyone else theirs upstairs, but he'd brought Kelly's down to his room.

"You're my present." Kelly slid his hand around to the waistband of Walter's jeans.

They teased each other until Sue called down good night and shut off the upstairs lights. Kelly dragged Walter back to his room, which made Walter laugh until Kelly pushed him backward onto the bed and started peeling off his own clothes.

They came quickly, no more foreplay, no teasing, just quick getting off against one another before collapsing in a sweaty heap together on the bed.

Kelly traced weary circles in the center of Walter's chest. "It's too bad we have this big bed we both fit in and can't share it all night long."

"Or use the ample space for extracurricular activities." God, but he longed to prop Kelly backward against a headboard and rim him good and proper, making him scream. The fact that Kelly would be facing an exceptionally girly *Tangled* poster while he did so made Walter want to enact that scenario *right now*.

He didn't, though, contenting himself with running his hand down Kelly's naked back. "What if we went to Minneapolis for New Year's? Stayed in a hotel, saw the sights? I showed you my city, now you show me yours?"

"Minneapolis isn't my city. I've been there a bit, but not as much as I'd like." He sighed and ran his fingers down to Walter's abdomen. "The theater district is nice. But I certainly don't have money enough to get a hotel there. Not even half."

Walter nudged him in the ribs. "Hey. What did I tell you about letting your boyfriend pay for things?"

Kelly propped himself up on an elbow and frowned at Walter. "It makes me uncomfortable that you do it all the time. I don't want you thinking I take advantage of you the way other people do."

Walter had opened his mouth to argue, then stopped, frowning back. "Who else takes advantage of me?"

"Who? Everyone. Your family, for starters. Cara

calls you for advice but isn't around when you need her. And don't give me the wedding excuse. She can do better. I don't want to be one of them."

Kissing Kelly's chin, Walter pulled him back down onto his chest. "You're not taking advantage if it's something I want."

"It is if it's always a one-way street, you paying for everything all the time, me never doing anything for you."

Walter closed his eyes and kissed Kelly's hair. "If you think that's true after today, you haven't been paying very close attention."

Kelly nuzzled him back, burrowing into his neck. "I'll ask my parents."

"You do that." Walter teased his backside. "I'll reserve a soundproof room so you can really howl."

Kelly arced into his touch and nipped at his neck. "Maybe...maybe if we go, maybe we can..." He nuzzled again, ducking his head a little. "Have sex."

Walter went very still. "I believe we've already done that, young Padawan."

Kelly licked Walter's neck. "Not all of it."

"It's still sex even if a cock doesn't go into an opening." Despite his words, however, his aforementioned organ swelled at the idea, and his voice grew rough. "Did you have a particular cock and opening in mind?" *Go on, Red. Talk dirty for me.*

Kelly slid his naked leg against Walter's hairy thigh. "Your cock, my ass."

Groaning, Walter flipped him over and kissed him hard, his dick telling him it'd be happy to go another round if this kind of talk kept up. Walter drew back from the kiss. "Oh yeah?"

"Yeah." Kelly looked wanton and hungry. A little guilty too, though, as he added, "Is that okay? I mean, I know you enjoy bottoming too…"

Walter laughed and ran his finger down Kelly's nose. "Sweetheart, I knew you were a nellie bottom a long, long time before tonight."

Kelly frowned. "I don't know what that means."

"It means you love to bottom and vocally show your enthusiasm while doing it."

"But I haven't even *been* a bottom yet."

Walter pressed his fingers against Kelly's hole, making him gasp and bite his bottom lip to keep from crying out. "I know, baby. I know." He teased him a few minutes until they were both good and riled, then kissed him slowly to take them back down. "I swing, sweetheart. I don't mind either way."

"But you like to be fucked too."

"Regrettably, only one of us can get fucked at a time." He drew Kelly's earlobe into his mouth and nibbled on it before responding. "I want to fuck you, baby. I want to fuck you until you come apart."

Kelly whimpered and drew his knees up to give Walter better access.

Their second go-round was rougher, and inspired by the conversation they'd just had, Walter turned Kelly face-down, spread his legs wide and thrust up against Kelly's cock from behind. It wasn't enough to make either of them come, but it drove them both crazy and gave them a foretaste of the feast to come.

When they finally met face-to-face again, they gripped at each other hard enough to leave marks, and Walter had to seal his mouth over Kelly's to swallow his cries when he came.

He vowed, as he drifted off to sleep beside his boyfriend, to make damn sure they got to Minneapolis and a proper hotel room for New Year's Eve.

In the middle of the night he woke and dragged himself out to the couch—they'd never blown up the mattress, but he wanted to respect Sue and her fussing and not have her find him tangled in her baby's sheets if she didn't have to. Even though it was short for him, he slept like a log. When he woke, he smelled coffee and breakfast food. Curious as to what food, exactly, eager for coffee and drawn by the murmur of voices drifting down the stairs, Walter rose, hit the bathroom and headed up the stairs.

That's when it happened.

All he did was pad around the corner to the hall outside the dining room, hanging back because he could hear Kelly and his dad talking intensely at the breakfast bar, and he didn't want to interrupt. Kelly was in his line of sight, bed-rumpled, wearing a pair of sweats and nothing else, morning sun filtering through the window over the sink and streaming through the whole of the dining room. It lit up Kelly's hair, his bare skin, his face, his eyes. Something Dick said made Kelly smile, that shy, head-ducking one that usually came with a blush, and it caught at the corner of Walter's heart.

It held him and turned something in his gut, a key

that opened a door to a subbasement, a door Walter
hadn't even known was there. The lock clicked, the
door opened, and longing, soul-deep longing poured
out.

He tried to slam it shut, but it wouldn't go—
Walter wanted to hold on to the wall, but he leaned
into it instead, trying to control his breathing as he
desperately fought the emotions inside him. It was
futile. The longing burned at him, making his arms
ache, but that wasn't even the worst. *Wanting.* Behind
the longing was wanting, craving—a parched plant
facing a lake. Yearning that burned in his blood, that
made him heavy.

Need. It was need.

I want Kelly.

I need Kelly.

His heart beat so hard it felt as if he was going to
have an attack. It wasn't anything, though, next to the
pain of what he realized that fervent beating meant.

I love Kelly.

He would have run, would have gone back down
the stairs or into the bathroom, into the fucking street,
he felt so shaken, but at that same moment as his
revelation, Kelly lifted his gaze to Walter's and smiled.
He motioned Walter into the kitchen, and when
Walter didn't come, Kelly went to him, asking his dad
to pour coffee, letting Dick know just how Walter liked
it. Kelly asked if Walter wanted some breakfast casserole or a cinnamon roll, inquiring as to how he slept,
was he warm enough, did he have a crick in his neck,
should Kelly have made him go to a bed—Walter heard

him, but it was noise in his head. All he could do was stare at Kelly and think, *I want you. I need you. I love you.*

I'm terrified.

"Kelly, I think you want to let him wake up before you chew his ear off," Dick said, breaking the spell. "You fix him a plate, and I'll get him settled at the table."

"Oh." Kelly blushed, but he smiled too. "Sorry."

He vanished deeper into the kitchen. Dick came forward, pressed coffee into Walter's hand and looked him right in the eye. "Don't worry, son. We'll take care of you."

Walter blinked, and Dick took his arm.

"Table's this way," he said, and gently led Walter into the sunshine.

Chapter Twenty-Four

THEY ENDED UP not going to Minneapolis on New Year's Eve, partly because of a bad weather system in the forecast, partly because Kelly could tell his parents weren't into the idea. They would have let Kelly go if he'd pressed, but it would have been because they didn't want to show Kelly up in front of Walter, and they still would have had their reservations. When Kelly confessed his dilemma, Walter immediately voted to give it up.

"It's cool. This is the part where I give the tired old line about how it must be nice to have parents who care enough to set limits, and so on."

"Trust me, it's not the line that's tired." Kelly flopped onto his bed. "It'd be easier if they were hard-asses, because then I could get huffy and rebel. They never do, though. They always look so *concerned*, and they want to talk everything through. Damnedest thing is, usually I say no for them." He sighed. "I really did want to go, though."

"We'll go another time. No sense getting snowed in, and no sense upsetting your family. I like them." He stretched out beside Kelly and caught his ankle with his foot. "I'll even go so far as to admit I enjoy the idea of spending New Year's Eve at home doing stuff such as watching movies and playing games."

The mention of games made Kelly roll his eyes, though he smiled too. Walter and Lisa had a constant game of *something* going, and they always tried to round the rest of the family into playing too. "I warn you, I'm making you watch a Disney movie for every two hours of Monopoly you drag me into."

"I can live with those terms." Walter nudged Kelly's arm. "Hey, actually, we should do that. Plan a movie marathon. You can show me your favorites, and I'll show you mine."

Kelly turned to Walter as realization hit him. "I don't know what your favorite movies are."

"*Cold Comfort Farm*, *Ocean's Thirteen*, and *Fight Club*."

"I haven't seen any of those."

"That's it. Movie marathon. What are *your* three?"

Kelly considered a moment. "Top three is hard. Hmm. Well, with only *three*, I'd have to say *WALL-E*, *Tangled*, and *French Kiss*." He glanced at Walter. "Go ahead, make fun."

If anything, though, Walter looked intrigued. "I heard *WALL-E* was good, so I'm already there on that one. *Tangled* is left field, I'll admit, though curiosity has me on your hook. But *French Kiss*? Live action? Can you list that and still keep your Disney Princess street cred?"

Kelly swatted him on the arm. "It's a great movie. So romantic, and funny too. It's what every romance should be, real and fictional."

"Then it's settled. Now all we need is a menu of munchies, copies of the movies, and command of the television."

The only requirement that posed any difficulty was getting Walter's shows, which he managed by having Tibby overnight them from home. Once all movies were on hand, Walter arranged them on top of the entertainment center in the order they planned to watch them—alternating between the two of them and going in ascending order toward their most favorite. The stack, when viewed as a whole, was completely schizophrenic.

"I look at this, and I can't believe we're dating," Kelly said, staring at it and shaking his head.

"Opposites attract, remember." Walter clamped a hand on his shoulder. "Come on. Showtime begins in less than twenty-four hours. We have cooking to do."

It surprised Kelly, though maybe it shouldn't have, to find that Walter was something of a budding gourmet. He didn't just make vegan kettle corn, he made vegan kettle corn with cinnamon and vanilla. Together they tried out a vegan-spring-rolls-with-peanut-sauce recipe Sue had been eyeing. They had trays of vegetables, pita breads and dips, as well as a mini-pizza bar ready. They had a variety of sodas, and when Sue quietly made it known she and Dick had no problem with a bottle of wine or some beer, Walter shrugged this off.

"Oh, no, we're fine." Walter licked off a bit of homemade hummus from his thumb and glanced at Kelly. "Unless I'm wrong?"

No, Kelly thought it would be way weird to drink with his parents around. God, what if he got drunk? "I'm fine with soda."

"Well, I hope you don't mind if Dick and I have a bottle of champagne," Sue said, though Kelly knew Walter had just managed to carve himself a whole new point level on the good-boyfriend scale.

"You guys are going to watch with us, right?" Walter asked as he rolled out some pizza dough.

"Oh, maybe some. That many movies in one day will make my head explode." Sue wiped her hands on some towels. "I wouldn't mind seeing *Ocean's Thirteen* though. I missed that when it was in the theaters."

"That one's set for the second showing. I'll let you know when it starts," Walter promised.

They really did have a schedule too, on a marker board Walter propped up beside the entertainment center. The movies were listed under the heading SHOWTIMES and had little cartoon drawings next to their names giving a visual summary of the plot.

Their first movie was Kelly's choice: *WALL-E*, which of course had a robot as its doodle. Kelly hadn't seen the film in a few years, so it had a fresh feeling that thrilled him. Walter seemed to like it too. "This is actually some pretty cutting cultural commentary."

"I love how there's no dialog for a huge chunk of the movie, but I get so invested every time." Kelly leaned against Walter's arm. "The dancing-in-space part is my favorite. It always takes my breath away. I have the soundtrack, and I listen to 'Define Dancing' whenever I get depressed."

The space-dancing scene was as wonderful as ever, and when the movie closed, Kelly felt very, very good.

Ocean's Thirteen was next (visual was a pair of dice). Sue came down, and so did Dick, so they watched as a family. Kelly enjoyed it, and told Walter he'd be open to watching the others in the series sometime.

"We'll do *Ocean's Eleven*, though you may want to skip *Twelve*. It's only okay." Walter grinned as he changed out the discs. "I love a good heist movie. Plus, the eye candy in this series can't be beat."

Kelly had to agree. Matt Damon in particular had him going when he was seducing the manager, even with that stupid fake nose.

They took a short break after that, heading upstairs to stretch their legs. When Sue and Lisa found out *French Kiss* was next, they became excited and ordered the boys to wait for them. Dick went back to the game on the living room TV.

"Wow," Walter said, as they headed back downstairs with a new round of snacks. "House favorite?"

"Yes," Kelly admitted. "On many a Friday night when my peers were out getting laid in the back of pickup trucks, I was at home with my mother and sister watching *French Kiss*. I know, the irony bleeds."

Walter smiled and ruffled his head.

It turned out to be very fun to watch *French Kiss* together, because Lisa and their mom called out favorite lines with him, and their excitement seemed to drag Walter along. When it was over, all four of them walked around in dramatic poses, saying, "I want you," with bad French accents.

Movie marathons were awesome, Kelly decided. And since they'd started with their least favorite of their favorites, he could only imagine things would get better.

Then Walter put in *Cold Comfort Farm*.

It wasn't so much that Kelly didn't like it but that it was weird. It was definitely funny, though a lot of times it was as if he had to turn his head sideways to get it. This movie, it turned out, was a Cara and Walter favorite. He texted her several times during the movie—*It's Urk! He's 'orrible!*—and when the show finished, Walter kept coming up behind Kelly and saying, in his best Ada Doom voice, "I saw something nasty in the woodshed." Kelly laughed, but he privately he was glad *Tangled* was next.

Lisa had watched *Cold Comfort Farm* with them, and said she enjoyed it, but she was off to a party of her own by the time *Tangled* got started around nine, and Sue said she wanted to spend some time upstairs with Dick. This meant it was just Kelly and Walter, which was fine with Kelly. This was, hands-down, his *favorite* of his favorites. It was the newest, which had made him suspect at first he'd been attracted to shiny, not calling it his favorite out of merit, but as time had gone on, its appeal had only cemented. He had it on DVD and a digital version on his laptop. He had the soundtrack. Lisa had given him a plush Pascal last Christmas, and it sat prominently on his home dresser—too precious (and embarrassing) to take to school. For this Christmas, she'd given him the *Tangled* boat ride play set, very much a little girl's toy, but it was already displayed next to Pascal. All the trinkets and music and posters, though, were simply reminders of the main event, which Kelly was about to enjoy again, this time with Walter. He couldn't wait.

"I feel as if I've been building up to this for months," Walter teased as Kelly put the DVD into the player. "It's the one Disney movie you aren't embarrassed about liking."

"Well, it helps that there are huge fan communities, many of them headed by adults. Though mostly I simply love this movie. It makes me so happy."

"Then fire her up. I want to feel the love."

Kelly had meant to check Walter's face to catch his reaction during the show, but he got so caught up he forgot almost until the very end. Just as they escaped Gothel's castle and went back to reunite Rapunzel with her family, Kelly glanced at Walter.

Walter looked…weird. He was caught up in the film, which was good, but he didn't look at all the way Kelly felt when he watched *Tangled*. He looked very deer-in-the-headlights, as if someone had snuck up behind him. He seemed almost wounded, which made no sense because they were at the happy ending. Flynn had a close shave, yes, but he'd made it, and everything was good. Rapunzel was going back to her parents, and they were so fantastic that they didn't even say a damn word, just looked at her, touched her face, and knew she was home.

Oh.

Glancing back at the screen, Kelly saw the king, overcome with emotion, look into his long-lost daughter's eyes before he gave in to his happiness and embraced her and his wife both. They crouched to the ground, huddled like a unit. It was almost too cheesy, which was why it was so good—*almost* too cheesy. Right at the edge, which made it glorious. Flynn Rider looked on with a rueful smile, accepting the queen's hand when she held it out to him. Then she pulled him in, making him part of their family puppy pile.

Without turning his head, Kelly glanced at his boyfriend.

Walter looked as if someone had shot him in the chest, and he had tears in his eyes.

For the first time in the three years he'd been watching it, *Tangled* didn't make Kelly feel euphoric and free—even after he moved his eyes back to the screen, the memory of how Walter looked echoed in his mind, and it put a pall on the happy ending that hadn't ever been there before. In fact, things were weird until the cartoon montage over the credits and Grace Potter's snappy "Something That I Want". The tension eased, but Kelly still didn't know how to behave. Should he act as if nothing happened? Would that be worse?

Walter solved his dilemma by brushing a kiss against his cheek and murmuring that he had to use the restroom. Kelly continued to listen to the credits, going over various ways to diffuse the awkwardness, but when Walter returned, he was sunny and—mostly—acting as if he hadn't been brought to his knees by a cartoon.

"Well, there it is. Now I've seen the mighty *Tangled*." He gave a slightly exaggerated sigh and popped the DVD out of the player.

Kelly gave up all his scenarios. "You didn't like it."

Walter seemed to take great care in not meeting his gaze, getting very focused on putting the disc back into its holder. "Not at all. It was a charming movie. I completely understand why it's your favorite. It's about as Kelly as a movie gets." He put the case onto the watched pile and pulled out the last movie of the night. "The thing is, I can almost promise you that you aren't going to like *Fight Club*."

"Why?" Kelly panicked. First Walter didn't enjoy *Tangled*, and now Kelly wouldn't like Walter's favorite? Not good. "Why do you think that?"

Walter shrugged. "Just do." He frowned and shook his head as he put the disc in the player. "I should have said a different movie. You're not going to care for it."

"But it's your favorite," Kelly pointed out. "Your *very* favorite."

"Yeah, well—" Walter cut himself off and sighed. He waved a hand, as if dismissing the argument, and sat back down on the couch next to Kelly. "Okay, let's just watch. When it's over and you hate it, I'll explain why I love it."

Kelly was determined to appreciate the movie, if only enough for the evening, if only to prove Walter wrong. Unfortunately, Walter called it. Kelly hated *Fight Club*. He absolutely, completely hated it.

It was depressing. It made him feel sad and confused and hollowed out. It reminded him of how he'd had to fake it in high school, being "one of the guys" and acting like violence was great, when in reality it made him feel sick to his stomach. The bloody scenes made his stomach turn, and Tyler Durden simply upset him in general. He didn't get the big twist, either. He could think of three or four scenes right off the top of his head that made no sense given the reveal. Still, he was determined to put on a good face.

Walter saw right through it, but at least he laughed.

"I *told* you. You think it's the worst movie ever made, don't you?"

Kelly thought about fishing for a lie, but then he gave up. "Yeah. Sorry." He wrinkled his nose. "It's really not my thing. But tell me why it's yours." At this point, Kelly *needed* to know.

Walter settled back on the sofa and threaded his fingers behind his head, staring at the still-rolling credits as he spoke. "The first time I watched it, I got so caught up in Tyler it was as if I'd found God. I was twelve, and miserable, and angry, and I just wanted to be him. I watched it over and over, parroting lines, posting the rules of Fight Club on my wall, lying in my bed and imagining my Club Mayhem contributions." He shook his head, smiling ruefully. "Then, on about the fifty-first viewing, I realized that I'd missed about six layers of the movie. I realized the Fight Club guys were just replacing their corporate lives with another version containing fistfights. It bummed me out, because of course I had to look up and see I'd done the same thing. Then a few viewings later I realized I didn't want a Fight Club, I wanted Sex Club—Gay Sex Club—but that it would probably be just as fucked up as Fight Club. For a while the movie made me very depressed. Except I kept watching it, like maybe I could find my way out if I did. And that's exactly what happened. When I was eighteen and I watched it again, one day in my dorm room when I hated everyone, especially my roommate, I realized I could be my own Tyler without self-destruction. Yeah, maybe the world is fucked up and there's no way out, but I could control me, and I could make myself strong. I could ride the tide of our corporate world and make it out okay, so long as I stayed in touch with myself."

Kelly listened to this, turned sideways facing Walter with his head leaning on the back of the sofa. He listened, tried to digest it, because it was clearly important to Walter. He wanted to understand, too, if not find an appreciation for the movie, find an appreciation for Walter's viewpoint.

He couldn't.

"I guess the thing is," Kelly began, "that was another one of those movies where everyone was depressing. I never connected with anyone. Everyone was a jerk or a loser or so downtrodden it made me feel down too. The whole story stands on an assumption that everyone sucks, and in the end they still suck. I don't get how that's any fun. I like to be happy."

"Yeah. You do." Walter had turned to Kelly, and as Kelly waited for Walter to tell him he was being insensitive and rude, Walter smiled a sad smile and touched Kelly's cheek. "I think that's my favorite thing about you. You're a happy-seeking missile. The damnedest thing is, you almost always find your joy." He glanced toward the stairs, where the sounds of Kelly's family could be heard drifting down. "I used to wonder how you managed it. I don't anymore."

That made Kelly feel bad, reminding him of Walter's reaction to the end of *Tangled*. It reminded him too of how the few times Walter had checked in with his mom since he'd arrived, the conversations had been tense. He recalled the way Walter hunched over his laptop, typing up things for Rose's Facebook group and sending emails to alumni. He'd heard Walter's angry phone call with Cara too, because she hadn't wanted to get involved in the letter-writing campaign.

Kelly's one complaint in life was that they still didn't know about his mom's job, but even that was minor. The Davidsons all had cheery smiles, and they would, always, because no matter what happened, they'd simply find a way to carry on. He had Walter, he had his family, he had Rose—Kelly led a charmed life. He just didn't understand exactly how it had happened.

He also didn't know what to say.

With a heavy sigh, Walter snapped the TV off with the remote and pulled Kelly closer to him. "Sorry. I put a bummer on the end of our movie marathon."

"Shut up. We were equal-opportunity bummers." He snuggled back against Walter. He spied a clock on the other side of the room and saw that it was one thirty in the morning. He smiled, a little ruefully. "Happy new year."

Walter lifted Kelly's chin. Kelly caught a sad smile playing on Walter's lips before they came down on Kelly's in a soft, sweet kiss.

They had talked, earlier, about maybe making tonight The Night to have some sexual adventures, even though they weren't at the hotel in Minneapolis, but Kelly knew the big sex ship had sailed. They made out in bed for a bit, but nobody so much as came. They ended up spooning, Kelly behind Walter.

"We go back in three days," Walter pointed out as they lay there in the darkness.

Kelly stroked his arm. "What are the plans for Williams? Is there anything I can do to help?"

Walter caught Kelly's hand with his and squeezed it. "I might have some freshmen you can approach, if you're game. We gathered a list of longtime families who might have some sway with the board, and some of their kids are first-years."

"Anything you need. Just let me know." Kelly pressed a kiss into the back of Walter's neck. "You guys are so organized. This has to work."

"I wish that were the case." Walter's thumb stroked Kelly's fingers. "I wish life *were* like those Disney movies. I wish people weren't mostly depressing and weird the way they felt to you in *Fight Club*. The truth is, usually people disappoint you."

I'm not going to disappoint you. Kelly wanted to say that, but he knew better. He simply kissed Walter again and held him until he fell asleep.

Kelly took longer. He ended up finding his iPod and queuing up the *Tangled* soundtrack, listening to it all the way through until he got to "Waiting for the Lights". He put that on repeat and listened to Alan Menken's hopeful, happy swells, pressing his class ring into his palm as he let the music carry him off to dreamland and the promise of a better tomorrow.

Chapter Twenty-Five

WALTER WAS GLAD to be back at Hope, but at the same time he wasn't.

Being with the Davidsons had been a good break from his usual family chaos and the hell that waited because of Williams's job debacle, but at the same time seeing such a happy family reminded him how messed up his own was. It was hard to watch them be so connected. And Kelly—Walter didn't even know where to start thinking about Kelly. Walter loved him, more every day, which was a huge fucking problem. Because Kelly didn't just want, he *expected* his life to end up like that damn Disney movie. He failed to see how removed from reality that storyline was. Reality was the only thing Walter knew, and he'd learned long ago never to turn his back on it.

Where that left the two of them, he didn't know. Happily, once they got back to Hope, he was too busy going to war to think about that too much.

Classes had always been something that happened vaguely on the side of Walter's life, but they were pushed so far to the periphery now they were an annoyance when they had to be dealt with. Skipping was never an option at Hope—even the "large" lecture classes of one hundred students took attendance and cast penalties for too many absences—so Walter had to work them in around writing letters, staging demonstrations, and pounding campus pavement as he and Rose and the rest of the communications students did their best to enlist soldiers.

Kelly was one of their recruits, and he proved to be a surprisingly good one. He had better personal-relations instincts than most of the communications majors—give him a few years and he'd be able to help someone run for office. While Rose and Walter huddled over laptops, consulting spreadsheets, and arguing over what would be their next move, Kelly visited the student lounges with other volunteers, shaking hands and handing out flyers and sample letters to the editor. When their team held a Google Hangout with interested alumni, Kelly became the spokesperson in their window, passing forward information.

He was a great face for the movement because one, he was still the super-cute good boy from Mayberry, and two, unlike most of the upperclassmen, he wasn't angry. Well, he was, but not so far down into his core that it came out in cold fury. Best of all, though, Kelly had a great backstory. At the Occupy Hope rallies that popped up on the main lawn, Kelly stood on the speaker's bench—wearing the super-hot leather jacket, always—and turned the random rage at an overly mothering college back to the matter at hand. Yes, he was prepped for hours by Rose, given key words and sound bites, but it was Kelly's authenticity and, frankly, downright Disney charm that kept winning the day.

"I came to Hope because it promised to be a community that took care of me. I was just coming out and wanted somewhere safe to practice being publicly authentic to myself. I have allergies, so I wanted somewhere that respected my health needs. I'm from a small town, so I wanted somewhere that felt intimate and not overwhelming. Hope seemed all of that to me. Sure, it came with a high sticker price. My family and I decided it was worth changing our budget to make it work.

"Yet being here in person has not always been what was promised. I'm in an allergy-friendly room, but it's a single being used as a double in the one dorm known for being unfriendly to gay men. I've had a lot of near-misses in the cafeteria with foods that would send me to the hospital. Now I'm finding out Hope is cutting a whole department, a department I was considering settling my major in. Hope for me looks less and less every day like a family that supports me and more and more like an institution eager to take my money but unwilling to deliver its promises."

He gave variations on the same speech to the paper and letters to the editor, and every time it was a hit. Everyone knew Kelly now. He was the campus celeb, and if he weren't already spoken for on the dating front, he'd be skimming the cream of the crop and sampling all the wares.

Occasionally Walter felt bad that he was in the way of that, but if he even *hinted* at that guilt, Kelly either got angry or got them both naked. The latter was more usual, especially as Kelly learned how quickly it shut

Walter up.

This became Walter's life: working to rile up the student body and alumni, strategizing with Rose, skating through on classes, making out with Kelly. Every moment he was out of his dorm room, he was working. Before break, he and Kelly had gone out to movies, gone to Moe's, but now all they did was rally, plan, and come back to the room to crash.

They'd opened the futon to share it as a bed, using the loft as storage. They were still two sardines wedged into a sliver of space, but they made it work. Walter had wanted to try and find them a bigger room, somewhere away from Porter, because while their heightened profiles might make them the toast of Hope in most places, this was not the case on their floor. Kelly was against the move, though.

"The administration is so angry at us. If we try to get anything out of them right now, they'll either squash it for spite or use it as leverage against us. We're fine how we are."

They were lying on the futon, naked and spooned together, Kelly's head on Walter's shoulder. Walter stroked Kelly's hair and trailed fingers down his back. "Are things okay with our resident meatheads? No one's giving you any shit?"

Kelly shrugged. "Sure they are. I'm not worried, though. It's as you said. They're just teasing me. They can't do anything. There's a lot of power in knowing they can only taunt me, not act. I've finally figured that out, and it's changed how I deal with them and let them affect me."

"If they so much as make you sweat—"

Kelly lifted his face to kiss Walter's chin. "You'll hit them with a frying pan, Flynn Rider. I know."

Walter worried, though, about more than simply Porterhouse. He *did* want to keep a frying pan handy when it came to Kelly, at least metaphorically.

He hugged Kelly tighter. "Just be careful."

You're the only sure thing in my life right now. Everything else is going to shit, and I can't bear to lose you too.

It made him feel raw to even think that, and he knew he couldn't ever say it. Kelly seemed to hear it anyway, because he kissed Walter's cheek tenderly and stroked his face with a reassuring gesture.

Then he slid his hand beneath the covers, teasing Walter's belly, then his cock, and Walter surrendered, letting himself be distracted from his fears.

KELLY WOULD HAVE been the last person to peg himself as a rabble-rouser, but lately at Hope, that shoe definitely fit.

Since he barely knew Williams, being a mouthpiece for him sometimes felt odd. It helped that he'd picked up some communications classes at the semester switch. It helped even more that he enjoyed them. The classes were smaller than his gen-ed and business courses, and the heightened intensity around the department's consolidation with humanities made everything feel more alive. Williams led his Introduction to Communication Theory class, which was about the logic of small group and interpersonal communications. It felt like a more formal version of Philosophy Club with different textbooks. Suddenly Kelly thought he had a pretty good idea how that group had been started.

In his two communications courses—he had small group communication too—Kelly felt at home and oddly happy despite the cloud hanging over Ritche Hall. He'd shied away from education courses, wanting to explore gen-ed first to see what stuck. What he found weird, though, was that he also enjoyed the management class his advisor had made him keep. "A liberal education is good," Dr. Lindon insisted. "I applaud the communication studies, especially the two you've chosen. Combined with Introduction to Psychology, you're well set. Keep the Fundamentals of Management, though. You have an excellent head for business, and you're a natural leader. Try it one more semester, and if you still feel it isn't what you want when we sign you up for the fall, we'll put you in whatever new direction you want to go."

This had all been in December, before Kelly couldn't read through an issue of *The Hope Journal* without seeing himself quoted. Lindon wasn't the only one who thought Kelly had leadership potential. One of the student senators had asked him to run for office. Kelly was considering it.

He *did* enjoy the management class, though. It wasn't as boring as the econ class had been, or the math. It was kind of fun, thinking about how systems worked. It was slightly surreal to have that course, plus the comm theory course, running alongside the Williams campaign. Kelly felt as if he didn't need to write his weekly essays. He only needed to direct Lindon to YouTube.

On a dreary Tuesday morning in early February, while Kelly headed back toward Porter, his phone rang. Nodding hello to someone who recognized him and waved, he ducked into the Sandman overhang to escape the light drizzle and pulled out his cell. It was his dad, which was weird. Wasn't his dad at work at this time of day?

The dark thought about what this call could be resonated in Kelly's brain, and his heart sank. No. Shit, no. Except he knew, even before he answered, that he'd guessed right.

"Hey there, Dad," he said, trying to sound bright. "Good to hear from you. What's going on?"

The heavy sigh confirmed the truth before the words did. "Your mom got her notice today. By the first of April, she won't have a job."

The wind blew around Kelly, rattling the door to the dorm, but the chill Kelly felt had nothing to do with it. "Oh no."

"She's looking into positions in Mankato, because there's nothing around here."

Mankato was over an hour's drive from Windom, and it could be hellacious in the winter. "Does she have any leads?"

"Nothing yet, unfortunately. But we're going to keep looking until she finds something."

Kelly clutched the phone tighter. "Is there anything I can do?"

"Don't spend any money you don't have to."

"I won't." He already wasn't. "Tell Mom to stop sending me meal bars. That'll save fifty dollars a month right there."

"I'll try, but I bet you'll still get them. She has to feed her boy."

"Tell her that her boy is doing pretty well." Kelly shifted to the side to let someone pass, and they nodded and waved at him with a smile. He smiled back.

"You still fighting for that professor? How's it going? We keep seeing you in the online paper."

"Pretty well, I think. They're talking about going to the board of regents over spring break. They're hoping they can get them to call a special meeting over this issue."

"Well, we wish them luck. Just don't get your name so muddied you get in trouble, you hear me?"

Kelly smiled, missing his dad so much. "I'm always careful, Dad."

"Do well at school, son. I don't want you feeling guilty about what education costs. So long as you use your time wisely and well, whatever we have to do to make it work will be worth it."

"Okay, Dad." He swallowed, but his throat was lumpy. "I love you."

"Love you too, Kelly."

Hunching into his coat and cutting across the green to Porter, Kelly felt the reality of his father's message sink in. *No job.* He didn't know how his mother would get a new one, and he hated that it might be out of town. He knew his dad did too. Despite what his father said, Kelly did feel bad, because he was a huge part of the cost. He was the expense that put the family on the edge.

As he climbed the stairs to Porter 4, gaze to the floor and ears closed to the cockroach comments, Kelly thought about the speeches he made for Walter and Rose, about how he'd questioned Hope and what it stood for. Those had been his words, and Rose and Walter had declared him brilliant, saying he had a career as a speech writer if he wanted it.

The thing was, Kelly *did* wonder if Hope was worth it. As he bore hallway insults—again—as he faced his too-small room, as he dwelled on the fact that his tuition alone was thirty-six thousand dollars, not to mention the four grand for room and five for board...he had to wonder, was Hope worth it?

No, Kelly admitted to himself. The only things he cared about at Hope were Williams, Rose, and Walter.

As two football players swore and fought in the hall, slamming hard into his locked dorm door, Kelly pulled out his laptop. He opened the browser and navigated to the University of Minnesota at the Twin Cities and started to click around. He looked at the academic majors, at the colleges, and the grad programs. He looked at the dorms, and he read the Equity and Diversity document he'd glimpsed last year but dismissed because it wasn't as intensive as Hope's.

He read the tuition and fees, which including room, board, and books were less than flat tuition at Hope. There wasn't one word about having to live on campus.

Someone slammed into his door again, but it didn't

even make Kelly jump. He closed the laptop, put on his iPod and lay in bed, listening to the soundtrack to *Tangled* as he tried, in vain, to think of what he should do.

Chapter Twenty-Six

BY EARLY FEBRUARY, the effort to save Williams's job began to wane. The novelty of shouting on the campus lawn and getting angry at The Man got old for most of the students, especially as the unseasonably warm weather gave way to a wave of snow and ice and bitter wind. The paper posted daily rants on the web, but there were only so many ways to spin the same outrage, and people complained they wanted to read something new for a change. Walter wished he could say he hadn't seen this coming.

"I knew we should have given ourselves a name." This complaint came from Rose as they sat up in her room one night, Walter, Kelly, Rose, and Ethan Miller. Walter ran through the Facebook group on his MacBook while Kelly rested with his head on Walter's thigh, and Rose and Ethan pored over her planning binder, which had started to look like John Nash's bulletin board in *A Beautiful Mind*.

"Why a name?" Ethan asked.

"Because if we had a name, we'd have more focus." She pursed her lips as she flipped a page. "It's always the four of us at the core, with a few other people getting serious on occasion. We have meetings, and a few people show up, but nobody does anything. They're always waiting for us to do everything."

"That's because people want leaders." This came from Kelly, still lying on Walter's leg. "Or so my textbook tells me." He stretched and turned to look up at Walter with a lazy smile and reached up to stroke his face. "It'll be okay."

From anyone else, the platitude would annoy Walter, but since it was Kelly he smiled back and brushed a kiss against his fingers.

Ethan watched them with a vaguely guarded jealousy. "We should plan something for next weekend. Something big."

Rose looked up from her binder, nodding. "Yeah, good idea. We need an event. Another rally?"

Kelly had gone back to daydreaming, and Walter stroked his hair. "No event, not next weekend. Wait until March—let the lull go on a bit and renew everything before the midwinter break. We need to come up with something big for when we come back."

Rose frowned at him. "You think it's *good* to let things cool down?"

"Sure. Gives the administration a false sense of security. Meanwhile, we do two things: plan something they won't see coming, and raise the communications department profile."

Ethan brightened. "We could do singing Valentines for people as a fundraiser!"

Walter gave him a withering look. "Please. We're a communications department, not a high school glee club. We should make a film about Williams, like a documentary. It could have a companion format across all available media: newspaper, online mag, and so on. We could do YouTube snippets and plan a launch when we get back. Jax would do it in a heartbeat. This would be the distraction—they'd think that was what was coming, what they should brace for."

"What would the other part be? The one they won't see coming?" Kelly asked.

"That we have to figure out." He nodded at Rose. "How's your intel on Regent dirt coming?"

"Not well." She flipped through her binder. "The best thing we can do is highlight what they're spending their money on versus how much they charge us and what they're cutting. Which we've already done, kind of."

"Then we focus on getting more details, as much as possible, and we hammer that. The documentary goes up, but so do posters and Twitter streams about what they're spending money on. I wish we dared have a hacker get in to the campus system and broadcast from there."

Rose snorted. "That wouldn't be hard to make happen. Those computer guys are always looking for a reason to fuck the system."

"It can't be connected to us, though. We need them to pick it up on their own."

"I could work on that," Ethan volunteered. When Walter gave him a long look, he held up a hand. "I know. It can't come back to us."

"It can't come back to *Williams*."

"I know, I know. I get what's at stake." He slumped

against the leg of Rose's desk. "I just hope this works. It's not going to be Hope if they fire him."

"If they don't restore his position, I'm transferring," Rose declared.

Walter lifted his head. In his lap, he felt Kelly's body stiffen in attention as well.

Ethan out-and-out gasped. "You'd *leave*?"

She shrugged. "Sure. I'm only a sophomore. Perfect time to transfer. My parents are always telling me this place is too expensive anyway."

"But leaving. God, it's so…final." Ethan frowned at the floor. "Wish I weren't a fucking junior. It's not an option for me."

"Why not?" Rose asked. "Do you know how many colleges and universities in Chicago alone are cheaper and better accredited than Hope? You might have to put in an extra semester or two, but in the long run it'd be worth it. What's your degree going to be worth from here now?"

"Our degrees will be fine," Walter said, losing his patience, "because our major and our advisor will still be here."

The subject had dropped after that, thankfully, and they'd spent the next hour making plans for both the documentary and what they'd started calling the counter-blitz. By the end of that week, they had a buzz back again, quieter than the rallies, but Walter rested easier because they looked productive, not stuck in a rut. Everyone enjoyed the idea of being in a movie, especially because Jax, who was one of the campus's mini-celebrities, served as official director. Meanwhile,

Ethan's computer friends were hunched over their laptops doing wicked things with code. It began to feel as if they were moving forward again.

On Valentine's Day, Walter took Kelly down to St. Louis, to an upscale bistro restaurant with a price-fix menu and a vegan option. They knew about the almond allergy too, and promised there was no chance of the evening ending in the emergency room. Kelly knew none of this, only that they were going out of town to dinner, so when they went all the way into the city and sat at a fancy booth with a moonlight view of the arch, he blushed and effused and pretty much made every minute of the wrestling Walter had done worth it.

"We could have just gone to Moe's," Kelly scolded him, but he played with the heavy silver spoon while he did so, watching its surface sparkle in the candlelight, looking enchanted.

"I've been appallingly inattentive," Walter said as he scanned the wine list. "We've been so caught up in the campaign for Williams that I've only ever taken you out for pizza, and that I think happened twice."

"You're never inattentive." Kelly looked dreamily out the window. "Oh my God, it's so beautiful."

Walter smiled to himself, feeling very pleased.

He ordered them a bottle of champagne, which prompted the waitress to ask for their IDs—she glanced at Kelly's class ring as she did so. Kelly caught her glance, and he blushed as he handed over his fake ID.

"Sorry," he murmured, still red-faced after she left. "Rose is right. I should stop wearing it."

Walter rolled his eyes. "Forget Rose. You want to wear your class ring, you wear it. It's kind of cute that you do, really."

"Cute," Kelly repeated, making a face.

Walter grinned. "Yes, dear. I'm sorry, but you're cute."

Kelly laughed and reached across the table to catch Walter's hand, which Walter readily gave.

"This is nice," Kelly said. "Thank you."

Walter swelled with pride. "For you, anything."

Kelly kissed their joined hands. He looked relaxed and easy, and the simple sight of him was restorative for Walter. Not for the first time, Walter wondered how he would have gotten through this hell over Williams without Kelly beside him.

He played with Kelly's hand, loosening their grip on each other and rubbing his thumb over the stone of his class ring. "You haven't given me a home-front update in a while. Is that because it's good, or bad?"

Kelly shrugged. "It's the same. Still no new job for Mom."

Walter had figured as much. He teased his fingers against Kelly's palm. "She'll find something."

Kelly smiled, but it was a sad, tired gesture. "What will you do if Williams's position really does get cut? Will you stay at Hope?"

Just the question made Walter go cold. "He's not going to lose his position."

"But if he did?" Kelly's fingers pressed against Walter's wrist. "Would you stay?"

Walter wanted to pull his hand away, but he

couldn't, so he looked out the window. "I haven't thought about it. I don't want to think about it."

Kelly squeezed. "I'm sorry. I shouldn't have asked."

Their champagne arrived, but Walter held fast to Kelly's hand. When the waitress left them again, Walter turned back to Kelly.

"I wouldn't leave you." Walter tightened his grip and swallowed against the vulnerability that confession left in its wake. He meant the words, but they made him feel raw and exposed. Still, he forced himself to meet Kelly's gaze, because reassuring him mattered more than anything else. "Whatever happens to Williams, I'll be staying at Hope. And you'll be the only sophomore living in the Manors, because those bastards owe us both big time."

That was meant to lighten the moment, but Kelly appeared as stricken as he had when Walter had first made his promise. "You can't say something like that. You can't stay at Hope just because of me."

Something in Kelly's tone made the yaw inside Walter gape wider. "Why not?"

Kelly wasn't blushing—which was weird. "Because you can't." He rearranged their hands so his was on top, pressing down hard. His class ring glinted in the low light, and the arch lit up behind him. "You can't sacrifice your life for other people. Look what happened with your mom."

"You are so *not* my mother," Walter said, still trying to turn this into a joke.

Kelly refused to so much as crack a smile, and his grip on Kelly's hand got tighter. "If you want to transfer, Walter, you'll transfer. If you want to follow Williams to Hawaii, you'll follow him. Do you hear me?"

Now Walter was getting annoyed. "I'm not choosing Williams over you, for Christ's sake."

"You shouldn't choose Williams or me over *you*." The waitress appeared, and Kelly waved her away, not breaking his heavy gaze on Walter. "Walter, I will *not* be the person you sacrifice yourself for."

"Kelly, I'm not going anywhere, okay? I want to stay. Anyway, nothing is going to change."

"Things happen. We can't always control them."

Walter held up his free hand. "*Stop.* This is supposed to be a romantic dinner, not an interrogation."

Kelly glanced back over the river behind them, a sad expression on his face.

"Hey." Catching Kelly's chin, Walter turned him toward his own gaze. Kelly smiled, and the waitress came to try again for their order.

The smile had shadows, though, Walter couldn't help but notice, and it worried him.

SOMEHOW IT DIDN'T surprise Kelly that Walter had gotten them a hotel.

He wasn't even surprised that it was a swanky, upscale number on the river, not far from the restaurant, and that their room had a view of the arch. What he hadn't been ready for was the bouquet of roses, the box of vegan chocolates, and the sea of lit candles floating in a sunken in-room hot tub. When he realized a hidden set of speakers played Sia softly in the background, Kelly became overwhelmed. Half-laughing, half-weeping, he sank onto the silky sheets of the king-sized bed and pulled Walter down with him.

"Is it okay?" Walter asked, smiling, but clearly nervous.

Kelly laugh-sobbed and hit his boyfriend gently in the chest. "You're *crazy*, you know that? You're absolutely insane. How can you even ask? Of course it's okay. It's beyond okay. It's *amazing*." He looked around again, sank back against Walter and caught his hand to squeeze it tight. "You know, one of us in this relationship is a hopeless romantic, and it's not the one who owns over thirty Disney movies."

"It's Valentine's Day. I wanted to do something special." Walter wrapped an arm around Kelly and pulled him closer, nuzzling a kiss against his temple. "I like making you happy."

The kisses along Kelly's ear began to slow, turning seductive. Kelly closed his eyes and leaned into them. "You make me happy all the time." He broke from the drugging kisses and turned to Walter, nuzzling his nose. "I love you, Walter."

Tucking his chin, Walter rested his forehead against Kelly's, hands skimming up Kelly's sides. "I love you too."

The echo of vulnerability lingered in Walter's words, and Kelly caught his mouth to ease him, reassuring his lover with kisses long and lingering. It didn't take long for passion and the promise of what pleasure there was to be had in a private hotel room, a large bed, and no parents or jocks around to make them self-conscious. Lube and condoms waited on the nightstand.

Kelly was losing his anal virginity tonight.

Nervous, giddy, impatient, terrified—Kelly felt everything at once, but he felt it with Walter, so he didn't care. He stripped off his shirt and shucked out of his pants, but before Walter could pin him to the bed, Kelly pressed Walter back, sliding down his chest to nuzzle his groin as his hands worked deftly to free Walter's cock. A second later Walter gasped and Kelly hummed around the warm hardness in his mouth, smiling around his mouthful at the familiar smell and taste of Walter. He wondered if all men smelled and tasted like that or if they were different.

He hoped, in the quiet of his mind where no one could tease him for his sentimentality, that he never got to learn the answer.

While he blew Walter, Kelly also stripped him out of his clothes, first pants and socks, and then, when Walter pulled him up by the hair with a warning that the show was about to be over way too soon, Kelly tugged at the panels of Walter's shirt until the buttons strained. Laughing, Walter pushed Kelly's hands away and yanked the whole thing over his head.

They stood a moment, nude, breathing hard, regarding each other.

Kelly grabbed Walter's waist. They came together in a kiss, cocks and bellies brushing, hands seeking, mouths claiming, and in that tangle, they fell back to the bed again.

Within a minute of making out, though, Walter had Kelly on his belly, knees parted, a pillow beneath his hips. Tense, but in anticipation of pleasure, not pain, Kelly shut his eyes and curled his hands against the mattress. He knew what was coming.

Walter's hand stroked a lazy trail down Kelly's spine, and Kelly shivered. Walter laughed, softly. "Don't worry, hon. You can squeal as much as you want this time."

Kelly blushed. They'd tried this once back at the dorm, and in addition to bruises on their knees and arms from wrangling into position on the futon, Kelly had made so much noise the linebacker and fullback across the hall had beat on their door and promised to knock it down if they had to keep hearing "cockroaches having sex." So they hadn't tried again.

Until now.

Cool hands spread Kelly's cheeks, a warm tongue pressed against his entrance, and Kelly felt brain cells die from sheer pleasure.

He cried out, a long arpeggio of a gasp that gave way to a tortured moan. His upper body felt like electric spaghetti, aching and splayed and completely void of the ability to move. He could feel Walter's tongue everywhere—it was as if there were eight of them, laving his hole, trailing up and down his crack, running down the line to tease at his balls. Kelly's jaw ached with want, and he had to actively keep himself from humping against the pillow in an effort to drive against Walter's mouth. Turning his face into the bedspread, he tried to muffle some of his sounds, sure he was carrying on far more than was normal.

Then Walter pulled his cheeks wider, tightened his tongue into a small, wet spear, and wormed his way inside.

Kelly came off the mattress.

For a second he tried to control himself, lest Walter think he didn't like what was going on, but Walter seemed to understand, holding Kelly in place and ignoring his struggles, leaving Kelly free to moan and flail and beg incoherently for things he wasn't sure what they were, exactly, but that he had to have them. He wanted more, he wanted harder, he wanted—

A slick finger poked in beside Walter's tongue, and Kelly's whole body short-circuited. Yes. That was what he wanted.

For a long time that was all he got—one finger, probing gently, Walter's tongue darting in beside it, Walter's breath hot against his cheeks. This, outside of the rimming, wasn't new. One of Walter's favorite games was to sit up late with Kelly, watching TV and driving Kelly crazy with his fingers while he whispered in his ear. "If you want me to fuck you," Walter would say, "you have to be ready. We have to stretch you, or it'll hurt."

"I'm stretched already," Kelly would complain, arching into the fingers that speared him, the smell of musk and lube heavy in the air. "Let's do it now."

"We'll wait," Walter always said.

They were done waiting now. Kelly clutched at the bed and submitted to the pleasure Walter gave him, as Walter relaxed him and teased him and spread him with two, now three fingers. He brushed that spot deep inside that made Kelly turn to butter, then rubbed against it so Kelly felt as if he were constantly shorting out.

The fingers slipped out, and after a kiss on Kelly's backside, Walter's mouth moved away.

Here it comes, Kelly told himself, feeling dizzy.

The crinkle of the condom seemed to echo like a gunshot. Walter had been tested already in October, just after the last time he'd been with anyone else, but he wouldn't be with Kelly sans condom, he said, until he had the follow-up in April. Walter's caretaking made him feel good, and this safety mingled with the truth that sex, always, was something a little dangerous—the whole business simply ramped Kelly's nerves all the way up to eleven. The lube slick against his skin felt cold, and his arms ached, a thin rust of fear sliding through his veins.

Walter nudged at his entrance, and he tensed. Walter's hand massaged the small of his back. "Relax, baby. Push into it." Kelly tried, he did, but all of a sudden he panicked, and he wasn't sure, and—

The tip of Walter's cock moved inside, and Kelly pushed up to his hands and knees, eyes wide open. For a long time they remained frozen in that pose, breathing hard, waiting.

Kelly shut his eyes, drew a breath. "More."

More came, tighter and more impossible than before. Kelly let out a sigh laced with pain.

"Breathe," Walter advised him. "Breathe and push, and we'll be at the good part."

The funny part was that Kelly had read about this—extensively, back in high school and again as he'd come closer to this moment with Walter. He knew to push as if he were trying to go to the bathroom. He knew once the sphincter relaxed, the game would change. He knew all of it. Except that was academic. This was his goddamn ass, which he was no longer quite sure was meant to have a cock in it.

Except he wanted a cock in it. He let out a breath and bore down.

With one good thrust and only one more moment of pain, the sphincter gave way, Walter pushed in deep, and Kelly entered a whole new world.

It wasn't so much that a cock was so much different than fingers. It was, but it wasn't about girth or length or even the sure, strong thrusts—though those were great. It was that he could feel Walter's heartbeat against his back. That he felt the nest of hair brushing against his ass, tickling him, teasing the strained, spread skin of Kelly's asshole. Their balls banged and danced together as Walter pushed deep and withdrew, sawing in and out of Kelly as his hands roved across Kelly's skin, as his mouth made love to the back of Kelly's neck. Walter was *in* him. Inside him. With him.

Kelly wanted more.

He tried to turn his head and catch Walter's mouth—he met his lips a few times, but it was a tease, not what he wanted. Figuring it out, Walter pulled out, leaving Kelly aching and empty until Walter rolled him over, pushed his thighs against his chest and pressed into him again, catching his mouth in a kiss as his cock resumed its previous engagement. Kelly moaned into Walter's mouth, shaking—from this angle, Walter could fuck deeper, and it made Kelly feel as if he'd die with want.

Walter nipped at his lips. "I have to be careful. This is your first time, and I don't want you to be sore."

"God, I want to be sore." Kelly nipped back, thrusting his hips against Walter's cock to take it deeper inside. "Oh God, please."

"We have all the time in the world, Red. No need to rush."

Kelly was done with all the time in the world. He wanted *now*. "Fuck me, Walter," he whispered. "Please. *Fuck me.*"

Walter did. Kissing Kelly with so much tongue it gave him goose bumps, Walter spread Kelly's legs wide and pounded against his body until their skin slapped, until Kelly's cock bounced between their bellies. Walter fucked Kelly hard, fucked him deep, fucked him long and slow and fast. He tucked Kelly's legs to one side, then another, placing Kelly's legs over his own shoulders until Kelly lay flat on the bed, speaking in sexual tongues as Walter both pounded into him and jerked his cock toward its inevitable end. Kelly came abruptly and hard, feeling as if his whole body exploded and shattered across the room. When he came around, Walter was winding up for his own release. Kelly watched him through bleary eyes, watched his lover's eyes close, his mouth open, watched everything strip away as he lost himself and came.

When Walter collapsed onto the bed beside him,

Kelly made his weakened limbs move enough to pull him close, twining them back together. His backside twinged, and he realized Walter was right. He was going to be sore.

He couldn't, however, bring himself to care.

Holding Walter tight, he pressed lazy kisses to his cheek and chin. Walter burrowed in against him, laughing with little breath to spare. "Shit."

Kelly kissed him on the mouth, slow and lazy.

I'll never leave you. Walter's words from the restaurant echoed in Kelly's heart, sinking there like lead. Kelly shut his eyes and threaded his fingers into Walter's hair.

I love you, and I don't want to ever leave you, either.

Except even as Kelly thought this, he thought too of his family's dwindling bank account, of his mother's lack of a job, of what three more years of Hope would do to their finances, what it would mean for Lisa's chance at going to school, any school—and Kelly knew that while he didn't want to leave, he couldn't promise, not honestly, that he wouldn't.

Chapter Twenty-Seven

THE DOCUMENTARY PRODUCTION went very well, and Jax promised an Oscar-worthy film by the time they returned from break. Ethan's computer nerds stood by ready to roll, and Rose printed the posters and prepared the graphics and copy for social media. Really, Walter thought, it was a shame they couldn't put all this on their resumes, because it was better than half the internships they could sign up for.

He had dinner with Williams before Walter went back to Northbrook—Thai takeout in Williams's office with the traditional bad coffee. They'd remained in their usual contact since the campaign began, but their conversations were always slightly stilted, and they kept the door wide open and their voices at levels allowing others to verify they weren't colluding on plans. Tonight, however, they were the only two in the building, and Williams declared he didn't care. Wearily, he shut the door and handed Walter a box of red curry and rice.

"Don't give me details," he said, "but tell me that you're not killing yourselves over this. If I lose my job *and* you all flunk out of college, I'll never live with myself."

"We're fine. You give us most of our grades, and last I checked, we're still working our asses off for them." He aimed his fork at Williams. "You're not losing your job."

Williams shrugged and dipped into his green curry. He looked so defeated. "Holtz says there's good odds that this Regent meeting will smooth things over."

Walter brightened. "There *is* a meeting then?"

Williams winced. "Shit, I wasn't supposed to tell you that."

"Already forgotten." Except he was so calling Rose on the way home. He didn't want to torture the professor any further, though, so he changed the subject. "How's the family doing?"

"Stressed. I have applications out all over the country, and a couple of colleges have put me into consideration for interviews. Karen wants me to wait until Holtz does his thing, but honestly, I have to have a back-up plan in place. Getting a new position isn't easy in any event, but add my age and lack of publishing and it's almost impossible. But she doesn't want to move, and neither do the kids. So it's hell." He sighed. "Sorry, I'm a real Debbie Downer."

"I hate that they're doing this to you. It makes me insane."

Williams reached over and squeezed his arm briefly, then fussed with his mouse, scrolling through his email while he continued to speak. "I'll make it through. It's you I worry about. Tell me good things about your life, Walter. I know you're hopelessly in love with your roommate and he with you, so I assume that's all good.

Doing anything together over break?"

Thinking of Kelly made Walter ease a little. "No, he has to go back home. His mom got laid off, and he wants to be with the family. I think he has some crazy idea about getting a job over break, but yeah, that's what he's doing. I'm heading home to do First Attendant prep work with Cara."

Williams stopped messing with his mouse. "Is Kelly's family okay? Do we need to look at some scholarships for him?"

"That's probably a good idea, though they'll have to be academic, not need-based. He's in that crappy middle bit where his family still has income but is about to lose it. So he won't qualify for loans until next year. I know too that his dad won't want him taking loans, either. But Kelly's obsessed because his sister is on deck to go to school."

Williams frowned. "Hope is pretty damn expensive. I hope he's able to continue."

Walter went still. His shoulders tightened, so much so that he felt a sharp pinch in a tendon on his left side. "What do you mean?"

"Just that if he's in that much of a financial snarl, he may have to transfer out." When Walter went white, Williams swore and sat up. "Shit. God, I'm an idiot. I'm sorry. He won't transfer, Walter. Ignore me."

Walter was having a hard time breathing. "You think he'll have to leave Hope?"

"I don't think anything. Debbie Downer, remember? Like you said, scholarships. There are a few that are for need-based but don't have anything to do with

FAFSA requirements. I know a few people who know a few people. We'll get him sorted, okay?" He studied Walter's face for a second, then sank back in his chair and wiped his forehead. "Okay. Good. That's settled. Just don't ever look at me that way again."

Walter blinked. He felt dizzy and off focus. "What do you mean? Look like what?"

"As if I'd killed your dog in front of you. Though God knows I've already let you down enough this year." He pinched his forehead. "Seriously, ignore me. I'm not in a good head space. It's funny, I prepared all year to be told I was losing my job, but somehow I still wasn't ready."

Dimly, Walter was aware something significant had just happened. Some part of him was able to pull back and assess the situation, observing both that Williams had brought up a valid point about Kelly and Hope and that Walter had pretty much freaked out at the idea of Kelly leaving. Worse than Williams leaving. He couldn't observe this long though, because even acknowledging it made him feel very...bad. He swallowed and put the Thai down on the edge of the desk.

Williams swore under his breath. "Subject change. Tell me about your Valentine's Day. I don't even care if I hear something inappropriate. Tell me about your date, because knowing you, it was spectacular."

Walter thought about the trip to St. Louis, the fancy dinner, the way Kelly's face had lit up at all the special touches, the way he'd felt in Walter's arms. He meant to tell Williams about that, but instead when he opened his mouth he said, "He gave me a Disney movie."

Williams raised his eyebrows. "For Valentine's Day? Which one?"

"*Pete's Dragon* on Blu-ray." Walter stared at the Thai container, smiling to himself as he remembered. "He kind of has a Disney fetish, and I told him once that I loved that one as a kid. So he got it for me. We've watched it twice already."

Williams smiled and eased back into his chair. "Perfect. What'd you give him?"

Walter told the story of their St. Louis trip, which ended up bleeding into the story of how they accidentally got lost on the way home and had dinner in some weird barbecue joint where Walter personally inspected the kitchen for allergens and Kelly sat mortified in the booth. Williams laughed, and they ate their Thai, and when Walter finally got on the road for Chicago, he was still smiling as he thought of hanging out with his advisor. It had been the same old times, after the bumpy start. He was determined to make sure they had one more year of doing so, and that any time he felt like visiting Hope he could do that again, for as long as Williams wanted to be there.

Northbrook of course put an immediate damper on his bliss, but he had been ready for that. His mother had been frosty at best since he'd run away at Christmas, and he would have skipped coming home entirely, but he wanted to check in on Tibby and he'd promised he'd help Cara. He took care of his sister first, booking several full days at the barn to watch her ride and promising to go to a Saturday show after he had his big prep meeting with Cara.

Tibby seemed to be doing well—their grandparents had shown up the week before, and Grandma Claire had been keeping tabs on Tibby, it turned out, making sure she was okay. Walter made a mental note to send her a bucket of flowers and chocolates and an album full of pictures of him and Kelly. His mom was also a happy surprise. She told him she'd switched to a new therapist and was working hard, always taking her meds. She'd fired the cleaning service too and did the work around the house herself because it made her feel productive, like that time they'd worked together. Something told Walter there was no way his mom was now in perfect mental health—there would be more awkward moments and nasty shifts—but the fact that she was clearly trying meant a lot.

Cara wasn't as easy. She was in full bridezilla mode, with the wedding only two months away, and every message from the caterer or florist contained a potential international incident and opportunity for every woman in the room to break down weeping. In Cara's defense, Walter could tell her mother and grandmother and her mother-in-law-to-be only threw oil on the fire and made sure it had plenty of coals. So on the Friday night before he went back to Hope, he took her down to Boystown, plunked her at the bar at Roscoe's and got her completely smashed.

"I just want to go to Vegas," she sobbed into her appletini. "I want to marry Greg. But I can't do this wedding."

"It's going to be fine," Walter told her for the thirtieth time and signaled the bartender to switch her over to water for a bit. "Give me the list of things you want me to do, and I'll do them. Tibby will help too."

"You can't. You have Williams to save." She sobbed harder. "I've been a horrible friend because I haven't been helping you."

She pretty much had been horrible, but after watching for a week what her life had become, Walter understood why. He wiped her face with a bar napkin, wondering if he should tell her that her mascara had pulled a Tammy Faye or if it was best to let that ride. "Kelly's helping me, and Rose. Even that dingbat Ethan Miller is pulling his weight. We've got Williams. You keep working not to lose your mind before you walk down the aisle."

"I tried so hard. I tried not to let it go crazy. I don't know how I lost control." She hiccupped. "Then my work has been bad, and Greg is all stressed—" She picked up a napkin and blew her nose into it.

Walter stroked her back, kept her hydrated, repeated soothing refrains. When the bars closed, he got her home, stopped on the way to let her vomit, and spent the night at her house and made sure she was done emptying her stomach. He woke before she did, went downstairs and had a long talk with her mother about Cara's stress level.

Checking his phone, he saw he had about two hours before they were supposed to start stuffing wedding-favor bags and take Cara to her final fitting. Slipping out to a local coffee shop, he ordered a soy latte in honor of Kelly, then called him up and smiled as his boyfriend answered the phone.

THE POST-BREAK BLITZ to save Williams went, Kelly thought, as well as it probably could. The documentary was well-received and seemed to renew the interest in saving the communications department, and the negative side campaign, including the hacking, helped make the administration look particularly bad. Walter had said there would be a meeting of the board of regents, and true to form, they had one scheduled for the last week in April. They planned to discuss the departmental issues and announce their decision the last week of classes in May, which also happened to be the week before Cara's wedding.

"They're doing that so if they decide negatively, there can't be any more pushback," Rose complained.

"There won't be any more pushback if they decide in favor of keeping Williams," Ethan pointed out. "I just can't believe they'll drag this out that long. If he doesn't get to keep this position, he has to find a new one."

"That's probably what they're counting on, that he'll have to get another job first and save them the trouble," Walter said.

Kelly agreed that he wished they'd decide sooner rather than later, though for different reasons. He and Walter didn't discuss the next school year much, only during the week Walter had been eligible to sign up for housing. They were now secured for a room in the upper story of Hampton, which was great—except

Kelly didn't know that he could come back.

He hadn't said a word to Walter about what his family's stark financial situation might mean to their plans, but sometimes Kelly thought Walter knew what might be coming. He wanted to talk about it, but every instinct he had told him not to bring it up until he had no other choice. When Kelly found himself in Williams's office discussing some scholarship opportunities, he decided to lay everything out on the table and see what Walter's advisor thought of the situation.

Williams sank back into his sagging office chair with a sigh. "Normally, I'd tell you to shoot straight and be honest. With this? With Walter, right now?" He shook his head with a grimace. "Let's just say I'm hoping one of these donors comes through with a full ride for you."

Kelly blinked. "Is that even a possibility?"

"Only if we're living one of your Disney movies." Williams ran a hand over his face. "God, I hate this. I don't know how much he's told you about his past, but your boyfriend is the poster child for abandonment issues. Doesn't help a damn thing that he has such a big, giving heart. He tries to hide it, but he has to have at least one or two people he can shower affection on as a kind of outlet. That would be you and me right now, kid, and we're both poised to abandon him the way nobody ever has."

Kelly felt sick. And trapped. "Dr. Williams, I can't make my family pay thirty-six thousand a year just because I don't want to make Walter feel bad." He hugged himself and hunched over. "Maybe I could go part-time until he graduates and I can transfer."

"No, Kelly. You were right the first time. You can't make your family strain just to avoid a nasty situation for your boyfriend." He rubbed at his temple. "Let me keep working on this. Or are your parents pressuring you to make a decision right now?"

Kelly shook his head. "They're ready to send me here again if it's what I want. The thing is, the only thing here specifically that I want is Walter."

"Yeah, that's what I figured." He shook his head. "If the appeal falls through, I hope he goes elsewhere. This has always been settling for him. I know he says it doesn't matter, but it does. He's so smart. Brilliant, even. But he needs to have somebody supporting him, or he's not okay. God, he'd hate us talking about this. Except it's true." Williams looked at Kelly over the top of his glasses. "You get that, right? That Mr. I-Don't-Need-Anyone only says that to keep people from suspecting what a big fat lie that is?"

Kelly smiled sadly. "Yeah. I've known that for a while now."

Williams went back to skimming his computer screen. "We'll find a way to fix this. I don't know how yet, but we'll find a way."

The talk helped Kelly. It made him feel less like he was keeping a secret from Walter and more that he was working on a solution.

The April meeting of Philosophy Club was on Francis Herbert Bradley and the philosophy of idealism. While Kelly still thought the whole philosophy thing went a bit above his head, he enjoyed Bradley and his good self vs. bad self. His favorite part was Bradley's suggestion people lean on religious teachings to find their way. Kelly had started becoming a regular church-goer, much to Walter's chagrin, and he found the hour to reflect and remember what was important in life centered him, helped him pilot better through the rest of his week.

He held Walter's hand as they headed back to the dorm after the Bradley meeting. The usual herd was headed for Moe's, which hopefully meant Porter would be a bit more isolated than normal. It was hard to believe in a month he wouldn't have to live there anymore, one way or another. He'd be either in the air-conditioned Manors with Walter, or he'd be…somewhere else.

"Three weeks until the decision," Walter said as they crossed the common and headed past the student union. His voice was quiet, and he sounded sad. "I hope we've done enough."

Kelly squeezed his hand. "If it isn't enough, you'll know you gave it everything you had."

Walter looked so tired. "Kelly, I don't know what I'll do if they don't keep his position. I honestly have no idea."

"Whatever it is, we'll face it together."

Walter pulled him close, and Kelly slipped an arm around his waist.

As they made love that night, though Kelly hadn't set out to plan it, he found himself subtly shifting the tables. It was he who pressed Walter into the mattress, he who covered Walter with kisses and urged him to let go, give in to pleasure. It wasn't the first time he rimmed him or added a combo blow job, but it was the first time he ever felt so intent on caretaking, on giving Walter a safe space. What came next, in the end, was only a natural extension.

They exchanged no words to confirm their switching of previous roles, but when Kelly began to ease him open, Walter opened his legs and helped him along.

As soon as Kelly began to push inside, feeling the heat and tightness around his cock, he quietly vowed he'd be doing this again and soon. Being fucked felt good, but fucking wasn't bad, either. Walter seemed to appreciate the change as well—he shut his eyes and let go, gasping and clutching at the futon, urging Kelly on. Kelly didn't hesitate to give his lover what he asked for.

When they came down, breathless and sweaty and sated, they spooned together, the smell of sex wrapping around them. Walter smiled sleepily and twined his fingers lazily in Kelly's hair.

"I can feel your spunk leaking out of my ass," he murmured, laughing. "I haven't felt that since I was too stupid to demand condoms."

Kelly fought not to shut his eyes against the gentle massage at his scalp. "I like that feeling too."

Walter nuzzled Kelly's lips, his fingers in Kelly's hair slowing to a more deliberate caress. "Thank you."

Kelly nuzzled back. "You're welcome."

Chapter Twenty-Eight

WHEN WALTER WAS five, he'd been lost in a department store. One moment his mother had been standing at the perfume counter while Walter touched the shiny rows of dangling necklaces, admiring the way they danced in the light, and the next his mother was gone. He'd wandered the gleaming white counters, heart pounding, wanting to call for her but not daring to shout and get in trouble for making a scene. Though the adventure had probably only been a few minutes, it had felt as if it were hours that he wandered up and down the center aisle, hoping for a glimpse of her red coat, until he couldn't hold back his tears and a saleslady took him to customer service. He'd been reunited with his mother right away, and she'd even fussed over him, giving him hugs and telling him never to wander off again, but that horrible feeling of what it felt like to be lost, hopelessly lost with no idea of how to find himself, had never gone away.

Whenever he was particularly stressed out, Walter replayed variations of that moment in dreams. The night before Williams's decision was to be announced, he had the version where he was lost in an airport—still young, still looking for his mother, but it was seas of suitcases and suit legs he navigated, not white counters and rows of perfume. In his nightmares, unlike real life, he never found his mother, and no one ever rescued him. He always woke agitated, hollowed out, and sick to his stomach.

That Thursday morning when he climbed out of the dream, Kelly was there, asleep beside him on the futon. They were both naked and twined together, pulled close in one of their last nights together until whenever they visited one another this summer. Walter intended to put in an appearance for a week or so in Northbrook and then head for the Land of Ten Thousand Lakes. He had, without telling Kelly, priced apartments in Windom and looked for part-time jobs so he didn't seem stalker-ish. He hadn't committed to anything yet, but he hadn't ruled anything out either. Their room was almost completely packed. Kelly's parents were coming on Saturday to move him out, though Kelly himself would be in Northbrook at Cara's wedding with Walter. They were taking Walter's things too, in a little trailer they'd borrowed from a neighbor for the occasion. Walter felt this was a sign his apartment idea was a good one.

At that moment he wasn't thinking much about apartments, though.

It was early, but he couldn't stay in bed any longer, and he didn't want to wake Kelly, so he dressed quietly and headed out to wander the campus. He skipped the cafeteria, meandering around the pathways that led to the lake instead, stuffing his hands in his jacket pockets and letting his caged thoughts spin out across the early morning mist. The leaves were in bloom, but they still had that stark green that came with first leaf. The flowerbeds were lush and primed for the marigolds the seniors would plant as part of their graduation ceremony on Sunday. The swans swam serenely as ever. Everything was quiet and beautiful, and it gave Walter hope, something to hold on to while he waited to hear what the future would bring. He wanted to sit at Williams's office, but he knew Williams was at home, waiting for the 8 a.m. phone call that would decide his fate.

Walter paced the length of campus and back again, waiting for it too.

At 8:16, his phone rang. He held it in his hand a moment, heart tight, arms aching. Then he swallowed hard and answered.

"Hey, Williams," he said, trying—and failing—to keep his tone glib. He looked up at the beauty of a magnolia tree in bloom above him, fixating on the frail, pink blooms. "Tell me the good word."

He had his answer before Williams spoke, in the heavy, painful beat of silence. "I'm so sorry, Walter."

Walter shut his eyes, breathing against the heaviness that hit him, pulling him down and down into a sorrow that did not stop.

"Walter, listen to me." Williams's voice sounded broken. "You did everything you could. I know that. I saw it. I watched you, watched everything you did. I know you got to them, and I think you moved a lot of the regents. You did amazing things, worked miracles, and moved mountains, and that counts."

Walter's throat was so thick he almost couldn't speak. "Not enough."

"Yes, enough." Williams's voice grew stronger. "You did far more than enough. You were amazing, Walter, the way you always are."

Walter felt sick. He swayed on his feet and put an arm out against one of the magnolia branches to steady himself. "They can't do this. They *can't do this*."

"They can. They did. They're selfish, idiot bastards, and I don't have to play nice for them anymore—but yes, they can do this. Right now, though, I don't care about them. I care about you. Where are you, Walter? I'm halfway to campus, and I'm coming to find you."

Walter opened his eyes at that, panicked, as if Williams might already be there. "No. I want to be alone."

"The hell you do. Listen to me: we're going to be okay. Both of us. You get that? I don't care what they did or didn't do. I'm not leaving you, and you're going to be okay."

Walter's laugh was hollow and dangerously watery. "I didn't lose my job."

"No. But you and I both know, Walter, that you feel you lost something a lot bigger than that. I'm telling you it's not true. I don't care where I am next year, or where you are. I will not abandon you. Understand that, please, because I'm going to keep saying it until you do."

Walter wiped at his eyes and moved away from the tree, heading to the other side of the union. He could see the lake in the distance, the cove on the far side where the swans liked to hide in the shadows. He saw them now, swimming silently together on the mirrored surface.

He wiped his eyes again.

"I have to go," he said, choking on the words.

"*Walter.*" Williams was almost shouting. "Walter, don't you dare hang up on me."

Walter kept looking at the swans.

Kelly. Kelly would go too. He knew it in his bones. He'd known it all along. He'd known Williams would leave, Cara, Kelly—they all would. They all did, in the end.

"*Walter Lucas,* you get your ass to my office right now, or so help me God, I'll send the SWAT team out to find you."

Kelly would leave. They all would leave.

Walter's stomach lurched, and he almost fell on his face. "I have to go."

He hung up the phone. He turned off the ringer.

He let tears stream down his face and stumbled toward the lake.

KELLY WOKE TO someone pounding on his door. The knocking was so insistent that he didn't bother getting dressed, only wore the sheet to the door, where his equally rumpled RA stood holding a piece of paper.

"You're supposed to call this number, right now. It's some professor."

Frowning, Kelly took the paper, wondering who could want him to call. Then he remembered what day it was, saw the time, and he fumbled for his phone.

"Kelly," Williams said as he answered. "Thank God. As usual, I've fucked everything up. I told Walter about the board's decision over the phone, and he got upset and now he's gone."

So it had been a bad decision. *Shit.* Kelly tucked the phone into his shoulder and started putting on his clothes, a task made difficult by his shaking hands. "Gone where? Is his car still in the lot?"

"Yes. I checked that first thing." Williams swore under his breath. "I'm such an idiot. I should have waited."

Shoes. Where were his shoes? "Where have you checked?"

"All of Ritche Hall, but that was probably stupid. He doesn't want me to find him."

Kelly grabbed his room keys and buttoned his shirt as he headed for the door, his sweatshirt over his arm. "I think I have an idea where he is. Is this your mobile? I'll text you when I find him."

"Yes, this is my cell. I'm sorry, Kelly."

"It's fine," Kelly said, though not very convincingly.

Pushing down his fear and worry, he headed out of Porter and took off at a steady jog across the campus.

At first he'd thought he'd guessed wrong, but just as he was about to try the back side of the PE complex, Kelly saw a familiar flash of dark hair inside of the campanile. When he caught enough sight of Walter to confirm, he texted Williams and broke into a run.

When he got closer, though, he slowed down. He took the long way to the edge of the lake, softening his footfalls, not wanting to alert Walter to his presence until he had to. Walter stood still and rigid, dark hair ruffling in the wind as he stared out at the water, where the swans drifted silently. Either Kelly hadn't done a very good job of sneaking, or Walter was dulled to the point that he couldn't be surprised, because when Kelly came up beside him, he didn't even glance his way, only said, "Kelly, go."

Kelly didn't, but neither did he try and argue. He came up beside Walter, tucked his hands into the pocket of his sweatshirt, and watched the swans too.

It was an oddly comfortable silence—all the panic Kelly had felt before he'd found Walter bled away, because now that they stood together, Kelly felt sure everything would somehow be fine. He let himself marvel in that a moment, not sure if it was real or made up in his head. He decided the truth didn't matter. He believed it would be, and believing otherwise certainly wasn't going to help him out.

He watched the swans a little longer, feeling their calm and gentleness seep into him.

"I think," Kelly said at last, "that Lancelot and Gawain were the reason I decided to come to Hope."

Walter gave no reaction, not that this surprised Kelly. Kelly settled into his story, though, smiling as he remembered.

"I saw their picture on the website above the caption that told their story, but even before I knew they were gay, I'd fallen in love. It was like they called to me. Told me if I came here, everything would be okay. So I did."

Walter snorted.

Kelly resisted the urge to turn to him. "They didn't lie. It was a good decision to come here. Not everything I learned this year was what I expected to learn, but there's nothing in the world I would trade for my year at Hope. I think I'll look back at my freshman year of college for the rest of my life and realize things that I picked up during these nine months. The swans were right. They told me to come, that it was a good decision, and so I did, and I'm not sorry."

"You're leaving." Walter's voice was raw and rough, accusing. "You're going to transfer for the fall."

He did turn to Walter then, still calm, still carrying the gentleness of the swans. "I'm not sure yet. But it's something I need to consider. Whatever happens, though, Walter—*whatever happens*—I'm not leaving you."

Walter's glare was full of anger and hurt. "You and Williams trading bullshit this morning? Yes, if you transfer, you're leaving me. If he leaves Hope, he's leaving me. Trust me—long distance is not the same. Wherever Williams is next fall, it won't be in Ritche Hall, and that's leaving. You're leaving too. You're both leaving me."

"I'm not leaving you." Kelly took a step closer and reached for Walter's hand—when he tried to pull away, Kelly caught him and held him fast. "Listen to me, Walter Lucas—I'm *not leaving you*. I'm not transferring unless you come with me. I'm staying if you're staying. We need to talk about this, a lot of talking, but the bottom line is that I'm going where you're going."

Walter faltered, but only for a moment. Then he stiffened and tried to pull away again. "You can't do that. I'm not stupid. Hope is expensive. If you don't have the money—"

"I have the money. Barely, but I have it. I won't lie to you—if we stay here, I have to transfer to the University of Minnesota or somewhere a lot cheaper the second you graduate. I'll have to work all summer and every break and probably get work study. I'm doing it, though, if that's what you want."

"You can't stay for me. You can't give up everything for me."

"You were set to stay on my account when you thought I wanted to stay. You came here for Cara. You stayed in Chicago for your mom. You gave up this whole semester for Williams, for the department." Kelly reached up and touched Walter's cheek. "Don't you think it's time someone gave up everything for you?"

Walter shut his eyes and tried to duck away, but Kelly caught him, drew him closer, held him tight. He held him until Walter's body eased into his, until his arms gave in and closed around Kelly, until he rested his face in the crook of Kelly's neck.

"I don't know what to do," Walter whispered. His voice was broken and thick, and Kelly felt warm tears against his skin. "I did everything I could, but it wasn't enough."

"You did enough. You were amazing. You still are amazing." Kelly nuzzled Walter's ear and held him tight. "We'll work it out. It's okay. I promise. We'll figure out what to do together. Because I'm not going anywhere, Walter. I will not leave you. I will never, ever leave you."

Walter's body began to shake, slowly at first, then steadily as he gave in, sank against Kelly and wept.

Kelly held him, rocking back and forth beneath the campanile, watching the swans swim quietly on.

Chapter Twenty-Nine

WALTER COULDN'T DECIDE if the obligation of attending Cara's wedding was an aggravation or a relief. The only thing he did know was that if it hadn't been for Kelly, he wouldn't have made it through.

Part of him noticed Kelly took up the role that Walter himself usually played, though of course he played it in a much more Kelly way. He engaged in cheerful patter with Walter's mother and sister, keeping the peace so much that even Walter felt a little hopeful when his mother smiled at him, though he noticed Kelly made sure they only lingered in the house when absolutely necessary.

When they were at the rehearsal dinner, he was never far from Walter's side unless Walter was practicing walking up and down the aisle, and then Kelly was always visible, always right there with the other spouses and significant others, always smiling and waving at Walter when their gazes met.

On the day of the wedding as Cara went into full-on wedding hyperventilation, it was Kelly who came in as the voice of calm when Walter didn't have it in him to play clown. Kelly took up some of the managing

Walter had been meant to do, talking with the ushers about getting the gifts out of the church and to the hotel room and arranging for the same at the reception. Kelly never missed a beat, was everyone's right-hand man.

Especially Walter's. Whenever they were together, his hand was on Walter's arm, his waist, his shoulder, or clasped inside his palm.

Some of Walter's fog lifted during the ceremony, and as the minister droned on about love and commitment, Walter looked at his boyfriend, who happened to be watching the bride—and in that moment he knew that he wanted, more than anything else, to have this with Kelly. He wanted the promise. He wanted the rings. He even wanted the three-ring wedding circus.

He wanted to be married. To Kelly. Forever. As he stood listening to Greg and Cara's ceremony, he thought, mostly, about when it would be okay for him to ask for his own.

The reception was in a pretty garden room of Greg's family's country club, and everyone, once arrived, seemed to relax. Walter made it through the wedding toast with a plastered-on smile and borrowed goodwill, and if Cara felt he'd phoned it in, she didn't say anything. He danced with Greg's sister for the attendants' dance, and with his obligations filled, he sought out his date, eager to slide off into the shadows with him for some quiet.

Except when he took Kelly's hand and tried to lead him away, Kelly took him back out to the dance floor.

Walter had his mouth open to object when the opening strains of piano arpeggios filled the room. He stopped short and looked at Kelly, who winked.

"Come on. I played this just for you."

Walter really tried to pull away then, but he didn't have a lot of fight in him, so he went, dissolving against Kelly and shutting his eyes, letting his lover lead as Helen Reddy's soft, familiar voice assured him she'd be his candle on the water.

"It was a nice ceremony, don't you think?" Kelly's hand shifted down to Walter's lower back, pressing reassuringly. "You look so handsome in your suit. Though I have to say, I can't wait to get you out of it."

Walter tried to take a deep breath, but it was shaky.

"My parents texted to let me know they got everything from Hope. They said you're welcome to stay with me as long as you like when you come back." His fingers splayed against Walter's hip. "Apparently someone is trying to rent an apartment downtown, and the word on the street is it's someone from Chicago. My parents said if that's you, if you think you can't stay in our house as long as you need to, they have a long lecture ready when we get there."

Walter tried to laugh, but it caught in his throat. He hugged Kelly tighter.

Kelly brushed a kiss against his ear. "Don't worry. They just guilt you a little, and then it's over."

The music was killing Walter. Thank God the song was almost done. He wanted to get out of there, needed to get away from the dance floor because he wasn't in the mood for anyone to see him come undone. As the song wound down, Walter began to relax. It was a nice gesture, the song, and he appreciated it. God knew he had it coming after all the rigging of shit he did for Kelly. It worked too, because while it played, life did feel like a Disney movie. The ship would come home. Pete would get away from the bad guys. Everything might just be okay.

Kelly slid his hand down Walter's arm, twining their fingers together, placing something into Walter's palm. It was small and round, and heavy.

It was, he realized, Kelly's class ring.

As the strings and piano slowed and the song ended, Kelly slipped the familiar piece of jewelry onto Walter's thumb, closing it tight into their joined hands as he leaned in and whispered into Walter's ear.

"I'll never let you go."

Walter laughed. And cried, and hugged Kelly, and laughed and cried some more. He forgot the rest of the room, the rest of the world, everything that wasn't Kelly, that sappy, stupid song, and this perfect, shining moment.

He forgot it all, because he didn't think, he *knew* that everything would be okay.

Epilogue

November
Minneapolis, Minnesota

ALL KELLY WANTED was a quiet weekend with his boyfriend.

Since this was Thanksgiving and everyone they'd ever known was coming to dinner, Kelly had resigned himself to the fact that there wasn't any way he was going to get in much quiet cuddling on the couch with the latest Disney release. The only consolation he had was that it was warm, which in Minnesota was about as rare as a church picnic without Jell-O salad. Sure, they were going to stuff every last one of their friends and family into their tiny apartment and hope they didn't kill each other, but at least they'd be able to open a window.

The day started out pretty well, though, much better than Kelly had anticipated. Normally Walter was so swamped with his pre-law courses he didn't have time to breathe, but the meal had been important to him, so Walter had cleared his schedule and even was home the night before. Of course, he spent the whole time cooking. Kelly's family had come in early, as had Shari and Tibby—they were all staying in a nearby hotel, though they were only sleeping there. The rest of the time they were completely underfoot.

At the moment, Sue and Shari were busy in the kitchen peeling potatoes. Rose had arrived at ten and promised to help, though Kelly privately doubted she'd do much but stare adoringly into her girlfriend's eyes unless the place was on fire, and even then he wasn't holding his breath. Cara and Greg were with Williams and his family in the living room, listening to Dick tell them all about Sue's new adventures, his face flush with pride. Kelly had heard the story a zillion times, but it was a good story, so he went into the room so he could listen again.

"The office is paying for her classes and her realty license," Dick explained, "which they don't normally do, but they wanted her there, so they're working hard to keep her happy. She already has several people who promise to give her their houses as commission."

"That's fantastic." Williams stopped to look down at his daughters, one who was coloring dangerously close to the edge of her paper. "Sweetheart, not on the table."

"I hear you're doing well in Iowa City, Professor?" Greg prompted.

"Yes, I'm a Hawkeye now. Karen is loving working at the University of Iowa Hospitals and Clinics, and the kids are happy in school. They all tell me they wish I'd have lost my job a long time ago."

Dick saw Kelly and smiled. "Kelly's doing well too. He's finally settled on a major."

Williams turned to the doorway. "Oh? Do tell. I've

been wondering."

"Nothing exciting," Kelly confessed. "I'm back in the business world."

Dick huffed. "It's very exciting. He wants to do public relations, he says, so he's focusing on marketing and accounting. I have an old school friend who teaches in the Carlson School of Management, and he tells me with the way Kelly's taking to his classes, he's going to have no problem getting into graduate school."

"That's brilliant." Williams smiled at Kelly. "A lawyer and a public-relations wizard. Match made in heaven."

Greg nudged his wife. "Cara has a new job too."

"Oh?" William asked, and Cara launched into the story.

Kelly slipped out, heading to the dining room, where Walter was instructing Tibby and Lisa how to arrange the table settings.

"We're a bit crowded, so do your best. For the kids' table, just make sure it looks fancy like the adults while not actually containing anything that will get any of them grounded." He looked up, saw Kelly and smiled. "Hey, you. Everything okay?"

Kelly nodded, though his return smile was a little forced. "Just waiting for something to go wrong."

Walter wagged a finger at him. "Listen here, Eeyore. We're having a Disney Thanksgiving, and don't you forget it."

"Even Disney movies have a villain," Kelly pointed out.

"Don't worry," Tibby said. "Grandma will be here at one."

Grandma Marissa did arrive on time, but so did Walter's other grandmother, Claire, the one who always begged for pictures of the two of them, and when she saw Kelly, she squealed in delight and hugged him. "I'm going to get the two of you in a picture with me before I go."

Nothing did go wrong, not really—oh, there was the occasional tension between Shari and her mother, and the kids broke into three fights before their mother threatened them within an inch of their lives, but other than that, the dinner went fine. Everyone had enough to eat, and Kelly didn't have an allergic reaction. The whole fiasco was poised to go off without a hitch.

All the way up until the end of the meal, when Rose and Cara came from the kitchen, looking grave.

"There's something wrong with the dessert," Cara declared.

Kelly frowned. "The pumpkin pies? But they're fine. I saw them when I went into the kitchen."

"No, not the pies," Rose said. "The other dessert." The door to the kitchen opened, and she waved Kelly out of his chair. "Here, Walter's bringing it. See for yourself."

Rising, Kelly tried to figure out what other dessert they had, and when he saw their cast-iron frying pan, he thought maybe his boyfriend had lost his mind. It must have been some extra thing he'd tacked on at the last minute, and from the grim expression on Walter's face, whatever was under that tea towel wasn't pretty.

"See for yourself," Walter said, and held out the pan to Kelly.

Kelly lifted the tea towel.

He stared for a second—only a second. Because after that, he had to press his hand over his mouth and try not to cry. When he realized he heard the soft, familiar sounds of "Waiting for the Lights" coming from the kitchen stereo, he did cry. And laugh.

Walter took the ring out of the center of the empty frying pan. He held it close so Kelly could see the engraved swans on the outside of the gold.

Smiling, just a little shyly, Walter said, "Kelly Davidson, will you marry me?"

Kelly wiped his eyes. He could see his family out of the corner of his vision, though none of them bothered to hide their tears. He could see Rose, holding her girlfriend tight. He saw his future mother-in-law, looking happy and sad at the same time.

He saw Walter, down on one knee now, still holding the damn pan as he held out the ring. Walter, who had managed the silliest, sappiest, most wonderful proposal ever.

Walter, who today, as he did every day, wore Kelly's class ring.

"Well?" Cara prompted from behind him. "Are you going to say anything?"

"Yes," Kelly said, beaming, laughing, his heart soaring as their friends and family cheered, as Walter slid the ring onto his finger and stood, taking him into his embrace, into his life, his love.

Into their happily ever after.

About the Author

Heidi Cullinan has always enjoyed a good love story, provided it has a happy ending. Proud to be from the first Midwestern state with full marriage equality, Heidi is a vocal advocate for LGBT rights. She writes positive-outcome romances for LGBT characters struggling against insurmountable odds because she believes there's no such thing as too much happy ever after. When Heidi isn't writing, she enjoys cooking, reading, playing with her cats, and watching anime, with or without her family. Find out more about Heidi at heidicullinan.com.

Did you enjoy this book?

If you did, please consider leaving a review online or recommending it to a friend. There's absolutely nothing that helps an author more than a reader's enthusiasm. Your word of mouth is greatly appreciated and helps me sell more books, which helps me write more books.

MORE BOOKS IN THE LOVE LESSONS SERIES

Love Lessons is also available in audio and German

Frozen Heart (short story, coming soon)

Walter Lucas knows his boyfriend has been looking forward to the newest Walt Disney movie, *Frozen*, but he isn't prepared for the reality that is the front row seat of Kelly Davidson's cartoon obsession. However, there's more going on in November than just the movie—a certain question Walter has been waiting quite some time to ask.

Fever Pitch (also available in audio and German)

Aaron Seavers isn't excited about going to college until he meets (and makes out with) Giles Mulder at a graduation party. But Giles isn't so excited when Aaron turns up at his college, bringing dark memories of their hometown with him. Just when they begin to successfully navigate an undergraduate relationship, Aaron's parents and a campus tragedy threaten to bring their bright crescendo to a shattering end.

Lonely Hearts (also available in audio and German)

Until now, Baz's friends have kept his painful past at bay. But as college ends, loneliness drives him to hook up with emotionally-orphaned Elijah Prince, and the aftershocks crack his armor, and Elijah's.

Short Stay

Baz and Elijah, looking to escape a pressure-filled New Year's Eve party in Chicago, run away with Walter and Kelly to Las Vegas. But they accidentally packed their troubles in the Tesla, and it's clear what happens in Vegas isn't going to stay there. With the help of new friends and old, Baz and Elijah face—and confess—their fears together…and have a whole new set of adventures.

Rebel Heart (coming fall 2017)

Other books
by Heidi Cullinan

There's a lot happening with my books right now! Sign up for my **release-announcement-only newsletter** on my website to be sure you don't miss a single release or re-release.

www.heidicullinan.com/newssignup

Want the inside scoop on upcoming releases, automatic delivery of all my titles in your preferred format, with option for signed paperbacks shipped worldwide? Consider joining my Patreon. You can learn more about it on my website.

www.patreon.com/heidicullinan

THE ROOSEVELT SERIES
Carry the Ocean
Shelter the Sea
Unleash the Earth (coming soon)
Shatter the Sky (coming soon)

THE DANCING SERIES
Dance With Me *(also available in French, Italian coming soon)*
Enjoy the Dance
Burn the Floor (coming soon)

MINNESOTA CHRISTMAS SERIES
Let It Snow
Sleigh Ride
Winter Wonderland
Santa Baby
More adventures in Logan, Minnesota, coming soon

CLOCKWORK LOVE SERIES
Clockwork Heart
Clockwork Pirate (coming soon)
Clockwork Princess (coming soon)

SPECIAL DELIVERY SERIES
Special Delivery (also available in German)
Hooch and Cake (coming soon)
Double Blind (also available in German)
The Twelve Days of Randy (coming soon)
Tough Love

TUCKER SPRINGS SERIES

Second Hand (written with Marie Sexton) (available in French)
Dirty Laundry (available in French)
(more titles in this series by other authors)

SINGLE TITLES
Antisocial (coming June 2017)
Nowhere Ranch (available in Italian)
Family Man (written with Marie Sexton)
A Private Gentleman
The Devil Will Do
Hero
Miles and the Magic Flute

NONFICTION
Your A Game: Winning Promo for Genre Fiction
(written with Damon Suede)

*Many titles are also available in audio and more are in
production. Check the listings wherever you purchase
audiobooks to see which titles are available.*

CPSIA information can be obtained
at www.ICGtesting.com
Printed in the USA
LVOW12s2311011117
554606LV00002B/382/P